THE SEDUCTION OF CAMERON MACKAY

The Nightingales – Book 2

Sheri Humphreys

ALSO BY SHERI HUMPHREYS

THE NIGHTINGALES SERIES
The Unseducible Earl

OTHER BOOKS
A Hero to Hold
By the Light of a Christmas Moon

Boroughs
Publishing Group

www.BOROUGHSPUBLISHINGGROUP.com

THE SEDUCTION OF CAMERON MACKAY
Copyright © 2018 Sheri Humphreys

ISBN 978-1-718805-04-0

To my brother, Steve, your support and belief in me always gives me strength when I need it most.

ACKNOWLEDGMENTS

My sincere thanks:

To my awesome critique partner and friend, JoAnn Sky. Your critique skills are always admired and appreciated. I'm so grateful I've got you in my corner.

To the Rough Writers of Cambria for their collegial critiques: John Lamb, Patricia Heineman, Diane Tappey, Ken Renshaw, Sherry Eiselen, D. Arthur Gusner, Donna Kean, Anne Bennett, Robbin Miller, Barbara Snyder, Ted Siegler, Mike Broadhurst, Susan Chase, and Jennifer Smith.

To the Publish Dammit Critique Group for their insightful suggestions: Susie Bessinger, Phyllis Brown, Twyla Smith, Carrie Padgett, Terell Byrd, Karon Ruiz, Elizabeth Hiett, Toni Weymouth, Bethany Goble, and Ralaine Fagone.

To Steve Soldo, M.D., for his help brainstorming historical medical care.

And to editor Carly Hayward for her much appreciated story guidance.

THE SEDUCTION OF CAMERON MACKAY

CHAPTER ONE

April 17, 1855
Koulali Hospital, Scutari
Ottoman Empire (Turkey)

Elissa Lockwood pivoted toward the urgent call of "Nurse" ripping through Koulali Hospital's surgical ward.

Even from the middle of the room, she could see the intense expression of the officer walking with the aid of a crutch, and knew he'd been the one to call. He kept pace with the stretcher carried at his side, his free hand pressing hard against the chest of the patient. He looked at Elissa and lifted his chin, drawing her toward him.

"This man needs surgery. Now." His words shot out with the confidence of a sharpshooter hitting dead center.

Elissa pointed to an empty bed. "Put him there." The familiar, gritty tension that happened with emergencies seized her.

From the amount of blood, and the way the officer held pressure, Elissa knew the soldier likely had a life-threatening bleed. Maintaining pressure compressed the vessels and temporarily stopped the bleeding. And maybe, if they were lucky, it would give them time to save him.

The stretcher-bearing orderlies deposited the wounded soldier and she yanked the blanket up and tucked it around the redheaded man's legs. He was too pale and too bloody and too young—too like others who'd died—for her to have much hope.

An orderly ran through the door, a surgeon's bag clutched in his arms. Elissa waved him forward, took the bag, and set it on the bed.

The limping officer must be the injured battlefield surgeon they expected on today's steamer. He wore the scarlet coat of a Royal Scots Greys uniform and insignia of staff surgeon's rank.

"You're Staff Surgeon MacKay?" she asked.

"Aye." He released his crutch and let it clatter to the floor. With both hands he bore down on the bared right chest of the wounded corporal. "His saber wound reopened while they were taking him off the ship. He was walking. Whistling a ditty! Now, if I can't stop the bleeding—" His lips drew tight. Overlaid with a Scottish burr, MacKay's voice held certainty and grimness and anger. "This damn war."

"Smith," Elissa cried with lifted voice. "We need towels here, now." Smith, one of the ward orderlies, was near the end of the long room, tending a patient behind a privacy screen.

"Right away, miss," he yelled.

Elissa opened the wounded soldier's filthy, blood-soaked coat, tattered shirt, and small shirt as far as they would go. MacKay pressed against the bleeding wound so firmly, his bloody fingers blanched.

Smith dashed up with an armful of towels.

"Here," MacKay said to Smith. "When I lift my hands, ye take my place. I want as much pressure on the wound as ye can deliver." As soon as Smith accepted compression duty, MacKay stripped off his coat and began rolling up his sleeves.

Elissa wrapped her fingers around the wounded soldier's wrist and found his pulse. It was fast. Too fast. And thready. He had to be in terrible pain, yet he wasn't struggling or moaning.

For the first time since he'd arrived, she really looked at his face. Freckles sprinkled his skin like splattered paint, and his ears cocked from his head like a listening dog's. Most would consider him homely, but Elissa found his face endearing. If her brother had lived, he might have looked much like this soldier.

No. Please, no. She hated it when they looked like Freddy. Dread hit her stomach with the impact of an anchor heavy enough to hold the flagship *Britannia*.

She knew death. Knew how to protect her emotions. And knew patients who reminded her of Freddy reached a fragile, fearful part of her she couldn't shield.

The corporal shifted, blinked, and looked up with eyes a century older than his face.

"Mother Mary. Help me." The patient's gaze flicked to the surgeon standing over him.

"Easy, man," MacKay said.

The young corporal's face became pleading and determined, a starving beggar staring through a bakery window. "Please, Doctor. I don't want to die."

Officer MacKay looked straight into the soldier's imploring eyes. "I'll do my best."

Something about the way he said it made her think his best would be very, very good.

The corporal's eyelids closed. His jaw slackened. Moments like this, when patients barely clinging to life entrusted themselves to the medical staff—and most probably to God—always made a tight, hot sensation invade her throat.

"Get one of the surgeons," MacKay said. "He can administer the anesthetic while I explore the wound."

Elissa shook her head. "They're all down at the quay, sir, sorting the new arrivals."

Sandy brows bunched. Green eyes studied her. Glowed with expectation.

"Can ye give the chloroform?"

"I never have, but I've watched it done." For a moment, tension pulled tight within her. Then MacKay's calm, resolute gaze reassured her. She considered the injured corporal's ashen face then nodded at MacKay. The corporal had no time, and she had no choice. "I can give it if you help me, sir."

Little lines appeared at the corners of his eyes, and without smiling, he gave the remarkable impression he had. "Good, lass. The chloroform's in my bag."

Elissa opened the bag, located the bottle of colorless fluid labeled *Chloroform,* and the eyedropper and handkerchief beside it. Chloroform! Many of their surgeons lacked experience with the powerful drug, and on the occasions they were supplied with it, were hesitant to use it. Elissa regarded the bottle of innocuous-looking liquid and marveled. She was holding magic in her hands.

The next few moments went as if they'd worked years together. Positions shifted, MacKay directing them with a few quiet words. He spread a towel over the patient's abdomen and set surgical instruments upon it. Elissa placed the open handkerchief close, beside the corporal's head. She uncorked the anesthetic and inserted the eyedropper into the neck of the bottle.

She bent toward their patient. "I'm going to give you some chloroform so Staff Surgeon MacKay can attend your wound. You won't feel any pain." The soldier's eyelids blinked open, and she looked into eyes filled with fear. She grabbed his hand and squeezed. "What is your name, Corporal?"

His cold fingers barely reacted, returning only the slightest pressure, but she felt it all the way inside, as if he'd gently squeezed her heart.

"Riley, ma'am. Please, ma'am. In my pocket…"

She had to lean close to make out his gravelly whisper. She found the gold locket in the inside pocket of his uniform coat, and with her apron, wiped away every trace of blood. She opened it, glimpsed the interior, and her heart cracked. Thank goodness the seal had been tight enough to protect the locket's contents. She held it up to Riley's face. One side held the daguerreotype of a young woman, the other side a lock of red-gold hair.

A flare of warmth and life lit his molasses-brown eyes. "Evie…" Colorless lips pressed together, and he struggled to swallow. "Thank you, miss."

MacKay paused, scalpels and clamps, needles and ligatures, lint and towels arranged. "I'm ready."

Elissa snapped the locket closed and pressed it into Riley's hand. "We're starting now, Corporal." He seemed to have found some strength, for his fingers closed tight around the locket. Her heart squeezed again, harder this time, and a frisson streaked down her spine.

Riley's eyes locked on Elissa. "Will I…pull through?"

She never lied to patients. Never. Unless she feared the Grim Reaper would use the sharp edge of truth, and slice the ties joining soul to body.

She gave a sharp nod. "We'll have you back in England with your Evie faster than a peregrine falcon dives for dinner." She took a deep breath and positioned the handkerchief over Riley's nose and mouth, tenting it slightly.

Riley's eyelids slid closed, and he whispered, "Our Father which art in heaven, hallowed be thy name…"

"Fifty drops over the first three minutes," MacKay said.

Elissa filled the eyedropper, positioned it over the handkerchief, and counted drops of the sweet-smelling chloroform. Riley continued to pray.

"Thy will be done, in earth…" The corporal took several large, shuddering breaths. A tear leaked from the corner of his closed eye. She was glad he had the strength to pray and had that comfort as he succumbed to sleep.

The first fifty drops were followed with another fifty. It was easy to tell when the drug sedated him. Deep, shaky breaths ebbed, became quiet and shallow.

MacKay nodded sharply. "Give the last fifty drops and watch his breathing."

MacKay went to work on the wound. He cut the sutures placed at the camp hospital, and opened the saber slash.

Blood ran out. Too much. Too fast.

Smith, freed from his wound compression duty, mopped it up as quickly as he could, but his efforts weren't enough.

"I cannae see, damn it," MacKay said.

Elissa focused on her patient's breathing, and peeked under the handkerchief. Not a bit of color tinted his face. A bad sign.

The upper chest wound was extensive. MacKay probed the laceration, his commanding presence rock-solid steady. So was his concentration. When his eyes closed, alarm shot through her. Until she realized his fingers were exploring—*feeling*—deep inside the wound.

Smith sopped up blood and no more flowed out. MacKay's finger, buried to its second knuckle, had arrested the hemorrhage. His shoulders squared, his chest expanded as he took in a large breath, then slowly released it.

"It's a wonder he didn't bleed to death when he sustained the injury," MacKay said. "Nor was his lung pierced, which is close to miraculous. Bad luck he started hemorrhaging, but I've found the bleeding vessel. I've got my finger on it."

Thick-lashed, brown-flecked green eyes looked at her, sharpened, and she felt as if she'd tumbled into a primeval forest.

"I doubt I can repair this." His calm voice could have been commenting on any common occurrence, and his face showed no more than mild concern. But his eyes—oh, his eyes held deep disquiet.

"How can I help?" Elissa asked.

For long seconds he considered the wound. Then his face cleared and he blinked. "Ye can hold a retractor."

Once she had selected a steel retractor from the assembled instruments, he guided the end of the instrument into the wound. "Now, hold his flesh away from my hand. I need room to work the needle. I fear it's hopeless, but perhaps with luck—or God's benevolence…" He offered her a large wad of lint. "Use this." He guided her hand. "Press here. Hard."

He intended to try, then. Many wouldn't. Gladness warmed and lifted her. She applied firm compression to the wound with her free hand, and he prepared his needle and suture.

He glanced up. "What's yer name, lass?"

"Elissa Lockwood. I'm one of Miss Nightingale's cadre." For the moment, Riley's bleeding was stopped, and she felt grateful and hopeful enough to offer a smile. "Welcome to Koulali Hospital."

Creases appeared at the corners of his eyes, which seemed to regard her with warmth. The change in his expression, subtle as it was, buoyed her as a smile would.

He directed his gaze back to Riley and began suturing. She watched his large, long-fingered hands, somehow nimble enough to work flesh, needle, and a bit of thread-like suture with sureness and precision. Riley's chest rose and fell with reassuring regularity.

"Ye did well, Miss Lockwood, but I'm afraid we've ruined yer apron," MacKay said.

"Perhaps I'll be lucky and it won't have soaked through." There were plenty of aprons available to protect their woolen skirts. She'd replace the soiled one as soon as they finished.

Movement drew Elissa's gaze to the doorway to see Dr. Humphrey, Koulali's principal medical officer, pass through. He made his way to them and took in the situation with one sweeping glance.

"Good to see you again, MacKay," Humphrey said. "I didn't think I'd find you at work already. And in your assigned ward, too."

Hands busy, MacKay's quick look at Humphrey lasted no more than a second. "This is the surgical ward? I didn't realize." MacKay glanced at her. "Ye can remove the retractor now."

Humphrey folded his arms across his chest and leaned forward to peer into the wound. It remained free of bleeding.

"Yes, this is Ward Two," Humphrey said. "I take it you've met Nurse Lockwood. She's Ward Two's nurse and will accompany you on daily rounds and make sure your orders are followed. There's also a lady volunteer and a Sister of Mercy, as well as a number of orderlies assigned to the ward."

A last few sutures closed the wound. MacKay straightened, stretched his neck, twisted his head side to side.

Elissa was struck by how broad-shouldered he was. How strong he appeared. His chest breadth spanned several more inches than Dr. Humphrey's or Smith's. His cotton shirt, sleeves rolled to his elbows, revealed arms thick with muscle, yet his every movement was precise and controlled. His power carefully contained.

"Well," MacKay said. "We've cobbled him back together and stopped the bleeding, but I've no idea if it will hold."

Corporal Riley had a chance.

Relief unfurled inside her. Warmth filled her chest. She took a length of gauze, threaded it through Riley's locket ring and tied the locket to his wrist.

MacKay had said *we*. Right in front of Dr. Humphrey, he'd credited her with helping him perform surgery. MacKay's upper arm brushed hers and heat bloomed deep in her body. Awareness encompassed her. She darted a quick look at his face.

Thick, tawny hair. A strong nose in a chiseled face that hadn't seen a razor in days. A wide, unsmiling mouth. A handsome man. But it was his confidence and command and sincerity that drew her.

His gaze swept from the crown of her head to the toes of her boots. Then up, to hold her eyes for one brief moment.

She didn't know what the intensity in his eyes meant, but it left her as flustered as if they'd shared a waltz. She'd never had such a reaction to a man while engaged in nursing duties. Actually, she wasn't sure that *any* man had *ever* affected her like this. Had ever made her aware of him—and herself—in such an intimate way.

She stood in the middle of Koulali Hospital's Ward Two in a plain gray dress and a bloody apron, her lackluster, light brown hair tucked under a white cap, and disbelief swam through her head. Since her arrival in Turkey, she'd concentrated on her patients and ignored herself. Ignored the brittle tension of chronic exhaustion, the emptiness that rarely left her stomach, the loneliness that clung to her heart even with so many people around her.

Which was why it was nothing short of astounding that with one look, Staff Surgeon MacKay made her remember she was a woman.

CHAPTER TWO

Cameron MacKay liked seeing the sudden sparkle in the little nurse's hazel eyes and the hint of pink in her cheeks. The tenseness that gripped his shoulders and back drained away.

"MacKay, you're finished here, aren't you?" Humphrey asked. "Miss Lockwood will watch him until he wakes up. Let me show you to the medical officers' apartments. I imagine you'd like to eat something and look at the rest of the hospital."

"Aye. Let me clean up." He'd nearly forgotten Humphrey was there. After five days aboard a steamer filled with sick and wounded, he was eager to crutch about terra firma a bit. Even if his leg did burn like holy hell.

Miss Lockwood had sent Smith for supplies. The orderly returned with a basin of water and bar of soap, a folded towel over his arm. Cam dipped his bloody hands and worked the soap. Miss Lockwood used another basin and washed Riley's face, hands, and chest.

There were a few soldiers' wives in camp, but he hadn't talked to a woman in several months. Not an Englishwoman, anyway. He'd purchased eggs, cheese, chickens, and produce from Crimean farmers' wives, but none had looked as bonnie as Miss Lockwood. Even pale and drawn she was comely. Give her a bit of rest and food and he doubted another could outshine her.

This was his first experience with a Nightingale nurse. He'd been with his regiment, near the front and on the battlefield, since his arrival to the Crimea at the outset of the fighting. Ill soldiers who convalesced at one of the three Scutari hospitals and returned to the front regarded the nurses as angels. He now understood why surgeons spoke highly of their efficiency and abilities.

He considered his sleeping patient. By blindly throwing sutures into the wound, he'd somehow managed to tie off the bleeding vessel. Now it was anyone's guess how the man would fare. Infection, additional bleeding, or both were possible, even probable. He'd hope for the best and focus on Riley's most pressing need, which was nourishment.

Cam caught Miss Lockwood's attention. "Do ye have beef tea? Arrowroot and lemonade?"

She nodded. "Yes. We have all the regular sick foods."

"As soon as he awakens, he needs as much as ye can get down him. Whatever he'll take. Someone will have to sit and feed him almost constantly. At least a spoonful or swallow every five minutes. As much blood as he's lost, it's his only hope."

"Very well. Thank you, sir." Miss Lockwood's firm tone confirmed she'd keep a close watch on Riley.

"I'll be back to check on him, but if he starts to bleed again, send for me." Finished washing, Cam grabbed the towel and dried his hands. He gave Smith a nod of thanks, returned the towel, then retrieved his crutch from the floor and fit it under his left arm.

Miss Lockwood smiled, and Cam gripped his planted crutch like a drowning man grips a Kisbee Ring. He'd thought her winsome before, but smiling erased the deep-seated weariness in her face and left it with a rare loveliness. Loveliness that echoed the warmth and openness and wholehearted goodness in her smile. It left him downright heeliegoleerie, so he muttered something and turned away to follow Humphrey. How unexpected to find such a beauty here, in the middle of this Godforsaken place. And nursing! A vocation that required exceptional mental and physical toughness. He'd expected the women here to be simple, hardy petunias, not glorious roses. The way she'd cared for Riley proved she possessed kindness, too. He could hardly credit it.

He followed Humphrey into a large open yard, which the hospital buildings, originally a Turkish cavalry barracks, had been built around. Cool, sweet air, heavy with the briny aroma of the sea, made him lift his face and suck in a great draught.

One long side of the hospital sat on the bank of the shimmering, deep blue Bosporus. Hills rose from the water's edge, sides covered with the green of spring growth, colorful wooden houses scattered like children's blocks across a velvety carpet. The sun, bright in the blue-washed sky, warmed his shoulders.

Humphrey stopped, feet spread in the sparse grass. "Because of the depth of the water and our proximity to the quay, we've a great capacity for offloading sick here. Each doctor or surgeon oversees up to one-hundred-twenty patients, and typically the beds are filled as soon as they empty." He pointed to the end of the yard, where a one-story building sat. "That's the convalescent hospital. Once patients are ambulatory and no longer require main hospital care, they're moved there, where they can stay until they're either well enough to return to the front or can make the journey home. The building behind it is the nurses' quarters. Medical officer apartments are on the third floor of the main hospital. We'll cut across the yard and enter the far door there." Humphrey pointed. Frowned. "Will you be able to handle the stairs?"

"I'll manage. I've got my crutch." Cam lifted the appliance and tamped it on the ground for emphasis.

"Good." The medical officer resumed walking, his pace measured. "The report of the attack on you was riveting, MacKay." A choked laugh escaped Humphrey. "I've never heard the like. Engaged in stitching the wound of a prisoner of war when the man stabs you! He did quite a job of it, eh?"

Cam grimaced. "Buried the knife and yanked down."

"Good God, man," Humphrey said, shaking his head. "Didn't anyone search him?"

"The blade was in his boot. He'd lain on the battlefield through the night and been captured the morning following the battle. He came staggering behind our lines, half out of his head from loss of blood and pain. I don't think he understood I was helping him. He already had a fever."

"I'm grateful you chose not to be invalided home. As you know, we need every surgeon we've got. Price didn't mind going to the front for a time and letting you take his place here, and you'll find this duty easier. No standing, performing surgery for two days straight after a battle, eh?"

"Aye. I'm glad the exchange worked out."

"Our terrain is less challenging, except when it snows or rains and this yard turns to mud." They reached the far door. Humphrey opened and held it for Cam, and once inside started up the stairs.

Cam stifled his sigh, clenched his teeth, and climbed. He had more reason than his leg to be glad of his respite from the battlefield. The surge of relief as his ship pulled away from the Crimea shore had been so overwhelming, it shamed him. He'd nearly fallen to his knees and given thanks. Even after five days, the sense of liberation charged through his blood like mounted cavalry.

Here in Scutari the drumming in his head that commenced with each cannon barrage would be silent. He'd sleep more than an hour at a time. And, please God, he'd be able to control the trembling that seized him when he least expected it. He was sick to death of the hiding and the guilt.

The army needed every surgeon. He'd managed to conceal the palsy. He'd been free of it while doing surgery, but he lived in fear of quivers striking at the very moment someone's life depended on his steady hands. Of course, if the tremors struck, he'd call for assistance. *But what if the tremors had happened with Riley? Help hadn't been immediately available.* Fear and a crazed helplessness reared up inside. He couldn't suppress the growl that rumbled out of him.

Humphrey paused and looked back. "Did you say something, MacKay?"

"Nae. No' a thing," Cam replied, and Humphrey resumed climbing. *I'll know if I need to quit.*

He'd just performed flawlessly and saved a man's life. He'd never endanger a patient. He'd stop performing surgery first. Step forward and confess his incompetence. *Are ye* sure *ye shouldn't step forward right now?*

Cam held his free hand up to his face. Steady. Rock steady.

Deep in the marrow of his bones, quivers nestled like coiled snakes. He'd wrestled them into submission, but what if he couldn't keep the damn things contained? If they broke free and crawled out, more than his hands and his future plans would shake. His entire life would crack apart.

#

Cam's crutch produced quiet little thumps as he walked through the dark ward, headed for the soft light of a Greek lantern. The familiar sounds of men in all stages of sleep and wakefulness inhabited the night. The noise of restless bodies shifting and seeking relief, the tones of those uttering prayers, and the mutterings and groans of those lost in uneasy sleep accompanied him.

As he neared the light, the nurse sitting vigil beside Riley lifted and turned her head. It was Miss Lockwood.

Her mouth curved slowly, drawing his attention to pink, sweetly shaped lips. Lips like those in a place like this—it flummoxed him. Finding her sitting beside Riley at two o'clock was just as surprising.

His previous experiences with civilian hospital nurses had left him thinking them far from committed. He supposed there were a few kindhearted and honest women among their ranks, but the majority of nurses and other hospital workers were corrupt. Many were drunkards.

This young, comely, dedicated nurse was a wholly different sort. She gave proof that Nightingale nurses were different, their praise deserved.

"Miss Lockwood." He tipped his head in acknowledgment. "How is he?" He stepped to the opposite side of Riley's bed and wrapped his fingers around the man's wrist. Pulse regular, but fast. Skin bordering on hot, and moist to the touch. His condition seemed much better than what Cam had feared finding.

"He's aware, and responds appropriately when I rouse him to drink. If I'm not prodding him, he sinks into a deep sleep."

She had broth and lemonade beside her.

"He's been drinking?"

She grinned, and little glints of gold sparked her eyes. A good chunk of his weariness and worry fell away. To think a look from this woman could produce such a liberating reaction.

"Yes. He didn't want it, but I've managed to get a good amount of liquid down him."

"He most likely has ye to thank he's still of this world. I'm surprised ye didn't have an orderly sit the night with him, though."

She leaned against her chair's wooden ladder-back. "We've some fine orderlies on this ward, but many are young and inexperienced. His condition made me nervous, and I knew I wouldn't sleep if anyone else watched over him."

He nodded. She was being generous. Many orderlies sought the job to remove themselves from the fighting. Typically, they had no special leaning for the work. "Ye are planning on getting some rest, I hope?"

"Sister Margaret sat with him earlier, and she'll be along again in a bit. It's only recently that the nurses have been allowed to work in the wards at night. When it's necessary to keep a close watch on someone, Sister Margaret and I spell each other."

He checked Riley's dressings, pleased to find them dry. He shook the man to rouse him. Riley woke and coughed a few times, recognized Cam, and accepted a few swallows of broth from Miss Lockwood.

As soon as Riley was left undisturbed he dropped off to sleep again, just as his nurse had described.

"I couldn't expect more," Cam said. Successful surgery and the patient doing well was a good way to start his duty at Koulali Hospital. "Perhaps we can build him up a bit before infection sets in. I'm amazed he didn't arrive with a roaring fever."

"He looks young, but his rank indicates he's an experienced campaigner. He must be a hardy sort."

"And what of ye, Miss Lockwood? Ye seem too young to be an old campaigner yerself, yet I understood Miss Nightingale's nurses were quite experienced in caring for the sick."

Was she blushing? The light was dim, but he was nearly certain the color in her cheeks had deepened. An unexpected curl of delight twined through him.

"From a young age I knew I wanted to nurse. Our village midwife, Maddie Gray, took me under her wing. I lived in her home and worked alongside her for several years. When I wanted a wider range of experiences, I moved to London and obtained a position at the Institute for the Care of Sick Gentlewomen. That's where I met Miss Nightingale."

"Ye must have been very young when ye went to London," he said. "Excuse my prying, but ye appear no older than twenty-four years."

"I'm twenty-six, sir. I was twenty when I went to the city. I started nursing at twelve, so you see I have plenty of experience."

"Ye were permitted to nurse the sick when ye were but twelve? Och! What were yer parents thinking?"

Her posture went from relaxed to rigid. He regretted his thoughtless words. He was the son and grandson of healers, and he grew up knowing he'd follow that tradition. If anyone should understand, he should, but somehow thinking of her seeing such horrors as a wee lass stammygastered him.

Her lips tightened, the corners turning down, and her narrow chin firmed. "My parents, sister, and three brothers all died of cholera in 1840. I had it, too, but I survived."

Ah. The poor lass. "I'm sorry. Losing them made ye dedicate yerself to caring for the sick?"

She nodded and smoothed the edge of Riley's blanket.

"Ye honor them, lass. They'd be proud of ye." Hundreds must have benefitted from her care, but had her devotion precluded husband and children? He didn't doubt she had fulfilled her vow, but at what cost? It didn't seem right she wasn't some lucky man's cherished wife and mother of his children. If Cam ever had a woman like Miss Lockwood as wife, he'd keep her loved and happy.

Her eyebrows rose and her lips parted. He saw emotion flash behind her eyes. Sensed words hovering on the tip of her tongue. He waited for her to respond, a surprising amount of anticipation striking him.

Thoughts unvoiced, her lips closed. His disappointment was too great to let the moment pass.

"What? What were ye about to say?"

For a minute he didn't think she would answer. Then she flashed a smile. Too quick, too bright, too false. A smile to hide her pain.

"Your saying that means a great deal. I rarely speak of them." She fingered the lone ring she wore. Its small, dark red stone glittered. "I care for each patient as if he or she were one of my family." She smoothed Riley's hair from his forehead.

Cam tamped down his emotions to conceal his sudden yearning. How long had it been since he'd felt a touch as caring as the one Miss Lockwood bestowed on Riley? Too long to remember. "Well. Please don't ever doubt what I said." He cleared his throat. Adjusted his crutch. "Ye'll be here in the morning for my rounds? Ye'll need to show me how to go on. I've spent the past six months in a small battlefield tent."

"Doing lots of amputations." Her voice wrapped around him, low and soft, laden with sympathy and regret.

"Aye." He sniffed in a sharp draught of air as in his mind, the muted sounds around him evolved into torturous, ghostly cries.

Good Christ! Were the nightmares to accost him even when he was awake and focused? He shifted to hide the shudder that streaked through him.

He had no reason to feel ashamed for leaving camp and coming to Koulali, yet this gut-twisting self-reproach never left. He wasn't shirking his duty. His injury had forced him to leave his post. He should feel grateful for this respite away from the tension of the front, instead of guilty.

He straightened his arm and leaned on his crutch. "Goodnight, Miss Lockwood. I'll see ye in the morn."

"I'll be here, sir," she said.

He returned to his small room, lay on his bed, and tried to ignore the throbbing in his leg. He pictured Miss Lockwood sitting beside Riley, her graceful, long-fingered hand smoothing the edge of their patient's woolen blanket.

Cam woke to light streaming through the window. He'd slept, deep and dreamless. He yawned and stretched then folded his hands atop his chest and enjoyed the cozy warmth of his bed.

A long trill of birdsong breached the panes of his window. He lay still and listened to each perfect note. A busy and demanding day lay ahead, but for the first time in a long while he looked forward to it.

CHAPTER THREE

The moment Staff Surgeon MacKay appeared, Ward Two's staff gathered outside the ward room with Elissa. Everyone but Louis Archer.

Today MacKay wore the military surgeon's workaday uniform of blue frock coat and trousers. Freshly shaved, hair neatly combed, he joined the group and nodded to several staff members, the corners of his eyes crinkling.

Elissa turned her attention to the task at hand, and introduced Sister Margaret and Alice Blackwell. Sister Margaret, an Irish Anglican nun, had helped Elissa get her bearings when she first arrived at Koulali Hospital. No matter how dreadful a sight confronted her, the nurse's steady gray eyes never shied away. She met every challenge with grace, and the greatest compassion Elissa had ever seen. Elissa admired her tremendously.

"Sister Margaret and I share nursing duties for the ward," Elissa explained to MacKay. "She's here late evenings and nights. I'm here during the daytime, and early evenings. Mrs. Blackwell is our lady volunteer. Her son is fighting with the 11th Hussars." So many times, Elissa had seen Alice Blackwell, drooping with exhaustion, sit at a soldier's bedside to write or read 'one more' letter. She never said 'no.'

Elissa smiled when Jesse Jakeman saluted. It was hard to be around the orderly and not be affected by his enthusiasm. As determined as he was optimistic, not a day passed that she didn't give thanks for his assignment to her ward.

"If there's anything you need, sir, just ask. If I can't do it, I'll find someone who can," Jakes bragged.

"That's good to know," MacKay said.

The surgeon sounded polite, but Elissa wouldn't be surprised if Jakes's first impression fell a bit short. With his rangy build, bobbing Adam's apple, merry, sky-blue eyes, and sweet, closed-lips smile, Jakes looked younger than his stated age of twenty-one years. His always-smiling eyes and unfailing eagerness for work only added to his youthful image.

"Jakes has the unique ability to be there right when you need help." Elissa had lost count of the many times he'd stepped in to assist her. She'd never trusted or relied on a colleague more.

"That's quite a recommendation." MacKay's eyes swept Jakes's form a second time. "Sounds like I'm lucky, getting assigned to Ward Two."

"We have a very capable crew." Elissa introduced the other orderlies on duty. "That's everyone," she said. Each person, having welcomed MacKay, returned to work. "Except we're missing Archer."

As soon as MacKay's brows rose, she knew her voice had revealed her frustration. She enjoyed working with the orderlies. Most appreciated being singled out for instruction and praise. Archer was another story.

The orderly came through the door, his bearing all one might wish a military posture to be. He presented himself and saluted. "Here I am, Miss Lockwood. Sir."

MacKay returned the salute. "Ye're the ward-master, Sergeant?"

"I am, sir."

Each half of Archer's waxed, pointed mustache curled with an exactness that matched the other. His eyes, ringed with sparse lashes, were so dark it made discerning his pupils from his iris difficult. They reminded Elissa of hard, flat obsidian. She'd once had a disturbing dream about Archer's eyes. Ever since, she couldn't rid herself of the foolish notion that his eyes had the power to mesmerize her and suck her soul from her person, much as a hungry man will suck marrow from a bone.

She firmed her lips and tilted her chin. "I expected you here to greet Staff Surgeon MacKay when he arrived, Archer." She suspected he'd stayed away either to challenge her authority or to ensure he warranted a special introduction. Perhaps both.

"It couldn't be helped. We should have another steamer coming in tomorrow," he said, as if that explained his absence.

MacKay looked about the ward. "That'll mean fifty to a hundred new sick and wounded for Koulali. Are there men I can discharge to the convalescent hospital today?"

Elissa nodded. "I think there are."

"We could have a dozen or more dead before morning," Archer said. "We'll whisk them off to the dead-house first thing, sir." Archer's lips spread into a grin that exposed a crooked eyetooth.

Archer's smiles never reached his eyes, and she usually saw any number of disagreeable nuances in his expressions. Elissa found this one nothing short of macabre. "Lower your voice, Sergeant!" She scanned the closest beds. "And keep such thoughts to yourself."

The swine opened his mouth as if to defend the truth of his statement, but when she sharpened her gaze, he kept silent. After an abbreviated night's sleep, she had little patience for the man who never stopped jabbing her pincushion. She'd worked hard at Koulali to become comfortable supervising men. The nurses didn't have any military authority, yet the Medical Service expected them to oversee the orderlies and give them direction. She found some orderlies, especially the younger ones, eager to learn. Archer, though... She couldn't seem to strike the correct balance. Archer intimidated her, and he knew it. He expected women to be subservient, and she didn't possess the degree of command needed to counteract his attitude of superiority. Luckily, the anger he generated made her able to stand up to him when it mattered.

MacKay's frown made her step back. Oh, no. Had she repulsed him, a woman dressing down a man? Did he think her wrong to step in, instead of leaving it to Archer's army superior?

She was so bloody tired of navigating around men's attitudes and opinions. Yet if she wanted to be effective, she had to work within the bounds of acceptable behavior. Trying her best to smother her irritation, she gave Archer a dismissive nod.

She turned from watching the sergeant's retreating back to find MacKay looking at her. She forced up the stiff corners of her lips. "Shall we begin rounds?" At his nod, she went about explaining Ward Two's routine.

Thirty-one beds ran along each side of the ward. They started down the aisle, stopping at each bed. Elissa remarked on the soldier's wounds or sickness, his general condition, and how long he'd been in their care. She ignored her intense awareness of MacKay.

At every bed, MacKay listened to her report, and then moved from the aisle to the patient's side. Each man received some degree of his attention. Dressings were removed and wounds examined, strength and appetite and degree of fever evaluated. He pressed his ear against backs and listened to breath move in and out of lungs. Bellies were compressed. Every man spoken to and listened to. By the time they stopped for a reviving cup of tea, Elissa had developed a firm admiration for MacKay's abilities.

She led him to the brazier in the ward room, which was not an actual room, but a partitioned area for the staff, with two canvas screens conferring a degree of privacy. His sigh when they sat made her wonder if his leg was paining him. But of course it must be. The realization made her want to coddle the stern-faced man. A notion as ridiculous as it was inappropriate.

"You're very thorough, sir. It's wonderful having you with us." His compassion impressed her even more than his scrupulous examinations, and she believed the men sensed the concern he held for them. Ease came to the patients' faces as they interacted with MacKay.

He gave her the almost-smile that made his eyes gleam, and took a swallow of tea.

"Thank ye, Miss Lockwood. I value yer praise." He leaned forward, stretched out one long leg, and kneaded his left thigh.

She couldn't hold back any longer. "Are you all right? Are you in pain?"

He scowled. "Nae. It's uncomfortable, but getting around here is much easier than in camp."

The lines that creased the corners of his mouth attested to more than discomfort, but it didn't surprise her that uncomfortable was all he'd admit to. "You didn't need to go home to recuperate?"

"They wanted to invalid me home, but I'll be healed in a few weeks. Luckily, Dr. Price agreed to exchange places with me until my leg returns to full strength." He shrugged. "Any non-commissioned fighting man with this injury would have been housed in the camp hospital for a while, then returned to duty."

In Elissa's experience, neither officers nor gentlemen compared themselves to common men. Officer MacKay possessed a most singular attitude. She wanted to ask how he'd been injured, but feared he'd consider her impertinent. Well, it wouldn't take long for Jakes to find out and tell her.

They finished their tea and returned to patient rounds. It took the better part of the day to review the cases and check the conditions of the sixty-two men residing in Ward Two. MacKay proved generous with orders of extra food and drink for the patients.

"I'm convinced nothing is more important for healing than good nutrition," he said when Elissa commented on his liberal distribution of custards, puddings, negus, potatoes, fowl, and chops.

She made careful notes of his orders and later would ensure the orderlies followed his instructions. They were responsible for making sure the patients received their allotted foods.

Orderlies who specialized in cleaning and dressing wounds followed behind them, redressing the wounds MacKay unwrapped and examined. He paused and watched the re-bandaging of a man's leg stump. The patient, an Englishman named Nolan, yelped.

"Ease up there, man," Nolan said with a grimace. "This bloke hasn't the gentleness you've got in your little finger, Miss Lockwood. Slow down and take care," he directed the orderly.

Baxter, the orderly, stiffened but slowed. Elissa stepped to Nolan and grasped his hand. "Hold on." She gave his hand a squeeze and his fingers tightened in response.

"Would you have time to do my cleaning and bandaging tomorrow, ma'am? I'd be grateful." Body tense, he kept his unwavering gaze fixed on her. Probably to avoid looking at his stump.

She and Sister Margaret didn't have time to care for all the men's wounds, but they did try to care for the more complicated cases, as well as provide for the men who needed a little extra personal attention. Sometimes that simply meant sitting and spooning broth into a man's mouth, as she had last night.

"Of course I can, Corporal Nolan. Mr. MacKay won't need to look at every wound, as he did today. Now that he's examined yours, we'll keep him advised of your condition."

"Since the fever passed, my wound is knitting together, right?"

Baxter tied the final binding strip around Nolan's stump, nodded, and moved on. Nolan sighed and released Elissa's hand.

"Yes. It looks to be mending." Soon after he arrived, Nolan developed an abscess at one end of his incision. Thankfully, it had ruptured and drained. Now the stump looked much improved, and he hadn't had fever in a week.

MacKay took Baxter's place on the opposite side of the bed. "Aye, it's healing well, and ye're vigorous enough to get up. I imagine ye're mighty tired of lying on that bed. I've ordered crutches, and we'll have you walking with them tonight or tomorrow."

A huge grin spread across Nolan's face. "I'll soon be bound for England and me own mum, then."

Elissa admired Nolan's attitude. It would sustain him as he dealt with a future that included a wooden appendage. The Russian guns had taken too many limbs, turned soldiers to men struggling to find work and provide for themselves. So many left Koulali with broken spirits. They lived, but what would become of them?

There weren't enough jobs, or support, for the men they sent back to England. If only she could instill a bit of Nolan's optimism in all of them. "Where is home, Corporal?"

"Devon, miss. I'll be helping my father on the farm. Once I couldn't wait to leave. Now I think working the land, caring for the animals, will give me peace." Tight-lipped, he smiled and gave a sharp nod. "And I've a mind to marry and have children. Would you have a younger sister, miss, who might have a hankering for the country life and a devoted husband?"

"I'm sorry I don't." For a moment, Elissa's mind jumped to her sister. Mary would have been seventeen this year. She'd had amber eyes and a scattering of freckles so tiny, Papa used to joke she'd been dusted by fairies.

Elissa brought her mind back to the present. After fifteen years, she could enjoy memories of Mary and the rest of her family without grief immobilizing her.

MacKay clapped Nolan's shoulder and grinned. "Ye won't have any trouble finding a winsome lass, Corporal. She'll be a wise one, too. A woman who knows a good man when she sees him—and knows he's a man in a thousand."

Oh, dear. MacKay's broad smile did alarming things. Robbed her of her senses. Imparted a deep-seated warmth. Made Nolan, the ward, everything around her insignificant.

"Ah, Miss Lockwood, I can see the thought of home has put you to dreamin'," Nolan said.

Startled, Elissa looked from Nolan to MacKay, whose watchful eyes glinted as if he could read her mind. Her face filled with betraying heat. She nodded her head.

"Gentlemen, will you excuse me?" Without waiting for an answer, she hurried away to the ward lobby then out to the yard. Once outside, she leaned against the wall and looked up into a blue, cloudless sky. Breathed.

It didn't seem possible that MacKay, a man she'd met mere hours ago, could produce such a profound effect, but she couldn't attribute the awareness that blasted through her to anything else. When their gazes met, she could hardly drag her eyes away. He might have considered her scolding of Archer distasteful, but if he had, it didn't affect their rapport, which already seemed firmly established. His unpresuming manner increased the appeal of his very masculine, handsome looks. She'd seen his surgical skill, his dedication, his kindness, his considerable intelligence. She appreciated the positive aspects of his character. But that smile hadn't prompted another degree of admiration for the surgeon's nature.

That smile had inspired a hot tingling that shot to places utterly private and feminine. The sensation shocked her. It made her think not of his fine persona but of burrowing her fingers into his thick, tawny hair and smoothing her hands over his broad shoulders and back. Of wrapping her arms tight around him, pressing her body and her lips against his.

Elissa slammed her eyes shut and slapped her hand across her mouth. She rarely faced a situation when she didn't know what to do. But she had no idea what she should do about these extraordinary feelings for Cameron MacKay. The man.

CHAPTER FOUR

The next morning, two days after his emergency chest surgery, Riley's fever burned. Elissa wiped his face and neck with a damp towel and ignored the heavy pressure inside her chest. She'd expected him to develop some degree of fever, but the intensity of this one made it appear fearsome. His face, bright red and hot to touch, glistened with moisture. The pulse point in his neck throbbed with his rapid heartbeat. His hair, wet with sweat, clung to his head.

Riley's dry, cracked lips parted. "You've the touch of angels, miss." His tongue swiped over his lips, but left no moisture behind.

She was no angel, but perhaps, with this soldier who reminded her so of Frederick, she had the touch of a loving sister. "Can you drink?" With one hand, Elissa picked up the waiting cup and held it to his lips. With the other she supported his head.

He managed a couple swallows then coughed. "Ah!" He grimaced with each cough. One hand clutched his chest. "It feels like knives carving me up," he said, words punctuated with gasps for breath.

The coughing spell subsided and Riley sagged, boneless and exhausted. "It's a relief to have you beside me, miss. Seeing as how my Evie can't be here. Being near an Englishwoman again before...I die. I'm thankful."

Elissa placed her hand over his hot, moist one. "Corporal Riley, please don't consign yourself to the grave. I'm not ready to." As sick as he was, his mind was still alert. A good reason to sustain hope.

His eyes drifted closed. "You and Staff Surgeon MacKay have done your best. I've never been treated better. But I'm too weak to withstand the fever."

Elissa applied the damp towel to his forehead and crimped her lips together. His resolute expectation of death made her want to be strong for him. Riley was an intelligent man with a world of experience. He'd lost friends and fellow soldiers to infection, and knew in all likelihood his chances were slim. He didn't need a nurse overcome with the helplessness that weighed so heavy within her.

"Would you write out a letter for my wife, miss?"

The lady in his locket. "Of course I will." Elissa rose to retrieve paper and ink, but returned to find Riley asleep. She gazed at him a minute, then looked down the row of beds.

She'd arrived in the ward before daybreak. Now the men were waking, the day orderlies arriving and performing their assigned tasks. Louis Archer came through the door and strolled over.

He jerked his head toward Riley. "Looks like he'll be the next one for the dead house."

"Sergeant!" Elissa grabbed his arm and tugged him in the direction of the ward room. Once inside the room's defining screens, she spun toward him so fast, the hem of her skirt belled out.

"How could you say such a vile thing? What if he'd heard you?" Voice pitched emphatic and low, Elissa loosed every bit of her disgust.

Archer smirked. Her hands tingled with the desire to shake him.

"He didn't hear a thing, and I spoke the truth." Archer's narrowed eyes glittered.

"Keep your voice down! You couldn't know he wouldn't hear you. And I won't tolerate such cruelty."

He shrugged. His impassive face and veiled black eyes made anger pulse like flaring matches in her head, her chest, her throat. She'd warned him yesterday about this very thing. Archer didn't care that he'd displeased her. Was he trying to provoke her?

"You won't tolerate it?" He sighed. "Well, do what you must, then."

She longed to scrape the superior smile off his face. Nothing would please her more than getting him drummed out of the medical service, but the bloody little rodent knew she lacked the power to hurt him. He took every opportunity to openly mock her, not even pretending to follow her directions. He loved lording his independence over her, emphasizing her impotence.

"Here ye are."

She hadn't heard MacKay's approach. He stood in the space between screens that comprised the ward room's entrance. "Good morning, Staff Surgeon." How much had he heard? Miss Nightingale, who oversaw all Scutari nursing services, and Miss Hutton, Koulali's superintendent of nurses, wanted problems solved before they came to the notice of the doctors and surgeons. They didn't want nurses perceived as disruptive, creating problems that the officers would then have to solve.

For a moment they all remained quiet. Archer stood at attention. MacKay's eyebrows rose. His gaze moved between Archer and Elissa. "Good morning. Are ye ready to begin rounds, Miss Lockwood?"

MacKay didn't act as though he'd overheard, which relieved her. He always seemed to catch her at the most inopportune times. She didn't want him seeing her as a domineering troublemaker, and she very much feared he did. She squared her shoulders. She needed to put the vexations of her job aside. "Yes. I'd like you to see Riley first. He's got fever."

MacKay grimaced. He gave a dismissive nod to Archer and turned away toward the ward. Elissa followed.

Riley was still sleeping, but when MacKay grasped his shoulder, he woke and coughed. A rattling sound accompanied his breathing. MacKay examined Riley's wound, which was bright red and swollen, then pressed his ear to the soldier's lungs. Riley seemed to have grown too weak for conversation. He lay quiet, his quick breathing barely lifting his chest.

MacKay straightened and shook his head. "He has infection of the lungs and the wound."

His words confirmed what she already knew. "Would you object if I dosed him with yarrow tea?" Elissa asked. "Might I clean his wound with it, too?"

"Ye're knowledgeable in herbs, are ye?"

"I told you I'd lived and trained with a midwife?"

He nodded.

"She used herbs. I brought a number of them with me—all things I've found effective."

MacKay walked to the small table that held a water pitcher, basin, and soap, and availed himself of all three. "Yes, go ahead." He dried his hands and tossed the towel onto the table. "Ye can bathe him with the infusion, too, if ye like."

Surprise and gladness spread through her. His statement made it clear he knew the different applications for the herb. *"You've* treated with herbs?"

One corner of his mouth lifted, and he *winked.*

"Aye. We Scots love the land and its bounty. And from my great-grandfather on, my family's men have been healers. They passed the old remedies down. I received the very best formal medical education available, yet my father and grandfather taught me respect for the old ways, too."

He stepped close. Lifted the patient list and pencil from her hands. She caught the faint scent of soap and bay rum, and the pit of her stomach quivered.

"I'll begin rounds. Ye make the yarrow infusion and get Riley's treatment started."

She knew how it felt to be sick and near death, weighed down, drowning with pain and despair. She imagined being in such a condition with MacKay as her doctor and having the comfort of his eyes. Their green depths shone with patience and kindness. She nodded and stepped back before he could see how his proximity affected her. She was already much too aware of the man, and with every encounter, her admiration for the surgeon grew.

Farther down the ward, Jesse Jakeman's lanky form caught her eye. "Jakes," she called. Flashing his famed grin, the orderly started toward her. "Jakes can accompany you and make any necessary notes." She started to hurry away then stopped and turned back. "Thank you, sir."

He'd already moved on to the patient in the bed next to Riley. He looked up. "It was yer idea, Miss Lockwood."

She sped away toward her room in the nurses' cottage, where she kept her herbal supplies. Her foolish heart leapt in her chest. Elissa took a deep breath, trying to quell the exhilaration she felt. It didn't help. If anything, it made it worse. An irrepressible smile stretched her mouth.

She nodded at army personnel and convalescent patients she passed. Held her pace to a brisk walk all the way to her room. Dropping onto her mattress, she buried her face in her hands.

What was she about? She couldn't be growing enamored of Staff Surgeon MacKay. She was in the midst of war and dying men, not London society. Yet she felt as giddy as a girl with her first gentleman caller. She needed to keep her attention where it belonged—on her patients. Officer MacKay wouldn't admire a nurse whose romantic notions supplanted her duty. And her patients deserved better. What kind of nurse was she if she allowed herself to be distracted by fancy?

Poor Riley was waiting, she reminded herself. She'd best collect the yarrow and get to work.

#

Elissa's stomach grumbled. The arrival of new patients had meant extra work, and she'd stayed past her normal time to leave the ward. But maybe, now... She looked up and down the ward. Archer had the night shift orderlies clustered about him and was doling out assignments. Most of the new patients were settled in and already sleeping. What a relief it must be for them, after several days' journey across the Black Sea, to arrive here and be tucked up in bed—filthy uniforms removed, washed and garbed in clean nightshirts, fed and made comfortable. Every empty bed had been filled.

Before leaving for dinner and a few hours' respite prior to the day's final rounds, Elissa moved toward Riley for a recheck of his condition. Two weeks had passed since his arrival and his body couldn't seem to decide if it were going to heal or succumb to infection. His degree of fever varied, at times becoming so mild as to be almost indiscernible, while his spells of exacerbation frightened her with their raging intensity.

Quiet snores soughed from him. She kept her hand light so as not to wake him and felt his forehead. Hot and moist, but moderately so. She hoped, when she made final rounds before bedtime, he wouldn't be in the grip of another scorching monster of a fever.

"Sergeant, I haven't slept." Henry Smith's distraught voice brought Elissa's head around. "I...I worked all last night. Once the sun rose, I was told to move those selected for the convalescent hospital, then I helped tote the new arrivals up from the quay. Sixty-seven of them! You can't expect me to work tonight, too. That would be thirty-six hours straight."

"Can't I?" Archer asked. "You surprise me, Smith. For some reason you think I care about your opinion. I can see I'll have to disabuse you of the notion that you know better than your superiors how to manage troops."

Smith's rigid form, already at attention, seemed to vibrate.

"Orderlies at the front work for days without relief," Archer said. "Perhaps you'd be more eager to discharge your hospital duties if you had that experience to compare this to."

Elissa gasped and swept toward Archer and Orderly Smith and the other two orderlies who stood together a short distance away. Had Archer threatened Smith with a transfer to the front?

"Sergeant Archer!" Elissa stopped square in front of the ward-master, who looked at her as though he'd love to toss her into the yard.

"This isn't your concern, ma'am," he said, eyes narrowed to slits. "Smith's under my supervision, and he's insubordinate." He stepped around her to face Smith. "You can perform your duty assignment or present yourself to the guardhouse. If you stay, I'd better not catch you slacking."

Elissa grit her teeth. No matter that she lacked official authority; she was a woman. Archer considered her subservient to every man on the ward. When his army superiors were around, he became polite and respectful, but when absent, he acted as though she were beneath his notice. How she wanted to stamp and kick her feet and let loose some of this frustration. His forward-canted posture, the tension visible in his neck and shoulders, the aggressive jut of his jaw, all told her she was no match for the experienced campaigner. Except what he was demanding of Smith wasn't right. They weren't under fire, and there were others, more rested, who could serve the shift in Smith's stead.

The young orderly was still at attention. Did she imagine the swift look that wasn't a plea, but an apology? If she did intend to challenge Archer's dominion, she should do it in private. Not in the middle of the ward, watched by the men he supervised and any patients still awake.

"Yes, Sergeant," Smith said, throwing a sharp salute. "Permission to be excused to get a bite from the kitchen? I didn't have time to eat, and they've saved back a bowl of soup for me."

Archer stilled and the orderlies appeared to stop breathing. What was Smith thinking, to voice such a request now? He could have pulled her aside after Archer left, and quietly asked her help. She'd have watched the ward while he ate.

The ward-master's head fell back, his handlebar-mustachioed mouth opened, and a long stream of laughter erupted. "Blimey, Private. You must have been bashed in the head sometime or other. Your brains appear to be scrambled. I'd wonder at your ability to serve, but I want to keep you around. I find you devilishly amusing." The sergeant's jocular expression fell. "Now round the ward and empty the piss pots," he ordered.

The beast. Eyes glittering, mouth smirking, Archer appeared pleased. What was wrong with the man? He enjoyed humiliating and controlling others. How had he been promoted?

"I'll bring your soup," Elissa said. What made her say it aloud? She could have simply done it and Archer would have been none the wiser.

"He'll eat when he's relieved to go to the kitchen, and not before," Archer said.

"Then I'll relieve him," Elissa added.

She'd never seen meaner eyes, and the look they cast made a chill streak down her spine. She stretched herself an inch taller.

"I see I've been too lenient. I should have put Smith on report after all." He bowed. "Thank you for correcting me, Miss Lockwood. Private Smith, report to the guardhouse," he snapped.

He was not getting away with this! "You're not sending him anywhere," Elissa said. "I'll report *you*."

A laugh, quickly stifled, broke from the nearest patient bed. Then quiet chuckling farther down. Archer's face turned hard, and fear arrowed through her. A mantle of cold fell atop her shoulders.

Then Archer's black gaze swung away toward the approaching man wearing a surgeon's uniform. Stranglehold released, her starved lungs filled with air. She didn't know whether MacKay would use his rank to supersede Archer and fix this. The officer had never taken her side against the ward-master, but her instincts, and MacKay's habit of weighing his words made her think him a fair man.

"Good evening," Staff Surgeon MacKay said, joining them. He looked back and forth between her and Archer and his brows rose. "Everything all right?"

She didn't want to air this further in public, but Archer needed to be stopped.

"Working out a few last-minute details," Archer said. "I was just commenting to Orderly Smith and Miss Lockwood how distressing unexpected consequences can be."

He was warning her—or rather, Smith and her. What would he do if she appealed to MacKay? Or lodged an official complaint with Archer's superiors? Archer had ordered Smith to the guardhouse in response to *her* threat! What kind of retribution was he capable of? She couldn't let Smith go to the guardhouse, but what if MacKay backed the ward-master?

Archer cocked his head toward Smith. "Do you have a request, Private? Or a grievance you feel compelled to lodge?"

"No, Sergeant," Smith said.

The cold, amused expression on Archer's face made Elissa want to shudder. Somehow, she suppressed it.

"And you, Miss Lockwood? Having second thoughts?"

Inside, her hope sagged. Inclination to trust the Staff Surgeon aside, she had no real evidence he'd agree with her. If she accused Archer of misconduct and MacKay believed the sergeant's actions were justified, it could go much worse for Smith. She couldn't risk appealing to MacKay.

"Yes. I am," Elissa said. She couldn't bear to look at Archer, and see him glowing with triumph. "My proposal was…imprudent."

A low, satisfied hum came from the ward-master. "Disregard that last order, Private. I believe you were attending to the patients' personal needs?" He wished MacKay good-night, gave him a lazy salute, and left.

MacKay's gaze followed the sergeant down the aisle.

"I'll get your meal and bring it here," Elissa said to Smith.

"Thank you, Miss Lockwood. There's coffee in the ward room. I'll be fine. I'm sorry I caused trouble. My dad always did call me pudding-headed."

"Sergeant Archer was in the wrong, Smith, not you."

A patient called and Smith hurried away.

"What was that about?" MacKay asked.

"A disagreement between Sergeant Archer and Orderly Smith, and I meddled."

"Ye don't strike me as a meddler," MacKay said.

"Well, I was. I thought it necessary, but it went wrong."

He waited, as if expecting her to say more. "How so?"

Oh, he was a savvy one. He knew there was something off about the exchange he'd witnessed. And he'd asked a question that could apply to either—or both—of her comments.

She took a quick look around. If she lowered her voice, she'd be out of earshot of the closest patients. Shouldn't she be brave, take the risk and discover whether she was right about his being a fair man? She was letting Archer get away with uncalled-for intimidation, and blackmail. It took a moment to screw up her courage. "It's been difficult coming here, working alongside men, teaching and supervising while performing my duties. I wasn't accustomed to it. We're expected to give the orderlies direction, yet we have no official authority over them. Some men don't like a woman making suggestions."

"My guess is Sergeant Archer likes it less than most," MacKay said. The kindness in his eyes encouraged her.

"Well, yes." She hesitated. Since his arrival, MacKay had praised and thanked her, and she treasured his approval. He treated all with courtesy and respect. She didn't want him to think her incompetent in any way, nor did she want to be thought a complainer or gossip. Perhaps he'd sensed the ever-present conflict between her and Archer. The way MacKay waited for more, with the patience of a fisherman, made her think he wanted her to confide in him. Something in his face reassured her and made her think he would keep her confidence. "Archer is two-faced. He undermines me whenever he can. I don't know how best to counter him."

"Any subordinate, or even patient, who dares cross him, he shows no mercy," MacKay said. "The short time I've been here, I've seen him make orderlies shake in their boots. Don't be too hard on yerself. Archer is bloody-minded and strong-willed, and he'll take exception to *anyone* he perceives as not having the right to challenge him."

She didn't *want* to cross him, but…

"I need to be able to stop him when he doesn't treat the orderlies and patients right. What if he's even worse when I'm not here?"

MacKay frowned. "I'll pay attention, and see what I can discover. If he's abusing anyone he needs to be stopped. I'm glad ye told me. I'm an officer and my reprimand will carry weight. Ye've done the orderlies and patients a good turn. I hope ye realize how much they respect ye."

It was good MacKay would be watching, but it almost sounded as though he were dismissing her, and not expecting her to monitor Archer's behavior and correct him when he needed correction. "I'm relieved you'll be observing Archer, but if I see or hear him being cruel, or even unkind, I'm confronting him. Knowing I have your support makes a difference." So much difference. She felt stronger than ever. "I'm not letting what just happened, happen again." And she wasn't going to continually tattle to MacKay.

"Och." He winced. "Please don't. Unless ye're someone who outranks the sergeant, or someone he fears for some reason, he won't bend for ye. It would make things worse with him to try."

His wanting to protect her made her go soft inside, but how much Archer disliked her was her last concern. "I think you're right," Elissa said. "But I can't ignore it if he does something that borders on abuse. Even if it makes me a target."

CHAPTER FIVE

Twelve days later Cam sat in the company of Miss Lockwood and savored a sip of steaming tea. This daily, late-morning respite in the ward room had become the favorite part of his day. Sitting down and enjoying a cup of tea relaxed him and renewed his energy, but it was the time spent in Miss Lockwood's company that made him treasure the interlude.

Ward Two had a few empty beds, and the workload for all the staff seemed lighter than usual. For the time being, the front was quiet. Cases of dysentery, cholera, remittent fever, and the like continued to come in, but the numbers of arriving trauma cases were low.

Riley hung on. He'd seem to get a bit better, joking a bit, his appetite improving and his fever down, then, just when Cam began to feel hopeful, the man would succumb to another bout of high fever. Today, for the first time in three weeks, Cam had reason to feel encouraged.

"This is the fourth day Riley's been free of fever." It was the longest he'd gone, and Cam knew Miss Lockwood understood the significance of the man's afebrile status.

She gave him the smile that never failed to dazzle. "He's eating well and his breathing's better."

"The angels in heaven must be watching over him," Cam said. "Three weeks ago I wouldn't have given ye a half-penny for his chances. Of course, Riley assures me *ye're* an angel."

"How embarrassing," Miss Lockwood said. "I wish you'd disabuse him of that."

"I doubt I'd succeed. Perhaps because there's more than a little truth to it," he teased.

She dipped her head and looked at him through her lashes. "I'm not angelic."

Cam struggled to conceal his satisfaction. He'd made her blush. Seeing evidence of his effect on her filled him with pleasure. He'd become addicted to those blushes. He loved making her eyes sparkle. And nothing was as rewarding as earning one of her smiles.

He'd found joy in his work once again, thanks in no small part to the little lassie. The only remaining effect of the nervous condition that had seized him at the front were the dreams that locked him in hell, and what man in this war-torn corner of the world didn't have the occasional nightmare? Every other manifestation had slipped away. His hands were steady, his mind clear and decisive. There was no reason he couldn't enjoy the unexpected companionship of this amazing woman.

"Yer patients may think ye an angel, but I know ye're a woman as well as a nurse."

The tinge to her cheeks turned bright. She was flesh and blood all right, though she looked like one of Botticelli's angels. Nae. It was Botticelli's Venus she bore more than a passing resemblance to.

Her face looked very like the beautiful goddess the master had portrayed, and though he'd seen no more of Miss Lockwood's bare flesh than her neck and hands, he knew he'd find her form as alluring. Thinking of her as naked as the artist's goddess tightened his body in a rather uncomfortable and alarming way. He shifted on his chair. He'd best turn his thoughts away from the lassie's sweet form or he'd soon find himself in an altogether embarrassing condition.

"I know I'm different from most women," Miss Lockwood said. "I'm not adept in the activities most ladies pass their time with."

Did she mean needlework and sketching and watercolors? Singing and piano playing and dancing? She couldn't consider herself lacking because she wasn't accomplished in those skills, could she? "Ladies' pastimes," he said slowly. "Organizin' a large dinner party would be child's play for ye. Ye're graceful and kind, and ye have a knack for making others feel better. All sterling qualities. I find ye delightfully feminine and entirely admirable."

Her eyes widened. He held her gaze. Had she never encountered men who wanted more than a pretty girl adept at flirtation? She was so honest and forthright, he couldn't imagine her flirting. Although the thought of her teasing *him* produced a flickering warmth in his chest. She deserved to know there were men who found her captivating.

"I'm surprised ye've never married."

Her brows snapped down. "I've always been drawn to nursing. The vocation hasn't left the time or opportunity required to foster a romantic attachment."

"Is yer nursing a true vocation, then? Ye feel called by God?"

"No, I—" She stopped, rubbed the ring she wore on her right hand. "Perhaps I do, deep inside, but I've attributed my dedication to the way nursing has always made me feel. Connected to my family," she added softly.

He nodded. "Aye. Ye've paid homage to them. I know ye've derived great reward in comforting others, but surely yer parents would have wanted ye to know the love of yer own husband and children?" Her fisted hand came up to her mouth and the little red stone winked at him. "Ye'd make some lucky child an exceptional mother." The thought put an ache behind his heart.

With a jolt he realized her eyes brimmed with tears. Oh, damn. He captured her hand, interlocked their fingers, and squeezed. She squeezed back, twice as hard.

"I'm sorry, lass. I didn't mean to hurt ye."

Her lips tightened; she blinked and sniffed. "Don't apologize. You're being honest, and I daresay your words were ones my parents would have wanted me to hear. They and my brothers and sister would have wished me to live the fullest possible life." Her eyelids snapped closed. After a bit she dragged in a big breath and her hold loosened.

"It's not too late," he said. Could the same be said for him? Wouldn't Logan have wanted Cam to live a life abounding with love? Chock-full of joy? Thoughts of his brother made Cam's heart pinch. How many years now since Logan's death? Nearly eight.

Cam had spent those years acquiring experience, becoming a first-rate surgeon. His confidence and speed during operations, the attitudes of his fellow surgeons, the outcome of his patients, all told him he'd met his goal. Yet he wasn't happy. Hadn't been, even before the nightmares and shakes began.

He released Miss Lockwood—Elissa's—hand along with his pent-up breath. Yes, Logan would want him to know love and happiness. Miss Lockwood had produced a handkerchief from somewhere and was drying her eyes. The corners of her mouth tipped and his heart rolled over. Shedding tears hadn't made her self-conscious, as they would many women. Logan would have liked her.

Urgency gripped him. He wanted to pluck the worries from her mind and the mantle of weariness from her shoulders. He wanted to tug her outside and whirl her into the steps of a polka. Spin her and spin her, until her tears dried and her eyes sparkled, and she couldn't stop laughing. Dancing wasn't possible, but perhaps another form of entertainment was.

Cam cleared his throat. "We'll finish early today. Shall we collect Mrs. Blackwell and visit the gardens in Bebek?" Cam asked. "I haven't seen them yet." The gardens of the sultan's physician were much admired and they could do with a respite from this intensity. The gardens' owner had generously opened them to the French and English. "Or perhaps ye'd prefer shopping in Pera?" The French quarter in Constantinople was another popular destination.

Miss Lockwood spread her open hand over her heart. "I would love to go to the gardens, but we've a pressing need for cough drops and mouth drops, and the army stores have none. I know the market has sugar plums and licorice. They may have acidulated drops, too."

"Pera it is. I'll arrange for a caique and rowers."

"I'm sure Mrs. Blackwell will be grateful for the opportunity. You're positive the walking won't be too strenuous for you?"

Her concerned eyes caused a lightness to invade his chest and belly. He was happy to include their colleague, and her presence would prevent the gossip that might attend the two of them alone. "I'll be fine. We can hire a conveyance to take us from the dock to the market, if need be." They stood, ready to return to the ward. "It'll be good to get away for a few hours."

Miss Lockwood looked out the nearby window, to the deep blue glint in the distance. "The Bosporus is so beautiful. I appreciate the view every day, but being on the water is another kind of wonderful."

The little flecks in her eyes gleamed gold. *Another kind of wonderful, indeed.*

#

Three hours later, Elissa lazed on luxurious cushions in the bottom of a graceful little boat and enjoyed a water-level view of the gem-blue water and the colorful houses lining the banks. They headed toward Pera, situated in the Christian enclave on the northern side of the Golden Horn.

Sun-bronzed caiquejees, garbed in traditional white trousers and wide-sleeved jackets, bent their backs against what rowers called the devil current of the Bosporus. Each man's scarlet fez dipped in unison with the stroke of the oars, the purple silk tassel atop the headgear dancing.

The waterway bustled with darting caiques. Steamers and masted ships rode at anchor, creating a deep border of masts and smokestacks. Ashore, minarets thrust skyward, towering above the city landscape. Rolling hills of olive and cypress rose behind the city.

The British military hospitals were all situated on the Asiatic side of the Bosporus, in or near Scutari. Elissa had crossed to the European side of the strait once before. That visit had been to Stamboul, on the Turkish side of the Golden Horn, an inlet of the Bosporus that transected the European side of Constantinople.

The tangy smell of the sea filled Elissa's head. Her umbrella remained closed. They'd somehow managed to cross in between showers, and bright sunshine cloaked her shoulders and warmed her bones.

Today MacKay had exchanged his dark blue staff surgeon's uniform for the scarlet coat and gold-striped trousers of the Second Dragoons—the Scots Greys. Regimental surgeons wore the uniform of their regiment, but since his arrival, MacKay had donned the common uniform of hospital surgeons. It was good to see him back in his regimental dress.

For a moment she marveled at his battlefield experience. The Greys had earned a formidable reputation for their action at Balaklava. Charging uphill, they'd routed a division of Russian cavalry in a saber battle. That kind of fierce fighting must have resulted in horrific injuries. Must have meant MacKay on his feet, performing surgery non-stop for many hours, perhaps even days, assaulted by the screams of the wounded and the constant drumming boom of cannon barrage.

Elissa gave her upper arms a brisk rub to chase away a sudden chill. An unexpected, overpowering gladness erupted from her center. Gladness that he was away from the front for a time, that her patients could benefit from his fine care, that she had the opportunity to know him.

MacKay tilted his head back and closed his eyes. "The sun feels good."

His eyelashes and a few favored strands of hair glowed gold. After watching MacKay a moment, Mrs. Blackwell smiled at her. It was all too easy to read the older woman's appreciation of the big man. Every person in the ward admired his dedication and kindness, but seeing him at ease, his features softened and his strong neck thrown back, twisted something open deep inside her. Warmth flooded from her core to her fingertips. Her heart pressed against her ribs, too big for her chest.

Since their interlude at this morning's tea-time, she'd thought again and again of how MacKay had called her feminine and admirable. His voice, saying those words, repeated in her mind, and each time she experienced the same rush of delight and wonder. His eyes—warm, focused, sincere—she'd never forget the look in his eyes when he told her.

Elissa tore her gaze from his profile and glanced at Mrs. Blackwell. Thankfully, the lady was looking toward the shoreline and hadn't caught her lost in a daydream while gazing at MacKay. Every time Elissa was close to him she became distracted—assailed by something she didn't want to call desire, but couldn't find another name for.

Moments ago she'd started out thinking about his surgical prowess, but somehow ended up admiring not his skill, but his very masculine person. As much as she hated to admit it, she was in danger of becoming besotted.

Her life was full and rewarding. She rarely thought about the love and happiness a husband and children would bring to her life, the way she had this morning, but of course she knew. Today MacKay had taken her hand and spoken to her soul. What if this feeling wasn't one-sided? Shouldn't she welcome the opportunity to explore—and possibly grow—this attraction?

She focused on the water streaming past the hull of their boat. How could a war and Koulali be the time and place for romance?

Men as sick as those in Koulali required every bit of intelligence, discipline, and stamina she could muster. They deserved every bit of tenderness she held in her heart. She could save some of them. Others she could offer a tiny bit of peace in their last days.

No, this wasn't the time or place. She needed to stay true. To herself. To the promise she made at the graves of her parents, her brothers and sister. At least for now. Dreams of love—and MacKay—were unworthy of a dedicated Nightingale nurse. Somehow, she needed to ignore her dreams and these feelings, even though with each encounter, they grew stronger.

Should she request a different assignment? She liked Koulali and Ward Two. She didn't want to go back to the immense Barrack Hospital, and MacKay would return to the front in a month or two. She needed to somehow suppress these longings and be satisfied with MacKay's camaraderie.

She couldn't deny herself his friendship. It was too special and rare to toss away.

MacKay pointed down the coastline. "The gardens are about there, I think. I hope I have an opportunity to visit them before I leave. Today the market's a better choice, since we're in need of a few special supplies. At any rate, it's too early for most blooms."

A lock of hair fell over his forehead, and she was struck with an urge to smooth it back into place. She curled her fingers into a fist. She'd build a box around her heart and lock it. She'd avoid looking in his eyes and instead focus on the little chevron crease that resided in the space between his brows. Today would be good practice for when they conferred in the ward. There would be distance between them, and plenty of things in the marketplace to pin her attention on. She could talk to MacKay without looking at him. Grow more accustomed to being near him. Enjoy his friendship.

Mrs. Blackwell began telling MacKay about her previous trip to the gardens. Elissa kept her gaze steady on the lady. She'd soon be ashore and engaged in shopping and the sights of a bustling market. She could do this.

CHAPTER SIX

After landing, Cam hired a caleche to take them up the big hill in Pera. Leg well rested, he stayed beside his two ladies as they strolled through the marketplace. He needed to keep his eyes on the people around them and his mind on the women's security, instead of watching Miss Lockwood. He found doing so a challenge. Her face glowed—filled with delight at the sights around them.

While the market vendors were primarily men, most shoppers were Turkish women. Their cloaks, called feridjees, ranged from bright to the most delicate hues, and white veils covered their hair. Some had ornamented, head-hugging caps under the veils. Those eschewing cloaks wore colorful, long-sleeved dresses with matching bloused pantaloons under their skirts. The women were never alone but in small groups, often guarded by African slaves wearing dark green or brown feridjees. Small children accompanied some of the women, the mothers holding their children's hands and keeping them close as they navigated the aisles.

The people crowding the marketplace reflected the many different countries inhabiting the area. A Greek priest in a square cap passed, his long beard resting on the chest of his flowing black robe. A number of French and English sailors strolled the aisles. Sardinian soldiers mingled with Greeks and Armenians. During the Bosporus crossing, Mrs. Blackwell had entertained them with her memory of a Pasha on horseback, a train of people following behind.

Hungry-looking dogs slunk about, noses twitching at the odors of grilling meat. It smelled good to Cam, too. He guided his companions toward a man cooking over a brazier. The number of people waiting as the Turkish cook dished out food attested to its desirability. After a short wait Cam exchanged a few piasters for three squares of heavy paper holding kabobs and pilaf piled atop tender rounds of flat bread.

They huddled out of the stream of foot traffic and ate in silence. After a few hasty bites, Miss Lockwood and Mrs. Blackwell began giggling.

"What?" Cam looked between them. Both ladies were flushed. Miss Lockwood's fingers splayed over her mouth. Mrs. Blackwell bent and clutched her waist.

"We're inhaling it." Miss Lockwood chortled. "It's so good."

"It *is* good." But why were they laughing? Had he missed something?

"The lady volunteers and nurses don't have a cook the way you surgeons do. I'm guessing our meals are a bit more meager than yours."

The British doctors and surgeons had hired a local man to cook for them in their quarters. Cam contributed to the money pool that paid the cook and purchased food provisions. As officers, they also had military aides, who for all intents and purposes acted as servants.

"Ye're not well fed?" What was the bloody army thinking?

"We don't have the same resources as the officers." Mrs. Blackwell lifted her shoulders in a ladylike shrug.

Cam stiffened. He didn't like to think of the ladies doing without.

"We're enjoying the food today." Miss Lockwood pulled a cube of meat from her kabob.

No doubt Miss Lockwood's reassuring tone was meant to appease him, but he intended to look into the matter when they returned.

"My last market visit, strawberries were in season," Mrs. Blackwell said. "I'd never seen so many. Melons, too. They were delicious."

"This time of year, they'll have raisins, dried figs, and apricots. We'll buy some for ye to take back," Cam said.

Outside the entrance to a spice shop, Miss Lockwood's attention was caught by a parrot in a gaudy, painted cage. She stood in front of the bird, eating the remains of her meal, while the gray, red-tailed parrot eyed her.

"Aren't you a pretty bird?" Miss Lockwood said.

A shriek erupted from the parrot and they all jumped. The suddenly agitated bird stretched its neck up and down, bounced from foot to foot, and flapped its wings. "God save the Queen," the parrot screeched. "All hands on deck! Fire! Fire! Fire!"

A man, no doubt the proprietor of the shop, appeared in the doorway. He grinned, his teeth a white flash in his swarthy face. He stepped to the parrot's cage and pointed at the bird. "English!" He shook his head. He added something in Turkish, gave them a nod, and returned inside.

"He means the bird speaks English." Miss Lockwood's eyes sparkled.

"Ahoy. Ahoy. God save the Queen." The bird bobbed in an altogether comical manner.

They laughed. Good Lord, how long had it been since he'd laughed? So long, he'd forgotten how good it felt, how warm, laughter seesawing from his chest and belly. It flung open all his closed and locked doors, and left him feeling as wobbly as a babe taking his first steps.

He looked down. Swallowed. Pulled himself together.

"I think my speaking to him in English set him off," Miss Lockwood said. "You don't speak Turkish, do you?" she asked the bird.

"Attention!" The bird's feathers ruffled, settled, and he released a long, singular whistle.

"English, aye, but more specifically, he has the language of a British sailor. That whistle was a bosun's call." Cam hoped the parrot wouldn't start swearing like a man of Her Majesty's Royal Navy. "As entertaining as this fellow is, we'd best be on our way."

Miss Lockwood smiled. "Aye aye."

"Aye aye, sir," the bird corrected, and they all chuckled again.

They continued down the aisle, stopping at any stall or shop that caught one of their party's interest.

"Here they are." Miss Lockwood stepped to a display of candies, tobacco, and small edible treats. "Sugar plums and licorice. Dare I hope for acidulated drops, too?" After a bit of back and forth gesturing, the proprietor began wrapping up scoops of the sugar plums and licorice. Miss Lockwood walked along the displayed goods. She stopped and pointed at a basket of small egg-shaped, sugary candies. "Are these acidulated drops?"

"Yes, yes." That one accented word appeared to be all the English the nodding owner was capable of.

Miss Lockwood's hand hovered over the basket of candies. She plucked a candy out.

"Oh, my dear," Mrs. Blackwell said, frowning. "Are you sure that's wise? What if they aren't your drops, and they're something unpleasant?"

Miss Lockwood popped it into her mouth.

Cam didn't have to wait long for his reward of her pursed-lip smile. The lassie had the spirit and sense of adventure of ten women, her step light, her eyes looking everywhere as she browsed the marketplace, her smile directed at each person they passed. She'd tried the candy with the confidence and daring of an explorer. Her spontaneity delighted him. He looked down again, hoping his face hadn't revealed his appreciation.

"They're acidulated drops. Very tasty. Nice and tart, too."

"I see the ever-generous Miss Lockwood has a new supply of treats to offer her patients," a smooth voice said from behind them.

They turned to find Archer observing them. Miss Lockwood's shoulders squared. Her smile disappeared.

"You're taking advantage of our quiet spell, and seeing a bit of the country, Sergeant Archer?" Mrs. Blackwell didn't seem to have Cam's trepidation regarding the ward-master.

Archer's brows rose. "It's good to get away for a few hours, ma'am. Although I see even away from the hospital, Miss Lockwood has the welfare of her patients foremost in her thoughts."

The sergeant's words were acceptable, even flattering, yet something about the way he spoke them made Cam wonder if he wasn't mocking, rather than complimenting, her.

One corner of Archer's mouth quirked. "Did you see the lacework down the way, Mrs. Blackwell? You wear such pretty collars, I know you'd enjoy seeing what's there."

Mrs. Blackwell hurried away with Archer. Cam waited for Miss Lockwood to complete her purchase. He could see Mrs. Blackwell at the end of their aisle, looking over the table of lace finery and talking with Archer. Then she stopped browsing and faced the sergeant. The two appeared to be having a serious conversation, with Mrs. Blackwell leaning in as she listened.

Miss Lockwood collected her purchases and they wove their way down the aisle toward Mrs. Blackwell and Archer. As they drew close, his co-workers turned their heads in a sharp way that made Cam think they were checking on his and Miss Lockwood's approach. Just before they joined the couple, Archer quit talking. Was it Cam's imagination that Mrs. Blackwell looked worried? He wasn't imagining the crease in her brow.

The sergeant excused himself and left, and Cam noticed both women loosen a bit. Cam guided them back to the quay, thinking about the ward-sergeant. The man was arrogant. Archer didn't hide his dislike of taking orders from Miss Lockwood and Sister Margaret, but excepting the officers, he acted rude to everyone. He didn't single out the nurses. Perhaps the man bore a special resentment regarding Miss Lockwood, though. He'd been just short of inexcusable toward her on the ward. One thing Cam knew—he was going to find out what caused Mrs. Blackwell's frown.

CHAPTER SEVEN

In the ward the day after their trip to the market, Cam noticed Mrs. Blackwell approach Miss Lockwood, lean close, and whisper in her ear. When Mrs. Blackwell eased back, Miss Lockwood grew an inch taller. Back stiff and straight as a plank, she strode toward the makeshift staff room, Mrs. Blackwell on her heels. Tension radiated from both women. What was going on? He didn't like the look on either lady's face. Was there trouble of some sort?

He finished his notation and followed. If there was a problem, perhaps he could help. If it was something that didn't concern him, he wouldn't stay. Two feet from the doorway, Mrs. Blackwell's voice stopped him. She sounded nothing like the happy lady of yesterday's excursion.

"I feel you should know what Archer told me about you," Mrs. Blackwell's agitated voice said.

He'd wanted only to check on them, not eavesdrop, but found himself frozen in place, concealed by the canvas wall of the structure. Had the ward-master been gossiping about Miss Lockwood?

"He's noticed certain *looks* you've exchanged with officer MacKay. Looks he feels are romantic in nature. He suggested you and MacKay might be engaging in *an affair*," Mrs. Blackwell said, hissing the last two words. "I know you wouldn't do such a thing, but…"

Anger fired Cam's blood until he imagined steam rose from his skin.

"But what, Mrs. Blackwell?" Miss Lockwood's outraged voice reached him.

"I've seen how MacKay looks at you. He admires you. In the way of a man for a woman. I'm sorry to admit I even listened to

Archer, but you need to know what he is saying, and that others are watching. I don't know who else, if anyone, Archer has told. Mrs. Danvers, over in Ward Three, told me he's complained to the other ward-masters that you've criticized him. He said there was no cause for it, and that you've discredited him." A pause, then in a soft, concerned tone, "He's very full of himself. You need to be careful around him."

That bloody Archer! Cam rounded the edge of the screen. Both women jolted and turned wide eyes toward him. "Sorry, ladies," he said tersely. "I didn't intend to eavesdrop. I overheard my name, and froze." Then what he heard pulled him in. Judging by their expressions, he'd embarrassed both women. Miss Lockwood was avoiding his gaze.

He pinned Mrs. Blackwell with his eyes. "There hasn't been the slightest impropriety pass between Miss Lockwood and myself." Ach. He'd been too loud and forceful. Cam tempered his voice and spoke to Miss Lockwood, whose bottom lip was crimped between her teeth. "Archer's going to answer for this."

Her teeth released her lip, her eyelids fluttered, and she gave a tiny nod. Damn it. He'd tried to be discreet, but apparently, he'd done a bad job of it. Archer had seen Cam's eyes follow her, and noticed how often they exchanged words and smiles. Had others noticed? If not, they'd soon be aware, with Archer spreading his vile speculation.

Cam hadn't given enough thought to how his chats with Miss Lockwood might appear to those around them. He'd been lost in himself, selfish bastard that he was. How many times had he thought no further than provoking those blushes he loved?

"I never suspected either of you of being inappropriate," Mrs. Blackwell said. She looked back and forth between them. "Perhaps I should give the two of you a moment." The kindhearted lady left before he could respond.

Thank God she'd told Miss Lockwood. When he returned to the Crimea, he'd offer to carry something direct from Mrs. Blackwell to her son, by way of thanks.

Miss Lockwood turned to the small table, spooned tea into the waiting pot, then removed the always-steaming kettle from the brazier. Excepting the two red flags in her cheeks, she looked pale.

Cam fisted his hands. "I don't want tea."

She filled the teapot before replacing the kettle. She turned, smoothed her hands over her apron and clasped them at her waist. "I can't just stand here. I need to do something."

He nodded. A face-to-face conversation on such a topic while mere yards away from the ward wasn't on his list of desirables, either. "We need to talk." If nothing else, he needed to accept what blame was fitting, and apologize. "Why don't we meet in the yard at five-thirty? Ye'll be free then, until final rounds. We could take a walk before it gets dark."

"Won't that just cause more gossip?"

He grimaced. "It could, but it's far better than trying to meet clandestinely. I can't think of another way."

"All right," she said, her voice low and soft.

His stomach flipped. She looked shaken, and he couldn't think of a time he'd seen her like this. Damn it!

"Five-thirty in the yard," he confirmed, and left the ward room. He went to a nearby window and gazed at the overcast sky. Once he was off duty, he needed to give some thought to Archer. Cam thought he might shake the sergeant until his teeth rattled. He didn't think it'd be hard to stop the scoundrel telling tales about Miss Lockwood, but Cam wouldn't be here beyond another month or so. He didn't want to do anything that might give Archer cause to be vindictive toward her.

Archer's gossip might well have roots in his dislike of Cam. He'd been sharp with the sergeant a couple of times. The ward-master was the worst kind of leader, but he hadn't done anything flagrant enough to warrant a transfer or demotion.

He'd think of something. He wasn't about to go back to the front and leave Miss Lockwood at that little bastard's mercy.

#

Elissa had just enough time to hurry to the nurses' cottage and retrieve her bonnet and cloak before five-thirty. She returned to the hospital to wait under the small back portico and watch the falling drizzle in the waning light.

What would she say to MacKay? She felt like an abandoned bagpipe, air leaking out until all that remained was a limp, empty pouch, all the while her heart pounding like a regimental drummer beating a tempo designed to make her gasp. She could manage an apology, but how could she explain that she'd been watching him?

Movement alerted her to MacKay's coated presence. He opened a huge black umbrella and lifted it in a way that offered a share of its shelter. She stepped beneath the umbrella, careful to maintain a space between them.

"It'll be dark soon," he muttered. "We'll stay to the path."

The gravel path would also keep them out of the mud. The path went from behind the hospital and its outbuildings to the graveyard, which sat a good hundred yards behind the medical buildings. Not a desirable destination, but this wasn't intended to be a constitutional walk, nor an entertaining diversion. They were seeking someplace private where they wouldn't be overheard.

MacKay had replaced his crutch with a cane. His limp continued to slow him, enough so his pace matched hers in spite of his longer legs. He stayed as quiet as she did during the few minutes it took to negotiate the pebbled path. The gravediggers' work had stopped for the day, and when they reached the unmarked turf that was the British graveyard, they were alone. Elissa folded her arms and tucked her hands. Even with gloves, her fingers were freezing.

"Miss Lockwood, I hope ye'll accept my apology. I've been a dunderhead. Thoughtless and careless. And if your reputation suffers, it'll be on my head."

A jolt went through her. If anyone was responsible, Archer was. Not MacKay. The thought of repercussions that could come because of the rumor were terrifying. She could lose her position and be unable to attain another. Being the target of jokes and innuendoes would be humiliating and enraging, but the fear of losing her income was paralyzing.

"I'm willing to do anything ye think might help," MacKay said. "Talk to yer supervising nurse, return to the front early, whatever ye like. I'm just so sorry. I'll speak to Archer first thing, and stop his gossip. Impress upon him that any further gossip will end badly for him."

"It's not your fault," Elissa said.

"Aye, it was, and I've no excuse. I got so much pleasure out of making ye blush and earning yer smile. I will stop that, of course."

He didn't have to do much to make her blush and smile, but...he *liked* doing it? Could he feel an attraction for her, as she did for him?

Elissa closed her eyes. She needed to be honest and fair. To be as brave as MacKay. "I can't let you take all the blame. It's my fault, too. I encouraged our repartee. I tried to hide my feelings, but it appears I didn't do a very good job."

MacKay faced her. "What feelings are those, Miss Lockwood?" His voice sounded even deeper than usual, and gentle. "Please. Tell me."

He waited, face intent, while she searched for the necessary spunk. She didn't understand her compulsion to confess nor her certainty that she could trust him.

"I'm drawn to you," she admitted. "When we're together, it's as if I'm wearing my most comfortable shoes, and waiting to unwrap a present. I feel I can do or say anything, and you'll understand and not criticize me. I've never met anyone I immediately felt so…aware of and attuned to."

His head fell back and his chest expanded with a large breath. "I feel much the same attraction. I've tried to subdue it and I can't. It's rather remarkable. Especially given where we are."

"Koulali is not the place for romance," she murmured. "But working alongside you has given me a great deal of pleasure. So much so, it makes me feel a bit guilty." So much so, she didn't want anything to change.

MacKay nodded as if he'd had a similar experience.

"Please don't consider returning to the front early. Nor do you need to speak with Miss Hutton. I think, being aware that we've captured the speculation of those around us, I can avoid casting any further admiring looks your way." She'd tried many times before and failed, but somehow, this time, she'd have to succeed.

"As can I. I'm ashamed that I let my appreciation of ye—not as a colleague, but as a woman—show. Ye're right about this being the wrong place. It's the wrong time, as well. Even if the war should end tomorrow. At least for me it is."

Even if the war ended tomorrow? "Why is that?"

He grimaced. As if the question pained him.

For a long minute, he considered her. "Do ye think we have to earn happiness? Or do we have the right to all we can grab?" His voice dropped a full register.

The question startled her, and she wasn't sure what she *did* think. "What makes one person happy won't necessarily make another feel the same. If you're a starving man, eating food makes you happy. Every starving man has the right to food."

"Does he? Or must he earn the food? Either by earning the money to pay for it or, if it's being given to him, then by some act, even if only a smile or a thank you."

"What if he finds an apple tree growing in the wild?" Elissa asked. "Doesn't he have the right to pick and eat all he wants?"

"What if the tree bore a single apple, and by his taking it, a bird starves?"

"Then perhaps it's meant to be," Elissa suggested.

"So the vagaries of happiness can be attributed to fate or God," MacKay said, as if they'd been debating and he'd just made his point. "Americans feel they've a God-given right to the pursuit of happiness. They didn't list happiness itself in their Declaration, but instead its *pursuit*."

Something about this strange conversation didn't feel right. She wanted—desperately—to prove MacKay had the right to be happy. Wait. That wasn't what they were discussing. Or was it? She considered the tightness of his mouth. The tension around his eyes. "What if it's a baby that's starving?" Elissa asked.

He frowned. "I won't argue that an innocent baby must earn his milk."

The way he'd spoken the word *innocent*…Elissa's heart pinched. "Perhaps we're actually discussing whether some people deserve *un*happiness?" she suggested. A heavy feeling lodged behind her breastbone. "I understand how easy it is to think you've done something that deserves God's wrath. My family died when I was eleven. For a long time, I felt I was being punished, and I didn't know why."

Gaze pinned to her face, MacKay appeared to be paying close attention.

"Losing them, being alone… I couldn't imagine anything worse. I didn't regard my survival as a miracle. How could it be anything but a punishment? I know it's why I devoted myself to nursing to the exclusion of almost everything else. Caring for the sick, helpless, frightened—it made me feel good. As though I were showing Mama and Papa, William and John, Freddy and Mary how much I loved them. Showing them that if I'd been their nurse, nothing would have been left undone. At the same time, some part of me was trying to atone for whatever I'd done that caused God to punish me." No other man made her feel the way MacKay did. Perhaps her meeting him was God's way of saying He had other plans for her.

MacKay blinked. His eyes seemed over-bright. Teary-bright. She knew better than to think her story had brought him to tears. In a year's time, surgeons dealt with more tragedies than the average person saw in a lifetime.

"Are you...atoning for something?" Elissa asked softly. "So you can't allow yourself to be happy?"

Slowly, slowly, he nodded.

He'd hung the hook of his cane over his arm and stuck his free hand in his pocket. Elissa covered his umbrella-handle-hand with hers. "You've helped so many, and you must have sacrificed so much. When will the debt be paid?"

He turned his gaze back to the rows of graves. "I don't know."

"The pursuit of happiness has ended for those men," Elissa said, nodding to the expansive and ever-growing graveyard. "Perhaps we do them and our loved ones a disservice, worrying about what others think of our friendship? Perhaps we should just enjoy our association and let our friendship grow naturally?"

"What of your reputation?" he asked.

That was a worry, but they'd done nothing to cause her reputation to suffer. "The rumor is just a lie Archer is spreading. I'm not worried about what Archer thinks of me, and as far as I know, he's the only one criticizing my behavior. Mrs. Blackwell may be the only person he's told." She released her hold on his hand. "This feels too right to be wrong. I don't want to lose this bit of happiness I experience whenever I'm in your company."

"Neither do I," MacKay said. "It's meant so much. More than you know."

By mutual accord they turned to retrace their steps. Somehow the little space between them had disappeared, and with each step, their arms rubbed. Elissa filled her head with the pleasant scent of MacKay's soap and something uniquely him.

He stopped when they reached the cottage she and the other nurses shared, and exchanging smiles, they parted without a word.

CHAPTER EIGHT

Cam stood at his newest patient's bedside and stared down at ten ruined toes. *Hell.*

The patient watching him was an experienced campaigner, the 88th Regiment of Foot's regimental sergeant major. Unless they were very lucky, this would not only end the RSM's career, but turn him into a man unable to stand or walk.

"The frostbite should have been treated months ago." Cam tried to keep his tone level. He wanted to keep his anger at the war and this particular situation concealed. The poor blighter had ignored the injury into a state far worse than the initial frostbite damage. All ten toes were dead and resembled black leather. The gangrene on the left had spread into the foot.

Cam paused, rubbed his forehead, and then looked Percival Weatherley straight in the eyes. "Ye're losing the left foot, man. There's no help for it. I think the damage on the right is restricted to your toes. I think I can save that foot." If they were lucky, Weatherley would be left with enough foot to maintain balance, allowing him to walk with cane or crutch and a prosthetic on the left.

But holy hell. An RSM was the quintessential army man. How would Weatherley provide for himself, with legs almost as useless as the skills that once defined him?

Cam's weariness, improved since leaving the battlefront, grew heavy. Weighed down his limbs, shoulders, mind. He pulled up a stool and sat. "Why'd you wait so long?"

Even sitting, Weatherley maintained the posture of an RSM—stiffer and straighter than all other soldiers. A man who made no excuses. His chin tipped. "The 88th Foot needed me, sir. I didn't want to leave my boys, and I couldn't feel my toes much. I sawed off a tent pole for a walking stick and it kept me from falling. That is, until the past couple weeks, sir. Now the gangrene's spreading, I can't keep my feet under me."

"How bad is the pain?" The RSM's eyes were clear. The man wasn't taking laudanum.

Weatherley hesitated then gave a small nod. "The left foot's started paining me, sir."

Frostbite was a common winter injury. Cam had seen a lot of it this past winter. He stared at the proud eagle of a man before him. How had he managed to carry on all these months? Cam wished he had even a portion of the RSM's fortitude.

Miss Lockwood slipped past him to stand at Weatherley's bedside. She pressed her hand to his shoulder. So automatic, to offer the man comfort.

Cam caught her gaze. "The surgery shouldn't wait. I'll do it tomorrow." He turned to the RSM. "Ye'll have chloroform, so ye won't feel or remember anything."

Weatherley swallowed, the bony prominence in his neck bobbing. "Very well, sir. You think I might still be able to walk? After?"

Cam could tell the man was struggling to keep his voice even, but an edge of pleading still managed to bleed through. "I think ye might," Cam said.

Weatherley released a great sigh of pent-up breath. Cam stood and walked to the aisle. Miss Lockwood followed.

Archer entered the ward, and Cam waved him over. "Let's schedule this surgery for after morning rounds tomorrow," Cam said, indicating Weatherley with a tip of his head.

Archer's brows bunched; his mouth pursed into a regretful moue. "Sorry, sir. New arrivals are expected tomorrow and I've got two orderlies out sick. I won't have the necessary staff."

Archer was refusing to accommodate him? The bloody bastard. The man was fiendish. He looked just as innocent and regretful as the day Cam had confronted him about his rumor-spreading, and he'd waited more than two weeks to retaliate, but this refusal to carry out Cam's request was deliberate. There was nothing exceptional about the days new sick and wounded arrived, except that *all* of the medical staff were busier. It was Archer's job to find the men. Borrow them from the other wards, or as a last resort, help with the surgery himself. Why the ward-master had waited until now to agitate Cam, he had no idea. Weatherley being an RSM might have contributed to Archer's satisfaction. Perhaps his controlling the life and future of a regimental sergeant major, who held the highest possible sergeant's rank, gave Archer a heady sense of power.

Cam didn't have time for this. Weatherley needed that surgery. "Find a way to make it work, Sergeant. This man's having surgery tomorrow. I don't think ye'll like what happens if I have to make the arrangements myself."

The ward went quiet. *Ach.* He should have rebuked Archer in private, but Cam had lost all patience. And he wasn't tolerating the sergeant's maneuverings endangering his patient's health. Well, it was done. The ward-master would have to deal with the humiliation of being reprimanded in the middle of the ward. At any rate, Archer needed to be taken down a peg or two.

Archer's mouth got tight. His nostrils flared as he inhaled.

"Dismissed, Sergeant," Cam said.

Body rigid as a child's tin soldier, Archer snapped a salute. Cam returned the salute and turned to Miss Lockwood. Behind him, Archer's footsteps retreated. Miss Lockwood gave a tiny shrug and Cam almost burst out laughing. The lass had a lot of favorites, but as far as he knew, only one person she detested: Archer.

"I want ye there when I apply the post-surgical dressings, and I want ye doing his dressing changes."

"All right."

He heard the question in her voice. "I believe how a stump turns out depends in part on how it's wrapped while it's healing. I just wish I'd had more opportunity to test my theory."

"In part?" Miss Lockwood asked.

"The way the surgeon fashions the stump—the amount of muscle and tissue covering the bony end—determines how much pressure the stump can take when the man walks with an artificial limb. Of course, the design of the prosthesis is important as well."

Miss Lockwood's brows scrunched together. "I haven't noticed anything special about the stumps or their dressings."

"Most amputations are done in the field hospital, in the heat of battle. Surgeons don't have the luxury of adopting new theories and techniques. I know ye realize how common it is for a stump to have edema. The way I wrap them, edema doesn't form, which allows for better and faster healing."

"RSM Weatherley is fortunate to have landed here, and gotten you as his surgeon."

Perhaps. As long as I can hold my hands steady. Miss Lockwood's compliment made sharp pleasure jig down his spine and whirl in his chest, but it didn't rub out the voice that pricked his conscience.

"I'll be there tomorrow, sir." She started to turn away then hesitated and turned back. "Thank you for teaching me. For choosing me to teach. For trusting me, I mean."

She'd gotten flustered, which he'd never seen her become. Cam suppressed a smile. Miss Lockwood could make him go topsy-turvy, too. "No need to thank me. I'm grateful ye're here. Ye'll take care to do it right, and ye'll share your knowledge with those under you."

He moved down the row of beds, pausing at the foot of Riley's.

"All invalids for England, proceed to the shore." The call, at first distant, became strong. And then less clear again, as the announcing soldier worked his way through each ward. Mondays and Thursdays all men well enough to travel embarked and set sail for home.

Ten men were leaving Ward Two today. They'd been sitting on their beds, sharp in new uniforms, their kits ready beside them. Now grins lit their faces. Hanrahan and Dunn cozied up on each side of William Lynch, who was still a bit weak. Some of those too sick for discharge pressed letters into the hands of the departing men. For a few minutes all activity in the ward stopped as goodbyes were said.

"Do you think I'll ever be one of them?" Riley tipped his chin at the men's retreating backs. His freckles stood out plain on his pale face.

Cam could put Riley on a ship, but he didn't feel confident the soldier would maintain his health during the sea voyage. Every time Cam relaxed and thought Riley was on the mend, the man worsened again.

Cam stepped to the head of Riley's bed. "Ye've made a lot of progress." With a couple waves of his fingers, he motioned for Riley to sit up. Cam had to support the man's back and push to get him up the last bit. He instructed Riley to take deep breaths, and he pressed his ear to the corporal's back. When Cam straightened, his gaze went to Miss Lockwood, who stood at the foot of the bed.

She was chewing her lip, but stopped and smiled. Cam knew the corporal was a favorite of hers. Worry lines creased her forehead.

Perhaps she had an intuition regarding Riley. Cam didn't like what he'd heard in the corporal's lungs.

The deep breathing made Riley cough. Once his breathing settled again, his gaze narrowed on Cam. "Well, how's it sound?"

"I still hear congestion. The fevers aren't as high, but occur most nights."

Riley scowled.

"Yer wound has healed. Once we improve the condition of yer lungs, ye'll be off to England."

Miss Lockwood moved to stand opposite Cam. "I put aside an extra portion of pudding for you," she whispered to Riley.

The soldier settled onto his back. "You're too good to me, miss."

Miss Lockwood gave his hand a squeeze.

Cam looked at her and tried to impart a message with his eyes. She seemed to understand. She followed him down the aisle and into the ward room. He told her at once. "I'm afraid he has consumption."

She gasped and clapped her hand to her throat. As if her legs couldn't support her, she dropped into a chair. He took the seat beside her.

"It complicates the pneumonia, and it's why the infection has lingered so long. His fevers and sweats stem from both conditions. By this time pneumonia would have either killed him or he'd be recovered. I think he'd be well now, if he didn't have the consumption."

Riley's course had been atypical. He'd recovered from his wound infection, but the pneumonia had persisted, with Riley continuing to have the same moderate severity of symptoms. "His pneumonia and general illness disguised the signs of consumption. I attributed his weight loss to his infections and the small portions of food he was taking. Once his pattern of night sweats began, I became suspicious, but it wasn't until today that I was sure." Today he'd been able to hear the bronchial sounds of consumption in Riley's upper lungs, the crackles of his pneumonia in his lung bases. His sputum contained streaks of blood.

Pressure to his forearm made him look down. Miss Lockwood clutched his arm. Her eyes gleamed with tears.

He covered her hand with his own. "He's special to ye."

She nodded. With her free hand, she dragged trembling fingers under her eyes. "He puts me in mind of my brother. Freddy was a boy when he died, but I think if he'd lived, he would have looked much like Riley. They've the same hair and skin. The same eyes and sweetness. Riley makes me laugh. Just like Freddy did."

Cam nodded. Made a sympathetic noise.

"He had cholera. Like we all did. Half the village had it. So many sick, and few to take care of us."

She looked up at him, the corners of her mouth drooping, her face resigned. Cam fought against gathering her into his arms.

"William was seventeen, John, fifteen, and Frederick, nine. Mary was just a baby yet—only two years old."

He remembered her explaining why the local midwife had taken her in. "Ye survived and became a nurse." She'd talked about it before. She looked on her nursing as a sacred oath. Cam marveled at the resolve of a grieving twelve-year-old, dedicating her life to caring for others after losing her family.

"I won't lose Riley." Her tone turned ferocious. Not the ferocious of a tiger. The ferocious of an angel wresting back a soul already taken.

Cam gave her a sharp nod. "We'll just keep on, building him up as best we can. Push as much food down him as he'll take. Maybe we'll get lucky and the pneumonia will subside. Right now, he's too weak. We need to make him a little stronger. Get him up walking, perhaps. Then he'd be well enough to sail home."

Miss Lockwood's jaw firmed. Her lips pressed together. Her eyes shone. Clear, bright, determined. She'd regained control of herself. Somehow, thank God, he'd managed to say and do the right thing.

"Thank you for understanding," she said.

Such a straightforward woman. Her sincerity never failed to impress him.

"I was even younger than ye when I decided to become a surgeon." He wasn't sure why he'd shared that, but her widened eyes told him he'd captured her interest. "My father, grandfather, and older brother are apothecaries. I wanted to know and do even more. So I enrolled at Edinburgh University, along with my twin brother, Logan. We were the first in my family to attain a university education."

"You're a twin," Miss Lockwood confirmed, smiling. "He must miss you. They all must."

Miss him? They'd been glad to be rid of him. Everything changed after Logan's death. Cam abandoned his lifelong plan to join his father's practice, and instead joined the military.

"Logan is dead, but the rest of my family understood my leaving. I wanted to get a lot of surgical experience. The army is good for that." It was good for other things, too, not just learning how to repair a complicated throat injury like Logan's. The army hardened a man. Tested him. Made him unshakeable. Cam needed to live his life so bold, so fully, and save so many, that his guilt would drain away.

Miss Lockwood's forehead and eyes scrunched. "I'm so sorry," she said, her voice brimming with sorrow and regret. "Your family must be very proud. You've become an exceptional surgeon. I'm grateful I've had the opportunity to work with you."

The warmth in her eyes thawed his limbs, which always turned to ice when he thought of his twin's death. Logan's death had been Cam's fault. He couldn't talk about Logan, though. Not here, in the ward room, and if he were honest, not anywhere. Not even to Miss Lockwood.

"Thank you," he said, rising. "I should get back to work."

"We both should," Miss Lockwood said, and returned to the ward.

He *was* a good surgeon. He'd performed hundreds of surgeries. Been aggressive, decisive, fair, and compassionate.

But somehow he'd gained nothing. Because in that most important, deepest part of himself, he seemed to still be the man he had run from.

CHAPTER NINE

Cam woke Weatherley just before leaving the ward. The RSM blinked a few times. Cam saw when the man's eyes focused and his mind sharpened. He'd wakened earlier, after the chloroform cleared his system, but had fallen right back to sleep and continued to snore through the afternoon.

"The surgery went well," Cam said. "I removed no more than what we discussed. Ye should be able to get about on crutches. Maybe canes."

Weatherley swallowed and nodded.

"Be sure and ask for laudanum if ye have pain."

"The nurse gave me some a while ago, when she checked my bandages. Water, too."

"Good. I'll be back in a few hours. Try to rest and not worry."

"MacKay," Humphrey called from the open door. "Come see. The local residents are treating us to a bit of a festival." Humphrey disappeared into the yard and two orderlies moved into the doorway. An ambulatory patient joined them, gazing over their shoulders. They moved aside when Cam reached them, and he stepped into the yard.

Lively music filled the air. A small group of Turkish musicians were grouped at one side of the yard. Cam saw a large drum, two stringed instruments—one that looked something like a long dulcimer being played with a bow, the other a short, gourd-shaped instrument strummed with the hand—and two different horn-type instruments.

There was meat cooking, and trays of edibles being offered. The locals seemed dressed in their brightest and best. It appeared every off-duty orderly and nurse and every ambulatory patient were gathering, wide smiles on their faces.

Miss Lockwood and Sister Margaret stood a short distance away. Cam joined them.

"It's the last day of the Sugar Feast," Miss Lockwood said.

"The celebration marks the end of Ramadan, and the month-long time of fasting," Sister Margaret said. "This is the third and last day of the holiday. I'm told they wanted to share a bit of it with us."

"This is delightful," Cam said. The British bought much of their fresh food stuffs from the local residents, and the surgeons and physicians staffed a small clinic once a week, welcoming anyone with a need. "It appears all locals who wanted to contribute, could." He saw from their clothing there were Greeks and Kurds included in the mix, so they'd expanded the celebration beyond the religious observance.

Women circulated through the British, offering candies. Cam sampled a couple.

"This must be why it's called the Sugar Feast," Miss Lockwood said, taking a candy from a woman wearing a red caftan and gold-colored trousers. "All the sugar one could ever want to indulge in." She popped a candy in her mouth and looked so delighted Cam laughed aloud. There were fruit and cakes and meat, continual music and even a few dancers.

"I hope you ladies are being regularly supplied with soups and stews now," Cam said. He'd arranged for the surgeons' cook to make an extra pot of soup each day and deliver it to the nurses' quarters. All the surgeons had contributed to pay for the purchase of meat and vegetables, and the cook's additional labor.

Sister Margaret's hand fluttered to her chest. "Mr. MacKay," she said. "I—all of us—cannot thank you and the other surgeons enough." Her hand dropped and pressed against her midsection. "My stomach is filled every day. The food is such a blessing."

Cam gave a nod. "Good."

A boy garbed in Turkish clothing presented each of them with a wooden spool, a string wound around each central groove. The boy demonstrated, letting the spool fall while the string fed out, then with a tug, brought the spool back up the string. Down, up, down, up, the spool unwound and wound.

Sister Margaret excused herself and joined her sister comrades, showing off her new toy. Miss Lockwood seemed to have a knack for keeping the spool in motion. She didn't let the occasional undesired drop deter her, getting the toy back in motion without fuss.

Cam had the devil of a time with his, rarely getting it up and down more than twice without the string playing out and leaving the spool dangling. The sound of chuckling swung his gaze from toy to Miss Lockwood, who was laughing at him.

He managed to withhold his grin and produce a frown. "I never suspected ye'd be the sort to laugh at someone trying their best and bungling it," Cam said.

His pretend-grump didn't fool her. She laughed harder. And sent her spool spinning down and up with a snap.

"Ye shock me, ridiculing my lack of talent. I cannae help myself," he said, adopting an outraged tone.

"Well, I'm astonished by your poor sportsmanship," Miss Lockwood said.

She didn't do as well as he at managing her expression and voice, though. She tried, but wasn't able to constrain her giggles.

"How about a contest requiring *real* skill and concentration?" Cam asked. He pointed to several young boys engaged in a pea-shooting contest. "Are ye game? Or afraid of being bested?"

Her brows rose and her chin jutted. "I accept your challenge."

They wove through the gathering to the pea-shooters, who stood about fifteen feet away from a target fashioned of wood and moist clay. It stood on edge atop a barrel, and leaned against the wall behind it. After several minutes of gesturing, Cam was in possession of two fine tubes and a small bag of dried peas. He offered both shooters to Miss Lockwood. She lifted and examined each foot-long tube in turn, peering inside and giving each an experimental huff.

"This one," she said, showing her preference for the longer of the two.

"Very well." Using his boot heel, Cam drew a line in the patch of dirt at their feet. "Best of three?" he asked.

"Fine."

One of the boys offered a basket, and Cam turned the bag of dried peas into it. Another boy readied the target for a new game by wetting his hand and smoothing the moist clay that covered the bottom of a wooden tray. After drawing concentric circles in the smoothed clay, he stood the tray back up. The peas would leave a mark where they struck.

Cam and Miss Lockwood positioned themselves behind the line and faced the target. "Ladies first," Cam said with a sweeping wave.

Miss Lockwood took her time selecting the perfect pea. "Shouldn't there be a prize?" she asked, sorting peas with the tip of her finger.

"Hmm." Cam gave the back of his head a scratch. "The officers' cook makes excellent biscuits—good enough to sell in any English tea shop." Miss Lockwood gave him a wide-eyed look. "Shortbread biscuits," he added.

"That will do for me," she said, an unmistakable note of longing in her voice, "but what about your prize?"

"I have some socks that need mending," he said quickly, praying she was a better hand at darning than the servant he shared with another surgeon.

"Done," Miss Lockwood said, and dropped several peas into her apron pocket. She inserted one into her shooter, then slowly raised the tube and positioned it against her lips.

A large breath, then...*thwack*. The pea hit, leaving a small mark in the largest ring of the target. Cam loaded and fired his shooter quickly, having participated in many such contests with his brothers.

Miss Lockwood turned to him with mouth agape. Her open mouth snapped shut and her eyes narrowed. She pointed to the mark left by his pea, in the ring closest to the bull's eye. "I believe you forgot to mention that you are an accomplished pea-shooter, Mr. MacKay."

"Perhaps it would have been advisable to inquire, Miss Lockwood."

Jakes and several of Ward Two's recuperating patients strolled up and gathered behind them. "Aw, don't let him rattle you, miss," Jakes said. "The trajectory arcs. Tip your shooter up a bit."

Cam chuckled. What silly fun. Joy, pure and simple as a child's, filled his chest.

Receiving continual calls of encouragement, Miss Lockwood slowly raised and tilted her shooter. *Thwack*. She'd bettered her position, striking two rings out from center.

"Giving me a bit of competition, are ye?" Cam asked. Without hesitation he raised his shooter and blew. And again hit the ring encircling the bull's eye.

"You wouldn't deprive a lady of her biscuits, would you?" Miss Lockwood asked.

"You don't know how big the holes in my socks are," Cam returned. "It's mighty uncomfortable."

"You can do it, miss," Jakes said. "Don't get nervous, now. Just like before, only raise it a little bit higher. Blow quick and hard."

Teeth crimping her lower lip, forehead creased in a frown, the lass was concentrating hard. She nodded, raised the shooter, and...*thwack*.

Jakes groaned. Miss Lockwood turned a friendly glare on Cam and he laughed. He'd make sure she got a plate of biscuits as a thank-you for the darning.

Miss Lockwood grinned.

Cam collected her shooter and returned both, along with a coin, to the boy who'd supplied them. Jakes and Miss Lockwood began to talk. Relaxed and contented, Cam let their words flow over him, and he watched. Laughing eyes. A lovely face. She seemed completely unaware of how appealing she was.

She made him smile. Quite irresistibly. Today he'd been given a taste of happiness, and he'd grabbed more. It had been years since he'd felt so light, so carefree. So...happy. Could it really be this easy? Not without Miss Lockwood's special style of cheer, he didn't think.

#

Cam jolted awake, wrenched up, and threw his legs over the side of his bed. His damp undershirt stuck like frog's skin.

Had he cried out? He listened, but all was dark and quiet, excepting the scurry of a rat. The whole country was overrun with the cursed things.

He bent forward and clutched his sweaty head. *Christ.* Where in hell had that dream come from? It was the first nightmare in over three weeks. Was it payment for having been happy today? Of course it wasn't, but he'd begun to hope he'd stopped having the dreams.

He no longer had the pressure of fifty wounded waiting their turn for his care. Other doctors were trying to save those with severed limbs and torn bodies and souls blasted halfway to heaven.

A roll of nausea made him retch. He gripped the back of his neck, sucked in air, willed iron through his veins.

Further sleep was out of the question.

He got up, pulled a blanket around his shoulders, and went to his trunk. He could barely see it in the scarce light, but he wouldn't need light to find what he was after. He lifted the lid. His hand went to the flask like lightning to a rod.

He settled into his one comfortable chair and took a pull. The whiskey washed remnants of the nightmare down to the bottom of his belly, where they burned, burned, burned away. His chest eased as a great waft of air squeezed out of him. The smell, the burn, the warmth in his belly. They all soothed his pain.

Hours remained until daylight. Plenty of time for the effects of the alcohol to wear off before he went on duty. Sometimes a bit of whiskey helped chase away the demons. Helped him relax. Helped steady his hands, which—*damn it*—were trembling. Again.

Cam took another swig. He might seek temporary oblivion with whiskey, many did, but he'd never become a drunk. The burn of the liquor unfurled and snaked through his body, a winding rope of heat. Heat that swirled into his head and settled his mind.

Since his arrival at Koulali, his growing concern over his symptoms of neurasthenia—his riddled nerves—had waned. As had the trembling in his hands. Not that he'd ever voiced his worries. Not even on the Crimean Peninsula, when his nightmares were at their worst. Doing his job was the important thing, and he managed to do it well despite every hardship and challenge. Why should he worry? This war made everyone's nerves suffer to some degree, and neurasthenia was a temporary condition.

Did Miss Lockwood suffer as he did? He'd seen no sign of it. She was strong as the finest tempered steel. No matter how dire the situation, she never hesitated, never wavered. He doubted she'd ever given in to defeat, the way he had with his brother.

Logan had needed a skilled surgeon that day—the day he'd gotten Cam as his surgeon and died because of his lack of experience. Died because of Cam's weak nerves and indecision and trembling.

A dagger split his heart. His chest. Sliced him in half.

He hated each failure. Mourned each loss. But the day his twin died—that day Cam lost a part of himself. A part that never filled, never stopped aching, never knew peace. He'd garnered enough experience for ten and become a highly skilled surgeon, but it hadn't changed the way he'd failed Logan.

Cam drained the flask, cherished the burn and the release. He hurled the flask toward his open trunk, slumped deeper into the chair, and covered his eyes with his hand. He'd give five years of his life to be sitting with Elissa Lockwood right now, drinking tea.

Her gentle calm overlay bedrock, and the combination of the two settled the turmoil inside him. Even a few minutes in her presence buoyed him. What would it be like, to call such a woman his? To have her sit across from him every day, to make a home with him, to have her in his bed every night?

The day they stood at the graveyard and talked, she'd challenged him to be happy. Not knowing what tormented him, she'd managed to plant the idea that Logan would have wanted Cam to be happy. Even that Cam owed it to Logan to be happy. He hadn't been able to dismiss the notion. It circled 'round and 'round inside his head.

Cam closed his eyes and cautiously allowed an image of Logan to form.

There he was. Joyful. Smiling. The sweet, sharp pain that usually accompanied his envisioning Logan didn't come. Warmth, far greater than the whiskey warmth in his belly, wrapped around his heart. Of course Logan would have wanted Cam to be happy. His brother had loved him.

Logan would have liked Elissa. He'd have told Cam to woo her, marry her, make bairns with her. Was it such an impossible dream?

He held his hand a few inches from his face. Steady. The trembles were gone. A dream now and then needn't concern him. Who wouldn't have been shaky after a nightmare like that?

Far more significant was the hopefulness that seemed to have taken up residence in his person. After being slammed shut and locked for eight long years, the door of *Life* had swung open, and a fresh, fragrant breeze had swept through. He'd caught himself whistling the other day. He hadn't whistled in...he couldn't remember the last time. Now his days weren't long enough. Each brought more heady moments of a happiness so pure and sweet, he wasn't sure he'd ever known the like. He was healing.

Some of the men he treated suffered so horribly, they prayed for God to take them. Standing at those bedsides Cam could have felt guilty, that his happiness was disrespectful, but he didn't feel that way. He'd begun to notice easement in his patients' faces when he was near them. He seemed to carry a bit of that fragrant breeze around with him, somehow sharing it. Elissa had always had the knack, and he was learning from her.

Soon this war would be over, and when it was, Cam thought there might not be any more impossible dreams. They'd all be within his reach.

CHAPTER TEN

Four days after learning Riley had consumption, Elissa found Miss Hutton in her cramped office, working late, attending to correspondence.

"Miss Lockwood. Please, come in." The Koulali nursing superintendent rose, shut the door, and waved Elissa to a chair.

Elissa did her best to quash the anxiety bubbling in her stomach. She had a very disagreeable suspicion as to why Amy Hutton had summoned her.

Miss Hutton laced her fingers together and rested locked hands atop her desk. She looked cross with her forehead creased and her lips pressed tight. "I'm afraid I've received a complaint regarding your behavior. One I must address."

Elissa held very still as her body went hot. This couldn't be about the care she gave her patients. This was about her and MacKay, even though nothing inappropriate had passed between them. Even knowing the complaint was without merit, being brought to the attention of Miss Hutton was mortifying. Elissa had tried to hide her reactions to MacKay ever since Mrs. Blackwell's warning. Archer had been the instigator then, too, and who else would have complained? He watched her and MacKay the way a wolf watched a wounded lamb.

"I received an anonymous note that accuses you and Surgeon MacKay of—well, of forming an attachment, I suppose."

Righteous anger turned her spine hard and straight as an Enfield rifle barrel. She did *not* deserve an investigation or a dressing-down.

"You're accusing me of inappropriate behavior based on an anonymous note?" Elissa's voice snapped like a battle flag in high wind.

A pink flush spread up Miss Hutton's throat. "I'm not accusing you of anything. Given its anonymity, the note is suspect. Still, I believe I'm obligated to look into its charges."

Elissa held herself as still a possible. "Officer MacKay and I have done nothing to warrant speculation or censure."

Miss Hutton's brows rose.

"I assume mutual respect and friendship are permitted?"

The supervisor sighed. "Of course. I also know how attractive and dedicated MacKay is. You're lovely, and one of my best nurses. It's not difficult to imagine the two of you finding each other—appealing."

Elissa stayed silent. She'd choke if she tried to speak.

"Any romantic association between nursing personnel and surgeons or orderlies is prohibited. I know you understand this. It's possible some of your interaction with Staff Surgeon MacKay was misconstrued. Keep in mind that others are watching. You don't want your character called into question."

Elissa clenched her teeth so hard she feared they might crack. Whatever was between her and MacKay was their business, not anyone else's. What right did the army or the nursing service have, to declare what she and MacKay could and could not share between them, as long as they were discreet? What if destiny or God or serendipity had intended for them to meet? Were they to remain strangers, disregarding this compulsion that drew them together?

Archer wrote the anonymous note held by Miss Hutton. Elissa knew it. And there was nothing innocent about his intent. She didn't have any proof, though, and without it, Miss Hutton might doubt Elissa's accusation. She didn't need her judgment called into question.

"I'll be mindful that others are watching," Elissa conceded.

"Thank you. That's all I ask." Miss Hutton gave a dismissive nod.

Elissa stood. "Are you speaking to officer MacKay—or anyone else—about this?"

"No. This will go no further. I don't credit anonymous accusations or rumors. A nurse and doctor would have to be seen engaging in intimacies and reported. Still, I felt it appropriate to inform you I'd received the note, and to give you a warning."

Elissa strode toward the nurses' quarters, walking fast. Miss Hutton might be satisfied, but that didn't mean she wouldn't be watching. As hard as Elissa worked, as much as she cared about the men under her care, Archer had succeeded in casting suspicion and placing her beneath the eye of her supervisor.

She flung open the central door leading out to the yard and encountered MacKay. She stopped, skirts swirling. She looked at his face and felt a portion of her tension slide away. Just being in his calm, level-headed, sensible presence made her feel better.

His brows rose. "Yer *birse's* up, lass. What happened?"

"*Birse?*"

"Yer temper. Something's riled ye."

"Oh. I…" She itched to stamp her foot but tapped her toe instead and folded her arms. "If I talk about it here I'll attract attention we can't afford."

He frowned. "Where are ye off to?"

She tapped faster. Shook her head. "Nowhere."

"Walk down to the quay. Slow, like ye're goin' to take in the sunset. I'll go a roundabout way and meet ye there. We've got time before last rounds."

She filled her lungs. Slow, he'd said. She gave him a nod and headed for the quay.

Being by the water helped. One supply ship was moored at the dock, apparently already off-loaded, given its lack of activity. Reminding herself to stroll, she headed down the quay and gazed across the blue Bosporus to the European side. The sun hung low, sinking toward green hills, the sky a panorama of radiant red and gold. She sighed. So many beautiful sunsets here.

She hadn't gone a dozen yards before MacKay joined her.

"Ah, good, ye're lookin' easier. Now tell me what's wrong."

Elissa told him all. He looked thunder-smitten afterwards, but she felt appreciably better. They reached the end of the quay. The sun had dropped to kiss the earth, and a ruby-red wash colored the entire western sky. Without speaking they moved to a bench at the end, and sat. Nearby, a local fishing boat swayed, as though the Bosporus were rocking it to sleep. A bit more of Elissa's agitation slipped away.

"That bloody-minded bastard," MacKay said. "It had to be him, but there's no proving it. Wouldn't do any good even if we could. I'm proud of ye for keeping yer head."

"I wanted to give her a piece of my mind," Elissa said, "but she'd been decent about it, and I knew I'd be smart not to. At any rate, the regulation forbidding officers and nurses keeping company exists. It's controlling and unfair and senseless. But here we are," she continued, throwing her arms wide, "meeting in secret, as if we're criminals. And we don't even have a romantic association."

"Well…"

Something about the way he said it made her seek MacKay's steady green eyes. They held a look that made her feel he'd pulled the glowing ruby sky down and wrapped it around them.

"I've a mind to change that, lass," he said. "For weeks you've had me thinking about the future, and feeling things I've never felt before. We've already been accused, we're being watched, and you've received a warning. If we end up in trouble, it might as well be for something we actually did, instead of a rumor."

His words made champagne effervesce through her veins.

"My feelings have grown romantic, and I think yours have, too. If we ignore this opportunity, we'll squander what we should be treasuring. We haven't much time here, but there'll be more time later, when the war is over."

She wasn't sure she could catch her breath, or put two coherent words together. "You…want us to…keep company?"

"We'll be discreet. Careful. If ye agree, that is. I'd like to enjoy a bit of time alone with ye before I leave, with no one watching or listening. We can manage one or two afternoons, I hope." He rolled his shoulders and gave her a smile so quick, it vanished almost before it formed. "I want to know ye better. Want to be with ye and be free to express what I'm feeling, but it should be yer decision. It's not fair, but we both know as a man my code of conduct is more lenient than yers. If we're thought to be more than friends, ye'll be judged more severely. Ye're the one who's been warned. I'm willing to take the risk, but if we are discovered, the consequences could be worse for ye."

Would a romance with MacKay be worth the repercussions if it were revealed? "Yes. I want to be more than friends," Elissa said. She didn't need to think about it further. It'd be worth the risk.

His teeth flashed in a broad smile. The sun was down; the light fading fast. His hand settled on her low back, and drew her to him. A knot of excitement pulsed in her abdomen. His breath whispered against her cheek, and he kissed her. His lips were warm. Soft, yet firm. He smelled of soap and ocean air overlaid with a tinge of chloroform. Her lips parted and the tip of his tongue grazed hers before he eased away. Heat flashed over her neck and chest, and deep inside, she glowed like the moon on a clear, hot night.

Air rushed in and filled her lungs. His gaze swept her face, he made an impatient sound, and pulled her back. Their mouths connected solidly, and she forgot to breathe. His lips nudged hers apart. She mimicked every taste and touch and stroke while a turbulent waterfall of desire spilled through her.

He gave her a last, lingering caress of his mouth. Her heart beat like she'd run from the ground floor of Barrack Hospital to the top. She stared at him. Pressed her palm to her heart. Were all kisses like this? She didn't need others to know.

"I think you've melted me," Elissa said.

The corners of MacKay's mouth curved. He pulled her hand from her chest and held it. Elissa gazed at their connected hands, rubbed her thumb back and forth across his skin. She'd noticed his hands on his first day, during Riley's surgery. Strong and masculine, right from the start she found them beautiful. They were skilled and careful, capable of great gentleness. Always, they were sure.

She loved his hands.

"We need to get back," MacKay said. "It's nearly dark and time for final rounds." They stood, and still connected, headed for the hospital.

She'd once thought a romance would conflict with a dedicated nurse's calling. She'd been wrong. MacKay made her happy, and happiness wouldn't interfere with her patients' care. Just the opposite was true. Elissa wished the world's perception of a nurse's morality was as simple as her decision had been. "We could end up getting discharged, you know," Elissa warned. Such an outcome was unthinkable, but as awful as that would be, she couldn't pass up the opportunity to discover how deep these feelings between her and MacKay might grow.

"Aye." He squeezed her hand. "But first they have to catch us acting in an unbecoming fashion. That's not going to happen." He released her and waved her on. "Run ahead, now, 'Lissa. I'll be right behind ye."

#

Nine days later, a howling man arrived bound to his stretcher. Even though ropes stretched across his body and secured his one arm and both legs, the soldier struggled. A bandage circled his head and covered his left eye. The hurrying transporters trotted up the ward aisle and placed the new patient atop the bed Elissa indicated. As soon as they untied the man and slid the stretcher out from under him, he began flailing his shaking right arm and trying to sit up. His mouth stretched wide in a horrible grimace.

"Cannon barrage!" His wild eye swept the room, but Elissa didn't think he saw the ward. His mind formed a different image.

The older of the two stretcher-bearers paused before her. "Cannonball took his arm off at the shoulder. Shrapnel got his eye. He seemed all right until yesterday, when he started hallucinating. We found two empty flasks with his kit."

She hadn't been expecting wounded today. "Where did you come from? Who is he?"

"Ma'am, we're full of wounded, sailing direct from Balaklava to England. When he started yelling and acting like a madman, the captain said to put him off here. He's Lieutenant Richard Parker, ma'am."

Elissa dismissed them, collected towels and a pitcher of hot water. She could understand why the ship captain had decided to remove the lieutenant. As soon as she stepped close to the new patient, he swung his arm, hand outstretched and reaching. Elissa grabbed his hand and set the pitcher on the floor.

"Cannon barrage!" he cried. "Look out!"

The poor man appeared terrified. "You're safe." She held his hand with both of hers. "Easy now. You'll hurt yourself." He held on to her like she was a lifeline. His eye locked on her face.

Jakes stepped up to the bed and placed his hand in the middle of the lieutenant's chest. "Do you need help, Miss Lockwood?"

The orderlies were all out front, sewing and stuffing mattresses. It was like Jakes to check on her when he saw the new patient arrive.

After the activity the sick officer endured with the transfer from his ship, and his explosive hallucinations, the lieutenant appeared exhausted. Now quiet and quivering with tremors, he lay with eye squeezed shut.

"I think we'll be all right, Jakes. Thank you."

The orderly brought an extra blanket before heading back to mattress duty. He'd no sooner gone than Parker opened his eye and began trying to sit up. Elissa placed one hand on his uninjured shoulder. She didn't need to apply much pressure before he collapsed back with a low moan.

Delirium tremens. As if the loss of an eye and an arm weren't enough to bear, he had to struggle through this gut-wrenching affliction, too. He reeked of alcohol and uncleanliness. His exhaled breath carried the fruity odor caused by forced abstinence and lack of nutrition. She immersed a towel in the hot water, wrung it out, and began washing his sweating face. "Shhhh. You're safe. You're in the hospital now." The thought of facing cannon and rifle shot, mind hazy with alcohol and body craving more, made her shudder.

He stared up at her with a bewildered look. His small-shirt was soaked with sweat, and his body shook. Elissa kept up a constant stream of words, trying to keep his attention centered on her and his mind in the present.

Then his gaze moved to the ceiling and his agitation returned. Elissa shook his shoulder and called his name as panic seemed to overtake him and his breathing sawed in and out.

"Lieutenant! Parker!" Desperate, she tried to turn his head, but he resisted.

He mumbled words she couldn't make out. His shaking intensified. Wide-eyed, a tortured cry tore from his throat. "Aaahhhh!"

The ward was silent, as if all the collective pain and fear in the room had settled over Parker. And as if compelled to escape that horrific miasma, Parker struggled up.

"No. Lieutenant, lie back." Elissa tried to hold him, but his strength overcame her efforts. He climbed out of bed.

He stood, weaving, and with his one arm, held her away.

"Help! Jakes!" Why had she let him leave? The other patients were alarmed, sitting up, several trying to get out of bed. She couldn't let that happen. She needed to get hold of Parker, before he and others were injured. The men began clamoring, calling out for the orderlies. She grabbed Parker's arm, held tight, tried to pull him back to the bed. He cried out, stumbled, and shoved her away.

She went down, sharp pain spiking her hip when she hit the floor. Parker bolted for the door, knocking over a lunging patient as Jakes and Wright ran in. Wright grasped Parker's arm, twisting it behind him, and Jakes grabbed hold of his belt. Parker struggled against them, but Baxter joined them, and the three orderlies half carried, half shuffled Parker to his bed. Parker yelled, a wordless, drawn-out cry, as the orderlies forced him back down to his mattress.

Elissa sat up and pressed a hand to her aching hip. Archer and MacKay came through the door. With a few terse words, MacKay directed Archer to assist Johnson, the patient that Parker had knocked down. The surgeon gave a sharp look to the group at Parker's bed, but didn't pause. He crouched beside Elissa and put a supporting arm around her shoulders.

"Are ye all right, lass?" His eyes blazed.

"Yes." She nodded, rubbing her hip.

He slid one hand under hers and palpated her hip, his gaze focused on her face. She forgot about the throbbing, conscious only of his face so close to hers, his large hand stroking and rubbing her hip, her bum, and thigh. He bent her knee and straightened it, causing her hip joint to move. "How's that?"

"Fine."

"Let's stand ye up."

He brought her up with him, and before she knew quite what was happening, she found herself standing, his arm warm and steady around her waist, the side of her body pressed all along the length of his. His hold didn't feel like him steadying her, helping her stand; it felt like an embrace.

She looked at Parker's bed just as Jakes jabbed Wright with his elbow and in a low voice said something to Baxter, drawing the two men's eyes away from her and MacKay. The orderlies seemed to have subdued Parker. Each had one of Parker's limbs held to the mattress.

MacKay seemed to realize at the same time as she that they'd been standing together longer than necessary, and attracting the attention and speculation of everyone in the ward. His arm fell from her waist and he moved a step away, which made her legs wobble and her heart clench.

"Is Johnson all right?" MacKay asked Archer, who was just straightening after helping the patient to bed.

Elissa shifted her weight and found her hip sore but not to the extent that she need favor it. She walked to Johnson's side and took his hand. "Thank you for trying to help."

"I'm sorry I couldn't stop him. I hope he didn't hurt you."

"I'm not hurt."

MacKay examined Parker with his usual efficiency. When Elissa crossed to Parker's bed, she saw the patient's blue eye glaring at the men surrounding him.

"You sons of bitches!" he wailed.

"Archer, get a bottle of brandy from the storeroom," MacKay ordered. "Miss Lockwood, give him an ounce or two. That should quiet him down a bit, and with luck he won't start vomiting. We need to get him comfortable and make the shakes and hallucinations go away. Give him small measures every hour or so. He also needs to drink a lot of liquid. Lemonade, whatever ye have that has sugar, and get him to take as much as ye can. After he's back to a normal state, we'll worry about weaning him off the alcohol."

Elissa moved to Parker's side. She'd wait until after he'd had the brandy to finish washing him. He needed the usual haircut and beard trim, too. It was something they did for each man to make them more comfortable and help rid them of the vermin that most of them arrived with.

"I'll examine his wounds when I make rounds tomorrow," MacKay said. He started to turn away, but paused. "Give him enough brandy that ye don't have to tie him down."

"You expect them to hold his limbs that long?" Archer's voice held disbelief and outrage, making clear he'd rather tie Parker down.

Elissa wanted to tie the sergeant's tongue down. He was cruel as well as insubordinate.

"Aye. I do," MacKay said, voice hard. "And I expect *ye* to get that brandy." MacKay looked at the orderlies securing Parker. "Thank ye. Ye're good men, holdin' him so as not to hurt him. I'll let the other orderlies know to give ye relief."

The orderlies smiled, Jakes and Wright thanked him, and Elissa realized how much praise from one of the officers meant to the medical workers. MacKay had shown them he expected the medical staff to show compassion and treat even disagreeable patients with kindness. How could anyone not respect and admire the man?

MacKay started toward the door with long strides. He halted in front of Archer. "I gave ye an order, Sergeant. I'd expect a man of yer rank to set a *good* example and carry out an officer's orders promptly. Instead I find the opposite."

She'd never seen MacKay so disdainful and cold. And he'd admonished the ward-master in front of the orderlies. Archer stiffened, and with a twitch his scowl became grimness. MacKay continued to stand, staring at the sergeant. What was he waiting for? MacKay tipped his head, his brows slowly rising. Then Archer's hand sprang up in a sharp salute. A long time seemed to pass before MacKay returned the salute and strode past the ward-master. Archer spun and followed, but Elissa caught a glimpse of his face, and it wore the purest look of hatred she'd ever seen.

CHAPTER ELEVEN

Parker looked like a different man. Brown hair and beard clipped short, skin washed, a clean shirt on him, he had his senses about him today. Yesterday Elissa had been the one to spoon brandy into his mouth every hour, since he'd roared when any of the orderlies came near him.

Today his blue eye didn't glare. He'd eaten a bit of egg custard and cooperated when MacKay examined his wounds and Elissa redressed them. His shoulder wound looked mildly inflamed, but his empty eye socket was healing well and he was free of fever. While not resolved, the severity of his tremors had lessened. Whenever he was left alone, he slept.

Riley was the patient who worried her today. He seemed fragile, his cough weaker and more frequent. He lay on his side, gaze vacant, face expressionless and weary, when Elissa set a small table and chair next to his bedside.

"I have just the thing to perk you up." She placed the checkerboard and pieces before him.

His mouth tipped. "Draughts? How did you know I was yearning for a game with you?"

Elissa laughed. "Maybe because I've had the same wish."

They got down to the business of draughts. The ward was quiet and peace stole through Elissa as she appreciated Riley's obvious enjoyment of their game. He had such a young-old face. A dear young man who had experienced things she couldn't imagine, and whose brown eyes were windows that permitted a glimpse of a man worthy of the best life had to offer.

"You had a letter from your wife yesterday, didn't you?"

His broad smile lit his eyes. "Yes, and it was very welcome." Riley pressed his fist to his chest, as if trying to hold in brimming emotion. "It's been seven months since I last saw Evie. I know in army life, that's not long, but it feels like years to me."

Not all wives were allowed to accompany their soldier husbands on campaign. When they couldn't, it might be years before they saw one another again.

"She wanted me to thank you for helping with my last letter to her."

Elissa managed to keep her smile in place. He'd been too weak to sit up and write his wife. "It was my pleasure. Since you've shared parts of her letters with me, I feel as though I know her."

She turned back to the game board, jumped and collected two of his pieces, but he didn't react. Just stared at the board.

"Sometimes I feel I'll never see her again." His voice rasped like a file against rock.

Elissa's throat tightened. A brick dropped into her belly. She reached out and covered his hand with hers. "You mustn't lose hope, George." She'd seen enough to know recovery could hinge on that all-important spark. "You mustn't give up." She squeezed his hand.

"Some days, I can't see her face."

She didn't know how to help him, and helplessness surged, filled her with a heavy heat that threatened to overcome her. "You've got her picture," she whispered. His locket was always with him, but it would be small comfort compared to his Evie's arms.

He frowned. "It's not enough." He pushed the checkerboard away and let his head relax on his pillow. "I'm sorry. I'm too tired."

Elissa nodded and curled her lips over her teeth. She rose, moved the table aside, pulled his blanket up, and tucked it under his chin. Her eyes stung, and she moved toward the limited privacy of the ward room.

As soon as she entered the canvas enclosure, she pulled her handkerchief from her sleeve and pressed it to her eyes. She held in the sobs, even as her shoulders bent and shook.

Death was no stranger. She'd lost her entire family when she was still a child. After, working with Maddie Gray, Elissa realized many families lost half or more of the children birthed to them. Those who reached adulthood navigated life knowing how vulnerable they were. The Crimea had hammered the lesson home. It wasn't only rifle shot, cannonballs, and sabers that threatened soldiers. Disease took down twice the number weapons did. Typhoid, cholera, dysentery, consumption, remittent fevers, and lung inflammations were impartial killers.

Riley had survived a very serious saber wound. He'd come through surgery and infection, and that wound had healed. Now consumption and pneumonia threatened him. It wasn't fair. She hated death. *Hated it.*

She lifted her head. Dried her cheeks. Blew her nose. She was not going to let Riley die. She'd move him closer to the window, where the air was fresher. She'd feed him—*make* him eat. She'd turn him. Exercise his limbs. If she had to sit beside him day and night, she would.

A noise behind her made her spin. Archer lounged in the doorway. His mouth curled into a sneer. His shoulders began to shake. He positioned his index fingers below each eye and trailed them down his face. His mouth opened. "Waah. Waah. Waah."

She wanted to hit him. Smash her fist into his mocking face.

He threw his head back, cackled, and left.

Cold prickles chased over her skin and she shivered. Archer wasn't normal. He'd become military-correct around MacKay, but when not in the surgeon's presence, the ward-master was a beast. He'd become unbending with the orderlies and openly rude to her. She detested him, and judging by the looks thrown at the ward-master's back, the orderlies and patients did, too.

Elissa knew some people thought of death as the Grim Reaper— a ghost-like figure that stole away the living. She had never given voice or form to death, but she thought perhaps, if she did, Death would look a lot like Archer.

She caught herself. No. No sinister thoughts to cloud her mind. No thinking about Archer, thoughts which made her feel angry and even more bleak. No more thoughts about the *unfairness* of life. She was bone-tired, but no matter. They all were.

Riley might be losing hope, but she would not. She was his lifeline, and she would not let go.

#

To Elissa, the war seemed far away on this Friday in early July. Had she ever been happier than now, seated beside MacKay, the weather warm and perfect, and headed for the heavenly waters of Göksu stream, considered the loveliest spot on the Bosporus? As planned, Elissa had walked a short way down the road before MacKay came along in the hired caleche and took her up in the small, open carriage.

Ward Two was quiet, with the rare occurrence of numerous empty beds. A ship carrying wounded was expected tomorrow. She and MacKay had each arranged to be gone a few hours, but not announced their intent of picnicking. They'd decided to do what they could to minimize the chance of being seen together. The less notice they attracted, the better, but going on a picnic in a fairly populated area was not immoral or prohibited, and a number of Koulali staff members had done so.

The biggest obstacle had been MacKay, who didn't like the idea of her walking the road unaccompanied. Unable to think of an alternative, and reassured that she'd walked the road numerous times without incident when accompanied by another lady, he'd grumbled that she was too independent by half, and stubborn, and conceded.

What remained of the three-mile journey passed quickly. MacKay directed the driver along the stream for a distance, and then they left him waiting and walked on. MacKay toted their picnic supplies bundled and tied up in a cloth, and Elissa carried a folded blanket. Caiques with ornately carved ornamentation glided up and down the stream like graceful swans. Fridays were known as the day Turkish women took their leisure here. Accompanied by men or guarded by slaves, small groups of veiled and unveiled women and small children relaxed on colorful rugs all along the water, usually in the shade of a tree. The bright colors of the women's garments put Elissa in mind of exotic blossoms strewn along the grassy bank. There were a few braziers with fires going, and the rich smell of coffee floated on the breeze. They passed two unveiled women chatting and sharing a smoke from a water pipe, lazing in voluminous trousers topped by inner robes and embroidered outer caftans.

"I'm jealous of the trousers the women wear," Elissa said. "They must be very comfortable, and I can't even imagine the freedom."

"Ye should purchase a pair of the pantaloons before ye leave," MacKay suggested. "Ye could wear them inside yer home, or perhaps in yer garden."

"I think I will. The idea is appealing."

"Ye'll feel light as air without skirts." His gaze dropped to her skirts, as if he were imagining her legs in the silky, cuffed trousers. "With yer self-confidence, if ye're caught wearing them ye'll be thought flamboyant rather than scandalous."

"You see me as confident?" Elissa asked.

"Of course I do. Ye're thoughtful, an excellent judge of character and situations, and ye trust yer decisions. It's why the orderlies respect ye and accept direction from ye." He said it matter-of-factly, as though he knew it were true.

"I...thank you." Pride swelled her chest, adding even more pleasure to the day. "I suppose being independent, and stubborn," she flashed a grin before letting her more pensive feelings show, "and self-confident all stem from Maddie. My temperament is not unlike hers. She's one of the most valued and respected persons in the parish, but she's not free with her affection and she doesn't like to be bested. I emulated her."

"Maddie's the midwife who raised ye after yer parents died," MacKay confirmed.

"Yes. She's a strong, no-nonsense woman. I think, if my mother had lived, I'd be softer."

"Soft," MacKay said in a musing tone. "Ye mean feminine, warm, and generous? Forgiving?" He captured her hand and gave it a squeeze. "Ye're all those things."

To this day, Elissa could feel Mum's gentle hands lovingly plaiting her hair. Could Elissa have, at her core, her mother's heart? She could only stare at MacKay. She'd always felt robbed, but what if she'd acquired what she'd valued most in her mother?

"I can't imagine greater praise than being told I'm as loving as my mum," Elissa said.

MacKay stopped walking. Elissa faced him with a questioning look.

"I wish I'd known yer mum. She must have been a fine woman. But even having not met her, I know she was no more loving than ye."

The inside of Elissa's chest felt as wide and free as the blue sky.

"Ye don't show yer caring in a conspicuous way, so maybe ye don't see it for what it is. Ye share it quiet-like and close, but I see it every time I watch ye with the patients, and ye feel it deep. Maybe, all those years without yer family, ye never learned how to give it openly?"

Elissa shifted from one foot to the other. How did he see her so clearly? How had he known she'd always guarded her emotions? MacKay took her elbow, turned her, and got her walking again.

They walked until the number of locals grew sparse and the music from a stringed, gourd-shaped saz and a reed flute faded and became too distant to hear. Under the trees, wild snowdrop and cyclamen blanketed the ground.

"There," MacKay said, pointing. He led her up a rise and past a clump of bushes, to a small cluster of closely grouped trees. Handing her the bundle, he took the blanket and spread it in the shade. Elissa knelt and untied the makeshift sack, setting out the fruit, bread, cheese, and strips of cooked lamb MacKay had brought for them. At the center was a bottle of wine and two cups.

MacKay plucked up the wine bottle and went about opening it with a corkscrew he withdrew from his pocket. "I wanted to get away with ye before my return to the front," he said. "I'm glad today provided us with that opportunity."

She could no longer imagine Koulali or Ward Two without MacKay. "What will I do after you leave?"

"We'll write." His hands stilled; he lowered the bottle. "We have a future, 'Lissa. This war will end, and when it does, we'll figure out what to do. I can't conceive of a future without ye in it."

The words filled her with light and warmth—her own special variety of Cameron MacKay sunshine. "I want that, too," Elissa said. She remained in a bubble of happiness while he opened the wine, poured, and offered her a cup.

They ate, and Elissa began to realize what a solitary location they'd found. No one else wandered as far as they had, and from their elevated position they'd be aware of anyone approaching. Seated, the trees and bushes would shield them from any strollers walking along the bank. "We're alone here."

He nodded and set his cup aside. "I want to hold ye. May I?" He stretched out his legs and slid down to lay on his back. He was no more than a yard away.

Elissa's heart began to pound. She wanted this. So much. She eased down beside him. MacKay put his arm behind her shoulders and pulled her close. All down their two lengths, they touched.

Anyone watching would consider this scandalous. This wasn't a simple intimacy between an unmarried couple in a garden. They were *lying down*, their bodies stretched out, and touching.

She didn't care. Oh, she did not *care* what anyone thought or expected or deemed appropriate. There was a pulsing in her center that told her that nothing mattered but this moment with MacKay—with Cam.

They lay on their backs, her head on Cam's shoulder. He sighed. She closed her eyes and smiled, knowing she would always remember this.

He rolled her way and kissed her, lips brushing once, twice, then settling.

She discovered anew the wonder of kissing.

Her hands slid over the contours of powerful shoulders. Up a neck warm as bricks baked in the summer sun. Pushed her fingers through tawny hair so thick it almost bristled. How often had she itched to brush a lock of hair from his forehead?

She hadn't realized how this would feel, Cam's long, hard body lying alongside, and then atop, her. How his tongue, tangling with hers, and his hands, sliding under her skirts, up her legs, and gripping her buttocks, would make the feminine parts of her body tingle and...*crave*, the sensation so strong it made her press tight against him. She'd never imagined this. Never experienced anything like it, so how could she have known?

Now she knew. And she understood these feelings weren't because she was lying with a man.

It was Cam. She loved him. She'd never been so certain of anything.

The bodice of the summer dress she'd worn exposed just a hint of the curve of her breasts. She wanted Cam's lips lower, on her breasts and nipples, instead of kissing along the fabric edge. Her breasts strained toward him as though an invisible force drew them. Elissa pulled the shoulder of her gown down, exposing the top of one breast, swelling above her corset. The drawing, pulling sensation increased. Her impatient, clumsy fingers took twice the normal time to unhook the corset halfway down.

Cam gave her a slow, intense look. She couldn't tear her gaze from his beautiful, rugged face. No man had ever looked at her this way, with an expression that bespoke admiration, and impatience, and great pleasure. *Desire*. And *she* was responsible. All that emotion, focused on her. Prickles tingled her nipple. She'd never felt so aware of her body. At least, not *these* parts. One big hand cupped her naked breast and she arched her back. Pressed into his hand. She wondered if he could feel her heart, banging under his palm.

He pinched her nipple. Sucked her earlobe into his mouth. The drawing sensation spread between her legs, pulling her pelvis toward his. He lowered his head to her exposed breast and a shudder rippled from her neck to her toes. An involuntary noise escaped when his mouth closed around her nipple.

"Ye like that, *mo gràdh?*"

His husky voice stroked invisible fingers between her thighs. Made her breath hitch.

"Aye," she said, drawing out the word.

He chuckled, warm puffs of breath tickling her neck. His laughter died, and he kissed her. Slow and deep, wet and luscious, amazing and unforgettable. He drew bucketfuls of desire from a well she didn't know was in her. Until the well became a spring, filling her and spilling over.

"What does that mean—*mo gràdh?*" She didn't know a word of Gaelic and hadn't ever heard him speak the Celtic language, but she'd be content listening to Cam for hours. His voice almost caressed the words.

The corners of his eyes crinkled. "*Mo gràdh.* My love."

Elissa's heart danced like jingles on a Turkish tambourine. So much anticipation confined in her humming body. So much promise in the way her body responded to his smell, his taste, his touch. So much certainty that joining her body with Cam's would give her the most glorious experience of her life.

She kissed him. Open-mouthed, wet, tongues stroking. Already he'd taught her how. She'd learned a kiss was more than a kiss. It was a marvel that swept her heart and lungs and stomach into a whirlpool. A whirlpool that drained into her pelvis in a sharp, sucking rush. And made the flesh between her legs throb.

The front of her skirt and petticoats had gotten pushed up to her waist. Cam pressed his pelvis to hers, and she thought she might explode. She could feel his cock. So hard…she hadn't realized…but it couldn't be anything else, and he rocked his hips and pressed it against her sensitive bud.

She reached down, nudged her hand between them, held her breath when he unfastened his trousers and guided her hand inside first his trousers then his drawers. She explored the rounded head, the moisture beaded at the slit. She wrapped her hand around him. The organ was so much larger and harder than she'd ever imagined. She thought of it going into her, and she tightened. They both moaned.

"Here, *mo gràdh,* let me show ye." He was short of breath, his voice strained. He placed his hand atop hers, wrapped his fingers around hers, showed her how to slide up and down his length. He tensed, moaned. His pelvis thrust with each slide of her hand. Then he released her hand and rubbed his finger over the sensitive bundle of flesh nestled between the lips of her sex. Her hips jerked. She gasped. Her lungs heaved like she'd sprinted away from a hornet's nest. She rocked and yearned for relief. Yearned for more.

His finger pushed inside her. It burned a bit, and her body gripped his digit in a way she hadn't known it was capable of. He slid his finger out. Rubbed her again. She moaned. Couldn't hold the sound in.

She'd become wet. There, under his finger. Wet and slippery and hot. He pushed two fingers in, pressed her nubbin with his thumb, and the sensation made her clench. Made her nipples shrink tight. Made her belly contract and her hips lift. She gasped, moaned again, and he kissed her with a new power and intensity. His fingers continued to move, and she grew wetter, and hotter, and emptier. She wanted to be filled.

She released his cock and wrapped her arms and legs tight around him. He broke their kiss and pressed his forehead to hers. "What ye do to me, woman." His warm, husky voice conveyed something splendid and precious: happiness.

She kissed him, slow, sweet, sliding her tongue along his. She swept her open hands all the way up his back, then held his shoulders tight.

His eyes were green. So green and alive, like spring shoots. "We mustn't," he whispered, deep, ragged voice a velvet rake. "Not here, lass. Not like this."

Desperation scorched a swath through her, but before she could clutch, or protest, or beg, Cam levered away enough to slide his hand back to her heat. He stroked in a new, firmer way, while the tension pulled tighter and tighter. Until it burst. Like a quivering sail catching the wind, her mind and body soared. A wave of intense pleasure crested and filled every pore with satisfaction.

He held her, chest to chest, belly to belly, until her heart slowed and her skin dried. Then he re-hooked her corset and pulled the shoulder of her bodice back up. He gave her several short, sweet, closed-mouth kisses, sat up, and lowered her petticoats and skirt. Then he laid back down and pulled her head onto his shoulder.

Elissa explored the line of his jaw, his ear, and the ends of his hair with her fingers. "I wish we could stay here, just like this," she said.

Cam tightened his arm, hugging her. "We'll stay as long as we can," he promised.

CHAPTER TWELVE

Cam watched Elissa dress RSM Weatherley's stump, satisfaction sitting warm and contented inside him, like a big, lazy, purring cat. Her long-fingered hands were graceful and competent, applying the perfect tension and configuration to the bandage wrap.

Weatherley's stump was without edema or redness. His other limb retained a toeless foot that he managed, with crutches, to balance on. Cam wished all his patients could have even half the fortitude Weatherley demonstrated. Cam wished *he* had it. The regimental sergeant major faced his altered body and his unknown future the way Cam imagined Percival Weatherley had faced every challenge, and the man must have faced a God-awful lot of them.

The sharpest blue eyes Cam had ever encountered gazed from a lined, sun-bronzed face, aged beyond its years. Weatherley had never uttered even the mildest groan or grouse, and he encouraged the other patients in a resolute, forthright way that made it clear he expected them to hold their heads high. Yet when anger, pain, or depression of spirit overtook one of them, he'd heave himself into a wheeled chair and have an orderly push him to the soldier's bedside. He'd say a few low words, lay his large, calloused hand on the man's shoulder, and glare at the rest of the ward as if daring them to take exception to his attitude. The RSM didn't hide his dislike for the curt way Archer spoke to the men, and last week he'd put Archer in his place. The ward-master had since made himself scarce.

"You'll be letting me sail home soon, I hope," Weatherley said to Cam, his eyes watching Elissa's nimble fingers.

"Two more weeks, I think. The danger of fever will be past." Cam jerked his head toward the crutches propped beside the RSM's bed. "Ye'll be getting around on those well enough by then. Any idea of yer plans?" Amputees were awarded a shilling a day by the government, which was why many men preferred to lose a limb rather than retain a crippled one. Inadequate as the stipend was, Weatherley would at least have that.

"I'll become a saddler, sir. I learned at the hand of my father. My brother and I both did. He has his own business now, and he's offered me a place."

"You preferred the army?" Elissa asked.

"I had the foolish notions of a young man, to see something beyond Norfolk. I thought making and repairing saddles and harness too tame."

"You've had a fine career. You're a brave man." Elissa tied the ends of the bandage and Weatherley settled his limb on its cushion.

"A brave jackass, more like," Weatherley said with a grin. "But it suited me. Now the thought of making a home with my wife after all these years—well, it sounds wonderful. Mary's accompanied me to every post and campaign, until this one. I can't wait to see the old woman's face."

Elissa settled one hand on her hip. "And just how old is this 'old woman?'"

Weatherley's laugh rang, making the patients in his vicinity smile. "She'd be thirty-two. Two years younger than me."

Weatherley touched Elissa's arm. He nodded toward Riley, who was across the aisle and several beds down. "How's that one doing?" he asked.

Her gaze darted to Cam.

"He's not doing well, I'm afraid," Cam said, voice low.

Weatherley's face hardened. "Archer had best keep himself busy elsewhere. He bullied the boy into showing that picture he's got of his wife. Archer told him he needn't worry about a nice piece like her finding a man once Riley was dead."

Elissa gasped, her face stricken.

Weatherley grimaced. "Pardon me, Miss Lockwood, but he didn't say it quite that nice, either."

She gave them a look that communicated just how despicable she found Archer, gathered up the basin and soiled dressings and moved away.

Cam exchanged a knowing look with Weatherley. Devil take that bastard, Archer. The sergeant struck Cam as someone who felt superior when he belittled others. He'd be of better use at the front, where it was too busy for him to exploit men's weaknesses.

"I don't think he'd be such a loathsome meddler if he were at the front," Weatherley said. "A man tends not to make trouble when he's dodging bullets."

Cam just managed to choke back a bark of laughter. He and Weatherly were of like mind. "There might be a bullet or two to avoid, but in general, the medical service doesn't face the same risk as the regular army." It wouldn't be long until Cam returned to the front and he wouldn't be here to oversee Archer and his conduct with the patients. He didn't like to think of them—or Elissa—at the mercy of Archer's poison. "Some experience at the front might make him more sympathetic to his patients' situations," Cam said. Working on men received straight from the heat of battle would affect anyone. Even someone as self-absorbed as Archer. Cam had already reported Archer for being insolent and insubordinate. He'd leave a letter for Price, who'd replace Cam when he left, and warn him to keep a close watch on the ward-master. He'd talk to Humphrey before he left, too. The best course would be a demotion. Whomever had promoted the man to ward-master should be court-martialed.

"You never know," Weatherley said with a shrug. "Battlefront duty might be the making of him."

#

One week later, Cam timed it so that he left the ward at the same time as Elissa. As they exited the hospital, Cam touched her arm with his finger. Even through her sleeve, that slight contact sent heat sweeping over his skin and made sharp *wanting* twist him tight. He longed to slide his hand up her arm, wrap his arms around her, and press his nose to the angle where her neck met her shoulder. He wanted to breathe her in.

It had been difficult, concealing his feelings while they worked together on the ward. Soon, he'd be gone, and he wouldn't have the joy of being near her, nor even the comfort of seeing her.

She glanced down at her arm then up at him.

He dropped his hand. "May I have a minute?" he asked. They stopped under the portico. A few men stood smoking outside the convalescent building. Otherwise, the yard was empty.

Elissa folded her arms. The brisk wind plastered an errant lock of hair across her face. He wanted to grasp the silky, light brown strand, rub it between his fingers, and tuck it behind her ear, but he forced his arm to stay at his side.

She changed her angle to the wind, so it struck her full in the face. The wind blew the lock of hair back, but also made her rub her upper arms. The warmth of the day had receded and the coolness of night approached. Cam changed his own position and stood in front of her, his back to the wind, and managed to shield her from the brunt of it.

"I leave for the front in seven days," he said.

Her lips parted. For an unguarded moment he saw surprise, regret, fear, *pain*. Then she composed her face.

"You're not limping anymore, but I've been pretending this day wasn't coming." Her gaze left him, regarded the yard. "I'll miss you." The space between her brows creased. She pressed her lips together and tensed her jaw. She attempted to smile, but ended up looking more grim than reassuring.

He stuffed his hands in his pockets to keep from pulling her to him. He loved her. He wanted to comfort her. And in return, find consolation in her arms.

Miss wasn't quite the word he'd use. He already knew he'd yearn for her. "This isn't the end for us. It's a delay." Big hazel eyes gazed up at him, glinting toffee and gold. "I meant everything I said at Göksu," Cam said. "We have a future."

Her mouth curved in a *real* smile. Her face glowed.

"Ye weren't sure of that?" he asked, shocked. "Ye thought I lied?"

She reached out, stopping her hand two inches from his chest. "No, I'd never think that. But some days, what we shared by the stream seems too wonderful to be true, and the end of the war feels a long way off. I like hearing you talk about our future. What you just said, how certain you looked and sounded, will be a special memory I'll add to my growing collection. They'll help comfort me after you're gone. I'm not used to being loved, but I'm learning, and I'm finding it far easier than I ever dreamed."

He would shower her with love, until she forgot all the years of drought. "Never doubt how I feel, Elissa. I love ye." He hadn't intended to declare himself in the hospital yard, where they might be overheard or forget to take care how they appeared to others. He'd meant only to tell her of his reassignment. But seeing her now—happily glowing—he wouldn't have done it any other way. If he had, he would have missed *this*.

Elissa locked her hands together and pressed them to her chest. "I love you, too," she said with a little gasp.

The words made his heart grow arms and do handsprings.

Ward Four's physician walked past, his head turning back for a second look. No telling what the man saw in Cam's face, but if there were any possibility he and Elissa's conversation might induce speculation, he needed to settle down. He rubbed his hand across the back of his neck and took a step back. They'd lingered here together long enough. "Being apart will be hard," he warned. "Write. Every day ye can. While I'm on the peninsula…I'll need yer letters."

"I'll write every day."

"I may not have the same opportunity, so don't ye stop writing if ye don't hear from me." This time, when the Scots Greys came under fire, Cam would be different. He'd gotten the shaking and nightmares under control, and he'd keep them mastered by remembering Elissa and dreaming of their future. He had plans to make, and so much hope. It would carry him through. It had to, because he couldn't offer Elissa marriage unless he was steady, and sure of himself.

"It's likely you'll be sent back to England before I am," Elissa said. "Eventually there'll be an armistice, but Koulali will have sick and wounded to tend long after the fighting stops."

"I'll keep you apprised of where I am," Cam promised. "Do you have any idea of where you'll go when you leave Miss Nightingale's service? Would you take up your previous position, nursing at the institute in London?"

"I don't know."

A gust of wind whipped through the yard and Cam stepped back to his previous position, closer to Elissa. He needed a few more minutes with her. A week from now he'd sail, and a few days after, be with his regiment. It could be months until the war ended and they were together again, and so much could happen before then.

Koulali Hospital and the Greys' regimental field hospital were both dangerous places to work. Every day, he and Elissa could face contagious diseases and men suffering from delirium. Cam would have the additional risk of errant rifle and cannon shot. His hands clenched and his nails bit into his palms. He'd worry about her every moment they were apart.

"This isn't the last time we'll work together," Cam said, his firm tone making the statement a fact. "We'll have other opportunities."

Elissa made a small, happy sound. "Working on your ward has given me the best nursing experience I've ever had. I've learned so much from you."

He huffed in acknowledgment. "Ye've taught me how very valuable and fine a nurse can be. Florence Nightingale created something exceptional here, with her special cadre of nurses. She's done the world a great service. She did me an even greater one, bringing ye here."

Elissa's lips pressed together. "I'll feel lost after you leave, Cam."

It was the first time she'd used his name. He wanted to hold her, feel her warmth, her supple strength, and smell her lavender scent. "Och, lass, I already ache. I'll pine for ye the way a man adrift at sea pines for land."

Her eyes glistened, and she swiped her fingers over the moisture on her cheeks. Face dried, she tipped her chin up and took a deep breath.

"I wish I could do something special for ye," Cam said. "Something to make another fine memory for yer collection. If we were in England, I'd take ye to a fancy restaurant, or perhaps a concert."

She dipped into her apron pocket, rummaged a moment, and then withdrew her hand with something pinched between her thumb and first finger. He couldn't see what it was. Couldn't see that she held anything at all. He gave her a questioning look. She was grinning. Her eyes teary a moment ago, now they gleamed with amusement. "'Lissa?"

"Hold out your hand," Elissa instructed.

He stretched out his arm. A dried pea dropped into his palm.

"If you really want to please me, give me a re-match," she said. "My victory will make a fine memory." Her laughter pealed out, and

Cam's erupted from deep in his chest. They laughed until they were gasping for breath.

"Give that pea back," she said, presenting her open palm. He returned it and she slipped it into her pocket.

Without intending to, Elissa had made a special memory for *him*. He imagined it would be many months before he laughed like this again. It still amazed him that, of all the places in the world, he'd found her here. It was astounding that he'd found her at all, a woman who carried a pea in her pocket as if it were a treasure.

"We'd best get to our quarters," Cam said. They'd been standing outside a long time. The smokers had gone in, and the yard was empty.

"Stop worrying," Elissa said. "We haven't been chatting any longer than it takes to have tea. I'll see you at final rounds, yes?"

"Aye." He watched her walk across the yard, past the convalescent building, and enter the nurses' cottage. Part of him wanted to propose now, before he left, but in good conscience he couldn't. Once the war was over, he would. He closed his eyes, made the vow. *I will.*

Seven more days. Intense heat filled his chest.

He headed for his room. There would be another massive assault before this damn war ended, and it could well be the final siege. It would happen soon.

When he arrived at Koulali, he'd have laughed at the suggestion he'd someday want to return to the front. But he was rested now. Ready to return and save all he could, and prove himself capable and deserving of a future with Elissa.

#

Cam had been late to dinner. The other physicians had already eaten and left the scarred table where they shared their meals. When Dr. Humphrey came in and requested dinner from their cook, Cam was glad of the company. Much of Humphrey's time was spent doing correspondence, and he always had recent news from the front lines and from England.

Koulali's principal medical officer sat and gulped half a cup of coffee without taking a breath. Then he released a long, satisfied sigh and set the cup down. "One of the field hospitals lost their most experienced orderly to typhoid. They need him replaced. Any recommendation on who I should send?"

Cam's head came up and his hand froze, fork suspended above his dinner. It didn't seem possible that he had discussed Archer with Weatherley such a short time ago, and now Humphrey was giving Cam an opportunity to solve the Archer problem with the very solution he and the RSM had proposed. He couldn't squire Elissa to a concert, but he could do something far better—keep Archer away from her.

"Sergeant Archer has the most experience," Cam said. "He's accustomed to trauma, and the orderlies he's been managing are good blokes. They'd make do without him."

Humphrey nodded. "I'll sign the transfer orders." He took a bite of stew and chewed.

Satisfaction swept through Cam, followed swiftly by remorse. Being *glad* Archer was going to the front seemed unscrupulous. It was a dangerous place. Dangerous to a man's person, and to his mind.

Still, working near the front at the battlefield hospitals was part of the job. Medical personnel went where they were needed. Cam had worked in a field hospital. As much as the experience had wrecked him, he'd do it again without hesitation. He swallowed. He *was* doing it again.

It would be good to know that, after he left, Archer wouldn't be at Koulali, tormenting the patients and nurses. Cam had no reason to feel guilty for thinking that. Archer's bullying was to blame for Cam's opinion of him. And perhaps, what he and Weatherley suggested was correct. No man could work at the front and not be changed by it.

True, the work had given Cam nightmares, and the anxiety and shakes that went with neurasthenia. It was the most demanding work Cam had ever done. But he had also felt his compassion grow with each day spent caring for men gravely injured in battle. He'd absorbed those men's emotions, and they'd trusted him to do so, even as they lay dying. There could be no greater honor than having men put their lives in your hands. He hadn't known that before. He'd learned it in the Crimea, after the battles of Alma, and Balaclava, and Inkerman. He *loved* those men.

They needed an experienced orderly. Why *not* Archer?

"Archer will be ideal to send," Cam said. "When will he leave?"

"As soon as I can get the paperwork done. I'll tell him first thing and get him on the next ship headed for the peninsula."

Cam wondered how Archer would take the news. Chances were, once he got there, Archer would love it. He liked the status of being ward-master, but the work bored him. The front was fast-paced, and each man, no matter his position, was faced with decisions that had to be made at once. Archer was decisive and confident. He'd probably cope better at the front than Cam did. No doubt Archer's calloused nature would see him through the experience with soul intact.

CHAPTER THIRTEEN

As soon as she stepped onto the ward, Elissa knew.

A nasty, clammy feeling prickled her skin. A feeling she knew had nothing to do with her poor night's sleep or the headache pulsing at her temples. Smith, the night shift orderly, hurried to her.

"It's Riley, Miss Lockwood."

She hurried to Riley's bed then fought her brimming tears. She sank onto his bed because her legs wouldn't hold her. Sweat plastered his carroty hair to his head. She felt his burning forehead, listened to his labored, rattly breathing.

"Riley? George!" Elissa shook his shoulder. Then shook it again, harder.

Nothing. No response.

Elissa folded her index finger and positioned her second knuckle in the middle of his breast bone. She pressed hard. "George. Wake up."

Riley moaned. His hand made a lethargic swipe at the pain drilling his chest.

Elissa shook his shoulder again. "George, wake up!"

Molasses-brown eyes opened partway. Blinked. They looked glassy and unfocused. He moaned. "Hurts," he rasped. "Chest hurts." A hacking cough shook him and loose secretions gurgled in his throat. The coughing left him short of breath, the movements of his chest rapid and shallow.

"Smith, get a couple blankets and roll them up," Elissa directed over her shoulder. "Put them behind him when I raise him." She slid her hands under his shoulders, palming his upper back. His skin was hot as a stove top. She waited until Smith had the blankets ready then pulled Riley, lifting his head and shoulders. He grimaced and pushed against her. "George, you need to sit up. It'll help you breathe easier." They positioned the blankets and his pillow behind his shoulders, and she eased him back down. He moaned and her throat got tight.

That was not like Riley. Riley didn't utter complaints or vocalizations of pain.

"Smith. Get Staff Surgeon MacKay."

Smith took a step back. "I'm off duty, Miss Lockwood. Officer MacKay should be here any minute."

Elissa jerked around. "Get MacKay, Smith." She took a breath. "Now!" The word burst out, propelled by fear and urgency.

Smith's head reared back.

"I'm here." Cam's heels resounded against the plank floors, his long, steady strides eating up the long aisle.

Cam. At the sound of his voice, overpowering relief rocked through her with the strength of exploding gunpowder. He came to her side, and his presence, standing close, calmed and settled her.

"He's so much worse," she said, appalled to find her voice broken. She must get hold of herself and be strong. She dragged in a breath and looked up at Cam.

All his considerable intelligence was focused on Riley.

Cam glanced at her, and she stood, surrendering her place to him. He sat Riley up much as she had, and she held Riley as Cam pressed his ear to the patient's back, listening to the air moving in and out of his lungs. When they'd settled him again, Cam looked in his eyes, his mouth, and pressed his ear to Riley's heart.

When Cam straightened and faced her, green eyes full of regret, Elissa's hope sank, and a chasm opened inside her. He walked into the aisle, out of Riley's hearing. Elissa dragged after him, not wanting to hear, but knowing she had to.

"We're already giving him anything that might help," Cam said, his low voice gentle. "We've been fighting the lung infections for weeks. I'm afraid they've overwhelmed him." He studied the toes of his boots, and then met her eyes again, his brow furrowed. "Spoon as much liquid into him as ye can. And wait. That's all we can do."

Elissa nodded, her head bobbing like a mindless doll's. She pressed her lips together hard, trapping the wail that shrieked inside.

Not Riley! Why him? Just like Frederick. Just like her entire family. Why did she lose every person close to her? She whirled away from Cam, before her fear overwhelmed her restraint. It would be all too easy to fling herself into his arms.

She needed to get liquids down Riley. Sponge him off to lower his fever. Turn him. Encourage him to cough the suppuration from his lungs. Sit with him, remind him he had a beloved wife to live for.

Jakes appeared before her, reporting for the day shift. Today his usually bright face was a study in determination. Thank God. She'd have Jakes beside her today. And Cam. They had more strength of character than any two people she'd ever met. They'd support her. And she'd make sure Riley had everything that might help sustain him.

Was she a fool? She'd faced off death many times, and lost too often. But this was Riley. He'd already overcome what most men couldn't. He had to be able to do it again.

#

"Miss Lockwood." It was midmorning and Jakes stood opposite her, on the other side of Riley's bed. His unhappy frown sharpened her attention.

"Sergeant Archer has ordered us to help in the other wards. Our ward is full, but the others have empty beds and there are two steamers at the quay unloading sick."

Elissa sprang to her feet. "You can't leave me here alone." She couldn't give her undivided attention to Riley if she was left to do the job of four men and care for the entire ward.

"I'll be here." Archer paced down the aisle and stopped at the foot of Riley's bed. "The other wards' orderlies are overwhelmed. I'm sending my men to help for an hour or two. Until the new arrivals are settled."

That didn't reassure her. Jakes had been fetching whatever she needed, allowing her to stay with Riley. While the orderlies were gone, she'd have to leave him some of the time to attend to other patients. But she understood the need, and it would only be for a short while.

"I want to stay with Riley as much as possible," Elissa said, making her voice as firm as she could.

"I won't be able to play lady's maid for you," Archer said, making Jakes stiffen, "but I'll try to take care of the rest of the ward and leave *Riley* to you."

His snide words and tone of voice made her want to grab his throat and squeeze. He never stopped testing her. She shouldn't let him get away with such disrespect, but today she didn't have the time or patience or energy to deal with him. She needed to get back to Riley. She just hoped Archer held to this bargain. He rarely helped with patient care.

Jakes and the other orderlies left.

About twenty minutes later, Archer sauntered to the head of Riley's bed and gave the corporal a close look. "Billings is having a lot of pain, miss."

She'd instructed the orderlies to alert her when a patient was in pain. Sometimes repositioning, or massaging a tender area, helped. She adjusted laudanum doses so the men obtained as much relief as possible, without giving them so much they became insensible. The ward had been quiet, but Billings was at the end. Perhaps he was too far away for her to hear his groans. "I'll give him a dose of laudanum."

After she dosed the grateful Billings, Jones asked her to help him turn over. She helped while scanning the ward for Archer. Where was he? She'd barely gotten Jones settled when another man asked for assistance drinking water. Then another needed her help during a coughing fit. Tension squeezed her lungs. Archer should be doing these types of tasks, so she could care for Riley. Finally, she headed back to Riley, Archer still missing from the quiet ward.

She paused and listened. "Sergeant Archer?" Silence.

Lieutenant Parker, propped up and reading, looked up and down the aisle. "I don't think he's here, Miss Lockwood." Parker, now steady on rationed portions of brandy, had revealed himself to be intelligent and well educated. His wounds were clean and appeared to be healing.

Elissa's heart dropped hard and fast when she saw Riley. He was unresponsive. His slack mouth hung open and his breathing seemed to barely move his chest. Appraising the purplish color of his lips, she picked up his hand and checked the color of his nail beds. Blue.

She did everything she knew to arouse him, but he didn't even move with painful stimulation. Even through his shirt, his chest and abdomen felt searing hot, while his extremities were cold and so pale they appeared bloodless. His freckles stood out like splatters of brown mud on his milky skin. She pressed her fingers to the pulse point in his neck. She had to concentrate to feel his thready, runaway heartbeat. Riley was slipping away.

"Do you need some help?" Parker stood beside her. "Shall I go look for Archer?"

"Could you find Officer MacKay?" True, she needed Archer to attend the other men, but he wouldn't help her face what was coming. Cam would.

That cussed Archer. She wanted to bash him with her fists. He'd promised to mind the ward, so she could tend Riley. Until she stepped away, she'd been sponging him off almost nonstop. He'd still been responsive enough to reflexively swallow the small amounts of water she dribbled into his mouth. Those ministrations hadn't been much, but they'd made all the difference. Now the water pooled and trickled down his chin. His body hadn't been able to sustain the rapid rate of his breathing. His breaths had evolved from rapid to slow. A raspy rattling noise accompanied each inadequate breath, and long, silent pauses separated each respiration.

Parker left, bare feet slapping.

Elissa sank down on the chair she had positioned close beside Riley's bed. She wrapped her hand around his lax, icy fingers and bent her head.

Her own breaths sawed in and out of her lungs. She felt as cold as the dear fingers she held. Riley's lungs were failing. She parted the unbuttoned placket of his shirt and saw a purplish mottling covered his chest. Awareness of his impending death seared through her. She leaned forward and stroked his hair from his forehead. "I'm here, George," she said, not caring how broken her words were.

#

Cam knew she wasn't aware of his approach. She sat beside Riley's body, head bowed. She'd closed his eyes, smoothed his hair, and straightened his covers.

The patients were quiet. A few watched her, sorrow and compassion etched on their faces. Others had turned away.

"Elissa."

She rose and threw herself against him. He closed his eyes, love for her and sorrow for her suffering overwhelming him. Regret settled heavy in his chest. He pulled Elissa close, felt her arms wrap around him and her hands palm his back. He breathed in a faint, lovely smell, redolent of lavender and unique to Elissa Lockwood.

"Freddy's gone," she whispered.

She'd used her brother's name instead of Riley's.

He sensed her desperation, crooned, and tightened his arms as her shoulders began to shake. He had to get her away.

He separated them and pressed her against his side, keeping one arm wrapped about her. "Ye're in charge of the ward," he told Parker, who stood nearby.

He propelled Elissa along with him, down the aisle and to the inadequate privacy of the ward room. She pulled a handkerchief from her sleeve and pressed it to her eyes.

He half expected her to gather her fractured emotions and subdue her display of grief, but she didn't. She folded back into his arms and pressed tight against him. He muttered useless, senseless words. Pressed his lips to her forehead. Rubbed her back, his hands memorizing her shape, the feel of bones that were too prominent. She worked too hard, and wasn't eating enough. He must remember to tell his cook to add more rice and meat to the nurses' soup.

His mouth slid across the curve of a soft, tear-wet cheek, and he pressed a kiss to the corner of her closed eye. Her pain made him ache.

He wanted to ease her distress. He palmed the back of her neck, the ends of his fingers sliding into silky hair. "He's at peace," he whispered. "No more fighting to breathe. No more pain." Riley's death left a hole inside Cam, too.

Having major emergency surgery performed the day Cam arrived at Koulali, Riley had started out as a patient of particular medical interest, but Cam had gotten to know the man. He'd touched Cam with his humor and the way he encouraged the other patients on his "good" days. Cam knew he wouldn't forget Riley's unfailing optimism, nor his simple gratitude.

Elissa nodded and made a broken little sound. Riley had become her friend, and she'd grown to love him. Cam put enough space between them to see her face. Wet, spiky lashes hid her eyes. He tipped up her chin and her eyes blinked open, their luminous hazel depths unfocused. She was shattered. Thank God, he was still at Koulali, able to console her. She needed solace and love, and Cam's heart, brimming with love for Elissa, was bottomless.

Need radiated from her bleak face, and her fingers clutched him as though she were drowning. The desire to help her became overpowering. He surrendered, bent his head, sought her mouth, and with all the sweetness and gentleness and tenderness he was capable of, kissed her.

He forgot everything. He'd meant to be loving and comforting, but her lips moved, *asked*, and he became a man of surging want and need and only Elissa could satisfy the yearning. He deepened the kiss, and her response set him aflame.

It was Elissa's sudden withdrawal and soft, shocked exclamation that made him aware they weren't alone. Her handkerchief fluttered to the floor.

Archer stood in the entrance, face hard and dark.

"I've men in pain, asking for laudanum," Archer said, black eyes burning with condemnation.

Elissa darted from the room, turning her body sideways to avoid Archer, who continued to stand in the space that served as doorway. One corner of his mouth curled up, turning his expression into a sneer, and rage erupted in Cam with the force of an exploding Mount Vesuvius.

Cam strode across the space and planted himself in front of Archer. He stood close, wanting his broader, taller, and untethered body to intimidate the ward-master. Archer didn't move, and Cam tightened his fists.

"I'd best not hear ye've reported this, Sergeant," Cam said through clenched teeth. What he and Elissa had done was forbidden, and if reported, she'd receive a reprimand at the very least. Any other orderly would have apologized and left them alone. They hadn't been gone from the ward more than a couple minutes. He knew their absence hadn't compromised anyone's care, no matter what Archer might claim.

The sergeant's eyes widened in a parody of surprise. "You're threatening me? With what? Fear of being sent to the front? I've already been informed of my transfer." Pure hate glared from Archer's eyes. His gaze fell to Cam's fists. "You're too much the gentleman to use your fists."

Cam grabbed the front of Archer's uniform, jerked him into the ward room, and then released him with a shove. Archer stumbled back, but caught himself before he fell.

"I'm *not* too much the gentleman," Cam warned.

Archer straightened, and tugged at the hem of his uniform. "You're too ethical to strike me, MacKay. Not when *you're* the wrong-doer. And I think you know, If I wanted to report you, nothing short of death would stop me." Archer turned and left, shaking his head and chuckling. The man's nonchalant amusement spiked Cam's already prodigious fury. He took a deep breath and dragged his hands down his face. Archer hadn't said he was reporting them, and despite his bravado, Cam's rank and the thought of possible repercussions would likely prevent him taking action. Cam had instigated the kiss. If Archer did report them, it would be Cam's fault.

Elissa's handkerchief lay on the floor. He scooped it up. Fingered the delicate fabric's softness. Brought it to his nose and sniffed the delightful fragrance he associated with her. Then he folded it and tucked it into his inside coat pocket. The one positioned over his heart.

#

Six hours later, Elissa stood on the starboard side of the Lady Jocelyn and turned her head so the wind struck her full in the face. When they'd first gotten underway, one of the seamen had boasted they'd make record time to Plymouth, the ship being powered by both steam and sail. Elissa didn't care about the efficiency of the screw steamer, but she preferred being on deck, where the activity of the sailors and the passing view could serve as distractions from her distress. They'd soon be passing from the Aegean to the Mediterranean, and she'd have the Greek isles to gaze at.

An overcast sky warned of an impending summer rain, and the wind's momentum increased. The force of it felt good, because it penetrated the shroud of pain that encompassed her. Every part of her, excepting the tiny piece that sensed the wind, was shattered and hurting. There was nothing else. Just pain and the blessed relief of the normality of wind in her face.

She gripped the edge of the bulwark rail, and tried to concentrate on the rushing air and the familiar smell of the sea. She seemed to be instinctively shifting her weight to counter the ship's movement. That was reassuring. Her body appeared to be functioning, even while her mind struggled to process what had happened.

Was this what disgrace felt like? This all-consuming, burning, confusing mix of anger and disbelief?

She still wore her nurse's dress. She tugged her cap from her head and let the wind take it. It hit the water and soon became a distant white speck, winking in and out of sight among the sea swells.

She should change. Her clothing—all her belongings—were aboard, but she didn't want to move to the confines below deck.

The summons to Miss Hutton's office had come as Elissa's shift ended. The soldiers standing at attention, flanking the nursing supervisor's doorway, had puzzled but not alarmed her.

"Did you embrace, and kiss, Staff Surgeon MacKay in the ward room?" a stony-faced Miss Hutton had asked.

Elissa told the truth and was dismissed from the nursing service without delay. No explanation or excuse would condone her behavior. Elissa understood that.

As if she were under arrest, the waiting soldiers escorted her from Miss Hutton's office to Elissa's room in the nurses' quarters, stood by while she gathered her belongings, and carried them along as they marched straight to the ship. Elissa had asked to be allowed to go to the ward, tell the patients and staff farewell, and pass on her most pressing patient concerns, but Miss Hutton refused. It was policy, she explained, and she believed the rest of the staff would already be cognizant of Miss Lockwood's patient concerns.

Elissa wasn't permitted a single goodbye. She hadn't even been given time to write a note.

As soon as she boarded, the ship set sail. So she left without telling Jakes how much she valued his never-failing dedication, how greatly she admired his character, and how grateful she was for his friendship. She'd write to Jakes, and hope he didn't think too badly of her.

As painful as it was to depart in disgrace, without saying goodbye, it wasn't the worst thing. She left without seeing MacKay.

If only they could have said goodbye. Made plans. Promises.

Well, he had made promises during their Göksu picnic, and when he told her of his reassignment they'd both spoken vows of love. In truth, this only added a few days to their anticipated separation, when Cam returned to the front. They'd been prepared to spend months apart. Elissa just hadn't expected the months to start now.

What would he think when he learned of her dismissal? How would he find out? Would he and the orderlies be told at once? Or would they wonder why she was absent, ask, and then be informed of her circumstances?

A huge wound pulsed in the pit of her. In a few short hours she'd experienced the agony of Riley's death, followed by the comfort of Cam's arms and the joy of his kiss. Then came the despair of shame, and being torn away from—her life.

Cam would blame himself. He'd be livid. She wouldn't want to be Miss Hutton when he found out.

Elissa's grip on the rail loosened and her shoulders slumped. Cam would be gone in a few days. Even if she wrote now and posted the letter when they reached Malta, it wouldn't reach him before he sailed. A sudden thought jolted her. What if Cam were discharged, too? He was a military officer. Would he be punished? How were officers reprimanded? A court-martial? A demotion in rank?

She couldn't bear it if he suffered for her lapse. She'd thrown herself into his arms. She'd *needed* him to kiss her. Wanted it more than she'd ever wanted anything.

As wonderful as the kiss had been, Cam receiving punishment would be too dear a price to pay. Being demoted or—God forbid— jailed could affect his current patients, as well as any future ones. He was such a skillful surgeon. The thought of his abilities not being utilized where and when they were most needed…How would she bear the wait for his letter, when she'd learn if his career had been damaged in any way?

She'd go to Maddie, she supposed. Elissa couldn't love the aging midwife more if she were Elissa's grandmother by birth. Maddie would understand how Elissa had been sent home in disgrace, even though Elissa didn't comprehend it herself. She'd been an exemplary nurse, not an immoral one. It was so unfair, and could affect her ability to obtain employment for years. Now that the shock was receding, she wanted to rage at Miss Hutton.

Just getting to Maddie's home in Nottinghamshire would take every bit of determination Elissa possessed. But she need only stay strong until she reached Maddie's cozy cottage. Then she could rest, enjoy being with Maddie, and visit with her good friend, Grace. She'd write to Cam every day, as she'd promised, and be waiting when he returned to England. Having even a semblance of a plan helped settle her. She'd need to keep herself busy and her mind occupied while waiting for Cam, whether he went to the front as planned, or experienced repercussions of some sort. To demote such a fine officer and surgeon would be criminal. She doubted a kiss was a court-martial offense, even given the rigidity of the military. More likely, punishment would come by way of Cam's future postings. If he were discredited, she wasn't sure how she'd contend with her guilt. For his career to suffer because of her—it was too horrible to contemplate.

"Excuse me, miss." A soldier stood beside her, hat in hand. This man wasn't part of the crew, but a passenger like herself.

"Yes?"

"Sergeant Stephen Fleming, at your service." He gave her a half-bow. "Is it true you're one of the Nightingale nurses, ma'am?"

The question made her feel like a wounded animal with wolves nipping, knowing collapse was near. "I was. Yes."

"We've a large number of wounded and sick aboard. I'd be grateful for any assistance you could give, Miss—"

"Lockwood." Thank God. *Thank God.* There were sick aboard who needed her. "Miss Lockwood. Please, lead the way, Sergeant."

CHAPTER FOURTEEN

Cam sprawled on his cot and groaned. Other than Peters, taking advantage of his own cot down the way, the Scots Greys officers' tent was empty. After being up most of the night, Cam planned on putting the spare hour he'd found to good use napping. He grabbed sleep when he could, and when the snooze was short, he usually didn't dream. He'd been back at the front a month and it felt as though he'd never left. Constant exhaustion dogged him, and the nightmares had returned. He'd begun to tremble again. Not during surgery, but how long would it be until he did?

He longed for Elissa. Longed to be strong for her and their future, but he was helpless, once again beaten down by the constant firing of cannon and an unending stream of wounded. No matter how many times he re-read her letters, sleeplessness and neurasthenia plagued him.

In the beginning, he'd managed to carve out a bit of time to write, telling her how Humphrey had turned a blind eye to Cam's part in the incident that got Elissa discharged. He'd filled his pages with guilt, and love, and questions. He thought she might prefer that he leave the military medical service. They could live in the countryside and work together. Where would she like to live? Or would she prefer London and working in a hospital, as she'd done before?

When the neurasthenia returned, he'd stopped writing. Even knowing how desperate she must be for word from him, he couldn't write. He didn't know what to say, so he said nothing.

He'd lost four men today. Four men he'd tried, and failed, to save. His other patients survived, but his failures, although smaller in number, loomed so much larger. There was word a major offensive was being planned. How was he to get through another?

Movement drew his gaze to the tent entrance where a hand shoved aside the flap. Cam sprang to his feet the moment he recognized the man entering. Dark eyes glittering, mouth twisted in an ugly sneer, thickly bandaged right hand held before him, Archer stomped to Cam. The flushed, sweating orderly stopped and thrust his appendage's soiled bandage inches from Cam's face.

Cam went still, locking down the powerful longing to deliver a physical pain to equal the hurt the devil had caused Elissa. This son-of-a-bitch was responsible for her dismissal from Miss Nightingale's nursing service. Guilt hammered Cam's conscience. If he were honest, the blame was more his than Archer's.

"Here you are, you sanctimonious bastard," Archer growled. "I wanted to show you that I'm still alive and whole, in spite of your getting me sent to the front. In spite of your surgeon friend trying to chop off my hand. You tried your best, but I won and you lost."

Aw, Christ. In addition to being despicable, the man was now cracked. Cam didn't want to deal with him. If he never saw Archer again it would suit him fine. He'd heard the sergeant had taken a shot while evacuating wounded from the battlefield, but he'd felt no obligation to check on him. Unfortunately, now that Archer had sought Cam out, he was going to have to involve himself in the orderly's medical care. His hand reeked of infection and proximal to the dressing his wrist was red and swollen. Archer's sleeve covered his arm, so Cam couldn't see how far the redness extended. Aw, shite. Why couldn't some other medical officer have intervened? Cam didn't want to help Archer, but his medical oath superseded his wants.

"Ye need to get that hand looked at," Cam said. That much infection, the hand was beyond saving. The obvious signs of fever meant more than the limb was at risk. If—no, *when*—the infection moved into Archer's bloodstream, he'd die.

"You'd like nothing more than to take your saw to my arm, but I'm not letting you or any of your cronies have at me. I'm taking care of it and it'll heal. I've seen it happen."

The man was a danger to himself and edging for a fight. *He'd love it if I attacked him.* But doing so would result in an official reprimand, at least. Even worse, he'd be sinking to Archer's level. Providing proof that the sergeant had the ability to make him lose control. Cam wouldn't give him the satisfaction.

"MacKay?" Peters. Cam had forgotten he was in the tent.

Cam tipped his head toward Archer, who was cradling and rocking his hand, and gave the major a look. They managed to communicate without saying a word, and Peters nodded.

"Excuse me," Peters said, and left.

Cam heard the officer whistle, heard voices, and knew he'd have help in a moment. Christ, he wanted a drink. *Needed* one, to subdue this violent urge to put Archer down and exact retribution. Cam's hands began trembling and he tapped his fingertips against his leg to hide the finer involuntary movements.

"Ye're going to kill yourself if ye ignore that hand any longer," Cam said. "Ye know how gangrene looks, and what it means. I can smell it. Use yer head, man."

Archer's lips pulled back in a snarl. His nostrils flared. "You always think you know better than anyone what to do. Even when it's none of your concern. You had my orderlies looking to you instead of me, their ward-master. You criticized the way I handled the ward? You should have taken lessons! I'm man enough to deal out discipline and demand the respect owed me. Unlike you, I'm a leader, not a *friend*." The last word was spoken as though there was no worse designation.

"Archer, ye're acting irrational," Cam said, "and ye need help. How high is yer fever? Perhaps it's affected yer mind."

Peters returned, bringing four soldiers with him. The soldiers saluted, and Cam acknowledged their address. "Here, men," he said, pointing to Archer. "He's out of his mind. Sick. Take him to the general hospital tent. If he resists, carry him. Subdue him if ye have to."

Two of the soldiers grabbed Archer's arms. They wrangled with him for a minute, but it didn't take long for the tussle to exhaust Archer. One soldier in the lead, the fourth pushing from behind, they shuffled him out. "You'll be sorry for this, you bastard," Archer howled, head thrown back, heels digging.

Cam's desire for whiskey was so intense it pulled like an anchor chained to his leg and plummeting to the bottom of the sea. He rubbed his hand over his mouth. Peters was watching, and Cam didn't know how he could snatch a drink without seeming too anxious. With a glance toward his kitbag, Cam sighed and followed behind the soldiers and Archer.

Once at the hospital tent, he waited a distance away while a surgeon examined Archer's hand. Afterwards, the officer found Cam.

"He owes you thanks for forcing him in," the surgeon, Matthews, said. He had tired eyes and an apron liberally splotched with blood. "He might be dead tomorrow or the next day if that hand isn't taken off straight away. I'm astounded he's been working. After he sustained the wound, he refused my colleague's recommendation to have it amputated." Matthews shook his head. "It's coming off now no matter what he says."

Cam nodded. He'd expected as much.

"I'd think a sergeant in the medical service would have better sense," Matthews said before he turned away.

Cam would, too, but then, Archer existed outside the realm of the expected, in a vain, self-serving, and incomprehensible world. Cam turned away and headed back to his tent, trying like hell to maintain a steady pace and not run. Damn this bloody palsy. He shoved his shaking hands into his pockets. Today's surgeries were done, and he no longer needed a nap. He needed oblivion. He needed Elissa. Neither were available. But whiskey was.

#

Forty-five days that Cam had been back, and rumor had it the three-day British bombardment of Russian-held Sevastopol was over, and that this would be the last siege of the war. Christ, it had better be. He wasn't sure how much longer he could last.

The wind changed and Cam caught the smell of smoke from the cannon over a mile away. The Regimental Field Hospital tent sides were tied back, allowing for quick access by those carrying wounded in from the ambulances. It provided Cam with a view of bare ground sweeping to distant rolling hills. Not one bush or tree marred the dirt. The sky was a cloudless, solid gray.

The regiment's assistant-surgeons were in the field. They'd apply dressings to stop bleeding and stabilize, and send the wounded behind the lines to await a more thorough tending of their wounds. Most of those men would live, as long as they didn't succumb to infection. The more seriously injured, those needing immediate surgery, the assistant-surgeons would send to Cam. Most of those wounded would die. The tent was empty now, but the ground assault had begun. Soon there'd be lines of Scots Greys and other regiments' soldiers waiting. Cam gave one last look around the space. A tray of instruments: knife, probe, lancet, trocar, saw, needle, and ligature. A basket of towels, lint, and bandage rolls. Chloroform. Orderlies.

"Wounded coming in!"

Cam's fingers jerked. *Oh, God, not the trembling. Not now!* He prayed the jerk meant nothing, and the quivers held off. Cam thrust his hand into his coat pocket and gave the flask a squeeze. It was there. Just in case. When the quivers struck, a swallow or two was the only thing that would settle them. They'd never occurred during surgery, but after listening to cannon fire night and day, doubt began to creep into his head. Yesterday the doubt had turned to fear. He faced many hours, maybe even days, of continual surgery. Having the flask near reassured and relaxed him. Anything that helped him get through the next couple days was good, so he put it in his pocket. Yes, he drank every night to ward off the dreams, but of all days, God wouldn't strike him with quivers today, would He? For a moment his mind flashed to Parker, the delirium tremens patient Cam had cared for at Koulali. Was this how he'd started? Trying to get through the fight while doing his job? Perhaps, but for now, Cam had no choice.

The litter-carriers ran from the ambulances, the first litter holding a pale man with blood saturating the front of his uniform. Open mouthed, rasping, he worked to draw air into his lungs. "Here." Cam pointed to the table he stood beside. Time to batten down his emotions. With a few jerks he opened the unmoving soldier's coat and tore his undershirt away to reveal a bullet hole in the man's right upper chest. Cam lifted the young soldier's eyelids then gave his shoulder a shake. Unconscious. Cam pushed his finger through the opening in the man's skin, sinking into the warm, bloody chest cavity. As deep and wide as his finger would go, he felt for the bullet. He connected with a splintered rib, but no metal. Not good. He removed his finger and with the assisting orderly helping, checked the soldier's back. The bullet hadn't gone through. That meant Cam would have to try a probe, and the likelihood of a successful outcome had just fallen dramatically.

Others waited. He needed to hurry. For a moment he heard the cries of pain and distress. He glanced up and saw a row of men lying on the ground, waiting. Another ambulance, its horses' sides heaving, was being unloaded. He picked up the probe, and using a light grip, inserted it. Bending his head, he brought his ear nearer the chest, hoping to both feel and hear the click of probe meeting metal. Oh, damn it! Blood spurted from the wound. The orderly sopped it up with a towel, but the heavy flow continued. Cam withdrew the probe and thrust his finger back in, feeling for the source of bleeding and hoping to tamponade the torn blood vessel.

Another orderly, another towel. The hand holding it a familiar and most welcome one. Cam glanced up then returned his gaze to his patient's wound. "What are ye doing here, Jakes?"

"Your regiment is taking heavy fire. You're getting more wounded than some of the others. They sent me and one other to help."

"Glad to have ye," Cam said. Jakes had arrived at the front a week ago, having been pulled up to replace Archer, who'd sailed for England two days after his amputation. Jakes had stopped by Cam's tent a couple of times, but was assigned to the general hospital.

The chest under Cam's hand stopped moving. Slightly and almost gently lifted...fell. Cam removed his finger. No blood surged. The chest lifted...fell...and didn't lift again. Cam shook his head, plucked a towel from the waiting stack, and dried his hands. Two other tables with men waited. "Who's next?" he asked.

He was happy to see a man whose leg had taken a cannonball hit. The tourniquet applied in the field had saved him. He needed a clean amputation, and if infection didn't get him, he'd do fine. Cam gave the man's shoulder a squeeze. This one looked even younger than the last, his jaw bearing a sparse covering of golden whiskers. Pleading blue eyes met Cam's.

"I'm going to fix that stump so ye can comfortably wear a prosthesis," Cam said. "Ye won't be able to soldier, but ye'll be walking, riding, standing as tall as any other man."

The boy—damn, Cam couldn't think of this one as anything else—gave a shaky smile, dropped his head, and sniffed. Hiding tears, no doubt. Cam wanted to ask his name, ask where he was from, ask what his dreams were, but he didn't have time. Many waited, and Cam was the only surgeon in the Scots Greys' medical tent.

"I'm going to give ye some chloroform," Cam said. "Ye'll go to sleep and won't feel a thing. Ye'll be on a ship home in a couple days."

Smile quivering, the lad threw his arm across his eyes and nodded. Cam gave Jakes a nod and they got started.

It helped to have Jakes with him. In between patients he thrust a canteen at Cam and made him drink. He anticipated Cam's needs. Pushed food into his hand. And he somehow made Cam feel he could make it through.

Day turned to night. Orderlies hung lamps, and the smell of burning oil mixed with that of blood and unwashed men and the waste that spewed in the last throes of life. Cam's back and neck and shoulders and legs ached, but he ignored the pain. The soldiers he plied his lancet on had it far, far worse.

Sometime after midnight the tremors began. Bloody, bloody hell. It had never happened during surgery, but happening it was, and that fine tremor would transfer itself to every instrument he held. There was no one to take his place, and he knew, the more time that passed, the more pronounced the shakes would grow, until he couldn't safely perform surgery. So between patients he stepped into the dark, fished the flask from his pocket, and guzzled a couple swallows. Enough to banish the tremors. An hour later he avoided Jakes's questioning gaze and disappeared into the dark again.

During the early morning hours Cam noticed he was treating men faster than they were arriving, and that the number of waiting soldiers had declined. Thank God. Oh, thank God. He was staying steady and focused. Each time he stepped away he was careful to take only two swallows, and he began to feel that he could maintain his current pace as long as needed. Some of the tightness in his belly eased. The wounded should have all been collected from the battlefield by now, and word was the Russians were in retreat. Rogers, one of the assistant-surgeons, arrived just prior to sunrise, which meant two medical officers performing surgery.

A last few soldiers waited. Eyes burning, beyond exhausted, Cam's legs had turned to tree trunks. Stiff, unbending, and somehow not quite part of him. He waited while the orderlies carried his previous patient—alive and patched up—to the larger tent where his surviving patients rested. Some were bound for England and discharge, some for Barrack or Koulali Hospital and the care of the Nightingales. He'd saved a good number, but many would have infection to battle. Those with uncomplicated wounds, primarily those soldiers the assistant-surgeons had tended, would remain here under his care to recover and return to service.

Cam twisted his head side to side. He'd done it. No question now but that he'd make it through. For a moment pride lifted the cloak of weariness. He'd entered the army medical service in order to gain experience, and modesty aside, this night had proved him a surgeon of extraordinary skill. Many of the wounded had been Scots Greys. He'd known some of them, recognized others. Later he'd grieve for those lost. Now was the time for rejoicing those saved.

Och. A last ambulance was pulling in. He clamped his teeth together to hold back his groan. He should have expected it. Now that the sun was up, they'd be finding more wounded who'd been overlooked in the dark. Jakes met the first litter and pointed to Cam's waiting table. Faces grim, the litter-carriers hastened into the tent and deposited their man on Cam's table. A man wearing the scarlet coat and insignia of a Scots Greys sergeant.

Everything inside Cam dropped and he grabbed the table edge to steady himself. Christ. Shrapnel had torn the soldier's throat open. Cam forced air into his lungs. Why this? Why now? This was too much like Logan. The sergeant's trachea was already open, and Cam had opened his brother's with a knife, but Cam was too tired to care about the differences. Images of Logan fired in his mind at the rate of the recent cannon bombardment. *Focus, man. Focus!* He glanced at Rogers, wishing he could turn the sergeant over to the assistant-surgeon. But, no, the soldier's injury was too severe. Rogers was a competent surgeon, but this patient was going to need more than competence. Cam gathered himself and examined the man's torn larynx. There wasn't much hope. So little, most wouldn't try. Unconscious, the man inhaled not through his mouth, but through his neck wound.

Christ. Cam jammed his hands into his pockets. The quivers. Far worse than any he'd ever had. He looked at Jakes, who frowned at him from the other side of the table.

"Wipe away as much blood as ye can," Cam said. "I need a good look." Cam sucked in a sharp breath and squared his shoulders. "I'll be back."

Jakes hesitated then gave a terse nod. Cam stepped away and looked about. No darkness to hide in now. He headed for the nearest tent, a giant fist of panic squeezing his chest. If he was seen...but there was no other cover. He walked around to the back and stood as close to the canvas wall as he could. Confidence and relief surged as his hand slid around the welcome contours of the flask. He tipped it back, swayed a little, and drank. He had to drink fast, which increased the burn, but if anything, the blaze made him sharper. He swayed again. Oh, God, was he intoxicated? His heart skipped then raced as fast as his most terrified patient's. No. He couldn't be. He held too much tension to be overcome by the whiskey, and he'd been careful. He held up his hand. Steady. No! Still a little tremor. He straightened his fingers. Willed them still. But, ach, no, the finest quiver remained. He tipped the flask. Drank. Slipped it back into his pocket, empty.

He returned to the surgery tent and his table, never looking at Jakes. He kept his eyes on that horrific throat wound. *Help me.* He jerked his gaze to Jakes. Had Cam spoken the plea—the prayer— aloud? No. And his hands were steady.

He'd lost so much, most recently his belief that he deserved to marry Elissa. *This patient* he could not lose. Everything since he'd joined the medical service had led to this moment. This impossible throat injury. *Help me.* God wouldn't abandon him again, would He? Logan had been Cam's biggest failure. This man, his injury so like Logan's...

The sergeant coughed, his open, ravaged trachea spraying blood. Cam picked up needle and ligature. He'd reconstructed his shattered life once, but if he failed now, he didn't think his life would be mendable. He *had* to repair this throat wound, and save this man. He had to.

CHAPTER FIFTEEN

Elissa's dearest friend's face lit with a smile that embodied joy. Grace Abbott stroked her infant daughter's pink cheek with a gentle fingertip. "It's so wonderful having you home, Elissa. Your serving as midwife for Amelia's birth... Maddie is a proficient and beloved midwife, but your presence made everything easier."

"She's beautiful," Elissa said, rocking the newborn cradled in her arms. "And she appears very healthy." Elissa glanced at Harrison, Grace's middle child. The toddler was engrossed with a short tower of blocks on the parlor rug. Martha, Grace's oldest child and Elissa's goddaughter, was at school.

She'd arrived home at the end of July and now Christmas was a mere two weeks away. Working again as a midwife, helping Maddie, her mentor, had finally begun to ease the heavy weight of hurt and anger she'd carried since leaving Turkey. Work had become her panacea. She still felt angry when she thought of how she'd been forced to leave Koulali in disgrace, but that event had been eclipsed by her loss of Cam.

"I've never laughed during childbirth before. Or heard of anyone else who did," Grace said.

Amelia's birth had been two weeks earlier, and Grace had weathered pregnancy and delivery well. "I must admit that my other mothers kept the laughter to a minimum." Elissa grinned when Grace chuckled. Elissa cuddled the warm baby closer, the infant filling her arms with a weight at once insubstantial and heavily momentous.

She could have had a home and family not unlike Grace's. She'd wanted that with Cam. Elissa gazed down at the now sleeping Amelia. A fragile tracery of veins was visible in the baby's delicate eyelids. Elissa had delivered many babies and cared for many sick children. As precious as they all were, she'd never been envious of what she'd forgone.

Until now. This visit, and this baby, were different.

"Sometimes our school days seem very, very long ago," Grace said. "I confess, I'm envious of your experiences. You lived in Turkey. Made a difference." She released a gust of air. "You've saved lives." In Grace's tone Elissa heard the admiration of someone who didn't realize that along with the reward came pain and loss and uncertainty.

Grace's housekeeper appeared with tea, and Grace stood and began pouring. Elissa settled the sleeping baby in her cradle and stood looking down at her.

"Perhaps you envy me the tiniest bit, but no more than that." Not as much as Elissa had begun to envy Grace. "Your life is full of love." Elissa had friends and work. Good work. But it wasn't the same. It wasn't close to what Grace had, and what Elissa had imagined having with Cam.

Elissa turned away from the cradle and sat. Grace served Elissa tea and returned to her chair. Resting teacup and saucer on her knee, she stared at Elissa. For a time the only noises were Harrison gurgling unintelligible words and pounding his blocks together, and the snapping of the fire.

"You're not happy," Grace said.

Elissa shrugged her shoulders. "I enjoy midwifery, but it wasn't enough when I was twenty, and it isn't enough now. I've enjoyed these past five months, but I'm not busy enough. I hate to admit it, but I'm bored." Would her friend think less of her for the admission? She was doing good work with kind, deserving people, yet as honorable as the work was, it didn't compare to her work in Koulali. As self-important as it sounded to confess, it was a relief to share her true feelings.

"At Koulali, the men and women I worked with, and my patients, inspired me every day. How am I supposed to find that again? I can't provide a reference from Koulali. Any position I apply for, they'll want to know why I left Miss Nightingale's service."

Grace began tapping the toe of her stylish shoe. "Have you gotten anything positive back from your inquiries?"

"No. Maddie thinks I should move to a parish in need of a midwife. I'd at least be busier if I were the only one."

Grace became quiet again and Elissa knew Grace was wondering if she should mention MacKay.

She'd received two letters written from Koulali, before he'd returned to his regiment and surgery in a battlefield hospital tent, and several from the Crimea. He'd been outraged. He'd tried to get the decision reversed, had assumed responsibility for their indiscretion, but Miss Hutton had been immovable. Dr. Humphrey had shrugged and refused to involve himself. And of course, a few days later MacKay had sailed for the Crimea.

Over the next several letters, he was once again caring for injured during the heat of battle. His manner had turned from loving and excited for the future to—remote. Very correct and reserved. Those pages held nothing of the man she'd known in Koulali, the man she'd lain on a riverbank with. She'd worried he wasn't getting enough rest. If not for the familiar, bold, and distinctive script, she would have believed the author someone else.

His letters began arriving further and further apart, but she'd told herself the war and his work didn't leave time for letter writing; he was too tired. She'd written faithfully each day, telling him details of Nottinghamshire and how she busied herself, waiting for the war to end and him to come home.

Then mid-September the last letter arrived, after weeks of silence. The goodbye letter. Written aboard ship as he returned to England. Telling her he'd changed his mind about building a life with her. That their attraction had been based on loneliness. He was certain once they were no longer seeing each other, she'd have experienced much the same revelation as he—that he didn't love her. She'd wanted to write, demand answers and ask to meet him, but she didn't know where to send such a letter. He'd left the Army Medical Service. She had no idea where he'd gone.

She'd read that last letter over and over, and with each reading, a bit more of her heart shriveled and curled. Now it was little more than a crumpled husk.

Grace opened her mouth, and Elissa spoke before Grace could utter something about MacKay. Talk of children, of Grace's husband Daniel, of Elissa's prospects for a position, any of these topics Elissa could converse on. She just couldn't bear to discuss Cam. Not even with Grace.

#

On her way home from Grace's house, as Elissa approached Maddie's cottage, a man removed himself from the front stoop and headed toward her. Elissa knew that tall, lanky body, knew that quick stride. Could it be? They drew closer. She saw light brown hair, then a lopsided grin, and finally, unforgettable, twinkling blue eyes.

She ran the last couple steps. They clasped hands and Elissa squeezed. *Jakes.*

When they parted, Elissa laughed. "Jesse Jakeman, this is wonderful, but what are you doing here?" She took a step back and looked him over. "And you're out of uniform."

"I'm on leave."

"And home from the Crimea." Home safe, thank God. "Come inside." She led the way into Maddie's small cottage, and then went straight to the kitchen. She gestured him into a chair at the kitchen table and busied herself with tea preparation. Maddie was calling on her patients, so Elissa and Jakes had the cottage to themselves. "Now, tell me everything."

"Did you know Archer was sent to the front?" He scowled. "He was the one who reported you and MacKay, wasn't he?"

She should have known Jakes would want to discuss Koulali and her upset. She didn't want to hear about Archer, though. She shrugged. "I think so, but it doesn't matter now. I didn't realize he was reassigned to a battlefield hospital."

Jakes nodded. "At one point Archer was sent to retrieve wounded while they were still under fire. He was wounded and removed from duty, so then I was sent to fill the open orderly position. You know how it is. They need a full contingent of medical personnel on the peninsula, and don't want to wait for someone to be sent out from England, so they pull staff from the hospitals in Turkey."

Elissa set the teapot on the table, along with cups and saucers. She took a chair, began pouring, and asked. She had to. "Did you see MacKay there?"

Jakes stilled. Went quiet. Shifted on his chair. He picked up his cup and took a long swallow. "When Sevastopol fell and the firing ceased, he quit the army."

"I heard he left." Elissa tried to keep her voice matter-of-fact, but wasn't sure how successful she was. "Do you know why? Or where he is?"

Jakes shook his head. "He's in London, I think."

London. How could he be so close, and not have come to see her? To at least say goodbye. She didn't feel as though they were finished. How could he?

Jakes took another drink of tea. "I came to tell you about a specialist hospital I discovered. It's a small charitable institution for the treatment and rehabilitation of soldiers who've lost limbs. They're provided with custom-made arms and legs, and when necessary, their stumps are revised. Many of their amputations were rushed, performed in the midst of battle, or to prevent impending death, and the resultant stump doesn't hold up under the pressure of use with a prosthetic limb." Jakes tapped the lip of his cup with his fingertips. "I'm hoping to convince you to come work there."

The unexpected suggestion startled her. It also made a pulse of hope surge in her chest. She needed a few minutes to accustom herself to the idea. "A hospital for veterans? It's a wonderful idea, but I've never heard of such a thing."

"The Duke of Carlisle founded Primrose Hill Hospital for Former Sailors and Soldiers. He and several benefactor friends support it."

"It's a charity hospital? Exclusively for veterans?"

"Yes. They converted a vacant building not far from Regent's Park."

"Bless Carlisle for establishing such a hospital."

"You would like it," Jakes said. "They need good nurses. They need you."

Those simple words were so welcome, and so needed, Elissa had to hold her breath to keep the resultant emotion in check.

"I have no references to present, Jakes. They wouldn't accept me."

He gave her a sheepish grin. "I've already spoken to those that matter, and they're anxious to have you join them. If you come, you'll be welcome."

Welcome? The thought staggered her. She liked midwifery, but helping rehabilitate men that the country owed so much to—it was vastly appealing. Koulali had given her a special affection for men who'd fought in service of the Crown. They were so very deserving.

"Jakes, is this true? They know I was discharged from the nursing service in Turkey?"

"I swear it." His forthright gaze left no doubt of his sincerity. "I'm so taken with the place, I've been helping them out. I've explained all to Mr. Fletcher, the chief surgeon, and to Mr. Howell. He's the duke's man of business for the hospital. They've approved your engagement."

Could it be that simple? Her work would speak for itself, if she were given the chance.

"I took the liberty of finding a room for you." Color pinked his face. "One of the hospital volunteers—she's a military widow—has agreed to let you a room. The home's nearby, and I know you'll find Mrs. Emerson agreeable."

"I—Jakes! I don't know what to say." Excitement brimmed over, and she reached out.

He grasped her hand and held firm. "Say 'yes,' Miss Lockwood."

This was the answer—work that would fully engage her. "Yes!" Laughter broke, providing some much-needed emotional relief. She turned her face away and dabbed at her mostly happy tears.

After a bit, Elissa refilled their teapot. She added bread, butter, and cheese to the table. They talked about how soon she could be there. It shouldn't take her but a couple days to transfer the care of her patients to Maddie and say her goodbyes. Part of her found it hard to believe she'd be in London in two days, immersed in a new life. What would she do if she happened upon Cam? He'd greet her as he would Jakes or any other person he'd worked with in Turkey. The possibility made her heart hurt.

"What of Archer, Jakes? You said he was wounded? How badly?"

"He took a ball through his right hand, and a putrid infection developed. They amputated."

A raw satisfaction turned her heart to lead, and her chest felt so cold, for a moment her lungs froze and wouldn't work. Perhaps an angel, one whose mortal form had suffered under the hand of the Koulali ward-master, orchestrated the injury and amputation as a measure of comeuppance for the arrogant, cruel sergeant. How fitting if Archer now craved the kindness and compassion he'd denied his patients.

Guilt crushed her thoughts. She didn't truly wish debilitation on anyone, not even the detested Archer. She imagined it would be especially hard for a man like Archer, who appeared to have few if any friends, and who'd never mentioned family.

Jakes's eyes rolled up and he shook his head. "You feel sorry for him, don't you? You're a saint."

"Not as sorry as I should be, and you can't fool me. I know you're sorry, too."

He gave her a teasing look that clearly said he thought her unhinged. The corners of his mouth curved up and dimples indented his cheeks.

Elissa had to ask again. "Do you know anything else about MacKay?"

Jakes pulled the teapot close, lifted the lid and peered inside. Then he filled his cup and added sugar. Elissa almost growled in frustration as she waited for him to finish stirring.

"I don't think he ever intended to stay in the army," Jakes said. "He once told me he joined to gain surgical experience, and he has a surfeit of it now. I imagine there're any number of positions he could take. Perhaps he'll go home to Scotland."

The deep disappointment that struck was irrational. Cam had hurt her. Terribly. How was she to stop thinking about him? He crowded her mind at unexpected times, and no matter how much she wanted to, she couldn't seem to expunge those brooding thoughts of longing. More than the confusion, hurt, and anger, she missed him.

At least in London she'd be busier, her brain and emotions engaged in her work. She'd work hard, become so tired, she'd sleep. No more endless nights lying awake, thinking of his face as he greeted her each morning, his voice sparked with humor, as it was several times a day, his kindness as he took the time to give each patient a few minutes of his complete attention.

Most important, she'd be too tired and too busy to remember that amazing time by the heavenly waters.

CHAPTER SIXTEEN

Primrose Hill Hospital for Former Sailors and Soldiers was the strangest and most marvelous institution Elissa had ever seen. One long room held sixteen patient beds. Elissa would work here, caring for amputees who had undergone surgery to have their stumps reshaped. It was the second room Benedict Fletcher led her to that contained a sight Elissa had never imagined—a gymnasium appointed with all manner of exercise apparatuses. Scattered throughout the room, men lifted dumbbells, did calisthenics, and boxed in a small roped enclosure. Every man was an amputee.

One man appeared to have weighted throwing clubs attached to his forearm stump with a wrap. He raised and lowered his weighted arm, building muscle in the limb. Another man, a prosthesis on one leg, held himself between double rails as he practiced walking.

"This truly is a place of rehabilitation," Elissa said. She hadn't been familiar with the term. Dr. Fletcher had explained the word, and the hospital's goals. The concept stunned her. She could see that the men's attitudes and potential would be enhanced as their ability to compensate for the loss of their limb rose.

"Primrose Hill's primary purpose," Mr. Fletcher said, "is to make the men not only able to work again, but to help them find placement, as well. They leave here without pain, with a prosthetic fitted to the individual's stump, and they're practiced in the use of the prosthetic. Many have prosthetics specially adapted to their particular line of work. When a man leaves Primrose Hill, he's able to hold his head up. He can support a family and take his place in society."

Fletcher motioned her back out through the gymnasium's double doors. "A man receives all the skills he needs to live and work with his amputation. If he needs new job skills, he's taught them before his discharge."

"The surgical service is just a small part of this, I suspect," Elissa said. "They don't all need their stumps reshaped, do they?"

"No, they don't. About half of our sixteen beds hold patients who have had their stumps refined. I want your nursing skills for them, of course, but I want your organizational skills, too. I want you to keep track of each man's progress. We don't want to overlook a key element in a man's recovery. You'll document and review each man's daily appointments and accomplishments."

He stroked his hand over his chin, smoothing his golden beard. "I admit, I'm hoping to find a suitable ward nurse so that you can concentrate on each man's overall needs. I wouldn't expect it of most nurses, but I know it's well within the abilities of a Nightingale nurse."

He was correct. In Koulali, the coordination of Ward Two had been her responsibility. She could do this, and do it well. The thought of such a challenging, comprehensive job made her heart patter like excited children's feet. Still. Did Mr. Fletcher truly understand she had left Turkey in disgrace? Jakes had reassured her Fletcher knew. She didn't want to bring it up, but how could she not?

"Jesse Jakeman said he made you privy to the circumstances of my leaving Koulali."

Fletcher bowed his head. When his head raised, his sharp amber eyes looked full into hers. "I'm well aware, Miss Lockwood. I assure you, I have no doubts regarding your ability to perform your duties here. Just the opposite, in fact. We'll be very pleased to have you as a member of Primrose Hill's staff."

He led her to his office, where they settled on her hours, responsibilities, and wages. Once their business was concluded, he showed her the dietary kitchen and laundry.

"The prosthetics shop is there," Fletcher said, pointing to a small building behind the hospital. "We'll leave that for another day. You'll like our prosthetist, though. He works miracles."

Every staff person she'd met exuded enthusiasm and dedication. It seemed too good to be true, to be part of it. To be valued. To be doing vital work. Unbidden, Cam came to her mind. He'd taught her how to care for amputated limbs. She wished she could show him this place. He'd be pleased she'd found a position here. The thought made a little ache take up residence in her chest.

Pleased? Not likely. When would she get it through her head that Cam didn't care about her circumstances? When would thoughts of him stop invading her mind? And how could she have been so wrong about him?

#

"Look at my hand, Miss Lockwood," James Storey said, almost bouncing with excitement in Elissa's office door.

Elissa obliged him by standing and motioning him into her small office, where she could examine the patient's new prosthesis. He'd just returned from the workshop and wore the new hand fashioned special for him.

Elissa knew on the inside, the stump socket conformed to the shape and size of Storey's stump. The exceptional fit assured stability of the prosthetic, and a stump free of irritating pressure points. As Storey aligned his natural hand alongside his wooden one, Elissa turned her hands palms up and cradled Storey's in hers.

His wooden hand looked much like his natural one. The length, width, and curve of the wooden appendage, the bulge of each knuckle and shape of each nail, matched its flesh-and-blood mate. Affixed to the wood, and running from the tips of the curved first and second wooden fingers to the wrist, a wide strip of metal provided the same unbendable strength as a metal hook. Not only did the flesh-colored paint match Storey's skin, but the painted-on nails gave the hand a realistic look.

Storey was being trained in the skills of a clerk, so it was more important for him to have a natural-looking hand, as opposed to one used for strength work.

"It's very fine, Mr. Storey," Elissa said. She'd made it her practice to drop the patients' military ranks and use the same address they'd use when they took up their new lives.

"I'm not self-conscious," Storey said. "Not in the least, and with the training I'm receiving, I'll be able to earn more than I did in the army." He sighed as if exhaling a great weight. "God bless the duke and the other patrons."

A shuffle in the corridor drew their attention. Mr. Fletcher stood outside her door, flanked by two other gentlemen. Elissa's office could hold three in a pinch, but no more, so she led Storey into the hallway.

"Mr. Fletcher. Good morning."

One of Fletcher's companions, the tall man in the impeccable, tailored suit, removed his top hat. The other unknown gentleman doffed his bowler.

"I'm glad to see our efforts are paying off." The tall gentleman's speech was no less elegant than his person. The slightest smile curved his mouth, accentuated by a neatly trimmed mustache and small beard.

"Your Grace," Mr. Fletcher said, "may I present our rehabilitation supervisor, Miss Lockwood. Miss Lockwood, this is His Grace, the Duke of Carlisle, and his man of business, Mr. Howell."

"I'm honored," Carlisle said.

Elissa made an appropriate response and introduced Storey. Storey, bless him, proudly offered his prosthetic hand for examination. The men exclaimed over it and Storey was effusive in his thanks. Carlisle listened with a pensive expression, his lips tipped in a pleasant yet subdued smile.

It seemed odd. Mr. Fletcher and Mr. Howell grinned at Storey, while Carlisle—without whom Primrose Hill Hospital would not exist—appeared only mildly appreciative of Storey's progress.

When Storey excused himself, Mr. Howell asked Mr. Fletcher to look at Howell's most recent financial report, and the men went along to Fletcher's office. Which left the duke with Elissa.

Without so much as a word, Carlisle strolled into Elissa's small office and sat. She trailed behind, took refuge behind her desk, and looked into intelligent, alert gray eyes set below a cap of black, silver-threaded hair. His short beard emphasized the very masculine planes of his face.

"Tell me how you supervise the men's rehabilitation, Miss Lockwood. Mr. Fletcher praises you and how well you've organized the place."

Elissa pulled Storey's folder from the file cabinet behind her desk and handed it to the duke. He opened it and began leafing through the pages.

"I keep notes on each patient. What treatments, surgeries, education, and physical training each man receives. His ongoing physical and mental progress. They undergo so many different sorts of rehabilitation, we must evaluate the men's progress along with their needs. We don't want to miss something or leave some aspect of their recovery incomplete. I make sure each man who leaves here has a place to go, a position or way of earning his living, and is as physically strong and able as it's possible for him to be."

Carlisle's gray eyes studied her. Initially, their intensity made her uncomfortable, but she was growing accustomed to their keen scrutiny and beginning to find them appealing. Compelling.

He was handsome in a refined, austere way. Before she'd come to Primrose Hill she might not have recognized the lean, athletic strength hidden beneath his tailored suit, but since her arrival she'd learned the look of muscles honed through long hours in the gymnasium. There was a controlled power in Carlisle's body. Elissa sensed the dominance of a panther surveying its territory.

"I'm impressed," Carlisle said. "And very pleased with the achievements of Primrose Hill. Its success is important to me." His hand fisted and bounced on his thigh.

"I'm grateful and happy to be contributing, helping men who are so deserving," Elissa said. "What we're accomplishing here must be very satisfying for you, Your Grace, having created Primrose Hill. It's a special place."

The duke's mouth tightened. There was something more than pride or appreciation in his eyes. A glint of profound sadness sat deep in those silver recesses.

"Yes, it is," Carlisle said. "The idea was inspired by my youngest son. He lost both legs at Alma."

"Oh. I'm so sorry." The man hardly looked old enough to have a grown son, but she supposed he could be in his early forties. "You must be very proud of him. Is he a member of the hospital's board of directors? His advice during planning must have been invaluable." She saw a flash of pain before his gaze lowered. His eyes narrowed, as if the light was hurting them, and she knew the answer wasn't good.

"Please, excuse me," Elissa said, horrified at her faux pas. "I'm used to my patients pouring their hearts out to me. I often say things designed to make them share what they're thinking and feeling.

They always feel better afterwards. It's put me in the habit of asking people whatever comes into my head. It's very impolite of me."

"It makes them feel better?" Carlisle asked.

"Disability and sickness frighten people. Talking about their fears somehow makes them less afraid. Or makes them feel strong enough to face their fears," Elissa said gently.

Carlisle considered her for a moment. "Perhaps you're right, Miss Lockwood. Michael wouldn't talk about what had happened to him. I knew he was melancholic, but didn't realize how deep his depression went."

She didn't know Carlisle, so she wasn't sure how she knew his sharing these details was extremely difficult for him, but she could tell. She sat too far away. She left her chair, moved around her desk and eased onto the chair positioned beside Carlisle. She waited as he stared at his silk hat and stroked the brim.

"I discovered how hopeless he felt when I read the letter he left. After he hanged himself."

The quiet desperation in his voice worsened the pinching in the vicinity of Elissa's heart. She wasn't sure how to offer her condolences to this contained man. Helplessness swamped her.

When he looked at her, she ignored the etiquette due his title and placed a comforting hand upon his forearm. Years ago, nursing taught her that whether of the greatest rank and wealth, or the humblest of origins, grieving people appreciated a caring touch. For a moment his gloved hand covered hers, and he squeezed. She caught a small movement in his shoulders—a little shudder, or a relaxation of tension, perhaps.

"I'm so very sorry," she repeated.

"Thank you." He dragged in a breath and Elissa removed her hand. "Establishing Primrose Hill Hospital has helped my grief."

"You've done a fine thing, something to be proud of, and I believe we'll become a model for rehabilitation. There's never been an institution that puts such services together, and we've been successful. Being with others in such similar situations encourages the men. It's not just the staff, but the men themselves who are instrumental in our success."

"Being here, seeing Storey today, has been uplifting. It's reassured me that Primrose Hill is everything I wanted it to be. I don't know why I procrastinated, delaying my visit."

"Perhaps you feared seeing men in the same condition as your Michael would be too painful?" Elissa suggested.

His mouth firmed. "Perhaps."

"I love this work more than any nursing I've done. All because transformations happen here. We're helping these men develop new, productive lives. You should pay us regular visits. Give yourself doses of Primrose Hill's optimism."

Carlisle stood. "I believe I shall." He cocked his head and listened. The rumble of Howell and Fletcher's voices was still audible from Fletcher's nearby office. "They appear to still be at it. Can I convince you to accompany me to the prosthetics workshop? I want to meet this artist miracle worker."

"I'd like nothing better! I'm not sure why I haven't yet made it there myself. I've been here two weeks! Each day I mean to visit, but something always occurs to interfere." Twice she'd been halfway there when Jakes had stopped her with an urgent request. And now here it was, past Christmas and mere days until the new year.

The workshop sat a hundred yards behind the hospital. Elissa led Carlisle down the bricked path that led to the cottage-like, two-story building.

Carlisle pushed the unlocked workshop door open and ushered Elissa through. She entered and blinked, eyes adjusting to the decrease in light.

A man sat holding a wooden arm, working sandpaper over its length. Sawdust powdered his tawny hair and his clothing. Something about the man's broad shoulders, bent over his work, seized Elissa and held her immobile. His head lifted, and all she could see was unforgettable forest green eyes set in an intense, masculine face. Cam.

Her lips parted, but no sound came out. She stood, befuddled and staring. Carlisle said something, but his words whirled about the room without her ever taking their meaning.

The legs of Cam's chair scraped the floor as he stood. He brushed his hands over his shirt and apron, creating a flurry of sawdust. Still brushing absently at himself, he approached them.

He'd changed, and the differences were both glaring and harsh. Her throat tightened. These were changes borne of deep distress.

Lines scored his now bearded face. He was lean to the point of being underweight, his hair overlong and shaggy. He looked like a man who'd gone months without a good night's sleep.

Cam's movements slowed. His arms dropped and a thunderous frown furrowed his forehead. "What are ye doin' here?" he rasped, gaze riveted to Elissa.

Oh, dear God. What was *he* doing here? *Cam* was the prosthetist? This was all *wrong*. "Jakes," she croaked. Jakes knew. He'd lied when he'd come to see her in Nottinghamshire. He'd arranged her coming here, to work at the same hospital as Cam. The past two weeks she and Cam had been a mere hundred yards apart and never known.

"Why are you doing this?" she asked, making a vague gesture and raking the room with her eyes. Everywhere she looked she saw the components of prosthetics—woodworking tools, bins of metal pieces, soft knitted stump socks to cushion the stump within the prosthesis, and blocks of lumber awaiting shaping and sizing. The air was redolent with the clean, sweet tang of fresh wood.

Cam's face hardened. "We're revolutionizing prosthetics here." His speech was slow, precise, and stern, as if she needed a careful explanation in order to understand.

This wasn't Cam. This wasn't the man she knew. Cam would never speak to her this way. He'd never look at her with this look that was so cold and sharp, it shot barbed needles straight to the most vulnerable, guarded part of her. Dislike, disgust, and aversion all swam in that chilling mix.

His red-rimmed eyes narrowed. "I've no cause to apologize or make excuses because I'm not laboring as a sawbones."

An empty, sick feeling knotted Elissa's stomach. "You're the finest surgeon I've ever known," she whispered. "Why would you stop performing surgery?"

He leaned forward like a pugilist poised for attack, teeth clenched. "Because I wanted to."

Elissa fell back a step.

Carlisle, silent until now, stepped closer, partially shielding her from Cam. "It appears the two of you are already acquainted," the duke said. "And that it's not the most cordial of acquaintances. I'll accompany you back to the hospital."

"No!" Elissa said. "Mr. MacKay and I are—" But what were they? Were they even friends? He'd cut all ties between them. This surly man wasn't the man she'd been longing for. He was a horrible parody of the surgeon she'd known in Turkey, the man she admired and carried deep feelings for.

"It might be best that *ye* go," Cam said to Carlisle, "so Miss Lockwood and I can speak freely." He adjusted his posture and his chest expanded, which somehow made him grow larger. "She dinnae need ye to protect her."

"Mr. MacKay! This is the Duke of Carlisle."

Cam didn't so much as twitch. "Well, I'm glad to know ye, Yer Grace. Yer money's being put to good use, and we're glad to have it." A muscle near Cam's eye began to tic. "But Miss Lockwood and I would be well served if ye'd take yerself out of here and leave us be."

Carlisle considered Cam as if such blunt speaking were unique in his experience. His brows rose.

The door flew open and Jakes rushed into the room.

"Jakes!" Cam barked. "Ye've some explaining to do."

CHAPTER SEVENTEEN

Cam's sudden surge of temper made his head sizzle like it was on the verge of exploding.

Jakes stopped, arms held up with palms facing out. "Let me explain."

The orderly looked pale but determined. Jakes might want to have his say, but Cam didn't care to hear it.

"I dinnae want to hear yer explanations, Jakeman. Playing God! Manipulating us! Ye bloody—" He stopped mid-curse, aware of Elissa's presence, the duke looking on. He fisted his hands. Bloody hell, but he wanted to take Jakes apart.

Jakes angled himself toward Cam. "You need her," he said, his tone and expression conveying desperation.

The pounding in his head, punishing Cam since he'd wakened this morning, intensified. He'd never have believed it possible for the nauseating hammering to worsen, but he'd been wrong. He squeezed his eyes shut and felt himself sway.

"Cam."

Elissa's soft, worried voice. Close. Her hand wrapped around his upper arm, steadying him. Jakes had built up the fire this morning, and Cam had removed his coat once the room warmed up. There was naught between her hand and his skin but the thin fabric of his shirt, and the heat of her palm seared. A shudder rocked through him.

He was afraid to look into her eyes—afraid of what he might see—but he couldn't stop himself.

He couldn't begin to read all the different emotions he saw brimming in their hazel depths. There were too many, and they made him ache. He pulled back, jerking his arm from her grasp. He backed up several steps, until he was too far away to make out the glinting gold specks in her eyes, or smell the light, elusive scent of lavender and Elissa.

"I'm all right," he muttered. "Ye needn't bother with me." Then he clamped his jaw shut, the emotions he'd glimpsed in her eyes echoing inside him in a hurly-burly tumble. Shock, sadness, hurt. Acute distress. The weight of them was crushing him.

"I don't understand," she said.

Her voice sounded strained, as though she held back tears, but he turned his head, determined not to look at her. "I've an appointment for a fitting in a few minutes," he said, sending Jakes a silent, glaring command.

Jakes and Carlisle looked as though they were both anxious to get Elissa out of there. They managed to make a few superficial parting comments and usher her out.

Thank God. Cam staggered to a chair and sank onto it. He bent forward and cradled his head in his hands. Was Jakes intending to finish Cam off, bringing Elissa here? Because her presence would put the last nails in his coffin. He'd been trying to push thoughts of her out of his head, with limited success. Now, knowing she was at the other end of the path, everything would change. Jakes had best stay away for a while, unless he felt like getting the stuffing knocked out of him.

Cam sighed. Scrubbed his hands over his face. He stood, went to the coat rack and fished in his coat pocket. Almost dropped the flask in his hurry to get the lid off. He welcomed the burn of the powerful drink. Whiskey would sort out the pounding in his head, release the god-awful squeezing in his chest, and get him calm enough to think rationally. He couldn't be acting like an overwrought, swooning female when his next amputee arrived for his fitting.

He took a second, deep pull from the flask. He'd figure out a way to keep Elissa out of his thoughts. He must, because reminders of what he'd lost were sheer torture. Even being her friend was beyond him. Any association would put his resolution at risk of dissolving.

She deserved a proud, strong-minded, tenacious man. One who could keep her safe and fill her life with joy. Cam was weak, his will crushed. He'd bring her nothing but worry and despair. He just prayed he still retained enough strength of character and integrity to keep his sorry arse away from her. Thank God he'd had enough backbone to end their romantic association. Blunt and full of lies, love had guided his hand as he'd penned the brutal letter. Once sealed and posted, he'd stayed drunk for three days. He knew he'd hurt her badly, but in time, she'd recover. Cam took comfort in having rescued her from life with him, and in having given her a future full of possibility and promise.

#

Cam woke, bleary and confused. He'd fallen asleep in front of the fire, slouched in his chair, legs sprawled on the ottoman. Now, nothing remained of the fire but a few glowing coals. His window revealed a sky gone from night to pre-dawn gray. Shadows cloaked the room, but there was light enough to see.

He looked around the small space that was his combination bed and sitting room, wondering what had awakened him. Quiet footsteps, advancing up the stairs, penetrated his haze. That's what woke him, then. Jakes's conscience hadn't let him rest. He wanted to explain himself to Cam. As if that were possible.

The orderly's footsteps stopped at the top of the steps and a long minute passed. Perhaps Jakes was mustering his nerve. Cam eyed the bottle that sat on the small table beside him, seeing he'd made a sizable dent in the liquor before he'd succumbed.

He put his feet on the floor and pulled his body more upright. The movement brought a stab of pain to his right temple and eye, and a roll of nausea to his stomach. He needed a bit of the hair of the dog that bit him.

"Well, come ahead, then," he yelled to Jakes, who still hadn't knocked. Cam's shouting resulted in a hammer-like bash of his brains. The pain made him want to wield his own cudgel on Jakes. He hoped the orderly was prepared for a bit of comeuppance.

Cam grit his teeth at the tremor in his hands, poured a hefty measure of whiskey into his glass, and got two swallows down before the door opened.

Only it wasn't Jakes.

"What are ye doing here?" he asked. "Have ye lost yer mind?"

Elissa stalked toward him, lips pressed tight, hands clasped together at her waist. She looked pale, and severe, and if he had to hazard a guess, he'd say she'd gotten even less sleep than he had.

Her gaze swept over him, the table and nearly empty bottle beside him, and stuck on the glass of whiskey in his hand. She stilled. Her mouth dropped open. "You've spent the night in that chair? Drinking?" she asked, dragging out the words, sounding horrified, disbelieving, and—hurt.

Her shock buried an arrow in his chest. He squeezed his eyes shut. Bloody hell. He didn't want to have this confrontation, but he had to.

He slammed the glass onto the table and surged out of the chair. Which was a mistake, as it made him want to clutch his head with one hand and grab onto a support with the other. "I've no proper room for entertaining a lady," he said through clenched teeth. "Ye'd best leave before ye're discovered and turned out in disgrace from this job, too."

Her chin tilted. "I survived it once, I imagine I can again." She stepped forward, stopping a mere arm's length away.

The air between them vibrated with her intensity. His legs nearly collapsed when he caught the sweet smell of her. Her eyes snared him, held him, while inside he railed. He was a shackled prisoner, freedom within reach, yet a world away.

Her hand hovered in the space between them. "Why aren't you performing surgery?"

The hitch in her voice cracked his heart open. Somehow, he stood firm. Kept his face stern. "'Tis my preference, is all, Miss Lockwood, and 'tis none of yer concern."

She looked outraged. "It *is* my concern. I…I…*care* about you. And I don't believe you prefer fashioning prosthetics to doing surgery."

Thank God, she hadn't said she loved him. Those words would have the power to gut him. He didn't want to hear them.

How could he make her leave? She was persistent, and he didn't think he could hold himself in check for long. Soon he'd be spilling his troubles, his feelings, wrapping his arms around her. Destroying her.

Fear of that made him burrow deep. He scraped together the shreds of his resolve, as he had when he'd written that last letter, and hardened his face and voice. As hard as, by some miracle, he'd managed to make his heart. "It doesnae matter what ye think."

Pain flashed across her face. "I…"

She stopped. He steeled himself to resist the compulsion to comfort and reassure her. It was almost overwhelming.

"What—what happened to you, Cam?" Her broken, whispered words tore like thorns dragged across his heart.

If treating her so cruelly hadn't already finished him, hearing her use his given name would have. No other woman, excepting his mother and cousins, had ever used it.

Elissa using his name told him, as clearly as anything could, she still had feelings for him. To hear her use it now, after he'd hurt her, devastated him.

Anger spurted through his veins. Months ago he'd ended what had existed between them. Why was she here? Twisting him. Torturing him. He'd told her to leave. Until yesterday, he hadn't had to witness the pain he'd caused her. He'd been thankful for that, but now there was no escaping her distress and desperation.

He took her arm, spun her, pulled her across the room to the door. Thrust her through the doorway and released her on the landing at the top of the stairs. He wanted to tell her to stay away, but he couldn't speak. If he opened his mouth, he thought fire might blaze out, dragon-like, and set Elissa aflame.

Mouth open, eyes wide, she stared at him and rubbed her arm where he'd gripped it. *Ah, shite.* On top of everything else, he'd managed to hurt her physically, as well.

Her mouth snapped closed. "I'm not leaving. We...we *loved* each other! I want to know what happened. That letter you sent told me *nothing.*"

He grabbed his head with both hands. "There's naught to explain. We were lonely and found comfort in each other for a time. Once you left, the intensity of my feelings subsided."

Oh, Christ. Her eyes were wet. And his chest felt like it'd taken a solid hit from a sledge-hammer.

"Now. Ye're leavin'. And ye'd better pray no one sees ye," he somehow managed to grind out. "Don't come back. Turkey was a different place. A different time. It's over and we've both new lives to live. I don't want to be held responsible for ye losing this position because ye've been seen leaving my quarters in the wee hours."

He knew he'd pierced her as surely as though he'd shoved a scalpel in her. She stood unmoving at the top of the stairs, pale and silent.

He slammed his door and leaned back against it. Waited for the sounds of her retreat. After a minute he heard her rushing down the stairs.

He couldn't resign, even though he should. This work was all that was holding him together. There wasn't another hospital or organization accomplishing what they were here. It was good work.

He didn't want Elissa to leave, either. He wanted his patients to have the benefit of her presence. After what happened at Koulali, it couldn't have been easy for her to obtain a hospital position. She might not find another, if she left Primrose Hill.

If they were both to stay at Primrose Hill, they needed to stay away from each other. Anything but the most infrequent of contacts would be unbearable. Hopefully, after this encounter, Elissa would keep as far away from him as she could.

CHAPTER EIGHTEEN

Somehow Elissa made it through the day. When she donned her coat and headed for home, the strangling tension she'd borne since seeing Cam that morning began to loosen. She'd gone no more than a block before Jakes joined her, matching her stride for stride.

Elissa kept her head facing forward. "You lied to me, Jakes. When you came to see me in Nottinghamshire, I asked you about MacKay. You withheld information and lied to me."

"I wanted to tell you, but I wasn't sure you'd come if you knew he was at Primrose Hill. I wasn't sure how things were left between you."

His speech sounded earnest, but Elissa wasn't in a forgiving mood. She shot him an angry glance, saw he was watching her, and turned her gaze back to the walk before her. "That makes it so much worse, Jakes, that you'd bring me here when you didn't know how MacKay or I would react to the other's presence. Since you didn't consider either of our feelings, let me enlighten you. MacKay doesn't want to see me or speak to me." She looked at Jakes again. His miserable expression was actually gratifying. "How do you think that makes me feel?"

She responded to his gentle tug on her sleeve, stopped, and faced him.

Pleading blue eyes begged her to understand. "I'm sorry, Miss Lockwood. I was desperate to get you to Primrose Hill." He paused, squeezed his eyes shut. When they opened, he delivered the blow. "MacKay's not right in his head."

Her anger drained away. Dear Jakes. He'd done it for Cam. She knew that.

"How bad is the drinking?" Elissa asked.

Jakes showed no surprise at her question. He jerked off his cap and thrust his fingers through disheveled brown hair. Stared at his boots. "It's bad." He lifted his head. "He's always got at least a little drink in him. He's pretty straight during the day, but once his workday is done, he dedicates himself to getting drunk. As though a state of drunkenness were a great prize."

How could a man of the fortitude and goodness of Cam become a slave to drink? But she'd seen the truth of it yesterday, when she'd mustered every scrap of courage she possessed and crept up to his room at daybreak. There he'd sat, newly awake and still in the previous day's clothes. Wrinkled, bleary-eyed, and already imbibing.

Something drastic had wrecked him after she left Koulali and he returned to his regiment at the front. The letter he'd written had broken her heart, but now she understood that *her* Cam hadn't written it. The Cam who'd loved her beside Göksu stream, and kissed her under a red sky, and engaged in a pea-shooting match with her, was lost, or locked away. She bent her head and squeezed her eyes shut. He might even be dead. A stranger had inhabited his body.

"I try to watch over him, but he won't listen to me. Don't you see, Miss Lockwood? I *had* to bring you here. You've got to help him."

She'd give anything to help Cam overcome whatever demons he ran from, but how could she help him when he refused to see or speak to her? "Jakes, I—I don't know if I can. I don't think he'll let me."

"He'll listen to you," Jakes insisted.

Elissa looked around and saw a bench positioned in front of a shop window. "Let's sit down." They settled themselves. Thankful the bench caught the rays of the lowering sun, Elissa crossed her arms and tucked her fingers into her armpits. Even through her gloves, her hands felt cold.

"Has he confided in you at all? Explained anything?" she asked.

Jakes looked pained. "At the front, there was a time I saw his hands shake. He carried a flask in his pocket."

"His hands shook?" A picture of Cam's hands, sure and steady even in the heat of emergency surgery, filled her mind. An image of those same strong hands, gripped by uncontrollable trembling, was beyond her imagination. Only something horrible would create such a change.

Jakes nodded. "He returned to the front near the end of July, four days after you left Koulali. I arrived the following month, a few days after Archer shipped home. The war was building and tension was high. MacKay was already different. I suspected his drinking, even though he pretended to be fine. He seemed to have it under control.

"Then our final bombardment on Sevastopol began. We fired three hundred and fifty cannons. A hundred and fifty thousand rounds. It was God-awful. I wondered if he'd hold up."

Elissa imagined Cam, waiting through the endless barrage. Knowing when it ended, the ground troops would attack and the influx of wounded would begin.

"After three days of bombardment we mounted the second siege on Redan. We failed, but the French didn't. They seized the Malakoff redoubt, which was the turning point. The Russians began withdrawing from Sevastopol. We're still waiting for an armistice to be declared, but that pretty much ended the fighting."

"But what happened to MacKay, Jakes?" Elissa asked.

"The siege on Redan resulted in massive casualties. All the surgeons worked around the clock." Jakes stopped.

"And?" She wanted to shake the story out of him.

"He held up for hours. All day and all night and into the next day." The light was waning, and Jakes's blue eyes held shadows. "Then he collapsed."

Elissa pressed her fingers to her lips. The thought of Cam breaking down was unbearable. "He was ill. Or exhausted."

"He was drunk," Jakes said, his voice hard. So hard, it jerked her like a condemned man dropping through a gallows trapdoor, caught by a noose.

No. That wasn't possible. Cam was too responsible to do surgery while intoxicated.

"Physically spent, too, of course," Jakes added. "To give him credit, he never faltered during surgery. The last patient was an impossible one. He had a throat injury so severe, I didn't expect MacKay to attempt a repair, but he did. He did an amazing job, but the man died. The injury was too severe. Then MacKay seemed to exceed his ability to function. Once he went over the edge, he wasn't unlike Parker. Remember him?"

The patient who'd been removed from his ship because of delirium tremens. "I remember." The thought of Cam acting like Parker... A hot stone lodged itself in her throat.

"MacKay wanted to sell out, resign, and the chief medical officer decided to send him home. The need for surgeons had lessened." Jakes sighed, bent forward, put his forearms on his knees, and folded his hands together. "By then, I realized MacKay had been drinking far more than I ever suspected. After his collapse, he seemed a different man. Morose. Defeated."

"So he came back to England and left the army?" It was on the ship home that he'd written her that letter. Suddenly she understood. He'd resorted to drinking to hold himself together. How guilty and desperate he must have felt. "I think, when he collapsed, his entire life collapsed." A sharp tearing sensation split her chest. He'd written that letter and terminated everything between them right after he'd foundered.

Jakes nodded. "I came with him. I—just couldn't leave him to his own devices. I followed the army hierarchy all the way up to the colonel. Begged him to let me accompany MacKay. Because MacKay was a medical officer, a surgeon, and because he wasn't well, Colonel Creasey agreed. He wrote a long letter, too, so I could get leave once we arrived back in England."

"I know you like and admire MacKay, Jakes. Everyone at Koulali did. I'm sure your experience with him at the front intensified that. But to be such a champion for him...why are you?"

His face hardened and flushed. "You'll think me doltish, miss."

"I won't." She waited so long, she wasn't sure he intended to answer. At last he gave a little shrug.

"I'm an admirer of *Le Morte d'Arthur*—the King Arthur books by Sir Thomas Malory. My village schoolmaster had the collection. He let me borrow them, one at a time. I read all nine, again and again."

She imagined Jakes as a boy, engrossed in the books, enthralled by the Arthurian tales inside their covers. They'd given him a strong sense of chivalry. He'd put it to use by trying to protect Cam. It made her want to hug him.

"I suppose joining the army was the closest I could get to being a Knight of the Roundtable. It was pure luck they assigned me to the

Medical Service as an orderly. I don't think there's anything I'd like better."

It gave him a noble purpose. "Perhaps your fondness for King Arthur is partly the reason you're so unselfish."

He looked a bit alarmed at the compliment and shook his head. "I'm nothing special, Miss Lockwood, but Mr. MacKay is. And he was injured, just as sure as the men he treats are."

Elissa thought Jakes's earnest blue eyes might be the most honest she'd ever gazed into. She supposed she understood. Cam had been as fine and dedicated as the charismatic King Arthur. As his loyal knight, Jakes had taken up Cam's fallen gauntlet. He'd considered it his duty to protect Cam. Even when it meant standing up to a colonel to argue Cam's case.

Jakes dragged in a large breath and straightened. "I want to help him, but he tells me to leave him be. I don't think he can operate now, and I think he's always at least somewhat drunken."

Elissa stifled a groan. How could Cam have fallen so low? The knowledge rent her heart, her lungs, her belly, like a giant hand reached inside and tore through her most vital organs. Her earlier anger with Jakes reasserted itself. Cam had made it clear she had no influence over him. Being at Primrose Hill, seeing him in his current state and being unable to help him, would be pure torture. And Jakes would be leaving her.

"Your leave will be up soon," Elissa said.

He cringed. "It's why I brought you here."

She couldn't stay mad at Jakes. She understood why he'd done it, that Jakes had been watching over Cam, even without the surgeon's permission. Guardian angel wasn't a role she aspired to. Helping him recover his lost self was a different proposition, but given Cam's attitude, how was she to intervene? If she did, how was she to bear it when he rejected her again?

The sun had set, and full dark would soon be upon them. Elissa stood, and she and Jakes resumed walking.

"How did he come to start fashioning prosthetics?"

"He began in the Crimea. Every minute, when he wasn't engaged in surgery, he could be found with a length of wood in his hands, making limbs for his patients. He's a true artist, but I think he took it up to prevent him thinking."

"You found him the position at Primrose Hill."

"Yes."

"And talked Fletcher and Howell into hiring me."

Jakes nodded.

"Do they know about my history with MacKay?"

"Only that we all worked together at Koulali. They were anxious to have you. I didn't lie to you about that."

Elissa sighed. At least she could still look Mr. Fletcher in the eye. Of course, after the scene yesterday, Carlisle must realize she and Cam knew each other well. How much had she revealed?

They turned the corner and she saw Mrs. Emerson's home, where Elissa let a room. Welcoming light shone from the front window.

"I knew Mr. Fletcher would ask MacKay about you, so I went with Fletcher and guided his conversation with MacKay. MacKay just thought Fletcher was asking about our experiences in Koulali hospital. Mostly *I* talked about you, and MacKay stood there and listened. He nodded a few times, and Fletcher asked him if you were a good nurse. MacKay said, 'Aye. The very best,' and that was it. I'd already explained to Fletcher and Mr. Howell that MacKay had been comforting you after a patient died, and that the situation had been misunderstood." Jakes shrugged. "It wasn't so very difficult."

"I forgive you for lying to me," Elissa said. And she forgave Cam for breaking her heart. He'd written the letter in a state of despair, that was now clear. He *still* existed in a state of despair. She didn't know how to help him, or even if it were possible. One thing gave her hope. He'd chosen work that mattered, and he was doing it with exceptional care. Some part of her Cam was still inside him.

#

Elissa savored the crisp apple she'd taken from Mrs. Emerson's cellar. Today her office felt confining enough to make her brave the cold for her afternoon meal. Outdoor benches, chairs, and small tables occupied one corner of the yard behind the hospital. Even in the winter months patients enjoyed getting a breath of fresh air.

The blur of a fast-moving figure came around the end of her bench and Jakes plopped beside her. Four days had passed since she'd discovered MacKay in the prosthetics workshop. She'd mostly forgiven Jakes his deception, but making him squirm a bit longer seemed fitting. Elissa didn't smile or welcome him, just raised her brows and crunched another bite from her apple.

"Miss Lockwood, I need a bit of help."

She kept her expression questioning, chewed, and waited.

Jakes pulled something from his pocket. She knew the object as soon as she saw it, even before Jakes opened the locket to reveal a curl of red-gold hair and the daguerreotype of a pretty young woman.

Elissa took it from Jakes's warm palm. "Riley's locket."

"I didn't trust the army to see it safely back to his wife," Jakes said. "I kept it, so I could return it. I know you wrote letters for him. I think Mrs. Riley knew you were the one helping him, didn't she?"

"Yes. At the end I read her letters to him, as well as wrote his. She often included a note of thanks to me."

"Could you see the locket back to her? I have the address. I think she'd like it coming from you."

As irritated as Elissa had been with Jakes, she knew she'd never meet another with such a sympathetic and selfless heart. "I know the address. After Riley's death I wrote to her, and we've maintained a correspondence ever since."

"You'll see she gets it, then," Riley said.

Elissa closed the locket. "Of course. She works as a housemaid, here in London." After her husband's death, Evie Riley had been relieved to find work.

Jakes frowned. "Oh. I thought Riley came from a small village outside London."

"He did. But Mrs. Riley couldn't support herself there."

Jakes looked alarmed. "Didn't Riley have any family to help her?"

"There isn't much family, and you know how many people are struggling. I'm grateful she didn't have to resort to factory work."

The sharp crack of a slammed door drew both their gazes across the yard to the prosthetics workshop. A frowning MacKay strode straight toward them.

Elissa stiffened her spine. She hadn't seen him since her ill-advised visit to his second-floor room. She'd been mad to go there, but after their brief and frustrating meeting in the presence of Carlisle and Jakes, she'd possessed an undeniable compulsion to speak privately with him. She'd been desperate to understand. And so determined, that after a sleepless night she'd gotten out of bed, dressed, and arrived at her workplace while the entire hospital still slept. She hadn't hesitated, just marched to Cam's workshop and climbed the stairs to his personal rooms.

She still reeled from that visit.

Cam stopped in front of them. His hair and beard had been trimmed, and his appearance reminded her all too painfully of the handsome man she'd admired in Turkey. He seemed to issue some silent command, although Elissa didn't see anything more than a sharp jerk of Cam's chin. Whatever the message, Jakes appeared to receive it, for he stood.

"I went to see the Director General of the Army Medical Services about ye," MacKay said.

"What?" Jakes sounded as stunned as Elissa felt.

"Director General Smith is a Scot. He's acquainted with my father." MacKay raked his hand through his sandy hair. "I convinced him to assign ye to Primrose Hill Hospital. It's temporary duty. Ye're to be Primrose Hill's overseer of veterans' affairs."

"But Primrose Hill isn't connected to the government. It's not associated with the military. How can I be assigned here?" Jakes asked.

"Andrew Smith can decree whatever he likes as it affects those under his command in the Army Medical Services. There's not another institution like Primrose Hill, providing for veterans. I told Smith the way ye've been helping organize the place and making sure the smaller needs of the patients are met. He felt justified in having ye continue the service ye've been providing. Until the hospital is well established."

"I don't understand," Jakes said.

"These patients sustained their injuries on the Crimean Peninsula. Not the orderlies, nor even Mr. Fletcher, have the kind of knowledge ye do of military men who've lost limbs. Yer knowledge is put to good use here. Ye'll remain for a few months, Jakes, while receiving yer regular pay."

Eyes wide, Jakes shook his head. "Who do I report to?"

"Mr. Fletcher will keep Dr. Smith advised of yer duties and how ye perform them."

Jakes's mouth spread into a wide grin. "I don't know why or how you managed it, but thank you, sir."

Elissa considered Cam's frowning face and Jakes's smiling one, and a tiny, silly notion teased her brain. A ridiculous thought, but one she couldn't shake.

Cam had done this for *her*. Not for Jakes, the patients, or the hospital. For her.

Cam knew how confused and hurt she'd felt when she received his letter, and how distressed she'd been to find him here, in such a deplorable state. He knew she was fond of Jakes. Having her friend's support while she grieved over Cam would soothe Cam's conscience. The thought made the back of her throat burn.

She sprang to her feet. "That's wonderful," she said, and swiftly headed inside, clutching Riley's locket. Cam knew they wouldn't reconcile. He felt sorry for her. *Pitied* her. Pitied her so much that he'd met with the director of the entire British medical service and somehow obtained unheard-of, impossible orders for Jakes.

Her breaths came fast, until she was almost panting. If she'd harbored any doubt as to his true feelings, she no longer did. He wanted nothing between them.

This new Cam did not hurt as she did. He merely suffered pangs of conscience. And now that he'd arranged for Jakes to be assigned to Primrose Hill, Cam had absolved himself of guilt.

CHAPTER NINETEEN

A few hours later, Cam finished his work day and retreated to his room. He'd barely sunk into his chair when the door opened with a short burst of rapping.

"Sir." Jakes walked in without waiting for Cam's invitation.

Cam groaned. He needed to start locking his door. Jakes had already thanked him for getting him assigned to Primrose Hill, so this unexpected visit wasn't about that. Which meant Jakes wanted to discuss something Cam had no intention of discussing.

"Ye can turn right around and leave out of here," Cam said.

Jakes grabbed a wooden chair away from the small table where Cam sometimes took his meals, plunked it in the middle of the room, and straddled it. Jakes crossed his arms atop the chair back and leveled snapping blue eyes on Cam.

"How much longer is this," Jakes said, making sweeping, circular motions which included Cam, the room, *everything*, "going to go on?"

Cam scowled. This conversation was not happening.

"You're no longer drinking to stay steady for surgery. You're drinking to stop the shakes the need for drink brings on."

When had Jakes gotten so audacious? Cam had become fond of the corporal, but had concealed his partiality. In the Crimea, age, education, and military rank had separated them. When Jakes arranged to accompany Cam back to England, and after they'd arrived, Cam had held himself separate. He didn't want a confidant or a billie. He wanted to be left alone.

"'Tis not yer concern," Cam said.

Jakes smirked. "You needn't growl at me. I brought her here. Now it's time you got yourself right."

Cam surged out of his upholstered chair and paced across the room. "I never asked for yer help, Jakes. And I don't like ye presuming ye know what I need or want. Especially not when it comes to Elissa."

Jakes's brows shot up. Damn it to hell. Cam had used her given name.

Cam stopped pacing and palmed his forehead. "I can't begrudge her the position here. I'm sure she needs the income and likes working with the veterans." Jakes's blameless expression made Cam want to shake him. He recommenced pacing. "But there's nothing between Miss Lockwood and myself, and there's not going to be." Cam stopped, glared at Jakes, and fisted his hands. "Ye can watch over Miss Lockwood all ye like. In fact, I got ye assigned here so ye could do just that. But ye'll *not* be watchin' over me."

"I know you started drinking to unclench your nerves and lessen your trembling," Jakes said. "Do you think you're the only one who got the shakes over there? That suffers nightmares? The only one that fear sneaks up on, grips and chokes you so hard, you just know you're going to die?"

Cam stumbled to his chair and sank into it.

"Ask the veterans you're helping. Go over to the hospital at night and see how many are crying out in their sleep."

Others? Other men's fears and nightmares had nothing to do with his own. He wasn't like them. Even strong men could suffer from war terrors. Of course he knew that. He didn't think less of those men.

But his character was flawed. He shook even before the war. For years he'd denied it. Fought it. He'd even fooled himself into believing he'd overcome his deficiencies. Until that last ground assault of the war, and his final patient—the throat patient. Afterwards, he'd surrendered to the reality his father and brother accepted years ago. It was why he'd ended everything with Elissa.

Cam dragged his hand over his face. Dear God, he was weary. Did he need to physically throw Jakes out in order to stop him? The way he had Elissa? After he chucked her out, he'd suffered through self-condemnation more fiery than the flames of hell.

"Leave off, Jakes," he pleaded.

Quiet blanketed the room. Cam closed his eyes and let his head fall back against the chair. Damn it. He didn't want to wrangle with

Jakes and Elissa, who were trying to help him, but far better to quarrel than to let them believe he was fixable.

"How can you toss away the chance of having something— having a *life*—with Miss Lockwood?"

Jakes sounded like everything Cam felt. Despairing. Angry. Miserable. Only Cam was accepting, as well, which was what Jakes needed to be.

Cam opened his eyes and studied Jakes. Had an element of *envy* crept into the orderly's tone? Was the man so adamant because he yearned for the opportunity Cam was rejecting?

"Do ye want her for yerself, then?" Cam asked. "Ye have my permission."

Jakes flushed dark red. "You sorry bastard, MacKay."

Cam smothered the cynical laugh that itched for release. "No more 'sir,' eh? Ye're gaining some understanding then, Jakeman." And Cam was suffering from Jakes's enlightenment, a twisting pain wringing his belly.

Jakes stood, his chair clattering to the floor. The orderly's glare, before he stalked to the door and slammed his way out, would have split Cam and spilled his guts, if Cam's conscience hadn't already turned him to ash.

Cam rocketed out of his chair, opened his trunk, and grabbed the waiting bottle. The fire of the first swallow didn't burn. It cascaded down his gullet like the sweetest, most soothing of elixirs, and revealed itself to be the very necessary essence of endurance.

#

Two weeks later, Elissa looked up from her desk and saw a woman she knew to be Evie Riley. The moment she did, a warm certainty enveloped her. It wasn't unlike the warmth of feeling she and Grace shared.

Of course, Elissa had penned the letters Riley dictated to his wife, and read aloud the letters he received. After his death, while on that endless journey home to England, Elissa had herself written to Evie Riley. They may have never met, but Elissa knew the heart of this woman. Seeing her, Elissa felt the open acceptance she knew to be true friendship.

"Mrs. Riley," Elissa said. She hurried to her office doorway, clasped her visitor's hands and drew her into the room. Evie Riley was far lovelier than Riley's daguerreotype of her. The young woman had dark blue eyes, a creamy complexion, and pink lips curved in a sweet smile. Her bonnet hid all but a glimpse of her shiny, red-gold hair. Long eyelashes swept her cheeks and Elissa realized Evie was shy.

"I'm so happy to make your acquaintance," Evie Riley said.

Satisfaction swelled as Elissa urged Riley's wife into one of the chairs positioned in front of her desk. She sat in the other chair and considered the very pretty young woman. Riley hadn't been handsome, but he'd been earnest and kind. A good man. A man who adored his wife. Knowing Evie Riley had seen beyond George's looks to the beautiful man inside made Elissa's sense of satisfaction grow beyond mere pleasure, and become a press of happiness and sadness. All centered around her memories of Riley. His having had such a comely wife seemed right.

"I didn't know you were Irish," Elissa said. Riley never mentioned it, but as soon as Evie spoke, Elissa knew.

"I met George while his regiment garrisoned Ireland. When they were ordered to the Crimea, he moved me to London. I wanted to be somewhere I could work and save a few coins for our future, and I wanted to be close to the war news. When George died, I considered moving back, but I'm settled, with a good position, so decided to stay for now. I'm glad, since it's meant I could meet you, Miss Lockwood. It's strange, finally putting a face to a person I feel I already know very well."

"It feels strange to me, too," Elissa said, "even though I've seen your picture."

"That was taken just before we married," Evie said. "A lifetime ago."

For a moment they just looked at each other. Then Elissa retrieved Riley's locket from her desk drawer, reseated herself, and placed the locket in Evie's palm.

"You can't know what this means to me," Evie said.

"I know it was the dearest thing your husband possessed, along with your letters. He kept them bundled together, under his pillow."

Eyes closed and head bowed over the locket cradled in her hands, Riley's young widow nodded. "Thank you for taking such care with this." She looked up, blue eyes bright with unshed tears. "For honoring him."

"It was Jesse Jakeman who kept it safe. He's the one you should thank." Jakes wasn't on duty until late afternoon, so Elissa had asked him to accompany them to tea. She expected his arrival at any time.

"George wrote of him, too, although he called him 'Jakes.'"

"Everyone calls him Jakes. I'm fortunate to be working with him again. He's supervising the other orderlies, and he's a great example for them to follow." She'd begun to wonder about approaching the Duke of Carlisle regarding a scholarship for Jakes. He had so much potential. In possession of a small endowment, Jakes could obtain surgical or apothecary training, if he weren't bound to the army. Surely Carlisle could fix that. "Jakes is accompanying us to tea."

"I hope we can meet sometimes, Miss Lockwood. Tuesdays are my half-days, and the Burtons' home is an hour's walk from here. A good constitutional." Evie opened her reticule and placed Riley's locket inside.

"Are you ever permitted an evening off? I'm sure Mrs. Emerson, my landlady, would enjoy your joining us for supper."

"I think it would be permissible on an evening the Burtons were otherwise engaged."

"Please, let me know the next time they accept an invitation."

Jakes entered the room, and Elissa stood. Evie Riley was seconds behind her.

"Mrs. Riley, may I introduce Jesse Jakeman to you? Jakes, I'm pleased to present Mrs. Riley."

"Ma'am. I'm honored," Jakes said.

"*I'm* the one who's honored, Mr. Jakeman. I'm indebted to you."

Jakes turned beet red. Oh, dear. The always-in-command Jakes looked downright flustered. He couldn't be embarrassed of Mrs. Riley's recognition, could he?

"I'm glad I could be of assistance," he said gently, and something different in his voice made Elissa stare at him in disbelief. *Oh, Jakes.* Could he have developed an infatuation for Evie Riley while he had possession of Riley's locket? Jakes would have been privy to some of the same letters Elissa had been, and Riley's widow *was* uncommonly attractive.

Evie had lost Riley a mere six months ago. Her grief stood in her eyes. Elissa hoped Evie wouldn't recognize Jakes's admiration.

Given she was shy and grieving, Elissa couldn't imagine Jakes's regard would make Evie anything but uncomfortable.

"Shall we go?" Elissa asked. "There's a shop just down the street that serves an excellent tea."

Within a half hour they were seated in a sunny window, enjoying small sandwiches and cakes. Jakes seemed less engaging and cheerful than usual, and each time he looked at Evie Riley, his gaze lingered the merest blink too long. Elissa considered digging her heel into the toe of his shoe, and then realized such an action would be much like little brother getting a smack from his sister for bad behavior.

The thought made Elissa gulp too large a swallow of her steaming tea. Her vision swam and she blinked. She did feel sisterly toward Jakes. Just as she had with Riley. She'd lost Riley to sickness, as she had her brothers, but she'd eased his last days. And they'd shared a connection she'd feel to her own dying day. She felt just as much fondness for Jakes, with his broad grin and his open, honest face.

It had been chance, and Maddie Gray's generosity taking in a grieving orphan girl, that had led to Elissa becoming a nurse. How lucky she had been. How fortunate to be doing work that allowed her to see the core of men like Jakes and Riley.

A part of Riley resided inside her. Helped her and comforted her. And Jakes sat beside her, oblivious that he'd just avoided bruised toes.

Elissa gazed out to the sunny street, squinting a little. Her feeling for Cam went much deeper than her feelings for Riley and Jakes. How could she have been so wrong about him? She'd thought him the most compassionate of men. A man whose internal compass always pointed toward honor. Yet if he were kind and admirable, how could he have been so cold and uncaring to her? How could he ignore his calling? How could this man—this mean, drunken prosthetist—be the same man she thought she knew?

She'd hidden the grievous injury he'd inflicted, and wept in private. It pained her still, and the ugly, gaping wound didn't seem to be closing.

A startled exclamation jerked Elissa's attention back to her companions. She sighed. Once again she'd started out thinking about one thing, and ended up immersed in thoughts of Cam.

"What?" Evie Riley's chin dropped and she stared wide-eyed at Jakes. "Staff Surgeon MacKay works at Primrose Hill?" A smile lit her face. "I must see him, too, and thank him."

Jakes shot Elissa an alarmed look and shifted in his chair. "He's fashioning wooden limbs for the amputees. We don't see him that often."

Evie frowned. "Why is that? He's a surgeon."

Jakes's lips pressed into a thin, grim line. "He is. But he's not doing that work now."

Evie continued to frown, and to wait. Elissa remained silent, as did Jakes. How could they explain what they didn't understand?

"Well," Evie said. "He might not remember my husband, but I'd like to thank him." She turned to Elissa. "Could you ask him if we might meet? I won't take up much of his time, but I'd never forgive myself if I missed the opportunity to meet Officer MacKay."

Even now, the thought of seeing Cam didn't fill Elissa with dread, but with hope, and an army of frogs jumped in her belly. The involuntary excitement made her want to slap herself. Seeing Cam again wouldn't change anything, and would only cause her more pain.

"It might be best if I sent him a note," Elissa said. "I'll let you know what he says."

CHAPTER TWENTY

"Mr. Thorpe, Jakes asked me to speak with you," Elissa told the disgruntled patient who sat in a wheeled chair, arms crossed over his chest. He'd refused a lap blanket, and sat with empty pant legs dangling several inches from the floor. Thorpe had no feet, but from mid-lower-leg up, his legs were intact. With good prosthetics and the training they could provide, Thorpe had every chance to be ambulatory, but he was refusing his prosthetic feet. She knew several Primrose Hill patients who would consider themselves fortunate to be in Thorpe's position, but how other men felt wouldn't alleviate Thorpe's grief.

"You're another do-gooder, are you?" The man hadn't trimmed his bushy, black Crimean beard, and it seemed to bristle when he spoke.

Was the man serious? He was. Elissa could tell he was. "You think the staff here are do-gooders? That makes us sound rather ineffectual. We're not exactly trying to reform you, Mr. Thorpe. We're trying to help you gain some skills that will assist you."

"Help me carry on as a cripple, eh?"

Elissa was too tired to hide her reaction to Thorpe's attitude. She sighed, pulled the nearby hard-backed chair away from the wall, and subsided onto it. The small recreation room they occupied was a place where the men could read, play cards or checkers. The bird feeder positioned outside the window was kept filled with seed. It was a pleasant room, popular with those patients able to be out of bed, but empty now aside from herself and Thorpe.

She didn't blame him for expressing his pain and sadness and anger with a foul temper. The thought of losing her feet sent a shiver streaking down her arms and spine, but understanding Thorpe didn't mean she'd meekly consent to his refusing treatment that would help him. The problem was, standing up to Thorpe's temper and volleying with him would take spirit. Spirit she didn't have right now. She didn't even have the energy for the stare-down he was trying to engage her in.

"I don't think of you as a cripple, Mr. Thorpe. You won't think of yourself as crippled, either, once you get your new feet on and start walking again. Our prosthetist measured, and made gypsum plaster molds of your stumps, didn't he? Jakes said MacKay had your feet ready."

"Prosthetist?" Thorpe huffed. "He's a carpenter. And the 'new feet' you're referrin' to are slabs of wood. You can't stick wooden blocks on my legs and expect me to walk!"

Hearing Thorpe ridicule Cam swept away her fatigue. The patience and dedication Cam had exhibited as a surgeon was now evident in the exceptional appendages he fashioned. Even irritable, melancholic, and she feared, sometimes influenced by drink, he created wooden extensions that were unique, well-functioning works of art. "You may always need crutches or canes to help you, but you'll be able to stand and walk. Let me take you out to the workshop. You can start practicing in the gymnasium tomorrow." As much as she wanted Thorpe to receive his new feet, she wouldn't push him to the workshop without his consent. He needed to agree, and participate in his rehabilitation. Unfortunately, he wasn't giving an inch.

"I'd like to see you dancin' around on stilts. I imagine you'd be so good at it, the circus would make you their star performer. They'd dress you in feathers and ribbons and you'd captivate the audiences. A regular dancin' freak."

#

"Shut up, Thorpe," Cam barked from the door. Thorpe jerked and slammed his mouth closed. Cam wanted to throw the wooden feet he carried at the man's head. He paced over to Thorpe and Elissa. "I've got better things to do than wait on you." Which was true, and he'd never before come to the hospital when a man was late for an appointment. The truth of it was, he'd used Thorpe as an excuse to come, hoping to catch a glimpse of Elissa after close to a month of deprivation.

He'd exhausted himself with his internal arguments, denying himself her presence since the day he'd told Jakes and Elissa of Jakes's assignment to Primrose Hill. He'd assured himself that by maintaining distance, he did them both a service. Until today.

Last night he'd neglected to build up his fire, and today, after a rest—more nap than true sleep—he'd awakened to a cold room. He couldn't seem to chase the cold away, not even after donning his warmest clothes and drinking coffee so hot he felt it travel down his gullet and hit his stomach. He'd started thinking about Elissa. About how one glimpse of her sunshine would warm his bones.

He'd capitulated. Just this once. One glimpse couldn't hurt, could it? He'd had no idea he'd find her with his tardy patient.

"Mr. MacKay." Elissa stood. Her cheeks flushed.

"Miss Lockwood." Cam felt crazed with his desire to rake her with his eyes, but sudden fear kept his gaze away. He didn't think he could keep his face from revealing everything he felt. The control he'd always taken for granted was nonexistent when it came to Elissa. And once he looked, he knew he wouldn't be able to look away. Relieved when she backed up a few steps, he crouched in front of Thorpe.

Cam frowned. As much as Thorpe had cause for bad temper, Cam didn't like him giving Elissa a share of his grump. "Why are ye here, if ye're not going to take what we offer?" Cam asked.

If Thorpe were a cat, he'd be bristling, hissing, and humping his back. Cam had seen fear enough times to know it.

"These pegs are going to work," Cam said. "Ye're standing up today, and when ye do, ye'll be standing in fine new boots."

Cam had hoped Thorpe's attention would fix on the brown leather footwear, and it did.

His eyes widened. "Those are mine? I've never owned the like."

"Of course, they're yours," Elissa said.

Thorpe ignored Elissa and stared at Cam.

"Aye," Cam said. "They're yours, and it would be a shame for boots such as these to go to waste."

Mouth tight, Thorpe gave a little nod.

Cam twisted the chair's footrests aside and went to work, rolling soft, fine-gauge knitted socks over Thorpe's stumps, and inserting the man's residual limbs into the prostheses sockets. The socket insides were carved matches to Thorpe's lower legs. Soft padding cradled the distal stump ends. Stylish ankle boots encased the wooden feet. "It's a good fit. I'll remove them every day, after your gymnasium session, and check for red pressure points. The idea is to get a snug fit without applying undue pressure."

Thorpe's fingers gripped the ends of the chair's arm rests. He lifted one leg a few inches then tamped it on the ground a few times. After repeating the action with his other leg, he looked at Cam and without speaking, shifted his weight forward.

Cam stood, ready to provide support. Lips tight, Thorpe stood. He weaved a bit and Cam wrapped a hand around the man's upper arm. They stood toe to toe.

Thorpe's gray-blue eyes narrowed, the creases at each corner deepening. For a minute he looked down at his boots, then he locked gazes with Cam. Thorpe's eyes brimmed with tears.

Cam's chest filled with lightness, expanding like radiant sunshine. He locked his jaw to hold in the joy. The accompanying heavy satisfaction in his belly had once been familiar, and the sweet ache of it almost overcame him. He'd forgotten, or hadn't let himself experience the feeling, when his work made a difference in someone's life.

Blinking, Thorpe reached out. They grabbed each other's forearms. Thorpe gave a terse nod, and Cam began moving back. Thorpe stepped forward. One step. Two. Four steps. Six steps. Thorpe began to tremble.

Cam looked at Elissa and jerked his chin. She brought Thorpe's chair up close behind him.

"Enough for now. The chair's right behind ye." Cam leaned forward a bit, urging Thorpe to sit.

Thorpe dropped into the chair. Cam twisted the foot supports into place and set Thorpe's boots on them.

"You did so well," Elissa said. "With some practice, you'll be getting around easy as you please, all on your own." Her face beamed.

While she looked at Thorpe, Cam looked at her.

Only for a moment. That's all he'd allow himself. Just a few seconds, drinking her in.

His heart thumped, hard, and hot blood surged through his body, heated him, spiked him with an awareness that brought every cell alive.

Elissa and Thorpe were conversing. She laughed and—looked at Cam.

His breath, his heart—stopped. He rocked once, as he started toward her, then pulled himself up. Her eyes widened. The happiness that had shone in them dwindled away, leaving behind a yearning that somehow found its echo deep inside him. It twisted, squeezed hard, and he knew. It would never let him go.

He was a bloody damn fool. Why had he ever thought he could see her without stirring up a bubbling cauldron of desire?

He jerked his gaze away. Something sharp tugged his heart—as if a hook had snagged it and someone yanked on the attached line. He turned, headed for the door, and spoke over his shoulder.

"Thorpe, I'll check yer skin tomorrow, after yer stint in the gymnasium." Cam paused, one hand clutching the doorframe, and swept unseeing eyes over the figures of Thorpe and Elissa. "Good day."

Thorpe's called out "thank you" followed Cam as he strode away.

#

The next day Fletcher came through the workshop door waving an envelope. The surgeon looked more excited than Cam had ever seen him.

"Carlisle has invited us to spend the weekend at one of his properties, near Brighton." Fletcher slapped the invitation down on the table, where Cam sat working on a length of ash that would soon be a leg. "All the Primrose Hill donors will be there, and potential donors. Their wives, as well."

Cam continued working the rasp he held. He wasn't going to the duke's weekend party. Making nice to a gathering of wealthy aristocrats, gentlemen, and ladies wasn't something he intended to do. "I can't go."

Fletcher frowned. "Why not? You don't even know when it is, man!"

"I haven't any appropriate clothes. And I haven't the time, inclination, or money to buy new." It wasn't the real reason, but it was true enough. He'd worn a uniform for years. What proper suits he'd had—those fitting a much younger, less muscular self—he'd given away long ago. The life he now lived didn't require fancy dress.

Fletcher scratched his bearded cheek. "My younger brother's about your size. I'll get you something of his."

Cam laid the rasp down and sat back. "Ye needn't bother. I'm nae good at chitchat."

"You'll be talking about your work, MacKay. And I know you can make nice when you want to."

"Well, I didn't make nice with the duke when I met him. He cannae want me at his party."

"He does. You've an invitation." Fletcher picked up the envelope, waved it in front of Cam's face, then tossed it back to the table.

Cam shook his head. "I've too much work. I can't be leaving for two days."

Fletcher clamped his hands to his hips. "You're going, MacKay. This is important. We keep the donors happy, and they keep us in funds. You've every right to boast a bit. You're making a name for yourself with your prosthetics. These men appreciate invention and fine craftsmanship."

Cam raked his hands through his hair and sighed. One corner of Fletcher's mouth tilted up. Damn the man. The surgeon knew Cam was weakening.

Fletcher crossed his arms. "This means money for Primrose Hill. Money for *your* program. Patrons want to know their money is being put to good use. Meeting you, understanding what you're doing, could make the difference when they're deciding which charities to support. It might even mean being able to expand our services."

Oh, hell. "All right. I'll go. I'll need those clothes ye offered."

"Good!" Fletcher grinned. "Howell, Carlisle's man of business, delivered our invitations and train tickets. I'll meet you at London Bridge Station. Saturday, eight o'clock."

#

"Come on, man, get aboard!" Fletcher leaned out the door of a first-class compartment, waving Cam toward him. "The train's leaving!"

Cam ran the last few yards and leaped up the carriage steps, just as a conductor on the platform called a sustained "all aboard." The shriek of the whistle cut off any conversation with Fletcher, who took Cam's bag and turned away. Cam bent to clear the doorway, and the door slammed shut behind him. The train jerked, groaned, began to move, and Cam raised his head to face the compartment interior.

Where Elissa Lockwood sat.

While he hesitated and they eyed each other, the train began to pick up speed. Fletcher. That dodgy blighter! Cam gave the surgeon a look that should have set him ablaze, but the man was too busy adjusting his clothing and looking out the window to notice. Cam claimed the remaining cushioned bench space. Luckily, Elissa sat on the other side of Fletcher.

She'd turned her head to the window. Hadn't even greeted him.

"Good morning, Miss Lockwood. I didn't realize ye were included in our Primrose Hill party."

"Didn't I mention Miss Lockwood was invited?" Fletcher asked.

"Nae. Ye didn't."

That caught Elissa's attention, and her head whipped around. "You didn't tell me about MacKay, either."

Cam wished he could give Fletcher a thump. The man wasn't overly concerned about anyone but himself. He was a competent surgeon, but Cam knew he didn't offer his patients anything beyond his surgical skill and a few pleasantries.

Fletcher chuckled. "It made for a nice surprise, I'm sure. The journey will give us time for a long chat."

To hell with that idea. "I'm going to sleep," Cam said, slumping down and sliding his hat over his eyes.

"Perhaps we should let Mr. MacKay rest," Elissa said.

Cam heard the crackle of newspaper and knew Fletcher had decided to entertain himself with a morning paper. Good. This would take care of the next two hours, and it shouldn't be too difficult to stay away from Elissa in a huge house with twenty or so people swarming about. And that didn't include servants.

CHAPTER TWENTY-ONE

The duke called out just before she stepped outside. "You're braving this freezing rain to go outdoors, Miss Lockwood?"

Elissa lifted her arm, showing him the umbrella she held. Rain had been falling since early morning. "I'm going no farther than your glass house, sir."

She needed time alone. Being in proximity to Cam, yet staying at opposite ends of any room they occupied, was exhausting. Avoiding him kept her on edge, and there was no escape. Every room held wealthy, and frequently titled, guests of the duke's, engaged in different pursuits. Cards, conversation, or simply wandering about enjoying Carlisle's many works of art, were ongoing activities. She'd found the other guests interested in her and her work. They'd welcomed her in spite of her class difference. Maybe because of the way Carlisle treated her. As if he regarded her highly.

Carlisle strode to her side and drew the umbrella from her hand. "Might I accompany you?"

Something had changed since their introduction at Primrose Hill. Even after twenty-four hours in Carlisle's home, meeting his smoky gray eyes took her aback. Charles Covington, Duke of Carlisle, possessed the most piercing gaze she'd ever encountered. They searched beyond her words, beyond her expression, and looked inside.

Since her arrival, those warm eyes had reassured her, encouraged her, and admired her. They'd drawn her in. And made her nervous.

"I'd be delighted." Sharing an umbrella forced them to walk close together, and Elissa took his proffered arm. She caught the scent of spices and something earthy with a subtle underlay of fine tobacco, before the wind swept it away.

As they approached the magnificent glass house, Carlisle told her the history of the structure's design and construction. Two long wings extended from an entry that rose to the height of two stories. White-painted metal framework held the glass panes, with the metalwork of the sizable entry aswirl with decorative arches and curls.

They entered and Elissa was struck with the delight of faintly warm air smelling of flowers and clean damp earth. Rain cascaded over the glass panes, obscuring everything outside with a watery curtain, and enclosing them in a private world of their own. The vestibule, which was similar in size to the duke's dining room, held a profusion of large plants and trees, with a number of chairs and benches creating small areas for contemplation or conversation. The noise of falling rain filled the space, but the sound was soft enough to permit normal speech.

They strolled the length of one wing—the edible section as opposed to the floral section, Carlisle said—the air warming as they neared the wing's center where a coal stove sat. Elissa marveled at the variety of plant life. She identified fruit trees and bushes, and vegetable beds.

"This is my favorite," Carlisle said, pointing to a plant with long and narrow, spiny leaves. It had produced two sprouts resembling huge green pinecones. "Pineapple. I wish these were ready to harvest."

Elissa pulled off her glove and touched the bristly fruit. "I've never tasted it."

"No? Then when this ripens, I'll have it sent to you. You'll think you're eating sunshine."

It was merely food, but so special, the promised gift seemed almost intimate. Could she accept it? Oh, she was being ridiculous. It was *fruit*! "I—that would be wonderful. Thank you."

His eyes roamed over her face and glowed with apparent approval, while his mouth curved in a warm smile. She couldn't look at him without seeing his wealth and power, as much a part of him as any of his very masculine, physical attributes, but that smile transformed him from reserved aristocrat to a very approachable, handsome man. Self-consciousness swamped her. Any woman would find him an appealing man, but the way he looked at her made it seem her admiration might mean more to him than she intended.

Elissa felt her cheeks heat and turned away to admire a tree covered in oranges. He was a duke. And in a roundabout way, she worked for him. What a muddle.

She scrambled for something to say. "I've never seen an orange tree." Dark green, glossy leaves surrounded amazing, bright citrus. "There are so many oranges on it."

Carlisle stepped close, stripped off his gloves, and tugged an orange free. She watched his strong, long-fingered hands as he peeled the fruit, spiking the air with sharp fragrance. Juice spurted as he split the orange and offered Elissa half. She accepted the fruit then stood considering it.

"Go on." Carlisle tossed a segment into his mouth.

Elissa followed suit. Juicy sweetness burst on her tongue. What a wonderful treat.

They strolled back to the entry vestibule as they enjoyed their orange feast. "Let's sit for a minute," Carlisle suggested, taking her elbow and guiding her to a cushioned wicker bench.

The duke sat and angled toward her, pulling a snowy handkerchief from his inside pocket and offering it. Elissa accepted the linen and wiped juice from her fingers.

"Am I making you uncomfortable?" Carlisle asked.

There was that too-direct gaze of his again. She tried not to squirm and passed the handkerchief back. "Um...uncomfortable?"

"I've been showing a decided preference for your company. I know you're aware. Everyone is."

Oh, dear. The duke—*the man*—intended to be straightforward. No more telling herself she was imagining his attention.

"I find myself in a unique position, Miss Lockwood. Since that day in your office, when we spoke of my son, Michael, I've found my thoughts drawn to you again and again." He scratched the edge of his bearded jaw with his thumb. "There's a special quality about you. One I find quite appealing."

What? Tension curled from Elissa's belly to her chest, shoulders, and arms. She gripped her hands together.

A gruff laugh barked out. "I don't usually have so much trouble expressing myself."

He was having trouble? Not in her mind. He was making an impossible situation all too clear.

"I find myself wanting to get much better acquainted. I'd like permission to call on you."

Elissa stared. "But...you're a duke." She pressed her fingers to her mouth. Could she have sounded any more gauche?

"I hope that won't be an immovable stumbling block. I'm also a man. A widower and a father. While my lineage is a huge part of who I am, it's not the most important part." He looked down. His lips tightened and his jaw twitched. "I didn't always feel that way, but since Michael's death, I've found myself residing in a different world. To be more accurate, I've become a different man, and living in a privileged world has become infinitely less important. I don't care about the same things anymore." He looked up, and his smoky gaze paralyzed her. "Our world is changing. If you were an American heiress, no one would lift an eyebrow. I find your—heart—a good deal more desirable than lineage or wealth. I only hope you can find something in me to admire."

Oh, dear God. This man! His honesty rocked her. Enticed her. But she couldn't imagine something more than fondness growing between them. Even if she weren't out of his social mien, her mind was still tangled with Cam.

"Your Grace, I'm honored. But calling on me...well, it's out of the question. I'm a nurse. My father was a miller. I had a good education, but—you're plumb out of your mind if you think we'd suit."

A bark of laughter burst from Carlisle. The smoky eyes snapped. "Oh, there's no question you'd suit me, Miss Lockwood, and I assure you I'm of sound mind. How about you give me the opportunity to change your thinking?"

Charles Covington might be the most fascinating man she'd ever met. An image of Cam thrust itself into her mind, but she pushed it away. Cam wanted nothing to do with her. She needed to accept that.

"Ladies as intelligent, charming, and lovely as you have a way of being accepted into society when the need arises. You've found my other guests cordial, haven't you?"

"Yes." But they weren't seeing her as a woman who might through marriage dare to rise far above her proper station—to that of duchess. Were they? Even if Carlisle hadn't remarked on how his guests were watching, she'd felt their eyes upon them. As if his suggestion wasn't enough to disconcert her, his compliments made a rabble of butterflies whirl in her belly.

"Good. I'd expect no less." He retrieved his gloves from his coat pocket and pulled them on. "I think you'll enjoy dinner tonight. My cook is planning something special, and the last of my guests—who are potential donors—arrived today. After meeting you, Mr. Fletcher, and Mr. MacKay, each established patron and patroness has assured me they intend to continue their support of Primrose Hill Hospital."

It was all Elissa could do to hold her uncertainties in. Thanks to Grace, who'd insisted on giving her several of her castoffs, Elissa had dresses appropriate for a ducal weekend that included a country dinner. As generous as Grace had been, Elissa's wardrobe didn't include ball dresses or garb for other London amusements. The kind of entertainment Carlisle would expect to escort her to.

Carlisle stood. "Are you ready to return to the house?"

No. She hadn't gotten the private time she'd sought when she'd decided to escape to the glass house, and she needed it even more now. "If you don't object, I'd like to stay here a while longer." Except it was still raining, and they'd shared an umbrella. "Oh, but there's only one umbrella, isn't there?"

Elissa started to stand, but Carlisle motioned for her to stay put.

"A little water won't hurt." Before she could object, he went out the door. Through the rain, she watched him make a crouching dash for the house.

"You dinnae need worry, lass. Everythin's gonna be fine."

The voice came from a dark corner of the room. It locked up her brain as hard as a seizure, and she jumped like she'd been caught by the tip of a lash. It took a moment for her to settle and assign ownership to the deep voice with its Scottish burr.

Cam came from behind a palm that obscured the corner beyond it.

Elissa clutched her chest. Her heart knocked against her ribs like a prisoner banging on a cell door.

"I apologize for eavesdropping. It wasnae intentional. I dozed off back there."

He'd heard everything. *Everything.* Her cheeks felt hot enough to singe.

Quite the opposite of her distressed state, Cam radiated a calm collectedness. He seemed far better than the last time she'd seen him, his eyes less red, the lines of stress less pronounced. The country air and the rest had been good for him. And obviously, what he'd overheard hadn't upset him. She didn't get much more of a look at him, as he strode to the door and stood looking out. Accustomed to seeing him wearing either military uniform or casual garb and carpenter's apron, he seemed different in the clothes of an English gentleman. They added to the distance she felt. Cam had been evading her just as she had him, and his avoidance hurt.

"I knew that day in the workshop," Cam said. "His feelings for ye are strong."

"There was nothing to know. I'd just met him that day. And this idea of his—it's ludicrous." She couldn't even give voice to what Carlisle had suggested.

"Nae. He's a man who knows his mind. He's a good match for ye."

Cam's big, nimble hands could do the most delicate repair on lacerated flesh. She hadn't known he could tear hearts in two, but he'd efficiently done just that to hers. Her breath wheezed out and her shoulders curled.

And then, without even a glance over his shoulder, he walked out the door, head up, and strode through the rain.

Her lungs wouldn't breathe. She bent forward, and just when her vision blurred and got dark, and she knew she was going to faint, finally she was able to draw in several small gasps of air. More small gasps, then a long, stuttering exhalation. This hurt worse than the letter, and that pain had been acute.

She pressed her hand to the pain in her chest. She hadn't realized until now, but she'd never completely believed their love was dead. Hers hadn't died, so how could his? When she'd found him at Primrose Hill and realized something had changed him, a tender shoot of hope had sprouted from her heart like the first brave crocus stalk pushing through snow. She'd begun to hope he could change back into the man she loved. That somewhere inside him, his love for her was tucked away, and safe.

But, no. He didn't love her. He couldn't callously encourage a romance with Carlisle if he loved her. No more deluding herself. She doubted she'd ever stop caring about the man, but it was time to let her hope—and her love—go.

She rocked and cried for a while, and then forced herself to sit up. She pressed her lips together to stop their trembling, dragged huge breaths into her lungs, and willed everything soft and hurting inside her to go hard. She dried her face on her hem.

Whatever had happened before, he didn't want her now, and that's all that mattered. Somehow, she'd get past this pain. She'd done it before.

Living with Maddie, she'd found her way past the grief of losing her family by pouring herself into learning the art of nursing. Though she was well liked, she'd been different than other young women her age. She hadn't interested the young men in Nottinghamshire. "Young men dally with the girls who make eyes at them," Maddie had said. "You're too serious by half."

Elissa knew Maddie was right. Boys liked girls who laughed and teased, blushed and flattered. They weren't attracted to budding midwife nurses, who birthed babies, nursed the sick, and laid out the dead. The year she turned twenty, she moved to London and obtained hospital work. As much as she enjoyed midwifery, she wanted more knowledge. More experience. She wanted to test herself. She'd been proud and satisfied, and her arms never felt empty.

Until she met Cam.

Cam made her heart yearn for more than the satisfaction she found in nursing. He'd made her reimagine her long-abandoned dream of someday finding a man she loved and wanted to have children with.

In Turkey, she'd fallen in love with him. Now he'd made it painfully clear their interlude had been a mistake. He might appreciate her nursing abilities, but his admiration no longer extended to her womanhood.

Just minutes ago, Carlisle, the most improbable suitor she could imagine, said he admired her and wanted to know her better. Said he felt drawn to her. His words soothed the hurt caused by Cam's dismissive words.

Because of her feelings for Cam, she hadn't even considered entertaining such a farfetched notion as an attachment between Carlisle and herself. Feelings Cam clearly didn't return.

Perhaps the best way of putting her love for Cam to rest was by opening herself to the possibilities Carlisle suggested. If her lack of wealth, title, and genteel upbringing didn't deter him, why should his abundance of wealth and grand title dissuade her? Carlisle was admired and emulated. She suspected he was as deserving of respect as the Cam she'd known in Turkey, and Cam *wanted* her to favor Carlisle. She needed to smother the feelings for Cam she'd continued to cling to. Allowing Carlisle to engage her mind would make the task easier.

CHAPTER TWENTY-TWO

A few hours later Grace's castoff dress made Elissa feel pretty, until she entered the parlor, where everyone gathered prior to dinner. It took no more than a quick look about the room to remind her she—a dove among swans—didn't belong in this gathering.

Grace was a country solicitor's wife. Her pale pink dress was acceptable garb for a formal dinner with country gentry, but its quality didn't compare to the other women's dresses. It appeared even in Brighton, titled ladies and wives of entrepreneurs donned their finest for dinner with a duke. Their dresses shimmered; their necks and ears glittered with jewels. The men wore formal black and white. Elissa felt as if she'd arrived for dinner and found herself at a ball attended by royals.

Suddenly Carlisle was beside her, his head bent close as he whispered. "Your loveliness outshines every woman in the room. You've even put my roses to the blush."

The look in his smoky eyes made her skin heat. She'd placed two of his glass house roses in her hair. Pink ones. His eyes roamed from her rose adorned hair to the toes of her slippers. A very un-aristocratic warmth transformed his expression and made her feel as if *she* belonged, and the rest of the fine gathering were the interlopers.

"I'll be taking you in to dinner."

Which meant she'd be sitting beside him in the most desired seat of honor. That knowledge struck her brain as the couples nearest them shifted, and her gaze landed on tawny hair, a tall, broad-shouldered figure garbed in black kilt, coatee, and waistcoat. He stood out among the duke's aristocratic and wealthy dinner guests like a battle-honed clan chief of old, staring down the British from a hill overlooking Culloden. The effect was as if she'd slipped on ice—her feet shooting up, the sudden, helpless panic as she fell to the ground; then landing, hard, her breath driven from her lungs. All movement, air, reason stolen.

Tight-lipped, green eyes glittering, Cam stared back at her.

It was Cam's gaze moving to the man beside her, the slight adjustment to his posture, that broke her trance.

Carlisle was speaking, and she didn't think it was the first time. "Miss Lockwood? Shall we go in?" Appearing as taciturn as Cam, he frowned down at her, offering his arm. The guests nearest them seemed to be waiting for Carlisle to lead them into the dining room. She grabbed his arm and relief besieged her as he led her away from the watching eyes.

What followed was fine torture. Somehow she managed to smile, engage in dinner conversation, and eat a few bites. She avoided looking at Cam, who sat halfway down and across the table. As stringently as she held her attention apart, she remained aware of him, sitting just there. She'd had no idea she possessed such acute peripheral vision. They might as well have been at opposite ends of a magnetic field, one too strong to ignore. There was never a moment she didn't feel the pull.

This weekend had given her an opportunity to observe him, and she'd yet to see him acting affected by alcohol. He drank no more than some of the other men, and he appeared to have no difficulty conversing with Carlisle's guests. He'd even been popular. She didn't know what happened after he retired for the night, but while he mingled amongst these Primrose Hill patrons, his hands didn't tremble, and he didn't lose control. She hadn't seen an unsuitable deed or heard an impolite word.

Which made her want to kick him. He cursed at her, threatened and warned her off, yet played the gentleman with everyone else? How dared he treat her so shabbily?

Except she knew why he'd done so. He'd created a rift between them by hurting her. Intentionally and with forethought he'd rejected her and destroyed their connection.

"Has MacKay bothered you?" Carlisle asked in a low voice. The diners closest to them were all engaged in conversation with others. For a moment she and Carlisle might have been alone.

Had she given her thoughts away? But no, it appeared the duke simply wanted to reassure himself. "No. We've stayed away from each other." Aside from this afternoon in the glass house.

"I realized the morning I met you, you have some sort of history—some contentious history—with MacKay. I considered not inviting him, but he's a key part of the rehabilitation work. I knew my guests would find him interesting, and he's making a name for himself with his prosthetic refinements. Donors like being associated with successful enterprises. Groundbreaking ones are even better." He leaned a bit nearer. "I've made a point to keep my eye on him, and stay close to you."

One more affirmation of Carlisle's concern. He'd been guarding her. Protecting her.

"I haven't asked you about him, but—"

She frowned. The presumption of the man. As if her history with Cam were any of Carlisle's concern. She leaned back, putting a bit more distance between them.

"My apologies." His gaze swept the diners around them. "I don't know what I was thinking. This is hardly the place for such a personal conversation." He looked perturbed and perhaps even angry. "We'll talk later."

Could she tell him she'd been in love with Cam? *Should* she?

No. She owed no allegiance to this misguided notion of Carlisle's, that they might suit. She might have decided to let the duke distract her from thoughts of Cam, but they were a long way from her needing to describe her history with other men.

As if he knew they were speaking about him, Cam's gaze skewered her. No question, his unhappy face trounced Carlisle's. Her own gaze must have blazed back at him, judging by his look of surprise and the way his brows shot up. Carlisle and MacKay were both powerful, capable, intelligent men, and they could both become contrary. They liked things done their way, and assumed control of every situation in an unconscious, natural way. She found it extremely vexing. Sometimes, like now, their confidence made her feel boxed in.

Elissa turned to the wealthy widow seated on her other side. "Mrs. Warren, tell me what first drew you to support Primrose Hill Hospital."

#

Cam watched as one by one, diners turned to listen to Elissa. Her attention appeared centered on the two or three people closest around her. She didn't seem to realize that she commanded the attention of more than half the table.

"I'm reading Dickens to the men," Elissa said. "They call it book hour. It's quite popular."

"I don't imagine many of them read." Cam recognized the speaker as Simon Garrettson. A wealthy publisher, he recalled.

"For many it's the first time they've experienced reading a novel. The response has been extraordinary. Most are gripped by the story. They discuss it amongst themselves. They moan and groan when I stop." She paused. Leaned forward. "Several have asked if I thought it possible for them to learn to read."

Lady Something-or-other leaned forward as well, her generous bosom in danger of scooping potatoes from her plate. "Rough men such as soldiers wouldn't have the patience or, I'm sorry to say, the intelligence for such schooling. I admire your optimism, Miss Lockwood, but I fear you're being naive."

"I admire these men, Lady Curry. And I know they can be taught."

Cam stifled his grin. Elissa's tart-as-lemon-curd voice made it clear she had the spunk to stand up to the sour Lady Curry.

"I find them eager to learn," Elissa continued. "In fact, I hope we'll be able to increase our services and offer reading instruction to the men. Having been exposed to another world—the world of books—they want to learn to read. And I believe I've convinced some of them that it's very possible."

"You're to be commended," Garrettson said. "And I'm all for more readers who want to buy newspapers and books."

Cam couldn't keep one corner of his mouth from curving up. The publisher wasn't approving of the soldiers' desire to be literate, but his potential for making profit. Cam knew Elissa felt much as he did, but she didn't let a bit of cynicism show.

"If you could see their faces," Elissa said.

Her face, her voice, held the other diners spellbound. She radiated the light he knew resided within her.

"Some are in pain. Others fear the future. Their lives will never be the same. They've lost part of their *bodies*. Yet they appreciate everything we're offering, and each day I watch their excitement grow as book hour approaches. They forget about themselves and focus on the problems of David Copperfield. While they listen, they're happy." Eyes intent, her gaze roved up and down the table. "Such a simple thing. I want to give them the ability to read. To give them that, why, it gives them the world. No matter what, they'll always have the ability to lose themselves in a book and, at least for a little while, be happy."

It didn't surprise Cam that they looked at Elissa as if she'd spouted something radical. It was a common misconception— especially among the upper class—that the average soldier was a brute, living without a care for anything beyond his next cup of cheer and his present circumstances. If anyone could disabuse them of the misguided notion, Elissa could. What bravery and poise she displayed, speaking her mind to these people, so far above her in station.

"You've in mind a school at the hospital?" Mrs. Garrettson asked. She was a good deal younger than her husband, and sonsie.

"We're already training the men, giving them new skills. If we could teach them to read, too, we'd be opening up endless possibilities for them."

"This is such an intriguing idea. I want to help." Mrs. Garrettson looked at her husband. "And I daresay Mr. Garrettson will want to, also."

Elissa pressed her hand over her heart. Cam closed his eyes, memorizing the image of her delighted face. The lass had convinced them.

"I am grateful, and the men will be proud that you believe in them. You should visit Primrose Hill. It's an uplifting place. We're giving them futures."

Carlisle settled back in his seat. "Once again, Miss Lockwood puts her mind to something, and it happens."

Carlisle didn't even attempt to hide his admiration. Cam looked away. Watching the duke with Elissa unsettled him to such a degree, he had to fight the compulsion to leave the table. Her success in getting the Garrettsons to support reading classes made him happy for her, but it revealed how well she could fit into Carlisle's life. Her dress might be the plainest one here, but she shone brighter than any of the other ladies.

Carlisle, the arrogant arse, was a different man tonight. Relaxed, smiling, enjoying himself, he looked younger. He'd barely taken his eyes off Elissa, even to the point of engaging in the unforgivable sin of failing to give the diners near him an equal share of his time.

Cam shifted in his chair. How much longer would this interminable evening last? He sighed. He still had to get through whatever evening entertainment was planned.

He caught Elissa's eyes. How could she ask so many questions by simply looking at him? The gold-studded hazel depths were telling him things, too, but he didn't want to hear—or in this case see—what more she had to say. He'd had all he could take of her entreating him to change back to the man he'd been in Turkey. What she didn't understand was that he'd never been more than a mere impersonation of that man. He tore his gaze away and focused on the remains of the bird on his dinner plate.

After Logan's death, he'd convinced himself he could be mended, and his shattered world fixed. For a while, he even thought he'd succeeded. Thought he'd healed, and grown into the man Elissa had believed him to be. Until he returned to the front, where the truth lay in wait. Now he knew better.

He inhaled sharply through his nose and looked up. Carlisle was gazing back and forth between him and Elissa, frowning. The duke touched her arm, and she jumped and turned, wide-eyed. Carlisle's head bent toward her, and a moment later she laughed.

Cam retrieved his fork and knife, considered the sharpness of the blade, and sliced through the breast of his partridge.

CHAPTER TWENTY-THREE

A week later Mr. Fletcher strolled into Elissa's office and stood before her desk, hands in pockets, rocking heel to toe. "One of the new admissions is someone you know."

"Oh?" Elissa set her pen down.

"He and Jakes shared a rather contentious greeting. It surprised me, so I pulled Jakeman aside. He said Mr. Archer was your ward-sergeant in Koulali Hospital. Not well liked, I gather."

"Louis Archer is here?" A heavy unease sucked away her cheerful frame of mind and replaced it with dread. She didn't want to see or talk to Archer.

"Yes." Fletcher's eyes narrowed. He tilted his head. "Is that a problem for you?"

She liked Benedict Fletcher and they'd established a solid working partnership, but she didn't want to share the details of her history with Archer. At least not the part about his role in her dismissal from Miss Nightingale's nursing service. Elissa released a sigh laden with aggravation.

"I won't lie. I'm not happy he's here. But I'm capable of managing his hospitalization." Thank goodness she simply supervised the progress of each patient, and didn't provide physical care, as Jakes did.

"Of course you are. I never doubted that, but I could see his presence upset Jakes, and I think it does you, as well. I hope you'll let me know if I can be of any assistance."

"Thank you." She owed Fletcher some kind of explanation. "Jakes and I don't like Archer because he seemed to enjoy being cruel whenever he could. It's rather ironic that he's now on the receiving end of the most excellent medical care I've ever been part of or even heard of. I'm ashamed to admit, he's the last person I'd offer a place here. But I promise he'll be treated with the same kindness as every other man at Primrose Hill." She rolled her eyes and gave her head a little shake. "Archer deserves the same opportunity as every other soldier who sustained injury fighting for England."

"I wasn't worried. Just wanted to prepare you."

Fletcher left and Elissa stood. Better to face Archer now than let their meeting loom. Putting it off would increase her already prodigious apprehension. If she did it now, it would be behind her.

His smirk hadn't changed.

His back against the wall, Archer lazed on his bed watching Jakes wrap the wound of the patient across the aisle. From Archer's self-satisfied expression, and Jakes's stiff posture and heightened color, she surmised the two men were already at loggerheads.

"Miss Lockwood." Archer caressed her name as if she were a long-awaited prize.

Elissa suppressed a shudder. She forced herself to go right up beside him and look in those black, glittering eyes of his. "Good day, Mr. Archer."

He lifted his right arm and saluted with his prosthetic hook. She held back a gasp at the sight of the talon-like metal appendage. She must not have done a good job of hiding her repulsion for the stiletto-sharp prosthesis, for Archer held his arm up, turned it, and considered the prosthetic that looked like it would make an effective meat hook.

"Not sure I'm not satisfied with this beauty, but they tell me I can build my strength here and learn to better use my left hand. I suppose I wouldn't mind a different one for times I want to look the dandy. Or court a lady, maybe. Times I want to be—gentle." With his thumb and finger, he smoothed and curled one side of his mustache, then the other.

Always, intonation lent innuendo to Archer's speech. A chill streaked down her spine, and she rubbed the back of her neck.

"Mr. MacKay will design something—"

His dark eyes flashed. "MacKay," Archer snapped. "MacKay's here?"

"He's the prosthetist."

Archer's forceful, head-thrown-back laugh wasn't the kind to make her smile. It made her chill move on down her arms and cramp her fingers.

Archer's laugh subsided to a mean chuckle. "You and MacKay. Both here."

She sensed movement at her shoulder and knew Jakes had come up behind her. Archer's gaze flicked to Jakes.

"And Jakes, too. I'm a lucky man."

What frightened her most was that he sounded as though he meant it. He wanted them in his clutches, and he felt lucky to have an opportunity to do harm. She stepped back and bumped into Jakes, who—growled? She glanced over her shoulder. Jakes looked ready to grab a claw of his own, brandish it as he would a small sword, and command "*En garde, prêts, allez.*"

"Watch yourself, Archer," Jakes warned. "You're fortunate to be here. There's a waiting list, and any of those men would feel privileged to take your place."

"I'm appreciative," Archer protested, his voice a low rasp. He frowned. "Don't think you can lord over me because you've two hands and I've been invalided out. I was born strong-minded. You and MacKay—you may think you can take me down, but you'll never be the kind of men who can get the better of me. You could take all my limbs and *I'll still be here.*"

Jakes pivoted with military precision and left the ward. She guessed he had to leave to prevent his doing or saying something he'd regret. An action Elissa thought wise, and one she decided to copy.

Elissa left the ward and, rather than returning to her office, went to the yard out back. The yard that offered trees and benches and an opportunity to take in some much-needed crisp air. And where a walking path led to Cam's workshop.

#

The door opened and Elissa swept into the workshop. Two spots of red flagged her cheeks. Lips compressed into a tight line, her chin jutted like a boxer's fist. Someone had put her back up. "What's wrong, lass?" Cam walked halfway across the floor before he caught himself and stopped.

"Archer's here. He's a patient."

Archer. How could life be so unfair and unkind as to put them in a position requiring them to care for that weasel? Cam jammed his hands on his hips, let his head fall back, and huffed a great sigh at the ceiling. "Ach! He'll love it that I'm here. I recommended his transfer to the front. After he was injured, he went a bit crazy and hunted me down. He had a putrid infection. I had to restrain him in order to get him to the surgery tent. I probably saved his life, but he ranted that I'd induced the surgeon to amputate, when it wasn't necessary. How did he seem to ye?"

"As nasty as ever."

"What did he say?"

"Nothing terrible. It's just the *way* he says it. Mocking. And the way he *looks* at me."

She didn't expand on that, and Cam dropped his arms and curled his fingers. The bastard hadn't been here a day and he was already disturbing Elissa. "Ye'd best keep away from him. He has an additional heap of hate for ye, because ye told him what to do and corrected him, when ye were naught but a woman. In Archer's world, that's not allowed."

"How am I to manage staying away from him? He's a patient! Do you plan to stay away, as well?"

"I'm not worried about Jakes or myself."

"Maybe you should be. Just wait until you see the hook he wears. The thing is lethal."

Cam shrugged. "He might leave when he finds out I'll be making his new prosthesis."

"I don't think so. He knows. He seemed—pleased—that you were here."

Cam hadn't seen Archer since the day of their confrontation in the Scots Greys officers' tent, but the memory of the hatred burning in the man's eyes still lurked in Cam's brain, fresh as the day Archer confronted him. And Archer knew Cam had feelings for Elissa.

"He reported our kiss and got ye dismissed," Cam said. When Cam learned of Elissa's dismissal, and that she'd sailed, he'd wanted to pulverize the ward-master and feed him to the fish. "Miss Hutton refused to name him as the informer. She said ye'd admitted it. Archer denied it and *apologized* for telling orderlies what he'd seen." Cam had never been so angry, nor felt so helpless. "When I think of what ye must have gone through that day…"

"He hates you," Elissa said. "He never tried to hide what he felt. He was jealous of how the orderlies admired you."

Cam shrugged. "He had a more concrete reason than jealousy. I made an official complaint about him. It would have affected his advancement, if he hadn't received the medical discharge."

Elissa's brows pinched. She folded her arms and hugged herself. "I'm glad you reported him. He was mean to the patients."

Elissa had likely seen that more than Cam had, and Cam had seen enough. Archer was one mean rotter. "If he's pleased I'm here, it's because he sees an opportunity for vengeance. He might try to harm me. Maybe ye and Jakes as well. Whenever ye're in the ward, make sure Jakes is nearby."

For a moment they fell silent.

Elissa sighed. "There are men here in far worse circumstances than Archer. Perhaps they'll have a positive influence on him."

She looked so sincere. Warmth flooded his chest. Even knowing the kind of man Archer was, and having suffered from his ruthless cruelty, Elissa still expressed a desire that Archer be helped.

"Nothing can soften up Archer. Just keep your interactions short, and make sure Jakes is in the vicinity."

She nodded. "All right."

Cam needed to make sure Jakes watched Elissa like a shepherd guarding his most valuable lamb. It wouldn't hurt to deliver a threat of his own to Archer, either. Provide the sorry bastard with a little diversion.

The tip of her tongue emerged and wet her bottom lip. "You'll be careful, won't you?"

The woman was trying to kill him. The concern in her eyes—for him—and that glimpse of her pink tongue made his body go rock hard. "Aye."

She hesitated. "You've been all right? Since our return from Brighton?"

Her tentative smile made him clench his teeth. They'd had a conversation about Archer. Her need to be careful. Such a conversation he could do. But they weren't talking about anything else. He didn't want to know if she worried about him. He couldn't let her smiles fill him with this damned warmth, which bloody—well—*hurt*.

He didn't answer. Just looked at her. Her face fell, and his heart dropped to his stomach.

She turned to the door. Opened it. Waited, while his heart thrashed. And left.

The door closed, and the little bell affixed to it jangled. Then he answered her question. "Nae."

CHAPTER TWENTY-FOUR

Elissa marked her place and closed *David Copperfield*.

"Ahhh," Lawrence groaned. "You're cruel, Miss Lockwood. Leaving us there."

"You say that every day, Mr. Lawrence. You're giving me quite the reputation for being ruthless," Elissa teased. Lawrence, a rugged former sharpshooter, had become deeply involved in the novel, and was one of the soldiers who'd asked to be taught to read.

"She's enough reputation for misbehaving already, without adding more."

The ward went silent. Elissa knew that voice, speaking low enough to seem he didn't intend to be heard beyond a person or two, yet loud enough to reach her ears and at least half the patients in the ward.

"Shut your mouth." Jakes strode to Archer's bed and stood at the foot. "We're not putting up with your lies here at Primrose Hill."

"Still protecting her, I see." Archer appeared unperturbed by Jakes, who leaned forward as though held back by an invisible hand. "I'm not surprised. The orderlies at Koulali thought the two of you had an *unusually* close—friendship."

Elissa stared, motionless with indecision and horror. How did Archer have the audacity to say such things in front of her and the entire ward? Every man stared. But then, he craved power and control. She supposed it made him feel superior. If some of those hearing him believed his claim, he'd consider it a boon.

"You lousy bastard," Jakes ground out. Elissa leapt forward and grabbed Jakes's arm as he started for Archer.

"Never mind, Jakes," Elissa said. He strained against her hold.

Archer chuckled. "I'm sorry, Jakeman. After all, you weren't the reason she was dismissed. I believe her whoring around with MacKay was responsible."

His taunt hit like a slap, and she felt every man's assessing eyes. Humiliation stripped her and left her standing naked and exposed. Her stomach lurched. Retaining hold of Jakes served to keep her physically restrained. "Mr. Archer. Your remarks are distasteful and spiteful. You're getting everyone agitated, and if you don't stop, I'll have you removed." Which wouldn't accomplish much, since every patient had heard the truth of her dismissal from Koulali. She couldn't erase his damning words, which effectively condemned her. Even if his claim didn't get her dismissed, from now on, she'd always be scrutinized, her morals questioned.

"They're not lies, though, are they? I don't think you can put me out for reporting facts. I imagine these gents appreciate knowing what kind of woman has charge of them."

He wore his usual lazy, taunting smile. Elissa struggled to contain her anger, which was making her heart pound in her head so loud, she could barely think or hear. Her fingers tingled with the desire to slap him, or—or— strangle him. She gripped Jakes's arm a little tighter, just to anchor herself.

Lawrence stood up, his imposing frame taller, his shoulders broader, than every other man in the ward. "Are you an animal lover, Archer? I saw a hungry-looking cat in the yard yesterday. If you don't shut up, I'm going to cut your tongue out and feed it to the kitty."

Lawrence's self-confident, relaxed stance and calm, matter-of-fact words settled her a bit. He supported her. He'd heard everything Archer said, and he'd chosen to threaten Archer. Elissa looked at the other patients. They all looked outraged, but they stared at Archer, not her. An absolute cloud of hostility seemed to fill the ward. Several of the men, when they saw her look at them, met her eyes and gave her nods of encouragement. Her chest filled with heavy warmth. These men!

"Step away, Jakes," Lawrence said. "He's not worth your being reprimanded or losing a stripe over."

"Not sure how you're going to take out my tongue with one arm, Lawrence. Even if you could manage, you're too righteous to assault a man for being truthful. I've done you a service, telling you about her." If Lawrence intimidated Archer, he gave no sign of it.

Why did Archer do this? It was sick and twisted, the way he delighted in manipulating emotions. Hurting people. He was receiving help at Primrose Hill, yet he'd chosen to harass her. She considered his self-satisfied, mocking expression. What horrible fate had befallen him, that made him exorcise his demons by wounding others? And why her, especially? Her small reprimands wouldn't warrant this. She couldn't help but feel a part of his hostility was simply due to her being female. It was so unfair.

"Is everything all right here?"

The smooth, challenging baritone snapped Elissa's head toward the door. Carlisle strolled forward, gaze raking the room. In spite of his brilliant white shirt, perfectly tailored coat, and holding an expensive top hat, he gave the impression of nothing less than an ambling tiger, alert and able to attack at the slightest provocation.

She felt the fight go out of Jakes, and she released her hold on his arm. The tense undercurrent in the room eased. Most of these men had met Carlisle on his previous visit, but even those who hadn't seemed to realize they could relax. The pack leader had arrived.

She knew Carlisle was a powerful man, but somehow she always thought of his power as stemming from his social rank and wealth. In Brighton she'd gotten glimpses of a strength far more notable and fundamental than what would be expected to accompany his title. Now she saw his dominance made mere frivolity of privilege and fortune. Carlisle radiated controlled menace.

He searched her face and his expression gentled. One corner of his mouth curved up the merest fraction. "Is everything all right?" he repeated with less force.

She didn't want Carlisle to know what Archer had said. *He knows you were discharged from Koulali.* At least Mr. Howell, Carlisle's man of business, knew. She assumed Carlisle did, as well.

But Archer's accusation inferred something dirty and very improper had occurred in Turkey. Some would say what had happened at Göksu stream was sordid, but it hadn't been. It had been thrilling and wonderful. Perfect. She didn't have to defend herself from Archer's falsehoods. Why should Carlisle hear them, and be forced into giving the nasty claims even the briefest consideration?

Jakes and the men waited to hear her response. Archer, eyes closed and head lain back upon his pillow, arms crossed and hook resting over his chest, smiled. Elissa left Jakes and walked to where Carlisle stood. "A few testy tempers getting exercised, is all. Everything's fine."

Carlisle looked around the ward, his gaze lingering for a moment on Archer. "Might I have a moment?"

"Of course." She led him to her office.

"How much longer will your workday last? Are you leaving soon?" Carlisle asked.

"I'm finished for the day." Book hour was always the last activity of her day. Then she went home and the men received their dinner.

"Let me accompany you home, then. My carriage is outside, and we can talk on the way."

A little jolt of nerves raced through her. What did he want to discuss? He helped her with her coat and waited while she donned her hat. His intent became clear as soon as they entered his finely appointed carriage and began moving.

"My sister and her husband, Lord Marsh, are hosting a small musical evening. I'd be delighted if you'd be my guest."

As unbelievable as it seemed, he really did intend to court her. She couldn't think of anything to do but be honest.

"Your Grace, I don't understand why you're persisting in this notion of yours. That we'd suit. As if my lack of social status and unconventional experiences aren't important. I haven't changed my opinion since our conversation in Brighton. My accompanying you anywhere would result in speculation and gossip, I'm afraid."

His mouth firmed. "I can stand up to a little talk. I think you'll see, when you meet Avis, that my sister is not a slave to capricious society. I'm afraid my entire family has a rather remarkable sense of entitlement."

It went part and parcel with being part of a duke's family, she supposed, but the gleam of humor in Carlisle's eyes surprised her. She wouldn't have thought him a man who'd make fun of himself and his family. "You'd be the topic on everyone's lips. It's not pleasant, being judged. Censured for your actions."

He grew serious, looked at her a moment, and she felt her face heat. He must know she spoke from experience. Was he wondering what she'd done to warrant criticism?

"You have no idea how society reacted when Michael committed suicide. As though it were a scandal. As though it were my fault, or the fault of his brother. I was devastated by the death of my son. When society began whispering and pointing judgmental fingers—it consumed me with anger."

Carlisle removed his hat, ran his fingers through dark, silver-threaded hair, and resettled the head cover. "I was already struggling with guilt. That I hadn't seen how deep Michael's despair went. That I should have *known*. And then, for society to suggest there was something inherently *wrong* with Michael, that he'd done something they considered dishonorable." His eyes flashed silver. "How *dare* my associates—supposed friends—put blame on me or my boys?"

"I'm so sorry. It was unfair. Monstrous." She didn't realize she'd reached out, until his hand gripped hers.

"Michael's death—and the aftermath orchestrated by society—changed everything. My wife died birthing Michael. He and Richard were just one year apart, and I always kept them close. I've enjoyed the successes I've had in business and in Lords, but my boys and my daughter always held the key to my happiness. For Michael, his brother, sister, and myself, to be blamed for *anything*...I lost all respect for those who participated. *They* were the dishonorable ones."

He released her hand. Elissa curled her fingers and set her hand in her lap.

"I know," he said with intensity, "that you would never act that way. I no longer care about the opinions of anyone but my family and people I respect. People like you. Life is uncertain, and too short. I feel a great deal of admiration and attraction for you. I'm determined that we explore this attraction between us."

How could she turn him down? She couldn't deny she found him appealing, but the attraction was nothing like what she felt for MacKay. Who didn't want her. She had to keep reminding herself of that. She *liked* Carlisle. Should she give their friendship the opportunity to grow into more? There weren't many men straightforward enough to share what he'd just shared, and she admired him for that.

"Very well. You haven't convinced me I'm a proper companion for you, but you have convinced me of your sincerity. I'll enjoy meeting your sister and having a musical evening."

Rather than relief, his expression flared with triumph. Did he feel far more attraction for her than she did for him? She hoped not. She didn't want to hurt him if her feelings didn't grow.

#

Cam entered the dining room and looked for Archer. Time to give the little shite notice that Cam was out of patience. Except Archer wasn't there like the other men, waiting for dinner to be served.

Cam stopped next to Lawrence's chair. The big man's stump was nearly healed after the surgical revision he'd undergone. He'd soon be ready for Cam to measure him for his new hand and forearm.

"Where's Archer?" Cam rubbed his temples. His head had hurt all day.

Lawrence glanced around the room. "Hell, if we're lucky."

"He's been here, what, two or three days? Doesn't take long for him to make an impression, does it?"

"It's been four days. He didn't lose any time. Acted the devil to Miss Lockwood and Jakes yesterday. I thought he might behave insolently with everyone, but after that show yesterday, I know he has it in for them. Especially her."

"Jakes told me what happened." He'd also informed Cam of the duke's visit. Carlisle wasn't wasting any time. "I'm top of the list of people Archer hates," Cam said. "And I'm going to make sure he doesn't bother Miss Lockwood again."

Lawrence grinned. "Good. Need any help?"

"Nae. I've a mind to keep all the fun for myself."

"I'll bide my time. With luck he'll need a second warning."

Cam gave Lawrence's shoulder a squeeze and headed for the hall.

He heard voices as he approached Elissa's office. He'd never been in the room, but he knew which door was hers. The east wing held the dining room, gymnasium, Fletcher's office, Elissa's office, and classroom-recreation room. The west wing consisted of the ward and surgical suite.

He knew the voices. Archer and Elissa. It was past time for her to be home. He'd waited until the workday was over to seek out Archer, to avoid seeing her. He stopped just shy of her door and listened.

"After what occurred in Turkey, how is it you not only recover but improve your lot?" Archer's voice asked. "My entire life has been blown apart. And I find you here, all cozy with MacKay."

"Not that it's any concern of yours, but I rarely see Mr. MacKay. I know you were responsible for my being dismissed. You've no right to speak to me as you did yesterday in the ward. I don't want to talk with you about anything but your rehabilitation at Primrose Hill."

"I've a right to say anything I like, and it's all true. You pretend to be the good little nurse angel, when you're rutting with MacKay."

Rage exploded inside Cam. He came around the doorframe and saw Archer standing angled over Elissa, inches away from her. Cam surged into the office and grabbed the weasel, jerking him away from Elissa, whose pale face appeared stricken.

Archer yelped as Cam slammed his back into the wall. Holding tight to the bunched neck of Archer's shirt with one hand, and his hook-bearing arm with his other, fierce satisfaction stabbed through Cam with each thump of Archer's head and shoulders against the plaster. So sweet.

"Shut yer fuckin' mouth," Cam growled, shoving his face close.

Archer's one-sided sneer didn't falter. "I'll have you gone by morning. You'll be whittling buttons and selling them on the street corner."

Cam heaved the man through the doorway and sent him sprawling. Clapping drew Cam's gaze to Lawrence, who stood in the hallway looking on.

"Didn't want to miss the show," Lawrence explained.

"Your easy life just ended, MacKay," Archer spat.

"Why would that be?" Lawrence asked. "It's not MacKay's fault you fell on your arse."

"*She* saw him attack me, and she doesn't lie," Archer said, gathering himself and standing.

"She didnae see a thing." Cam swiped sweat from his brow. He hoped, given the circumstances, Elissa would lie, although he wasn't at all certain.

Archer stared past Cam's shoulder, where Elissa stood. Cam glanced back. There wasn't a lick of hesitation in her determined expression.

Archer straightened his collar. "No matter. This is too satisfying to end it so soon anyway."

Their quick little tussle hadn't delivered near enough wrath. "Consider yerself warned. I'm watchin' ye. I suggest ye stay as far away from Miss Lockwood as ye can. And if I hear of ye demeanin' her again, ye won't like the consequences."

"You might acquire some consequences of your own, MacKay. You'd better watch your own back," Archer warned.

Archer left, heading toward the dining room, which threatened to make Cam choke. After this, the whoreson was going to eat? Cam's stomach churned like butter being paddle whipped. His hunger had disappeared.

"I'll keep my eye on him," Lawrence said.

"I'm beholden to ye."

"No need to be. I'm happy to do the service." Lawrence ambled away after Archer.

Cam turned to face Elissa.

Frowning, she stood with hands clasped. "He threatened you."

Cam suppressed his grin. She sounded outraged.

"After I threatened him."

"I don't spout falsehoods, but I'd never support any tale Archer told about you. I wouldn't hesitate to lie."

She said it like a vow, a promise, and his chest tightened. Elissa might be the most principled person he knew. The thought of her going against her tenets, for him, was priceless. He'd never received such a commitment, and he didn't know how to respond.

Cam rubbed his hands together. "We can get him expelled for what he just said to ye."

"If you report him, it will drag up my history again. I'd have to tell Mr. Fletcher what Archer said in the ward yesterday, and explain myself. "

"Fletcher and Howell would support ye. They'd never condone how Archer acted in the ward, or what he said today."

"They might not like that you tussled with him."

He shrugged. "I doubt they'd mind. He deserved it."

"Maybe he'll stop now."

Cam gave her a pointed look. "Are ye serious?"

Her mouth flattened, and he shook his head. Of course, she didn't want to become the object of gossip again, no matter it was undeserved. Cam wasn't certain the patients would talk about them, but he didn't want to chance it. She'd been through enough.

"Archer won't have another opportunity to catch ye alone. Ye needn't fear him. And if he dares say anything else hateful to ye or about ye in the ward, he'll find himself being fit for prosthetic teeth."

Elissa's hand flew to her mouth. Her shoulders shook with stifled laughter.

Pleasure curled inside him. If he'd helped her find humor in all this, he'd done well. He shifted his weight from one foot to the other. They still needed to employ caution. "If he does or says anything to hurt ye, tell me at once."

She took her coat from the peg and had it on before his mind realized what she was about. She tied her bonnet ribbons with jerky movements.

"Shall I—would ye like me to walk ye home?"

She shook her head. "Just do whatever you can to get Archer's rehabilitation completed quickly."

He watched her skirt sway as she hurried down the hall and around the corner. He swiped his hand across his mouth.

He needed to protect Elissa. Archer would take any advantage he could, and at present, Cam possessed enough deficiencies to make the task easy for the weasel. Their brief scuffle had made Cam break a sweat and caused a wave of nausea to swell. He needed to be sharp; instead he felt sluggish. He didn't care what happened to himself, but dammit, he wasn't going to allow Archer to hurt Elissa again.

CHAPTER TWENTY-FIVE

The following day Cam had just closed the workshop and gone to his room, when someone—likely Jakes—knocked at his door. Cam had sent a note with one of the patients, asking Jakes to come see him before he left for home.

Things hadn't been right between them since Elissa's arrival, when they'd argued. It was time to repair that rift. He needed Jakes's help.

He didn't harbor any belief that his forgiving Jakes's interference would completely mend their friendship. There was still the issue of Jakes's disappointment in Cam. It had been months, and the loss of Jakes's regard still hurt.

When the orderly didn't enter when Cam opened the door, he curbed his annoyance and invited Jakes in. "Thank ye for coming. I need to talk with ye." Cam waved toward his sitting area. "Have a seat."

Jakes paused a long moment and considered the chairs, before sitting in one of them. "I heard what happened between you and Archer yesterday."

Cam nodded, and sat. "He's a bully. Can ye help keep an eye on him? Fetch me right away if he does anything to jeopardize Miss Lockwood. Lawrence will keep watch, as well."

"If your little fracas doesn't subdue him, how do you plan to control him?" Jakes was still acting a little stiff. His voice held a challenge.

"I'll do whatever's necessary." Cam leaned forward, put his elbows on his knees and clasped his hands. "He's not going to be spreading any more rumors about Miss Lockwood."

Jakes's blue eyes scrutinized him. Cam held his gaze.

"She's important to me," Jakes admitted. His chin tilted up. "She's my friend. I think she's something more to you, but I'm not sure you can be trusted to do what needs doing. That you're *able* to keep Archer caged. It'll take more than yesterday to prove to me you can."

God's breath! Jakes didn't cushion his blows. Cam bowed his head. Considered what he needed to divulge. Looked up and met Jakes's cold gaze.

"I know I've disappointed you. With the whiskey, and how I abandoned Miss Lockwood." Cam had watched Jakes's eyes go from admiring to shocked, to hurt, to angry, and finally, to dull acceptance with a glaze of disgust. Still, he'd as much as admitted he'd brought Elissa to Primrose Hill to set Cam to rights. Maybe, even after the failure of that plan, Jakes still held a small bit of hope for Cam.

Cam cleared his throat. He hadn't said this aloud yet, and the words dammed his throat like a log jam. "I'm going to stop drinking." After a long, sleepless night, he'd accepted that he couldn't protect Elissa the way he wanted if he got drunk every evening. He needed to be sharp. Archer would take every advantage Cam gave him, and not staying keen would be a huge boon to the man. Cam needed to be razor-edged.

"What?" Jakes asked with a mean-sounding chortle. "Do you expect me to believe you? You abandoned Miss Lockwood, and turned a blind eye to all the patients needing your surgical skill. None of them were as important as that bottle. Excuse my skepticism, but it stretches credibility to think the need to keep Archer in check is stronger than your desire to drink."

Jakes didn't understand. For years Cam struggled to escape a future he seemed fated for. He'd even convinced himself he'd been successful, until the Crimea taught him how wrong he'd been, and showed him Elissa had been no more than an unattainable dream. When he faced the truth and gave up surgery, he surrendered to the inevitable.

"I didn't stop being a surgeon because I wanted the drink more." At first the drink had kept the nightmares at bay. Then it stilled the tremors. "The war broke me down, Jakes." He stopped. Swallowed. "Broke me down to nothing. Whiskey was the bulwark that allowed me to carry on." Jakes had been there, but even so, he might not understand. Other men, men like Jakes, didn't break.

Cam waited, breath rasping in and out of his lungs.

"If nothing else, maybe you can physically intimidate Archer," Jakes said. "You didn't do too bad yesterday."

Relief eased through Cam at the change in Jakes's voice. Cam settled against the chair's cushioned back. "I didn't. But I took Archer by surprise. I won't have that opportunity again. I've already talked to Howell. I'll return to the workshop after I eat tonight, and I'll work the next few nights, as well. Then I'll be caught up with my work and able to take a few days for myself." At Jakes's puzzled expression, Cam added, "to detoxicate."

Jakes leaned forward. "Let me help."

"I'll be fine. Ye can help by staying close to Miss Lockwood while I'm incapacitated."

"It's going to be that bad?"

"Not sure, lad." It'd be bad enough, he knew. "I'd appreciate yer keeping this to yerself."

Jakes tipped his head. "Even from Miss Lockwood?"

"Especially from her."

"I'll look in on you. You can't stop me doing that. I can fetch anything you need."

He didn't want anyone to see him, not even Jakes. But agreeing to Jakes coming by was probably wise.

"Miss Lockwood will be happy when she realizes you've quit drinking."

"This won't change anything between Miss Lockwood and me. It just keeps her safe from Archer." Drunk or sober, he was not for Elissa. He'd accepted what he'd been denying at Koulali. He was broken, and stopping the drink wouldn't mend him.

Forehead creased, Jakes looked at him. The orderly stood. "I don't understand why you're opposed to a connection with Miss Lockwood. It's been obvious since Turkey that you feel something for each other. You're a perfect match."

"Don't tell me ye're a romantic, Jakes."

Jakes had matured. There was a time such a jest would have turned him red. Now he merely lifted his brows.

"None of my concern, I know," Jakes said, then made his good-byes.

Being sober might bring back the shakes, the nightmares, or both. But both were preferable to Elissa being at Archer's mercy. He could endure the nightmares, and it no longer mattered if his hands shook. It only mattered that his mind was sharp, his reflexes fast, and he could best Archer.

#

Carlisle's sister, Lady Marsh, met them in her foyer and clasped her brother's hands. She had Carlisle's black hair, but her eyes weren't the same solid gray. They were blue-gray, which Elissa suspected might appear blue or lavender or gray, depending on what color the lady wore.

When their hands released, Carlisle introduced them. "Miss Lockwood, may I present Lady Marsh. Avis, this is Miss Lockwood."

"Whom I've heard so much about," Lady Marsh said with a friendly, engaging smile. For a moment Elissa felt befuddled. Although his sister was a viscountess, he had chosen to introduce her to Elissa, as if Elissa held the higher rank. In a subtle way he was telling them both how greatly he valued Elissa.

Lady Marsh didn't seem the least affronted or surprised. As if they were best friends, Carlisle's sister slipped her arm through Elissa's and guided her into a large room arranged for the evening's entertainment. A quartet of musicians tuned their instruments at one end of the room, where a grouping of chairs and divans sat. She and Carlisle weren't the first guests to arrive. About ten others stood chatting and sampling food and drink.

A short, bespectacled gentleman crossed to them as soon as they entered.

"Marsh, here's Miss Lockwood," Lady Marsh said.

"Welcome. We're so pleased you could join us," Lord Marsh said. His brown eyes shone with kindness, and a bit of her tension eased.

Carlisle launched into conversation, relieving Elissa of the necessity. As the evening progressed and they advanced into the room, he took most of the conversational burden, always staying close. So close she caught the sandalwood scent of him. Near enough that she remained acutely attuned to his presence.

In the company of so many titled ladies and gentlemen, it was a great relief to have him beside her. She could see they were all the slightest bit deferential to him. He was a duke, after all. But the charisma so much in evidence wasn't owing to his rank. The man wore his masculinity with an easy, refined grace, and radiated self-confidence.

A trait she'd always found attractive. It was the first thing she'd noticed about Cam, how sure of himself he was. She remembered him striding into Ward Two that first day, snapping orders, yet steady and certain of every action. He'd been a stranger, yet she'd immediately trusted him. Elissa froze. She shouldn't be thinking about Cam now, when she was Carlisle's companion for the evening. She *must* stop thinking about him at every turn.

"Miss Lockwood?"

Carlisle's voice drew her attention.

"Shall we find seats? They're almost ready to begin."

"Of course."

He pointed her to a settee. Once they were seated, he gave her a warm smile, then cast his gaze around the room. The look on his face—her throat tightened. He looked...*proud*.

"Are you beginning to believe that you could be welcomed into society? Everyone greeted you with respect, and I believe the women are in awe of you. Many of these ladies are members of charitable societies. They have an appreciation for what you've done and are doing. You're intelligent, kind, and beautiful, and your speech and carriage is no less genteel than that of any lady here."

His flattery left her at a loss. A nervous little bird seemed to have flown into her stomach and begun to peck. Carlisle's timetable for their association seemed set at whirlwind pace, while Elissa desired something leisurely. A conversation was in order, later. She needed to slow the duke down.

These twenty or so guests had been cordial, but she'd never been without Carlisle at her side. They'd been so pleasant, in fact, she wondered if they might not have been hand-picked. Carlisle waited, obviously expecting her to comment.

"The woman who raised me was a school master's daughter," she said. "She'd been well educated, and held me to high standards."

Carlisle grinned as though her reply amused him. No doubt he realized how out of sorts he made her.

Elissa didn't hear much of Lady Marsh's introduction of the musical selection. The quartet's first notes floated around her, but the lilting music of Mozart didn't lift her as it normally would. She barely heard it.

Carlisle's enthusiasm for her company should thrill her. Instead, their very young romance gave her doubts, and she wasn't sure why. She could grow used to his privilege and wealth, and they were only beginning to explore whether they'd suit one another. With Cam, she'd discovered the happiness of loving and being loved, and been hungry for more. She'd realized how lonely she'd been, and how she'd offset her loneliness by working as a nurse.

After her family died, she'd discovered what *alone* felt like. Maddie had been kind and they'd grown to love each other, but having Maddie didn't fill Elissa's emptiness. She doubted such a chasm could be filled. After days of cholera sickness, she'd regained her senses and discovered that every person she loved had vanished from the world.

Waking, having that pain take her... She knew she couldn't bear such a tumult again. The deep connection with her patients helped, as did the gratitude she received from their families. Nursing was what she was meant to do, and that remaining bit of emptiness, well, it helped make her a better nurse, didn't it? She never forgot her own battle with cholera, when the disease reached its peak. How it felt when the fear fell away, when pulsing and light filled her head and her body ceased to exist. When there was nothing but the beat of angel wings.

She'd survived, been tossed back to earth, but she'd lost her family. She'd never expected to have another.

Elissa drifted upon the music's current. Did she think, because her family had been taken away, she didn't *deserve* a family? Is that why she hadn't put up a fight when she'd found Cam again, and he'd rejected her? Had she been *afraid* that he might fill the emptiness, and she'd once again be vulnerable to that all-encompassing pain?

In spite of what she knew to be more than passable looks, she'd never been one to turn men's heads. She'd accepted Cam's decision. Had she done that because she believed she was not meant to have love? Or because she wasn't brave enough to fight for what she wanted?

She thought herself strong. She'd stay at the bedside of a patient until certain of the person's outcome, even if that certainty was days in coming. Had she given up on *herself* too easily?

Men didn't appear proud and possessive, the way Carlisle did, unless they wanted the woman who engendered that look. He sat beside her, head tilted back, eyes closed, looking utterly content. He seemed to think they belonged together.

Had she been wrong? Was it possible for her to find love? Perhaps even have children? Carlisle was older than she. He had a son—heir to his title and estate—and a daughter, but he was still a vital man. A man who loved his children deeply, and who might receive more with joy.

The thought made a nervous, jittery feeling possess her. Made her shift, and drew Carlisle's gaze. Made her shudder as a soul-deep yearning burst free.

Dear God, but she wished that yearning was for Carlisle.

CHAPTER TWENTY-SIX

A loud, persistent rapping woke Elissa. She groped her way into her wrapper and down the stairs, arriving at the front door at the same time as Mrs. Emerson.

Clutching the edges of her shawl with one hand, her landlady parted the drapes of the window facing the street. "It's too dark," she muttered.

"Who's there?" Elissa called.

"Miss Lockwood! It's Jakes!"

Elissa exchanged a surprised look with Mrs. Emerson. Her landlady turned the key and opened the door partway. Elissa peered out. "Jakes? What on earth?"

"I'm sorry to disturb you in the middle of the night, miss, but you must come."

All their months in Koulali, no matter the urgency, she'd never heard Jakes sound like this. Elissa swung the door wide. Mrs. Emerson lit a lamp, and they all squinted in the sudden brightness.

"It's MacKay. He's sick."

Elissa squeezed the handful of gown and wrapper she'd gathered at her neck. Her entire body came awake. "Sick? What's wrong with him?" She couldn't imagine Jakes coming here like this unless the circumstances were dire.

"You've got to come. I've been trying to take care of him, but he's frightening me."

Frightening Jakes? She reached out, grabbed Jakes's arm, and pulled him inside. "*What's wrong with him?*"

"He's getting off the drink and he's half out of his head. The stubborn arse wouldn't wean himself off, he had to do it straightaway." He paused, studied the floor, and grimaced. His eyes, when they met hers, apologized and begged. "He's in a bad way."

She didn't want to leave Jakes to deal with something he felt unequipped for, but she knew Cam wouldn't welcome her help. She'd considered offering it before, but he'd made it clear he didn't want it. She'd borne his rejection twice, and she didn't want to suffer the humiliation and pain of a third rejection. This time he'd be rejecting her as a *nurse* when he was in dire need of her nursing skill. She wasn't sure she could ever forgive him for that.

"Can you manage until morning? I'll have one of the other nurses attend him then."

Jakes squeezed his eyes shut then peered at her with disbelief. "I wouldn't have asked if I thought there was any other way."

"Perhaps you should go," Mrs. Emerson said.

Elissa gave her head a sharp shake. "He'll be all right. His alcohol habit isn't so severe that stopping it will be dangerous. He keeps himself more or less sober during his work hours, and he has a strong constitution. He won't have seizures. You only need be there to make sure he doesn't injure himself." Elissa forced herself to harden her heart. She wanted MacKay to have more than a mere watchdog, but he wouldn't come to harm without more.

Jakes seemed to grow a little taller. "He won't let me stay," he snapped. "When I refused to leave, he started throwing things. He won't be happy to see you, but I think you may be the one person he won't pitch things at."

Her heart might have been a dishrag, the way Jakes had wrung it. "Wait here." She caught a glimpse of his relief before she whirled and took to the stairs. Inside her room, she ripped off her nightgown, threw on clothing, and tried not to give free rein to her nerves and worry. She chose items that were the fastest to put on—the bodice with the large buttons, her side-laced boots—and cursed as her mind outraced her fingers.

She clattered back downstairs, where Jakes held the door open. She said a quick goodbye to Mrs. Emerson as she flew out the door.

"I'm sorry I couldn't find a cab," Jakes huffed. The merest sliver of moon glowed, and their steps echoed as they rushed down the silent street.

Elissa made some kind of noise in acknowledgment. She was already breathing hard. He took her arm as they crossed a road, then kept hold, pulling her along a bit. She walked this route every day, and it took no more than twenty minutes to reach the hospital.

Tonight the walk, even as fast as they went, seemed interminable. Finally they reached the outdoor stairs to MacKay's rooms. A light glowed from the window overhead.

Out of breath, Elissa forged up the steps ahead of Jakes. She'd cared for a number of patients gripped in the anguish of detoxication, but she found when she stepped into Cam's rooms, breathing hard and pressing her hand to the pain in her side, those experiences hadn't prepared her. This was *Cam*, muttering, covered in sweat, writhing amid twisted bedsheets. He might as well have bundled all his misery and shot her with it.

She crossed the room. Bent over him, pressed her palm to his forehead, smoothed back his hair. Placed her hand atop the tawny beard and cupped the side of his face. "Cam?"

Glazed eyes roamed her face. "'Lissa," he sighed, as if he'd found her after a long, arduous search. He blinked and his face hardened. "What're ye doin' here?"

"I brought her," Jakes said, stepping up behind her as she straightened.

Cam's eyes blazed. He pointed a shaky forefinger at Jakes and spoke through clenched teeth. "Get...out." His hand dropped and his gaze swung between Jakes and Elissa. "Both of ye. I don't want ye here."

"I'm not leaving you alone," Elissa said.

Cam's mouth twisted and he struggled, pushing himself into a sitting position. Then he sat, hands fisted on the bed, green eyes glowing with the fire of the aurora borealis. "Get...outta...*here*," he bellowed. A weak spate of coughs followed the shout. He folded to one elbow then collapsed to his back. His eyes drifted shut and he resumed muttering.

Elissa clasped Jakes's arm and pulled him back. "Go. Go on."

Jakes's lips compressed to a thin line. "I'm going to stay right outside the door."

Elissa shook her head. "It's too cold. Go down to the workshop. I'll stamp on the floor if I need you." He hesitated. "I'll be all right, Jakes," she said. One thing she knew with absolute certainty: Cam would never physically hurt her.

With an expression that said he wished he were staying, but knew he couldn't, Jakes left. For a few minutes Elissa watched Cam, whose jerky twitches appeared involuntary. He'd removed his shoes and gone to bed with his shirt, pants, and socks on. He looked restless and uncomfortable, the bedclothes bunched and half under him, his shirt wrinkled and twisted, his hair wildly rumpled. He was one giant, disheveled mess.

She got busy. Broken crockery littered the floor, but she found his wash basin intact. Room clean-up could come later. No doubt thanks to Jakes, a healthy fire burned in the stove, and a steaming kettle sat atop it. She filled the basin with hot water, collected soap, a towel and small washcloth, and positioned one of the two ladder-backs beside his bed.

He needed fresh clothing. A nightshirt, perhaps? She went to the clothing chest and paused, fingers on the top drawer's pull knobs. He hadn't given her permission to look, or to touch his things. She knew his need was enough justification, yet guilt nagged her. These were Cam's private belongings. The room itself was bereft of personal items, so any items that held meaning would be in this chest or the trunk sitting at the foot of the bed.

She pulled the knobs and the drawer slid open. The pleasing aroma of soap and cedar drifted out. Neatly folded shirts lined the interior. She closed the drawer and went to the next. She found the perfect nightshirt in the bottom drawer. One that had been washed so many times, it had gone thin, and soft as a baby's cheek. The nightshirt completed her small stack, which included clean drawers, socks, and bedsheets.

She began to close the last drawer when a corner of lace at the back caught her eye. Almost of their own accord, her fingers edged socks aside and withdrew the fabric. She recognized the lace that bordered the scrap of cotton. A pattern of swirling roses and tiny blue blossoms. Her handkerchief. The one she'd misplaced in Koulali.

The unexpectedness of finding it here, in Cam's drawer, made prickles chase over her skin. Her mouth went dry. She crushed the square of linen and lace in her hand, turned, and looked at Cam, who gave a rather loud snore. All these months, he'd kept her handkerchief.

Something inside her fractured. Something she hadn't even known was there, barricading her emotions, holding her feelings for Cam confined. Safe.

Released, they flooded into her empty center and filled it. The tenderness hadn't died, in spite of being locked away and in spite of her having told herself she must let her love for him go.

She pressed her fingers to her curving lips. Over a smile impossible to suppress.

And pressed her hand to her chest. Over the fragile petals of her heart unfolding.

And released her hope from its prison. To let it soar and dance and dream.

He'd written and told her he didn't love her. He'd stood right in front of her and told her a second time. He'd been lonely and she'd comforted him, he'd said. But this changed everything. No matter how often or vigorously Cam protested and denied having feelings for her, it wasn't true.

She meant something to him.

Elissa folded her handkerchief, returned it to its back corner and slid the drawer closed. Mind full of her discovery, she retraced her steps to his bed.

When she placed the hot washcloth to his face, he moaned. A moan of relief and primal pleasure. He grabbed the cloth and held it to his face, his large hand pressing the heat to his skin.

"Ooooooch!" The weary sound rumbled out of his chest. "Be ye an angel?" He shivered. The heat of a low fever radiated from him.

Had he forgotten she was there? "It's me, Cam." She pulled the cloth away.

He blinked repeatedly. The glazed confusion in his eyes receded until sharp awareness looked back at her. He sighed. "Ye shouldn't be here, lass."

"Just for a little bit," Elissa said. She'd thought once Jakes left, Cam's anger would drain away, and she'd been right. He couldn't stay angry at her, not ill, his mind confused. He might not want her here, but she suspected he found her presence comforting.

His brow furrowed. "I dinnae want ye seein' me like this."

"I know you don't, but I'm proud of you. I'm so happy you're getting back to yourself. It doesn't have to be this hard. Won't you take just a spoonful of whiskey? Or perhaps laudanum?"

He pressed his hand to his stomach. "I deserve this godawful retchin' for lyin' to ye, and hurtin' ye." He began to laugh, and then the laugh turned into a grimace and a groan of pain. His hands cradled his head. "Me head's splittin' apart like it's rotten inside. This is the fastest way. I want it over."

Glistening eyes, greener than she'd ever seen them, poured strength into her brain, her body, her resolve.

He slid his hands from his head and pressed the heels into his eye sockets. "Why are ye temptin' me? Ye've been in me mind, now ye've taken the form of her? Ye devil, usin' *her* to tempt me."

Dear God. Seconds. Mere seconds had passed, and he'd swung from clear thinking to delusion.

She pulled one of his hands away and held it, palm to palm, fingers interlocked. "It's Elissa, Cam. I'm right here. I'm going to take care of you, and you're going to be all right." She tightened her hold on his hand and gave it a little shake. "Cam?"

He wrapped his free hand around their joined hands, and squeezed. His brows bunched and his lips thinned in a look of disbelief. "Elissa?"

Her heart cracked. "Let's get your shirt off and give you a wash. Make you more comfortable."

She'd already unbuttoned the shirt's front placket. She grabbed the hem and drew the shirt up. He didn't help much, but enough to allow her to remove it without too much effort on her part. The undershirt came next, and then his upper body was bare.

His muscles were well defined, his chest broad and furred with curly golden hair. She tried not to stare, but couldn't stop herself.

He splayed one trembling hand across the center of his chest. "Ye shouldn't be doin' this, lass."

It was peculiar, and humorous, that whenever Cam became angry or emotional his Scottish brogue grew more pronounced. For some unexplainable reason, hearing the pronounced accent now made her eyes fill. She sniffed, lifted his hand, and began washing his arm.

In Koulali, she might wash men's faces and hands, but she didn't bathe patients. The orderlies did that. But on the occasions she provided assistance with grooming, her emotions weren't engaged. She thought only of the care the patient needed.

Nothing about bathing Cam felt routine. She toweled his arm. Not with her usual brisk efficiency, but slowly, her fingers sliding over muscular bulges and valleys. The sight and feel of his flesh made ribbons of desire unfurl and heat every feminine part of her.

Her heart beat faster and harder. She couldn't seem to get enough air.

She clamped her teeth together. Cam needed a *nurse*, not a love-addled ninny.

"Cam. Can you drink something? Is your stomach sick?" She had to say his name sharply, twice more, and repeat her question.

"It churned aplenty, but seems to have settled a mite now."

His slow response managed to push everything from her mind but concern for his well-being. She finished his chest, rolled him to his side, and started on his shoulders and back. Once she had him comfortable, she'd give him tea. Come morning, Jakes could fetch some porridge from the hospital.

She kept him well covered by the blanket, exposing no more than the portion of body she was bathing, and never exposing his pelvis. Ready to wash his legs and feet, she moved to the bottom of the bed. "I need to get your trousers off. Unbutton your pants, Cam."

She kept her gaze locked on his blanketed knees while he fumbled under the blanket. The wait seemed to be forever, as her face heated. He muttered something about "ma breeks" she couldn't understand. Then he unbuttoned his trousers, and underneath the blanket, she slid her arms up each side of his legs. Keeping the woolen cover in place over his pelvis, she pulled the pants off.

She tried her best to get him to wash the part of his body she hadn't touched, but he was beyond understanding. She gave up and discovered pants were far easier coming off than drawers were going on, but by bending his knees, tilting him from one hip to the other, and with his half-hearted assistance, she managed to get the drawers up. Managed to keep her touch impersonal. Managed not to think about how it felt when the backs of her fingers slid over his hips. Managed to ignore the blissful expanse of Cam stretched before her.

Finished, she rolled him side to side, and changed the bed linens. Finally he was clean, lying on fresh sheets, smelling faintly of soap. The relief inside her felt as crisp and cool and correct as the bedsheet she covered him with.

Time to get some liquids down him. She let the tea cool and he gulped it down, spilling a little down the front of his nightshirt.

The bath, bed change, and tea drinking exhausted her. Cam seemed just as tired. He rolled to his side and closed his eyes.

Elissa sank onto the chair she'd placed beside him. The ladder-back. Which didn't comfort her spine, her head, or her shredded emotions. The moment Jakes appeared, he was helping her drag the room's one cushioned armchair to the bed.

CHAPTER TWENTY-SEVEN

Cam woke. He felt better. Alert. Like he was past the worst of it. Thank God.

Late afternoon light slanted through the window. A book open in her lap, Elissa dozed in the armchair Jakes had pulled to the side of Cam's bed. Elissa had insisted on helping Jakes move the chair, Jakes had refused to let her help, and the ensuing argument had given Cam the one bit of amusement he'd had in—he couldn't even think how long it had been since he'd felt like laughing.

He watched her sleep, admired her sprawled, curvaceous body, her open, transparent face, and the long sweep of her lashes. Something sharp poked his conscience. She was vulnerable and he was taking advantage, his eyes eating her up.

He sat up and stuffed a pillow between his back and the headboard. A pitcher sat on the bedside table, alongside a glass of water. He grabbed the glass and guzzled the water. Amazing that a simple drink of water could taste so good. A second glass tasted just as sweet. The nausea was gone. In fact, he felt hungry.

Unable to resist another look, his gaze slid back to Elissa. She wore a different dress, which meant another day had passed.

Jakes relieved her several times a day, which allowed her to go home, eat, bathe, and change clothes. This morning Cam had tried to make her leave altogether. He'd agreed to accept Jakes in her place, but she refused to leave.

Three days she'd been here. Ignoring his bad temper and his embarrassment and his shame. Howell had granted her leave to stay with Cam as long as he needed her care. Which meant Carlisle must be aware of Cam's situation. Or perhaps he only knew Cam was sick.

He held up his hand. The withdrawal tremor was barely noticeable. Much better. Tomorrow she'd agree to leave. Tonight he'd insist on a regular meal. He'd eat well, dress, and walk about. That should resolve the last of her hesitation.

She moved. Her breathing changed. Her eyes blinked open and, still half asleep, she looked right at him.

For one unguarded moment her eyes revealed everything. Revealed a yearning as intense as Cam's. A yearning she snuffed.

Her cheeks flushed and she wriggled in her chair like a Newmarket race horse awaiting the starting shot. "I fell asleep," she said. "Are you all right? How long have you been awake? Why didn't you wake me?"

"I woke a few minutes ago, and I'm fine." She needed more rest, though. She had shadows under her eyes. He'd insist she leave tonight. When Jakes brought their food, he'd tell his friend to walk her home. "I'm hungry, though. I want a good meal tonight. No more sick foods."

"How about tea and gingerbread for now? We've a couple hours before Jakes brings supper."

"Gingerbread! Ye're spoilin' me, lass."

Ah. A big, bright smile. It eased the worry gnawing at him. She popped out of her chair and within a few minutes they had tea, along with gingerbread fit for the Queen.

"Do you like it?" Elissa asked after he swallowed his first blissful bite. "My landlady, Mrs. Emerson made it."

He looked at her eager face, and for one perfect moment she wasn't his nurse. They were a man and woman, enjoying a quiet, sunny room, enjoying being together.

"Nae. I don't like it. I love it. How did ye know it's my favorite?"

"Is it? Jakes said you liked it, but I didn't realize it was your favorite. Did your mother make it?"

A lump, like a gluey ball of gingerbread, wedged in his throat. He swallowed, hard. "We had a cook-housekeeper. Mrs. Milligan. My mother died birthing me and Logan." The words spilled out of his mouth as if he'd intended to say them.

She gasped and her lips parted. And he couldn't look away from her shocked, dismayed face.

"I'm sorry. Sorry you never knew her."

"I don't even know *about* her. There're no pictures, no relatives, no stories." A devil had hold of his tongue. He should stuff his mouth with gingerbread the way a bricklayer filled holes with mortar. Stop the leaking words.

But he couldn't. His body had turned to rock.

"Hasn't your father told you about her?"

"He doesn't speak of her. What I know—which isn't much—comes from my father's parents. They lived a distance away, and didn't know her well. She and Father only had four years together."

"Why doesn't he speak of her?"

He took a moment. Placed the plate of unfinished gingerbread on the table beside him. "I think… He delivered Logan and me. It went wrong—too much hard labor, too much bleeding. She died under his hands. I think he blames himself." His father blamed himself for the death of Cam's mother the way Cam blamed himself for Logan's death. The similarity had never occurred to him before, but now the idea battered inside his head like the clanger of a great bell.

Her voice pulled him back.

"What a terrible burden." Elissa's voice came soft, sliding like tears. "Blaming yourself for the death of the person you love."

He nodded, slow and deliberate, a sage rewarding his pupil for understanding. "There's no way to put aside the guilt…and it's like carrying an Egyptian pyramid on your back." A pressure so great, it crushed your organs, your bones, your character. Your life.

"I'm so sorry you lost your twin, too."

He remembered telling her at Koulali, while they sipped tea. He and Logan had been so close, part of Cam died with Logan. Right there, in Sam Abernathy's pasture.

"Did you look identical?" She asked hesitantly, as though not sure if she should ask.

They had looked alike, but they'd been different men. Logan had been the peacemaker, always looking for a compromise. The one with a ready quip.

The urge to tell her about Logan burst from the pit of him, as if her question had opened Pandora's box. "We were identical. Logan died nine years ago. I have an older brother, Wallace." His speech was disjointed, but he couldn't find any other words.

Elissa knew loss. The day he met her, she told him about her family, but even when he knew he loved her, he'd been unable to do the same. He'd told himself it was better to wait until they returned to England, where they'd have more time and privacy, but he'd lied to himself. The truth was, he'd been afraid she might not love him if he told her. He'd known his fear was groundless, yet he couldn't tell her.

Now, he'd crushed her love, yet he trusted her. Elissa would never hurt him.

He saw her face mirrored his pain, and he had to look away.

Don't say it. Don't say it. Don't say it. He didn't want her pity. But he knew, even before he opened his mouth, the words were coming.

"Logan and I had just graduated from Edinburgh Medical School. We were just down the road from home, at Sam Abernathy's farm. Each of us needing to buy a horse." They'd been happy. Looking for mounts they'd use making home visits to their patients. Sharing their plans with Abernathy, an old family friend.

"What happened?" Dark foreboding stained her voice.

A sudden craving for whiskey called him like the irresistible song of Odysseus's Sirens. He needed a numbing, memory-clouding rush of drunken oblivion. He poured a glass of water, drank it down, and with careful precision, placed the empty glass back on the table.

Elissa's gold-flecked hazel eyes held steady. She seemed ready to listen, no matter what he said. Suddenly, he wanted to tell her. *Needed* to tell her.

"A wasp stung one of the horses and it kicked Logan in the throat. The blow crushed his larynx."

The kick had knocked Logan down. He lay in the dirt, hands gripping his throat, mouth working for air. Cam would never forget the fear and desperation in his brother's eyes, the way he clutched Cam's arm. The way his eyes pleaded. "There wasn't time to move him. He was suffocating. I tried to manipulate his throat, open his airway, but nothing helped. I had a pocket knife."

Elissa's gaze was riveted to him. "Cam…"

For a moment he was afraid she wanted him to stop, but nae. He saw she'd spoken his name in order to comfort. That was good, because he *couldn't* stop.

"I couldn't think of anything to do but a tracheotomy. I was desperate. I cut into his throat, but there was too much damage inside. I panicked. Wasted precious time feeling helpless. Then I—

saw Abernathy's pipe, sticking out of his pocket. I tried putting it in Logan's trachea, but...I was too late."

He squeezed his eyes shut, trying to block the image of Logan, a vertical incision opening his throat. Cam putting his finger into Logan's trachea, trying to create a space in the crushed airway. Feeling the tear in his trachea, and knowing it was hopeless. Even then, he'd still tried blowing his own breath into Logan's throat.

His father had heard. Had run to the pasture, where Cam still kneeled over Logan's body. Cam stood. Stood before Father with face and hands smeared with his brother's blood.

He remembered Father's pointing finger. How he stabbed Cam's chest so hard, Cam rocked back. "Look at you," Father shouted. "Your hands are *shaking.*"

And they were. Shaking so hard.

"How could you do this to your brother?" Father raged, a mad judge passing sentence, the verdict condemning Cam to a lifetime of guilt and despair. "How could you do *surgery*—here—in a *field*—with your hands *shaking!*"

That day, his hands trembled for hours.

In the Crimea, at the end, they never stopped trembling.

Elissa's fingers, curling around Cam's hand, brought him back to the present. Her mouth, pulled tight, made him want to rub his thumb over her lips, ease their tension until they resumed their natural, soft shape.

"Father couldn't bear to look at me. He blamed me. When Wallace heard, he did, too." Cam still heard their accusations. He'd been the hotheaded twin, and this time his impulsiveness had killed Logan. "I was inexperienced, and tried to do something I'd only read about. I'd already blamed myself, before Father arrived and had his turn."

"No." Elissa's voice squeezed out, sharp and raw as splintered bone.

The mattress gave; Elissa sat with her hip brushing his thigh. And then her arms were around him. Nothing had ever felt better, and he knew nothing ever would. He held her tight enough to feel her body move with each breath. She put her head on his shoulder. Tension spilled out of him and streamed away.

"It wasn't your fault, Cam."

He felt her lips on his cheek. Her nose pressed into his neck. Then her head settled back to his chest. She believed in him. He'd broken her heart, and yet there wasn't the slightest doubt in her voice, and she lay beside him, relaxed and loving. She trusted him.

"I'm an experienced surgeon now, and I know Logan's wound wasn't repairable. The injury was too severe." In his mind, he'd always known Logan's death wasn't his fault, but his heart had never believed. Until now. He thought, finally, he was ready to forgive himself.

He breathed her clean, piney-floral lavender scent. He wanted to close his eyes, lay here, and breathe in and out for hours. "Ye asked me, that day at Koulali's graveyard, if I was trying to atone for something. I was. Logan's death. Ye suggested I could never atone, but I could honor him by living a full and happy life. When I went back to the front, I planned to do that with you."

"What happened?" Elissa asked softly.

He ran his hands over her back, reacquainting himself with the shape and strength of her, loving the feel of her. "The war happened."

"There's no shame in that," Elissa said.

Utter relief cascaded through his chest and belly like a waterfall washing him clean, and he crushed her against him. She felt so good, so warm, so *right*.

He found her mouth, and desire exploded. So intense, so hot, it engulfed him and burned away everything but Elissa. Fireworks licked his brain and lit a raging need. He didn't want to put out the fire. He wanted to pull her into the flames and let the fire rage.

He deepened the kiss. Nudged his fingers into her silky hair. Pressed against her.

He slid down the bed. Pulled her down with him. They kissed—not just him kissing her, but *they* kissed—for a long time. He released a few of the buttons marching down the front of her dress. Enough to give his hands access to the flesh swelling above the edge of her corset. Enough to expose the skin that covered the ridge of her collarbone. It tasted sweet. So sweet, he couldn't resist a little nip. Her mouth, her skin, her form, made his entire body clench.

They weren't enough. He wanted more.

He unhooked the top part of her corset, edged his hand beneath her clothing, and cupped her breast. Sweet Jesus.

He wanted to be inside her, as intimate as a man and woman could get. Wanted her to understand how much he felt, how much she meant. She believed in him; she didn't judge. He'd been right in Koulali, to think he could do anything with her by his side. He just hadn't given her the chance. He wanted her next to him for the rest of his life. He loved her. Dear God, but he loved her.

"I want ye. Want ye to be mine." He spoke against her lips, punctuating each short phrase with sipping kisses.

She nodded. "I want you, too." Her voice sounded old and wise and young and giddy.

Her response burrowed straight to his heart, and tenderness engulfed him. He kissed the eyelids that descended when she felt shy, the space between her brows that creased when she was puzzled, the crest of her cheek that grew warm and red whenever he gave her a certain look. Kissed her temple, under which lay the organ that housed her kindness and intelligence and reason.

He rolled out of bed, strode to the door, turned the lock. Then went back and stretched over her.

He kissed her. Full, deep, each stroke of his tongue inside her sweet mouth tightening his body. "I don't know what I've done to endear me to ye, but however it happened, I'm glad of it."

"Don't you know what a fine man you are? How very much I admire you? You've overcome so much—the death of your brother and the misplaced guilt you've shouldered, the estrangement from your family, the overwhelming demands of war, and your battle with alcohol." She brushed a dangling lock back from his forehead then cupped her palm to the side of his face. "I have no doubts. I want to touch and taste and be filled by you." She paused. "I need to share my body and know yours." Her eyelids lowered. "And discover what happens when they join."

Her words speared intense desire through him. He kissed her again, thinking about what she'd liked when they explored each other on the bank of the Göksu. His sweet Elissa. There was no one else like her, so generous and forgiving.

She took a deep breath, her breasts rising and pressing against his chest.

He wanted, so much, to please her. "Our love will make it phenomenal," Cam said, surprised by how deep and husky his voice had become.

She slid her hands under his nightshirt, and soft fingertips explored their way up his torso. He pushed back, fisted the shirt, pulled it up and off, and tossed it to the floor.

She simply stared for a moment before kissing each side of his chest, just above his nipples. She opened her mouth and licked. He groaned and gripped her waist.

He nudged his fingers inside the waist of her skirt and felt for the strings tying skirt and petticoats closed. Perhaps a surgeon's fingers were nimble as a lady's maid's, for he located the strings, pulled them, and was sliding her skirts and petticoats down before a minute had passed. He sat up, drew the garments past her feet, bundled them together, and tossed it all into the chair. Then, with great care, he finished removing her bodice and corset.

He settled atop her again. Oh, dear Lord. Nothing more than his drawers and her shift separated them, and he felt every curve and swell and dip. Her shift lowered when he pulled at the neckline, exposing her shoulder and breast. Dear God. She was pink, and perfect, and beautiful. Just as he remembered her, only better. He licked, then took the peak of her breast more fully into his mouth and worked the tip with his tongue and teeth, loving the way she gasped and arched her back, and clutched him. She was salty and sweet, pure ambrosia.

He shifted his hips so he could slide his hand up the silky length of her thigh. She was hot and wet when he touched her, and they gasped together.

"Ah, *mo gràdh.*" He pressed his cock to her thigh. Christ, he wanted inside her. Ached with the need.

He stroked her clitoris, the rate and volume of her breaths increasing, while small sounds of pleasure came from her parted lips. He kissed her and slid his finger inside her. So hot and tight.

"Mmm." Her eyes closed, head tipped back, and the low sound was steeped in wonder.

He added a second finger, sliding, stretching, as her breathing hitched. The hands clutching his shoulders relaxed, slid down his back and pushed his drawers over his hips. Her hand curled around his cock.

"Please, Cam."

"Aye," he groaned. "Aye." His heart slammed against his sternum. This time, he wouldn't stop. He'd love her completely, as she asked.

He settled atop her, and knew he hadn't exaggerated. It would be phenomenal.

His cock was right there, rubbing over her entrance. So close. A small adjustment, and he'd be inside.

Her hands squeezed his buttocks. "Cam."

"All right, lass."

It was all he could do to hold himself back as he entered her. Quivering tightness. Heat. A barrier that gave and yet didn't. He wanted to bury himself in her.

He stopped. Somehow, good God, somehow, he held his lower body still. "Are ye all right, lass?" He kissed her mouth, her cheek, her neck below her ear. Already, her skin was flushed and moist.

"Is there…more?" she whispered.

He grunted. "Aye, *mo gràdh*. There's more."

"Yesssssss," Elissa said.

He thrust, and her breath hitched. He filled her, and she squeezed her arms around him. He'd breached her virginity. He wanted to comfort, and he murmured into her ear, though he had no idea what he said.

Prickles chased up his spine. He kissed her deeply. Pumped his hips. Short, slow strokes, becoming longer and faster as everything became both easier and more tense. Sensation sweeping, building, swelling. He didn't know if he could last until she peaked. Perhaps, this first time, it was too much to expect, but she was close, her tension growing in a manner not unlike his own. Their bodies became slick, their breathing labored. Their bellies slapped out carnal applause.

She moaned; her body locked, squeezed, quivered. He released, an intense surge of pleasure wringing him until all that remained was a puddle of bliss.

For a time neither of them moved. Their bodies calmed. Cam thought his satisfaction so intense, so deep and complete, he might be glowing. He rolled to his side, gathered Elissa, and pulled the bedcovers over them. Smoothed a loose lock of hair behind her ear. Eyes closed, she smiled.

He kissed her lips, angled his head, and kissed her again. Gave her lower lip a gentle suck. Took her hand, and threaded her fingers with his.

He took a deep breath. It seemed like years since he'd breathed with ease.

His ribs spread, his chest moved, and peace filled his lungs.

Her eyelids fluttered open. He was glad it was daytime, that he could see her clear hazel eyes. The green that was almost brown, graduating to dark amber around the pupils. The gold glints that gleamed brighter than ever before.

He lifted their clasped hands, kissed the back of hers. "I'll make the wedding arrangements right away."

Her eyelids fell. Too quick to be shyness. So quick, his stomach gave a nervous clench.

"You don't have to marry me." Pride shivered in her tone, like she'd barely managed to scrape it up, but was determined he have it. "I wanted you. I don't regret what we did. And I don't expect you to marry me."

Surprise and a little indignation bit him. Why didn't she expect him to marry her? Did she think he'd take her virginity and leave her? Along with his confusion, guilt pricked. He'd nearly done that before. He'd done everything but take her virginity, vowed his love, and disappeared two months later. Shame washed over him. He'd taught Elissa that she couldn't trust his word. And now she'd taught him a painful lesson in return.

She still stared at his neck, dammit. He needed to see her direct, honest eyes. He rubbed his thumb over the crest of her cheek. Tipped her chin with his finger. But her eyes remained hidden.

"Well. Ye might not expect me to marry ye, but I want to." With Elissa as his wife, the future would be better than he'd ever dared dream.

Her gaze lifted. What he saw made him jolt.

Uncertainty.

A messy mix of possibilities ran through his mind and tumbled into his chest with the force of a dropped boulder. Perhaps she believed he didn't want her, and he was lying. Or maybe she didn't want him, but didn't want to hurt him. She'd said she wanted him, but did she look at him and see a strong, admirable man? A man she desired? Or see a man she pitied?

She pressed the small, dark red stone of her ring to her lips. "Are you offering marriage out of gratitude? Because I believe in you? Because…I absolved you of blame for Logan's death, when your father wouldn't forgive you?"

"Nae." His voice broke. Hard. Like a key snapping off in a lock.

Why couldn't she believe he loved her? Maybe because she grew up without the love of a family. Or because it wasn't so easy to believe in him when he'd broken her heart once before.

"'Lissa. Are ye *afraid* to love me?" Because her family—all the people she'd loved—had left her. Him included, he realized with a heavy weight dropping into his belly. He palmed the back of her neck. Kissed her. A soft brush of lips. "I love ye. Ye make me so happy, lass. Do ye believe that?"

She crushed herself against him. Squeezed him tight, tight, tight.

He closed his eyes. Tightened his arms. Thank God. *Thank God.*

She relaxed. Drew back until they were face to face. "You made it clear when I first arrived at Primrose Hill," she said, "and again in Brighton, that you didn't want me." Her tongue darted out and moistened her lower lip. "Given what just happened, I know you desire me, physically. But I thought it might be more on my side."

Her cheeks grew pink. They'd be warm if he pressed his lips there.

"I wanted to make ye believe I didn't have feelings for ye." He'd succeeded, and knowing he'd wounded her almost killed him. "Ye deserve a better man, but in spite of my failures, we have something good between us. Something remarkable. It's not right to ignore feelings this powerful. We're meant to be together."

"You haven't failed. You've struggled. And you're overcoming every wretched problem you've faced." Her tone scolded him for suggesting otherwise.

She believed in him. The knowledge shot through his veins like a magic elixir, making him strong and sure and steady.

He captured her fingers, rubbed his thumb over her ring's red stone. "I hurt ye. Can ye forgive me?"

"Yes. Yes, I forgive you."

He kissed her. Hard. Deep. Long. He wanted her again.

But he should let her heal a bit. And he should propose like a gentleman.

"We'd better get dressed. Jakes will be bringing dinner in a while."

The corners of her lips tipped. "I should leave. If I'm here when Jakes arrives, I'll blush. I won't be able to look at him. He'll know." She began to roll away.

"Wait." He wrapped his hand more fully around hers. "Ye're not leavin' this bed until I get an answer." Her pupils were large and dark. The gold around them gleamed. He wanted to look into those eyes until the end of his days. "Marry me, *mo gràdh.*"

Mouth and eyes smiling, she answered with a kiss. Joy burst from the center of his chest and rushed to his arms, his legs, his head. This beautiful, laughing woman was his.

His to protect. Care for. Share a life with.

His to love.

"We'll need a house," Elissa said. "Can you—can we afford one?"

He chuckled. "We'll start looking right away." They'd marry at once. If they'd made a bairn today, no one would know they'd anticipated the ceremony.

"Will you find another position, or continue to work at Primrose Hill as a surgeon? Do you want to set up a surgery in the house?"

Cam's heart skipped then raced helter-skelter. He stood on the edge of a precipice, buffeted by the wind, trying to balance, and knowing, knowing, knowing he was about to fall. "I can't perform surgery any longer." Was that his voice? Shaky, cold-sweat fear snaked between the words.

Elissa frowned.

"Ye know I'm a prosthetist now." Elissa's hand went slack, and Cam tightened his hold. "What made ye think I was returning to surgery?"

Elissa pulled her hand away and sat up, sheet clutched at her throat. "What do you mean? Why wouldn't you return to surgery? You're the best surgeon I've ever seen." She looked helpless and confused.

Like a flea jumping dogs, Elissa's nervousness leaped to Cam. He needed to move. He grabbed his drawers, stood, jerked them on. "*Was* the best surgeon ye've ever seen. Not anymore."

224

"You haven't lost your skill. I know you haven't. You had some trouble in the Crimea, but lots of men did. The war is over, and you've stopped drinking."

A bad, bad feeling dropped into his stomach, like when a patient begged Cam to let him die.

"You're meant to be a surgeon." But instead of sounding certain, Elissa's voice pleaded. "I've seen you. Focused. Challenged. Refusing to give up on a patient. Why would you give up on yourself?"

How could this be? "I thought ye understood. I haven't given up, I've accepted." He held his open hands out. "I. Shake." He pressed his palm to his forehead. His skull felt like it was splitting apart. Of all people, how could Elissa not understand? "I can't do surgery if I shake!"

"I've never seen you shake. I know you did, but that's behind you. It's all behind you. You can be a surgeon again."

"I never know when the trembling will seize me. Ye don't know what it's like, but can ye imagine being in the middle of an operation and all at once not being able to control yer hands? While a man depends on you. For his future. Perhaps his life. And ye're trembling and helpless. I won't let that happen."

"When was the last time your hands shook during surgery?"

Irritation bit his nerves like a swarm of midges. He didn't enjoy having to strip his character bare because of her stubbornness. "There've been times I ate with my fingers, because I couldn't hold a fork. I didn't tremble during surgery, because whiskey kept the shakes away." If they shook, and a patient suffered for it, how would he live with himself?

"You were at the front. Under bombardment. How can you blame yourself for having a physical reaction to those conditions?"

The midges became wasps. His ears pulsed with their buzzing. "It didn't only happen in the Crimea." Their stinging stabbed his throat. "It happened when Logan died." His raspy voice sounded the way it had when he'd stood beside his brother's body. When he'd stood before his father and tried to explain.

That stopped her. The horror and pain on her face looked the way the noxious compound in his belly felt.

"I don't have the backbone necessary for a surgeon. When Logan died, I made excuses. Told myself I needed experience. Decided to gain it as an army surgeon. But now I've more experience than doctors a decade older, and the shaking's worse."

"No." Her voice spilled out, resistant and dejected. A woman grappling with the demon that had already gobbled him up. Grappling, and losing.

"Just accept it."

"Cam. You're the strongest man I know. When others are incapacitated with fear, you lead them through. Performing emergency surgery on your brother? Of course you shook. But you weren't responsible for his death."

He wanted to throw something. Break something. Destroy something. But not the intangible, new, wondrous something between him and Elissa.

He paced. Tried to find an anchor for his hands. Finally, he palmed the back of his neck with one hand. Fisted the other. Stopped and faced her.

"Ye think I'm strong? Sweet Jesus. I may drink again tomorrow. Tonight."

"I'm here. I'll help you. *You're meant to be a surgeon.* Not a prosthetist. If you aren't a surgeon—doing what you love—you won't be happy. *We* won't be happy." Her face went pale. She pressed her hand to her chest. "It's not just your opportunity for happiness, Cam. It's mine, too. *Our* chance will be gone if you remain a prosthetist. Marriage won't change that."

She was hammering his heart apart. A fountain of desperation shot from the poor, mangled organ. "Ye're wrong, lass. We can have a good life." He needn't worry about mere tremors. In another minute he would start shaking so hard, he'd shake apart.

She threw back the bedcovers and sprang from the bed. Began putting on her clothes. Face flushed, eyes averted, mouth tight. She jerked clothing strings—first corset strings, then petticoat and skirt ties—hard enough to cut off air. Face tight, she sat, pulled her shoes on and jerkily tightened the laces.

He realized he still wore nothing but drawers. He strode to his clothing chest, pulled out a clean pair of trousers and tugged them on.

Elissa stood. Her hands, one atop the other, pressed against her middle. When his focus shifted to the downward curve of her mouth, his small measure of hope shriveled and died. Nae. Nae, nae, nae. He clasped his hands, pressed his thumbnails to his mouth. Willed her to give them a chance.

She wrapped her arms around her waist. "Can you tell me you've been happy—even one day—since you stopped working as a surgeon? If you can, that changes everything."

He couldn't lie, so he didn't answer. "Ye'll make the difference, 'Lissa. Ye make me happy."

"No. I can love you—I *do* love you—but I can't fill your emptiness. I can't replace what you've given up. And if that hole isn't filled, our marriage is doomed." Her lower lip trembled. "I can't. Marry you."

Something inside his chest twisted and tore. She hadn't really ripped his heart out, but the pain felt as if she had. He might even be bleeding to death, as woozy as his brain felt.

"You're denying your true self, and I...I...I refuse—" Her choked voice faltered. She drew in two short, sharp breaths. Lifted her chin. "—refuse to help. The man I know—the man I love—is a surgeon. Not a prosthetist." Her eyelids closed.

"Lass, ye're not thinkin' straight. We—"

Her lids snapped open. "I am thinking straight. I see everything quite clearly, in fact. I could accept your being a prosthetist if it made you proud, and excited, and fulfilled. Like surgery did. But you see prosthetics as puzzles to be solved." She went to the door and placed her hand on the knob. "I know you enjoy helping the men. I'm glad that pleases you. But it doesn't fulfill you the same way. I admire what you're doing here, but if you don't follow your heart, you'll molder away."

"Ye say ye want me to be happy, but by refusing me, ye're takin' away my best chance. The truth is, ye don't trust me. Don't trust that I can make ye happy. Give me another chance, 'Lissa. I won't let you down." Not this time. Not ever again. Desperation and disbelief grew larger and larger while he searched her expression for something that would tell him she'd changed her mind.

Her eyes glistened. He took a step toward her, but she shook her head in a quick, frantic motion. He froze.

"I'd give anything to be wrong, but... Just don't start drinking, Cam. Please don't."

She left.

Left him staring at the door. What in bloody hell had happened? What was he supposed to do now?

Did she think he hadn't tried? He *hated* that he couldn't perform surgery. Hated that, as much as he wanted to put his past behind him, he couldn't.

His nerves jumped like chattering teeth. He needed to do something physical. Or drink.

He wanted to hit something. Hard. His mind flashed to the hospital gymnasium and the horse-hair-stuffed bag hanging from the ceiling, used for punching and kicking.

He could exhaust himself. Pummel the bag until he'd pounded the rage ripping through his chest into oblivion.

He might be able to subdue his anger. He hoped he could. But the raw hurt went too deep.

The horrible wound couldn't be sutured. Or ignored. He couldn't even use whiskey, which would have offered some anesthesia.

At least, no whiskey for now. Not until he learned their lovemaking hadn't produced a child. Not until Archer no longer posed a threat. Not until he knew Elissa faced a happy and secure life. A life without him.

CHAPTER TWENTY-EIGHT

Jakes walked through Elissa's office doorway, teapot held in one hand, cup and saucer balanced in the other. He set the cup and saucer on her desk, filled it, then set the teapot down.

Elissa sat back. For the past two weeks, since she'd returned to work after that momentous day with Cam, Jakes had appeared every afternoon with tea. His friendship helped get her through the day. So did her work, although she'd begun to think she needed to search for another position. Cam's unseen presence pulled at her constantly. He was so close...*happiness* was so close, yet she sat here, alone, mourning yet another separation. This one her fault. It seemed they were destined to never be together.

Jakes pulled a second cup from his pocket, filled it, and sat. From his other pocket, he withdrew something wrapped in a napkin. "Lucky we both take our tea without milk or sugar. I'm limited to only these pockets."

This ritual accompanied Jakes's daily tea service, so Elissa knew the last item would be a pastry of some sort. He sat the napkin-bundle on her desk and peeled each folded corner back like a mother unwrapping her newborn babe. The last corner unfolded.

"Cherry tart." From the pride in his tone, it was the best tart to be had in Britain.

It did look good. Elissa picked the miniature pie up, bent it in half, and pulled it apart to make two halves. The smell of buttery pastry and cherries wafted to her nose. She placed one half of the tart on the napkin and slid it toward Jakes. The other half she bit into. Sweet and tangy, the flavors burst on her tongue.

Since *that day* with Cam, her sleep had been fitful. Food had lost its appeal. Almost at once, the shadows under her eyes and lack of energy drew comments. She worried she'd lose her strength and health, and wouldn't be able to do her job.

Then she took herself in hand. She might not be able to sleep, but she could force herself to eat something at each meal. So she did, but she didn't enjoy the food.

Jakes's treats were the exception. His biscuits and cakes, presented as if he were offering a delicacy from the Queen's kitchen, were the tastiest she'd ever eaten. She relished those few minutes in her day, when she enjoyed Jakes's companionship and his sweets. She knew he'd created this daily respite out of concern for her.

He'd never asked why she'd stopped watching over Cam. That last day, when Jakes arrived with their meals, he'd have found Cam alone. She didn't know what passed between them, but she'd not given Jakes any explanation. And he'd never asked.

He knew something. And he must know what happened had been bad. Because Jakes served her tea with as much kindness as she gave the patients who hurt the worst.

Jakes stuffed his whole half-tart into his mouth. Chewed. Swallowed. "Archer's leaving tomorrow." One corner of his mouth hitched up. His brows lifted and fell.

A crumb stuck in Elissa's throat. She coughed. Took a quick drink of tea. "Already? Given his malicious talk when he arrived, and the scuffle with MacKay, I expected to be in for a great deal of misery. But he hasn't bothered me." Thanks to Jakes being her liaison, she'd been able to ignore Archer. She'd made sure Archer's gymnasium schedule coincided with the time of day she read to the men.

Jakes swallowed a mouthful of tea and rested the cup on his thigh. "Mr. MacKay warned him. Several times. Lawrence watches Archer, and reports to MacKay."

Between breaths, Elissa went from relaxed to rigged-for-storm tight. "Warned him?"

"Warned...threatened...he took care of it." Jakes laughed. A laugh unlike any she'd heard from him. Low. And nasty. "You should see Archer's eyes when MacKay comes to the ward. Lethal."

She shivered.

"It must have killed him, having MacKay make his prosthesis," Jakes said. "Checking his stump every day for pressure spots. All the men know, and the ward gets quiet as a church when MacKay's with Archer."

She froze. "The men know...what?"

"That there's bad blood between MacKay and Archer. There're still men on the ward who were here when Archer arrived, and heard the way he attacked you. The minute he did that, he became their enemy." Jakes's mouth curled with another smirk. "It hasn't been easy for him."

With her obsessive thinking about Cam, she'd almost forgotten about Archer. She'd had no idea Cam, Jakes, all of them, had been watching over her.

Jakes set his teacup on her desk, rested his wrists against his flat belly, and tapped the tips of his fingers together. "MacKay stopped drinking to get the upper hand on Archer. In order to protect you."

Jakes's words drove the breath from her lungs. "What?" squeaked from her throat.

Jakes nodded. A slow up-down of his head. His face scrunched. "I wasn't supposed to tell you."

Cam stopped drinking, and suffered through horrendous physical distress, out of concern for her? Why had she never asked what had motivated him to stop? She hadn't even wondered.

Jakes's confession meant, even when Cam drank and spurned her, his true feelings had been powerful. She'd felt that power when he'd made love to her. Was she wrong to refuse his proposal? He loved her. Would it matter if he wasn't quite as happy as a prosthetist, as he would have been as a surgeon, as long as they were together?

She'd been so sure he'd become miserable. If they married, it would make matters worse. She'd be worried and downhearted, and he'd blame himself.

She recalled his final accusation. That she didn't trust him. Was he right? Perhaps, in part, he was. But he'd broken her heart. As much as she loved and wanted him, a small part of her questioned if she could trust him not to do it again.

Do I trust myself? The thought wriggled in her head like a snake. The people she loved most—her family—had died. Was she capable of deep, wholehearted love? Unlimited, unrestricted love. The kind of love Cam deserved.

The thought of making a life with him, the risk of it, frightened her. What if she lost him, as she had her family? Had she placed conditions on him out of fear? She'd never thought herself a coward, but shame had shackled her. Each day she saw MacKay stride past her office door. That glimpse of him meant everything. She knew the cadence of his walk, and listened for his footsteps. When she heard them, anticipation twisted her belly. Thrashed her heart against her ribs. Held her breathless on a precipice of hope.

She waited for him to stop, turn, walk into her office. Take her in his arms.

He never turned his head to look in. Not once.

Day after day, when he passed her door, stride steady and purposeful, her anticipation and hope wilted and collapsed. Shriveled and died. Crumbled and blew away.

Then she remembered. *She* ended it. *She* left him.

Now they ignored each other. Was he angry? Had he forgiven her? She'd ended things as surely as he had when he'd returned to England. He must be going through all the same emotions she'd experienced. The thought brought her up short. Because she knew, deep in her heart, she hadn't quite forgiven him for throwing away her love. He'd hurt her.

Now she was hurting him just as badly. Unless her rejection had killed his love. Her shoulders and arms grew heavy. She set her teacup down and let her hands fall to her lap. An image of Cam formed in her mind, and the last thread of her anger and resentment snapped.

She forgave him. It felt good, freeing, but it didn't really change anything.

"MacKay's doing well," Jakes said. "Goes to the gymnasium every day."

A movement in the doorway drew Elissa's attention. Evie Riley stood there.

"I'm interrupting." The hesitation in Evie's voice matched the way she poised in the office entry. Like a skittish deer prepared to dart away.

Elissa stood and hurried to Evie. Jakes stood and turned.

"Not at all, Mrs. Riley. Please come in." Elissa turned to include Jakes. "You know Corporal Jakeman." The news of Jakes's promotion had been celebrated not long after his official posting to the hospital.

Evie's gaze darted to Jakes for a moment before dropping. Her cheeks flushed. Elissa did some rapid calculations. It had been a year and a half since George Riley's regiment left England and Evie last saw her husband. Eight months since she'd received news of his death.

"Good afternoon, ma'am." Jakes's voice held the delight of a child receiving an unexpected present. "May I get you a cup of tea? Miss Lockwood and I were just enjoying a cup."

"Thank you. You're very kind." Evie sounded like he'd offered an appointment with the Queen.

Jakes took the teapot with him, and Elissa showed Evie to a chair.

"I'm sorry I didn't send a note telling you to expect me, but the Burtons made a quick decision to visit family for a few days. Mrs. Burton told me to work half-days while they're gone, and use the extra time for myself."

"You must come to dinner," Elissa urged. Time had slipped away. Two months had passed since Evie Riley collected her husband's locket, and she and Elissa met. "I didn't intend for so much time to pass without extending an invitation. Could you come tomorrow?"

"I'd be delighted." Evie's head tilted. "I hope you don't think I'm here to coax an invitation from you. I hoped to see Mr. MacKay. I wrote, but I'd like to thank him in person."

"Jakes can check at the workshop and see if he's free." Could she invite MacKay to Evie's dinner party? She didn't think he'd come, but she could ask. She hated the anger and hurt between them. She saw him almost every day, yet they didn't even exchange greetings.

It had only been two weeks. But it felt like two lifetimes. She needed to see him and talk to him and make sure he was truly all right.

She wondered if he thought of her, and buried himself in his work, as she did. If he were as miserable as she was. If he'd changed his mind. Had she changed hers? She hadn't. She loved him. Wanted to be with him. Wanted to make him happy, but didn't think she could. He'd quit drinking for her, but that didn't mean she could fill what was missing because surgery was absent from his life. She might even increase his discontent, because he'd feel that he was disappointing her. Not because she made him feel that way, but because deep inside, he disappointed himself. She knew. There was an intensity about him when he performed surgery that she'd never seen in anyone else.

She needed to see him. Have his gaze sweep over her and make her body come alive. Hear him call her lass and feel her heart flutter. And she'd assure herself he was staying strong. See that she'd done the right thing. Know he'd be fine without her. So she could go on. Right now, obsessive thinking about him occupied her brain. *What if he isn't fine?* She shivered. He had to be.

She wasn't sure she could bear to see him alone and look into his unguarded eyes, as they might be if no one else were with them. She'd tried to write, but couldn't.

"Why don't I invite Mr. MacKay to our dinner?" Saying it made her blood fizz, her spine tingle, her brain turn somersaults. "I'll invite Jakes, too. We'll make a regular party of it."

Jakes returned with a full teapot and another cup and saucer. He set both on her desk. "Please excuse me. I'm needed on the ward."

"Before you leave, I've invited Mrs. Riley to supper tomorrow. I hope you can join us?"

Jakes's head jerked. His blue eyes glinted like sun bouncing off a lake.

"I'll be there," Jakes promised.

#

Muscles rigid, Cam bent his knees and lowered the barbell to the gymnasium floor. He released the bar, straightened, and swiped sweat from his forehead with his sleeve. He rolled his shoulders. Tilted his head side to side and stretched his neck.

Physical exercise had become his panacea, and he spent every evening in the gymnasium. Exhaustion helped subdue his craving for whiskey. Helped repress his nightmares. Helped control thoughts of Elissa—and the urges that accompanied those thoughts. It didnae keep him from wondering if she was right, though, that his not being a surgeon would lead to misery.

As far back as he could remember, he and Logan had wanted to be surgeons. While boys, they'd splinted and stitched wounded animals under the supervision of Father. The proudest day of Cam's life had been when he'd qualified as a surgeon. The profession had tested and matured him and never disappointed. In the war, he'd acquired a reputation as a practitioner of skill and compassion, but in the end Cam hadnae measured up. Not the fault of the profession, but of his own shortcomings.

He approached making prosthetics in much the same way as he'd approached surgery. He was good at solving problems, encouraging patients, using care and not being satisfied with less than his best. He enjoyed it and he'd met with success. Liked it a lot, in fact, but…it wasnae the same.

How would he feel in a year? Two? Three? Would his dissatisfaction grow? Would he be content with complacency? He'd been thinking about it for weeks now, ever since she left him. What if their situations were flipped? If he and Elissa were married, and she loved him, but wasnae happy with the rest of her life, how would he feel? Would her dissatisfaction bleed into their love and poison it? Would she resent his untampered happiness?

He held up his hands. Steady. *Could* he go back to surgery? The thought sent nervous excitement whizzing through his veins. He rubbed the back of his neck. The possibility didn't just excite him. It scared him, too. If he failed, what would stop his falling back into the bottle and back into the well of despair he'd been trapped in the past months? Would he be able to stay sober?

He chose a dumbbell and stood feet apart, back straight. Pulled the dumbbell to his shoulder, then let his arm relax to his side. Did it again. And again.

The door opened. Elissa stood there.

He tensed. *Hell.* She must intend to see him. He was alone in the room. He tightened his grip and increased the rate of his lifts.

She walked toward him, her steps slowing the nearer she came. She stopped. Offered a hesitant smile. Her gaze ran up and down his frame, and she swallowed. *Hell.*

"What are ye doin' here?" He'd been rude, but he didn't want her here, making his already turbulent emotions even more tempestuous. Reminding him that he was too much a failure to win her. Feeding his guilt with the efficiency of a stoker shoveling coal into a steam engine firebox.

"I'm here to invite you to a dinner party."

Anger shot from his twisted gut to his head. Pure luck held his brains together. "A dinner party? Delightful. We can make polite conversation and enjoy each other's wit."

She shifted from one foot to the other, making her skirt sway. "I've invited George Riley's widow. She wants to thank you. My landlady, Mrs. Emerson, and Jakes will also be there."

Cam let the dumbbell drop to the floor. It hit with a bang, and Elissa jumped.

"Have ye lost yer mind?" Cam asked.

Red stained her cheeks. "I...miss you. I thought we might be...friends."

Hurt, disguised as words, spilled from his mouth. "Oh, aye. Nothing I'd like better than being yer bosom friend. Have ye confide in me. Ye can share the details of yer engagements with the duke. Tell me how he makes yer heart go pitapat. When he proposes, I'll be first to hear the news and wish ye joy."

Her mouth tightened. "You're acting ridiculous."

He hated the strain on her face. He was a bloody bastard, talking to her this way. But having her pretend they could go on as if they hadn't shared their bodies—shared love... She'd sliced his soft belly open.

He focused his gaze on the floorboards. Fought the pull of her.

He'd managed to carry on as if he were fine—when he passed her open office door, heard her voice drifting down the hall, imagined he caught a whiff of her lavender scent. The nights were even more difficult, yet he hadn't blubbered or sought a bottle— even when he remembered the taste and feel of her, the sounds she made when he loved her, the way her face looked, aglow with love.

But he wasnae strong enough. He didn't have it in him to be pleasant and pretend his heart wasnae hemorrhaging. Not when she stood right in front of him.

He folded his arms. Made his voice so hard, the words ripped from his throat like shards of shrapnel. "We cannae be friends."

She flinched.

Ah, hell. Why did she think they might start over? Did she think they could forget all they'd shared? She might try to forget, might pretend she wasnae affected, but he knew better.

He'd been in her arms when she held him so tight, he felt her heart pounding against his ribs.

He softened his voice. Took the anger and hurt out, and left the truth. "*I* cannae be your friend. I still *want* ye. Being with ye, watching ye smile—would be torture."

The way she'd pinned her gaze to his folded arms, he couldn't see her eyes. He dropped his arms, but her gaze remained centered near his waist.

She nodded. Flicked a glance at him and turned toward the door.

Dread built in his chest like steam in a boiler. The pressure and burn so great, he expected his heart to become a rock she might kick down the street.

She was leaving.

"Elissa." She stopped. Face to the door, back to him. "Has yer flow come, lass?"

He almost groaned aloud. He hadn't meant to say that. Aye, he was worried, but he must be daft to bring it up now.

She turned her head enough to reveal the curve of her cheek. "Any day now." Her voice was hollow, brittle, absent of feeling. Three words that were splinters torn from his killing blow.

She went through the door and let it slam shut.

Cam's knees bent. He sank down. Crouched, head in hands. Fell onto his arse. And he roared.

CHAPTER TWENTY-NINE

The next morning Elissa rested her elbows on her desk and cradled her forehead, the heels of her hands pressed to her eyes. She'd already drunk tea made of feverfew and chamomile, but so far the tea hadn't affected her megrim.

A noise made her drop her hands. Archer stood in her open doorway. Revulsion smacked so strong, she had to grab her desk to keep from shrinking away. Her stomach rolled, and a ferocious throb of pain to her temple made her squint.

"I'm discharged. MacKay's given me a fancy hand, but I rather like the old workaday one." He raised his arm, showing off the hook fixed to his stump. Its lethal-looking tip glinted.

He strolled to her desk. Elissa stood as if yanked from her chair. The corner of his mouth curled in a smirk. She ignored the icy prickles that chased down her spine when his black eyes trailed down her form. She would not give him the satisfaction of seeing her hatred and fear.

Where were Jakes and Lawrence, her supposed watchdogs?

"Couldn't leave without saying goodbye to my old nurse supervisor. The woman who occupied the fantasies of the Koulali orderlies." He came around the end of her desk.

She swallowed her gasp. Her heart pounded in her chest. Drummed in her head. "Stop." She wanted to cringe at the weak breathiness in her voice. His eyes glittered. As hard as she tried to hide her alarm, she knew he must sense it.

She had nothing to prove. She should leave. Run. But this was *her* office. Her feet stuck as if no longer a part of her. He stopped an arm's length away. Close enough to touch.

"You should have heard the chorus of grunts and moans each night in the orderlies' quarters, once they were all abed. Just imagine twenty men in one room, all sounding like MacKay when he comes in you."

His crudeness crashed over her like an icy wave. Her feet released, and she backed up. He advanced. She palmed the back of her chair to steady her pudding legs. She tried to think. He was using the sex talk to intimidate her, to get close and make her afraid. She'd know if he lusted after her, and he never had.

He took one more step forward. Fear, shock, repugnance—all coalesced. Anger exploded from her core like cannon shot.

"Get out." She planted her hand in the middle of his chest and pushed. He rocked back. His face turned feral.

His hard, narrow hand grabbed her wrist and squeezed. The pain almost buckled her knees, it was so intense. Like he was crushing her bones.

He jerked her against him. Wrapped his arm tight around her back, pinning her free arm. Forced her captured hand down and, laughing, rubbed it against his erection.

Like an animal in a trap, she panicked. Tried to pull away. Struggled as hard as she could, but instead of loosening, his hold grew tighter. Until she was flush against him.

So close, she felt his breath on her face. Smelled the tobacco smoke scent that clung to him. Saw his eyes weren't black, but dark, dark brown, filled with obsidian chips. Felt excitement and satisfaction hum through his body and realized her fear and rage and helpless struggling gave him great pleasure.

She found her breath, her voice, and screamed.

He released her and ran. Ran right into Cam, who charged through the doorway and shoved the smaller man with enough force to send him flying. Archer crashed against the wall and dropped to the floor.

For a moment Cam stood, legs spread, fists clenched, and looked at Archer.

His grim face turned to Elissa. "Are ye all right, lass?"

Hot green eyes skimmed her from head to toes. Settled on her hand, rubbing the wrist Archer pinched. She'd have bruises tomorrow.

"Yes," she said, her voice steadier than the rest of her.

Jakes and Lawrence ran in, Jakes pausing in the doorway to dismiss some other men in the hallway beyond. By the time Archer scrambled to his feet, Jakes and Lawrence had his arms. Had him caught. She'd never felt such intense hatred, filling her mind, her core, the marrow of her bones.

Archer spat. "You yellow bastard, MacKay. You're not *braw* enough to meet me without your henchmen?" Archer's sneering voice made her stomach turn.

A muscle in Cam's jaw bulged. She'd heard him use the word braw—Scottish for brave. As if Archer's taunts weren't enough, he'd mocked Cam's nationality. Elissa moved toward the group of men. She wanted to be close to Cam, even if it meant she'd also be in Archer's proximity.

"Come on. Give me a chance to deliver a bit of comeuppance. I'll even take off the claw. You know I deserve the chance. You sent me to the front, man!"

Mouth tight, Cam shook his head. Elissa reached his side. She'd give anything to touch him. To take his hand. Instead, she thumbed her mother's garnet ring.

Archer's gaze flicked between her and Cam. "At least I sampled your strumpet."

Cam went rigid. Archer's gleeful eyes might have licked her up and down, the way they raked her body.

It was the last straw. And it was *her* right to punish him. Elissa stepped forward and slapped him.

The men jerked. Archer's mouth fell open and his cheek turned bright red. Her palm stung.

Cam put his hand to her waist. Drew her back until she stood in the curve of his arm.

"Toss him out," Cam said, low and quiet and with a hardness that made chills race down her back.

Jakes and Lawrence hustled Archer away. They cleared the door, and Carlisle stood there.

"What's this?" Carlisle asked. His gaze went to where Cam's hand grasped her waist. Elissa stepped away and Cam's arm dropped to his side.

She hadn't thought Cam's unhappy glower could become any more intense, but it did.

"It's over." Cam's decisive tone made clear he wasn't going to explain anything to Carlisle. He ignored the duke and focused on her. "Are ye all right, lass?"

No. She wasn't all right. Archer had frightened her. Hurt her. Brought out a violence she'd never before experienced. She wanted Cam's arms around her so much, her weight shifted to the balls of her feet and tilted her toward him.

His forest-green eyes were deep pools of regret and concern. "Elissa?"

Carlisle made a noise, and shock pitched her back to her heels. MacKay had used her given name in front of Carlisle, as if they were betrothed.

She lifted her hands—her shaking hands—to her temples, where devils' pitchforks stabbed. "My head's been hurting all morning. I'm going home." Getting away from Carlisle and Cam, each trying to claim his position as the man who held her affection, would help immensely.

"I'll take you." Carlisle's firm tone warned he'd brook no argument.

She nodded. Retrieved her coat and bonnet from the rack beside the door. Carlisle came into the room and helped her don her coat while Cam watched.

She stepped to the door. Paused, and looked at Cam. His lips pressed together into a thin line, as if in punishment for letting her given name slip through. A vessel in his neck pulsed.

She steeled herself against the yearning and passed into the hall.

#

That evening Elissa studied the faces around Carlisle's dining table. The last of her apprehension drained away. Her friends appeared relaxed, participating in the conversation, and enjoying the meal. She hadn't been certain they'd be comfortable at the home of the duke. She still wasn't sure exactly how they'd come to be here.

"I'm happy Father included me tonight," Carlisle's son, Richard, said. The duke had seated her at the head of the table, in the hostess's place. His son, Lord Peyton, sat on her right.

Elissa turned her attention to Peyton. "Meeting you is an unexpected pleasure. Carlisle took me by surprise, insisting I move my dinner party to his home. I don't imagine we're typical of his guests, but he's put everyone at ease." With the beautiful table and superb food, he seemed to have made magic happen in just a few hours. Of course, a duke's staff could manage a dinner party three times the size of this one, even impromptu.

That morning, when Carlisle escorted her home, he'd invited her to dinner. Said he'd spent the week out of town thinking about her. Said he couldn't wait another day to see her. Head pounding, shaken by the events in her office, she'd become flustered. When she told him Jakes and the widow of a former patient were dining with her and Mrs. Emerson that evening, he'd insisted they all come to his home instead. Somehow, he'd convinced her to agree.

She'd had to tell Mrs. Emerson about the change in plans, since they no longer needed a meal prepared. Her landlady had spent the day in a jumble of nerves. Elissa hadn't let Jakes or Evie Riley know. Being the guest of a duke for the first time was an event that could produce a state of anxiety in the steadiest person. Feeling certain Jakes and Evie would dress in their finest, Elissa decided to spare them the nerves.

She hadn't been nervous, but confused and agitated and on the verge of tears. Her head throbbed so hard, she took a teaspoon of laudanum and went to bed. When she woke the megrim was gone, leaving her pain free, if a little muzzy-headed. Carlisle sent his carriage, and Elissa bundled everyone in.

Her mind still felt a bit foggy. She considered Peyton. The young man bore a strong resemblance to his father. They had the same lean, elegant body, the same black hair. And though his eyes were not gray, but blue, they held the same sharp intelligence as Carlisle's.

Peyton nodded, acknowledging her comment about the unexpected invitation. "Father has never been a slave to convention. He's independent. Forms his own opinions and isn't afraid to act on them."

"So he's always been this…impartial? Dukes don't usually offer invitations to such plain people as nurses and orderlies and widows of soldiers." They didn't court them, either.

Peyton set down his fork. "He's always been a fair man, but not to the degree he is now. Michael's death changed him." Peyton's jaw firmed. "It was the so-called common people who offered genuine sympathy. Who shared and comforted. Who missed Michael and mourned his death. Those who knew him felt some form of guilt that they hadn't realized the state he was in." Peyton paused. He squeezed his eyes shut a moment then gave his head a shake.

"Father's peers were scandalized that Michael killed himself. Found it a topic for titillating gossip. Felt Father was better off not having a legless son."

Elissa placed her hand on Peyton's forearm. "Some people can be unimaginably cruel. I'm so sorry he had that to contend with in addition to Michael's injury and death." Thank God the duke had come out intact. According to Carlisle, everything he'd endured had made him a more compassionate and generous man. It was why he was so sociable with the Primrose Hill patients and staff. He shook their hands, talked with them, listened to them. All admired Carlisle, and commented on how his open friendliness was the opposite of what they expected from a duke.

"Michael's death was horrible enough. The attitudes of society's elite made coping with his death so much worse. Father became angry. Disillusioned. Disgusted. He began seeking out those he referred to as people with honorable souls." Peyton glanced down at her hand, patted it, then shifted. She pulled her hand away. "My sister and I were just as lost as Father. We tried out Father's new philosophy for ourselves. I'd never have believed striking up acquaintances with people who work for their living could add so much to my life."

The space between his brows creased. "I suppose Michael started it. He wrote about some of the soldiers under his command. One or two sergeants in particular. I know most officers hold themselves separate from the rank and file, but Michael wrote how fighting alongside his men changed him. He valued them."

Peyton took a drink of wine then leaned back against his chair. One corner of his mouth tipped. "As much appreciation as Father has gained of common people, he hadn't yet invited any to dine. It was your influence that caused him to do so."

Realization struck. This conversation wasn't just about Carlisle. Or his son. It was about Carlisle and *her*. Peyton's tone wasn't resentful or condemning. If anything, he sounded impartial and honest and kindhearted like his father.

"He's spoken of me?"

"Several times."

Today, riding home in Carlisle's luxurious carriage, she'd been overcome with discomfort. Everything had changed. The past week she'd become a different woman.

She'd given herself to Cam. Given her heart. And had it shattered.

Now Carlisle was back, his warm eyes trailing over her like caressing fingers. Whatever had been growing between them, she had to end it. Immediately.

She looked down the table. He was laughing at something Jakes said. What was wrong with her, that she kept hurting good men?

"Miss Lockwood?"

She turned to Peyton said. "Yes?"

"Father's fond of you."

"We've become friends. He's an admirable man."

His head tilted. "I approve, Miss Lockwood," he said, voice deep and soft. "Of you. That's all I wanted you to know. I approve of you."

He could tame wild beasts with that voice, but why had he used it on her? But, she knew. He wanted to reassure her, let her know he wouldn't object if Carlisle were to propose.

Evie Riley laughed at something Jakes said. Peyton straightened and turned his attention to the other diners. Relief washed over Elissa like the cold water of McGinty's Pond when she jumped in on a hot day. Jakes the storyteller had them all in thrall.

"She loves stopping at all the best parts of the story," Jakes said.

What? He was telling tales about *her*?

"You should hear the men moaning and groaning when she snaps the book closed. And then she gives them a grin. Kind of an imp-like grin, you know? But for all their grumbling, you should see the smiles the next day when she walks back in with the book."

Carlisle looked at her. Could the others see the warmth in his eyes? In his face? Of course they could. It was there every time he looked at her. She had to speak with him tonight.

Jakes glanced around the table. "Jimmy Banks's parents are part of a traveling theatrical troop, and Jimmy was born into it. Acted until he joined up. He says Miss Lockwood's as good at reading lines as the best of them. She can make the men laugh or twist with discomfort."

All but Evie, whose gaze was pinned on Jakes, looked at her and chuckled. Peyton's shoulders shook. "Jakes is the one who keeps them laughing," Elissa protested.

"And you make them laugh, cry, and hold in curses until they're right close to bursting. Right now she's reading a book by an American, Herman Melville. *The Whale*. I wish you could have seen the men when she voiced the ship's captain. Him vowing he'd chase the whale," Jakes said, dropping his voice, "'round perdition's flames before I give him up.'"

Elissa forced the corners of her lips up, and curled her toes. She felt like she was dancing around flames. And getting too close.

#

Carlisle stood at her side. With dinner finished, and tea and sherry dispensed in the sitting room, Elissa knew they'd soon be leaving. She tilted closer to her host and pitched her voice low. "Might we speak privately?"

He plucked her glass from her fingers, wrapped her hand around his arm, nodded to his guests, and escorted her from the room. He walked with purposeful gait to the main hall, paced that expanse, and steered her through a doorway that opened to the library.

Dark green walls. Brown leather chairs tucked close to a fireplace. A comfortable-looking chaise placed near a big window. At one end, an adjoining room held a large desk. And books. Hundreds of books.

Carlisle left the door open and guided her to a velvety settee. Nerves ramped to knife-edge keen, Elissa bent her knees and sat. He sat beside her, his knees a finger length away from hers. The space between his brows creased.

"Why do I think I'm not going to like what you say?" he asked.

The man was astute. Elissa rolled dry lips into her mouth, seeking moisture. *Blast it.* "I'm not sure how to say this."

He took her hand. Squeezed a little. "You can tell me anything."

She tugged her hand away. "We don't suit." The voice she used to comfort squeezed out, the undertone wary and regretful and apologetic.

His chin jutted forward. "I'm certain we do suit." He frowned. "What makes you say this?"

She shook her head. She couldn't explain *why*.

Quiet, he looked at her.

She avoided his eyes. Locked her hands together and stared at her white knuckles.

He took a sharp breath through his nose and growled, "It's MacKay."

She looked at him.

She knew hurt. Knew how it looked. This was anger.

A muscle at the hinge of Carlisle's jaw bulged. His lips clamped into a thin, tight line. His gray eyes turned dark, like thick, choking smoke hiding a snapping, roaring wildfire.

He took two more breaths through his nose. "May I offer my best wishes for your happiness?"

Her fingers began tapping against her leg as if possessed. She couldn't continue to sit, fingers tapping, insides jumping. She stood. Carlisle followed an instant behind, and positioned himself even closer.

His eyes narrowed. "No answer," he muttered. "I think I deserve to understand the situation, Elissa."

Oh, he'd used her name. And there was the pain, sparking deep in those dark eyes. The anger had hidden it.

"We're not engaged. Nor likely to be." One hand atop the other, she pressed them against her stomach. Forced her gaze to hold steady on his. Breathed. In. Out. Dredging up the words. "I love him."

His chin jerked up and he stepped back. Looked away.

She didn't feel close to tears, but her chest ached with the tightness that accompanied a crying fit.

"Has he wronged you?" An undertone of danger laced his words. Hard and intense enough to send a shiver racing down her spine.

He was asking if they'd made love. If Cam had refused to offer marriage.

She shook her head. Carlisle wanted to know too much. But, blast it, her eyes were hot and her vision was blurring and he was no doubt going to guess. "He proposed. I refused him." She pressed her fingers to her eyes.

"Here." A soft brush of linen against the back of her hands. Carlisle's handkerchief, carrying the faint scent of sandalwood.

She took it, dabbed at her eyes. Knew she couldn't delay any longer. She fisted the handkerchief and looked at him.

She'd hurt him. Even more than she'd expected to. His eyes were glassy, unfocused. His face grim. He'd already borne so much hurt in his life; he didn't deserve this additional wound from her.

"I'm sorry," she whispered.

He grimaced. "Can you find your way back to the sitting room? I'll order the carriage and be along in a moment."

She left him standing in the library. Retraced their steps, struggling to keep the guilt and regret from breaking loose. Entered the sitting room to find Jakes still entertaining Lord Peyton and the two ladies. It gave her a moment to collect herself, school her face, and think about keeping her voice pitched soft.

Jakes finished whatever he was saying and the three of them chuckled.

"Carlisle's calling for the carriage," she said, and thought perhaps Jimmy Banks was right about her acting ability. But then, after looking at her, her three friends exchanged glances between themselves, and the smiles dropped from their faces.

Blast.

CHAPTER THIRTY

Five days after Archer's expulsion, Cam sat on a stool in the workshop, working a wooden leg. Sawdust covered his thighs and dusted his sleeves and hands. When Elissa came through the door, he placed the prosthetic on the table and stood. His eyes went past her.

Shock jerked him straight. His brother, Wallace, walked around Elissa. She folded her arms and frowned, the way she used to do just before giving Archer a set-down. This time it was Wallace, not Archer she was watching, and instead of her patients, she was trying to protect Cam. A warm feeling filled his chest.

Wallace pulled off his hat. "Cam."

Cam's head reeled. Wallace. Here.

Cam might have been a frightened rabbit, the way his heart thrummed. His throat tightened. Cold sweat broke under his collar. "Wallace."

His brother's hands came partway up. Cam stepped back. Hardened his will. Licked his lips. Wished he could dispel the sudden desire for whiskey. The even stronger, gut-clenching need to make everything *right*.

"Thank God I've found ye," Wallace said.

The relief in Wallace's voice made anger curl in Cam's belly. "I haven't been lost."

"In the past six months, we wrote five times," Wallace said. "When we didnae get a response, Father wrote to yer commanding officer. Discovered ye'd left the army. Seven months ago." His last words burst out like a discharge of lightning. He tossed his hat to the table. Raked his fingers through his hair.

The ruffling made Wallace look younger, not unlike the way he appeared when Cam looked up to his older brother and wanted nothing more than to be like him. Cam and Logan had both admired

Wallace, who lectured them, guided them, and safeguarded them. But that was a lifetime ago.

"Eight years, Wallace. It's been eight years since you and Father disowned me. Eight years without a word. Not one response to my letters." He'd told himself he was crazy to send those letters, one or two a year, but he could never quite abandon the one-sided contact. Not until sometime during the war, when his last hope for forgiveness dissolved.

Cam squared his shoulders. Noticed Elissa standing behind Wallace. She was right. He'd been wrong to think he needed forgiveness. He hadn't killed Logan. He'd done his best to save him. Looking back with the eyes of an experienced surgeon, he knew no one could have done more. Or done better. Why had he been blind for so many years?

An image of Logan filled his head. Logan during his last seconds of awareness. The panic had faded from his eyes. He'd looked up at Cam with trust. Acceptance. Love. How had Cam forgotten those moments? Peace swept through him, a cool, cleansing wave.

Wallace dragged his hand over his mouth and chin. "We were wrong. And we're sorry. We want to make amends."

So much damage had been done. With each year, each unanswered letter, Cam's outrage had grown. He'd fashioned an impenetrable shield around his heart. Wallace's words didn't even dent it.

Wallace reached inside his coat and withdrew an envelope. "From Father," he said, and extended it to Cam. "We want ye to come home and join our practice. The way we all planned. The way it was always meant to be."

Cam took the envelope, *Cameron* written across the front in a spindly, shaky hand. He knew the handwriting, and yet he didn't.

Movement drew his gaze to the door. Elissa, turning and leaving. She'd stayed and listened. In case he needed her.

"What's wrong with Father? His hand shook when he wrote this." Cam raised the envelope.

"Shaking palsy."

Cam's belly fell like a lead plummet sounding bottom. A mix of regret, compassion, and indignation churned in his chest. "So he's buried his anger and blame in order to get me back to help support him."

Wallace gripped Cam's shoulder and squeezed. "Read the letter."

#

Three hours later, the Duke of Carlisle stood in Elissa's office doorway, holding two pineapples—the fruit she'd seen two months ago in his Brighton glass house. It seemed much longer than that.

He appeared to have an entire retinue of servants behind him. "They're ripe, and I insist you have a taste. You might remember. I said it was like eating sunshine. Come along to the ward."

The guilt she'd felt since telling Carlisle a romantic association between them was impossible had only added to her distress caused by everything with Cam. Sleeplessness, lack of appetite, and the lackluster looks that accompanied both continued to plague her. She'd filled her mind and her time with work, often leaving well after dinnertime.

Carlisle looked as handsome and commanding as usual, but she saw subtle differences. His expression seemed reserved. His eyes cool. She had no idea what he was feeling.

He'd made a point of including her in the pineapple sampling. Perhaps as a means of showing he didn't harbor ill will? She stood and crossed to the door. "I can't wait to try it."

The corners of his eyes crinkled and a slow smile curved his mouth. The coolness melted away, replaced by a warmth that seemed…tender.

Within a few minutes Carlisle's servants were serving pineapple slices to the patients and staff. The ward took on a party-like atmosphere, with cooks, laundresses, even Mr. Fletcher and Mr. Howell joining them. One of the men began playing an Irish melody on an accordion.

Elissa bit into the juicy fruit. Tangy and sweet and altogether remarkable.

"How do you like it?" Carlisle stood at her shoulder.

She pressed the napkin she held to her lips. "You were right. It is like eating sunshine." She looked at the laughing, animated men around her, Lawrence and Thorpe among them. "You've done something wonderful here." Michael O'Toole, a right-leg amputee who would soon be bound for home, began singing. The rest of the men quieted, listening and swaying to the music.

"Let's add to their pleasure, shall we?" Carlisle plucked away her plate and handed it to one of his servants. He took her hand and pulled her to the middle of the ward aisle.

"What? What are you doing? Stop."

He faced her. Raised their joined hands, put his right hand on her waist, and they were dancing.

Her feet seemed to move of their own accord. Men moved aside, clearing the aisle, and Carlisle swept her down, then up, the length of the room.

"I'm not giving up," he said. "You're not in love with me now, and it may be some time before it's possible for you to love me."

She couldn't look away from his watchful eyes. He swung them into a turn, and her skirt belled out. Her breath hitched.

"But I'm giving us that chance. The rest of it doesn't matter."

This man. So forgiving and stubborn and certain. She *liked* him. He deserved more than being second best. "We should talk."

He gave a short nod as the song ended. The room burst into applause, those with missing hands stamping the floor. Carlisle retrieved her pineapple and passed the plate to her. The accordionist began playing something lively.

Jakes tugged a sheet from a bed and tied it around his waist. Then draped a pillowcase over his head, and curtsied before Storey, who was not only the tallest man on the ward, but one of the tallest men Elissa had ever seen. Storey bowed and held out his prosthetic hand. The ward erupted in laughter. Storey and Jakes began to dance, Jakes fluttering his eyelashes and pursing his lips and in other ways playing the part of an ingénue. The audience began clapping and stamping in time to the music.

Carlisle barked out a laugh. "That Jakes. He is a sharp one."

She'd meant to talk to Carlisle about Jakes. Guilt jolted her. She'd been so immersed in her own troubles and her work, she'd forgotten about her idea for Jakes.

"He's even smarter than you know. And a kind, good man. He's been such a great friend to me." And to Cam. "He'd make a wonderful surgeon, and I want to help him become one."

Carlisle gave her his full attention. Lifted his brows.

Her face warmed. "I don't have the means. I don't know who else to ask but you. You've been so generous to the veterans here, and you have so much influence. Do you think it could be arranged for Jakes to receive a special warrant? Authorization that allowed him to leave the military. At least long enough to obtain an education."

Carlisle's brows drew together. "I'd have to go very high in the military hierarchy—possibly as high as the government. Cambridge is now commander in chief. He may not be the best choice. He's conservative and doesn't like change."

The Duke of Cambridge, Commander in Chief of the Forces. Supreme commander of the military. When she'd thought of helping Jakes to a different life, she hadn't realized it might take a man of such prominence. And Carlisle hadn't even questioned the idea.

"Or there's Panmure," Carlisle continued.

Lord Panmure. Secretary of State for War.

Carlisle rubbed his hand up and down his jaw. "Andrew Smith might be best. He's Director-General of the Army Medical Services."

"MacKay got Jakes temporarily assigned to Primrose Hill by going to Smith."

Carlisle paused. His gaze flicked to the doorway. Elissa looked, and saw Cam. How long had he been standing there with his brother, eating pineapple? She hadn't known he was here, but Carlisle had.

Carlisle nodded. "So Smith will already be familiar with Jakes. I doubt he'll discharge him, but he might permit a furlough while Jakes becomes educated and trained as a surgeon. He'd still have to fulfill his obligation, but he'd be an army surgeon then."

"He's been borrowing books from MacKay. Given the chance, he'll be successful."

"Yes." His gaze went to Jakes. He and Storey had finished their dance, and were bowing to the cheering men. "He impressed me last week at dinner. I'd like to help him. In turn, he'll help the hundreds of men who come under his care." Direct gray eyes met hers. "If Smith agrees to the plan, I'll pay for Jakes's schooling and his living expenses."

The joy and surprise and gratitude made a hard knot in her chest. "Thank you." She took a deep breath. She had to know. "Are you doing it for me?" She didn't return the affection he felt for her. She couldn't be beholden to him.

He shot another look at Jakes then returned his gaze to her. "No. I'm doing it for myself."

He was such a fine man, and she'd hurt him. She wished she had the same intensity of feeling for him as she had for Cam. But she didn't.

"Can we go to my office? Talk for a bit?" Elissa asked.

"Why don't we take a walk instead?"

They ended up on a bench in the yard behind the hospital. Tulips, daffodils, hyacinths, and primrose had transformed the area. A popular spot for respite, it had been abandoned in favor of the pineapple celebration.

Carlisle bent and plucked a single blossom of primrose from the plant beside their bench leg. Elbows on knees, he twirled the stem. He didn't look at her, but kept his attention centered on the bright yellow flower. "That night of the dinner party—you surprised me." He glanced at her then turned his gaze back to the primrose petals. "I won't lie and say what happened with MacKay doesn't matter. But I don't need to know the details. I want us to continue getting to know one another." The twirling stopped. He turned his head. "In time you'll forget MacKay. I'm convinced, when that day comes, we could have a happy marriage."

Elissa's breath froze. He'd never been so bold. This was tantamount to a proposal. "I'm not certain I'm suited to marriage with any man."

He straightened. Tossed the blossom away. Angled toward her. "Why do you say that?"

Because of the loss in her life. Because of her fear. Because she may not have given Cam—the man she *did* love—a real chance. Did she really think they couldn't be happy together with him a prosthetist instead of a surgeon? Or was his accusation that she didn't trust him more truthful? She'd been going back and forth for weeks; her mind couldn't seem to let go of it.

Carlisle had survived great loss. Like herself. And MacKay. They'd each been tossed into a foundry furnace of guilt and grief, been melted down and recast, and emerged different people. Carlisle would understand how the demise of her family still affected her today.

"Lately I've thought—I may be afraid. Afraid to open my heart. Afraid that if I lose the person I give my heart to, I'll lose myself."

As compassionate as his eyes were, she couldn't meet them any longer. She focused on her clenched hands. He slid closer.

"I know something of loss. I've lost a wife and a son. You may be hesitant to risk your heart, but I'm not afraid to risk mine. You think your ability to love stinted, but I know even damaged, your heart is ten times bigger than most. Whatever you have left to give me, I'll be content."

How could she convince him? She'd hurt Cam so bad, he wouldn't even agree to remain her friend. Carlisle might think her worth the risk, but she knew better. "Nursing—taking care of others—is special to me. I never want to stop." It was the objection that came to mind. Dukes' wives weren't nurses.

"Most duchesses are involved in charitable work. If we married, you could continue doing what you do now. You just wouldn't receive payment. Together, we can build more hospitals like Primrose Hill. You can help organize and manage them."

As raw as her emotions were, his acceptance was comforting. That didn't make agreeing with his plan the right thing to do. Even given how fond she was of him.

She could be with child. Even if she weren't, she couldn't imagine any man making her body feel the same rapture Cam had. Marrying Carlisle wouldn't be fair to either of them if she ended up comparing the two men and finding her husband lacking.

"You make a life together sound appealing. Reasonable. But I don't think it's possible. It wouldn't be fair to you."

"Let me worry about that. At least agree to continue as we have been. Getting to know one another. For now, that's all I ask."

He wasn't asking a lot, and yet it seemed huge. It would mean giving up all hope of Cam and giving Carlisle a real chance to win her affection. Movement caught her attention. The two brothers, returning to the workshop. Cam didn't glance her way.

Her chest felt as empty as a condemned house. Carlisle waited, eyes hopeful. She didn't want to hurt him. But what if she agreed, he fell in love with her, and she couldn't stop loving Cam? What then? "Why me?"

His head inched forward, his brows bunched, and one corner of his mouth dimpled. "Remember the day we met?"

She did. It was the same day she'd discovered Cam working here as a prosthetist.

"I'd only just met you, yet I told you about Michael. Would it surprise you to learn I rarely speak of him? Perhaps someday I'll be able to, but for now it's too soon. I'm still too emotional. Yet that first day, with you, it all spilled out. I showed you a part of myself—a very vulnerable part—I keep hidden. Afterwards, I felt peaceful. Happy. I felt as if our souls connected."

"That sounds like a foundation for friendship, not marriage," Elissa suggested.

Carlisle took her hand. His was still gloveless from the pineapple feast, and she didn't wear gloves at the hospital. The warmth, the gentle firmness, the certainty of his hold imparted more intimacy than she'd ever dreamed a mere hand could convey. "You make me feel I can do anything. You make me see what's important. The peace and happiness I felt that first day...I feel it every time I'm with you."

She began shaking her head, and his hold on her hand tightened.

"I'm bungling this. I'm not attracted to you because you're good for my character. I admire you and value you and like you for that, but—" His eyes flashed silver and grew intense. "You have the most beautiful eyes I've ever seen." His face flushed. "You're lovely. Every part of you is lovely. You carry yourself like a queen. I—" He closed his eyes and pressed his lips together.

Shock held Elissa frozen. She'd never seen Carlisle act any way but supremely confident. Until now. He was struggling to express himself.

His eyes opened, and right before her eyes, his chest expanded, his frame grew larger.

"I want you in every way a man can want a woman," he said, his tone gruff and warm, wrapping around her and squeezing the air from her lungs.

Dear God. Was he already in love with her? Her heart pinched. She didn't want to say it, because it would hurt him. But she had to.

"I wish I could say yes. Wish I could give you that chance. But I know in my heart, it's hopeless."

He released her hand. Rocked back as if she'd landed a punch to his solar plexus. He swiveled until he faced forward on the bench. Bent forward and covered his mouth with his hands.

She waited. Fought the desire to apologize, comfort. She imagined herself Carlisle's wife. A duchess. Thought of all she was giving up. A chance for a fulfilling life. A marriage shared with a man she liked and admired. A husband she could work beside. Have children with.

Her eyes felt hot and she blinked. She made her spine straight and hard as the trunk of a pine. To accept that life would be nothing short of stealing.

He dropped his hands, dragged in a couple big breaths. She should leave him alone to collect himself. He looked up when she stood. She wanted to cry when she saw his face, because she knew what his expression meant.

"Fair warning," he said. "I'm not giving up."

CHAPTER THIRTY-ONE

Cam jolted from sleep. Holy Jesus.

He scrubbed his hands over his face, trying to dispel the last traces of the dream. His skin was clammy, his sheets damp with sweat. He sprang from the wet, crumpled mess, stalked to the window and threw the sash up. Put his hands on the sill and sucked in air.

After a few minutes he felt better. He straightened. Took a huge breath and blew it out. Dragged a trembling hand across his mouth. Closed his eyes and leaned his forehead against the cold glass.

The dream had left him in a turmoil as bad as the worst of withdrawal. He clenched his hands, still feeling Elissa's hot blood on his fingers. In the dream, he'd been performing surgery on *her*.

She lay on the ground; he knelt beside her. Her chest—her heart—exposed, sliced open. Skin, muscle, and bone peeled back. He was suturing her lacerated heart together, but it wasn't beating, and his panic rose with each stitch. He'd started out taking tiny, perfect stitches—this was *Elissa*—but as the minutes passed without her heart contracting, his sutures grew hurried. Larger. Less precise. Until he became frantic, taking huge, sloppy stitches while her slippery heart bled and the knees of his trousers became ever more saturated with her blood.

While prayers stumbled from his numb lips. While his arm blotted tears from his blurry eyes. While his chest heaved with unvoiced, restrained sobs.

No matter how fast he went, how hard he tried, how desperate he felt, he remained clumsy, slow, incompetent. Elissa's life slipping through his fingers.

It was Logan, all over again.

Except this time, he pledged he would not stop. Promised he would not give up. Vowed he would not admit defeat.

Even though, deep inside, he knew she was dead.

Finally, with his lungs hurting so bad he couldn't draw air, he woke.

Cam straightened away from the window. The sky was pre-dawn purple. Still dark enough for the window of a lighted room in the hospital to glow. Elissa. Working early again. Yearning to see her, whole and alive, slid along his sinew, swam through his blood.

He tugged on clothing. Cleaned his teeth and splashed cold water on his face. Raked fingers through his hair.

The moment he saw her, seated at her desk with papers spread out before her, every jumpy nerve calmed. Relief eased through him, warm, heavy, and sweet as syrup.

She didn't seem surprised to see him. She pressed her lips together, leaned back in her chair and folded her arms. "You can stop worrying. We didn't make a child," she said. Her voice sounded resigned. Resigned to not attaining the dreams that mattered. Or perhaps his imagination had bestowed Elissa with his own regrets.

A giant fist squeezed his belly. He paced the few steps to her desk, collapsed in a chair.

He hadn't realized, until this moment, how much he'd wanted the answer to be different.

"You're going back to Scotland?" she asked.

"Not to stay. But I need to see my father."

Whose letter had said he'd been wrong to blame Cam for Logan's death, and he'd known it for years. MacKay men were stubborn, his father reminded him. Cam knew that only too well. Father and Wallace had both asked for forgiveness. A request easy to grant. He loved them.

Before Wallace left, he and Cam talked for hours. It had left Cam empty. A good empty, as if someone had reached in and plucked out all the burdens that weighed his soul.

"You'll come back to England? To Primrose Hill?"

He gave a single nod.

"You won't join your father's and brother's medical practice? You said you'd once planned to."

He'd told her that the day he told her about Logan. The day they made love.

"Wallace says it's my decision. He and Father will understand if I don't."

"And you've decided? You're sure?"

"I like working with veterans. Love helping them come to terms with the loss of their limbs. I work on making a prosthetic that feels like it belongs to the man. Sometimes they want function, sometimes appearance. It's a big part of the rehabilitation we do here, and what we've been accomplishing is amazing. We take men in despair, and when they leave us, they're looking forward to life. I like being part of that."

"I didn't realize you were so proud of your work here." The breathy uncertainty of her tone hung in the air.

Her words stung, made anger flare, and he felt his face flush. "Perhaps you've been wrong about a number of things."

Her mouth dropped open and she looked as devastated as if he'd struck her. She blinked several times. Remorse nipped the pit of his stomach, but he ignored it and told himself he didn't care. She *should* wonder if she'd made a mistake.

Her chin tilted. "Perhaps your feelings took root after you quit drinking."

His anger dropped away as if it had never been. That was his 'Lissa. Strong. Stubborn. Unafraid. He bit the inside of his cheek. She was fair, too, and later, she'd think about what he'd said. He owed her the same honesty.

"I've been thinking about how ye feel," Cam said. "How ye're not understanding why I'm not a surgeon, and yer not wanting to marry. I understand." He paused, bowed his head and rubbed the back of his neck. "I'm not the same man ye knew in Koulali. I do good work here and I'm proud of it, but it doesn't hold the same challenge or reward as surgery. Whether that has the power to make a marriage between us unhappy, I don't know."

Elissa rose, came around the desk and stood in front of him, hands clasped together. "I've been miserable. Topsy-turvy. When my flow came, I cried. It made everything so *final* between us."

He nodded. "I feel the loss, too." He dragged his hand over his mouth and beard. "In the Crimea, I broke. Thanks to you and Jakes, I'm patched back together, but I can't promise it won't happen again. I think, more than anything else, it's that fear that keeps me from going back to surgery."

For a time they gazed at each other. Then Elissa wet her lips.

"I'd like to get to know the Cameron MacKay of London and Primrose Hill Hospital," she said. "Could we do that in a leisurely manner? Perform our jobs, let the nervous tension unravel, and see what happens?"

"Aye, lass." He filled his lungs, silently gave thanks, and let himself be dazzled by joy.

He recalled the excitement he'd felt during his talk with Wallace, and wanted to share it with her. "Wallace encouraged me to write a book about the medical care and rehabilitation of amputees. I like the idea."

Her lips curved. "Everything from surgery and care of the stump to a man's mental attitude," Elissa said. Her eyes sparkled. She raised up on her toes and gave a bounce. "I remember in Koulali, you taught me how crucial it is to wrap the stump correctly. The book's a wonderful idea. It would be innovative."

Pride swelled in his chest. "I intend to write it." His voice rolled out, as strong and certain as he'd ever sounded during surgery.

Elissa's forehead creased. Her gaze roamed his face and she nodded.

He still wanted her. She didn't trust him, and she was afraid to love.

But he wanted her.

#

Two and a half weeks later, Cam kept his eyes trained on the passing scenery and tried to ignore the conversation between Carlisle and Elissa. It was difficult, because inside he seethed.

Carlisle was talking about founding more specialty hospitals for veterans. He wanted to offer more classes on reading and math. In spite of Cam's efforts, he couldn't block their voices, the animation underlying their words. Elissa's happy tone made Cam's heart squeeze like it was caught in a steel-jaw animal trap. How could he compete with Carlisle?

He stared harder. Made himself focus on the view outside the carriage window. Everything was different than it had been their last visit two and a half months ago. Brighton bloomed with early spring flowers. Trees stretched limbs heavy with buds, and the sky looked like Scotland. He saw the fresh mid-April beauty, but it didn't touch him. It didn't lift him. Nothing around him mattered enough to breach the dark moat of misery that surrounded him. His hope of repairing things with Elissa was draining away.

At least Carlisle and Elissa were leaving him to himself. He was grateful for that. Cam shot a glance at Jakes, seated beside him. The orderly had been quiet on the train. Cam couldn't tell what was going on in the man's head, but Jakes could well be out of sorts, getting thrust into this unexpected situation. Cam guessed Jakes, one of the best men he knew, would feel inferior to Carlisle's other guests. Cam hated that. This visit, Carlisle hadn't invited his aristocratic friends, but instead, a mix of wealthy industrialists, ship owners, and other powerful businessmen. He'd said the guests, most of whom had humble beginnings, would enjoy meeting Jakes. Cam hoped they'd be considerate.

Buildings grew sparse as they neared the edge of town. They slowed as they approached the road to Carlisle's estate, the turn situated near a combination inn and tavern. The man Cam saw standing outside gave him a jolt. He leaned forward and watched until the figure passed from sight.

"What is it?" Jakes asked.

Cam regarded Jakes, Elissa, and Carlisle, who each studied him. "The tavern we just passed? The Mermaid's Purse? Archer was standing outside."

Jakes looked like a hunting dog within nipping distance of a fox. "Archer. Are you sure?"

"Aye. I am."

"The man who insulted Miss Lockwood?" Carlisle asked, his voice taking on a hard edge.

"Aye."

"What is he doing here?" Elissa asked.

"Do ye know anyone at the Mermaid's Purse?" Cam asked Carlisle. "If it's a coincidence, I don't want him to learn we're here, but I need to know why he's in Brighton."

"I think we'd all like to know," Carlisle said. "My coachman, Samson, is a capable man. He'll find out without Archer suspecting a thing."

#

Cam sought out Carlisle as soon as he entered the man's drawing room. Elissa stood beside the duke, and her gaze swept Cam's figure, clad once more in his black kilt, coatee, and waistcoat. For a moment everything but Elissa receded. That look of hers made his chest swell. Made him glad his sporran hid another part of his anatomy.

He was accustomed to her dressing in dark colors at work, but tonight she shimmered in pink, and she'd done something different with her hair. He had trouble dragging his gaze from her lips. They looked plump, pink as her dress, and begging a kiss.

Cam steered his gaze to Carlisle and gave the man a nod. "Have ye found out anything about Archer?"

"He took a room for three nights under the name of Smith." Carlisle scowled. "He keeps to himself. Samson couldn't find out anything else."

"Not using his own name? He's up to no good." Jakes came through the door and Cam motioned him over with a jerk of his head. "Maybe Jakes and I should pay him a visit and convince him it's not the time for a visit to the seashore."

"Samson has a man watching him. It might be better to keep an eye on him, rather than send him packing and not know where he is and what he's about."

Cam nodded. Carlisle was right, and his sensible proposal made Cam feel like a hot-headed fool. But it grated at his nerves, knowing Archer was close. The man was irrational and dangerous. He didn't like Archer being anywhere near Elissa.

"Corporal." Carlisle gave Jakes a nod and looked at Elissa.

"The duke has a surprise for you, Jakes," Elissa said.

"For me." Jakes sounded a combination of stunned and wary. He looked fine, his uniform brushed and buttons shined. Cam hadn't expected anything less. Jakes was doing a good job of hiding his nervousness, but the rigid correctness of his posture gave it away.

Carlisle stepped back and faced his other guests, who were scattered about the room. "Friends, if you please. I have an announcement before we go in to dinner."

Elissa moved to Jakes's side. Her eyes gleamed and the corners of her mouth tipped up. She looked ready to grab Jakes and dance around the room.

The other guests quieted and gave Carlisle their attention. "For those of you who haven't met Corporal Jakeman, allow me to present him. He helped organize Primrose Hill Hospital. He trained the orderlies, and our surgeon tells me they're the best he's ever seen. Corporal Jakeman demands the highest standards, which means patients receive exceptional care. Miss Lockwood suggested he had the intelligence and dedication one expects of a surgeon or physician. I agreed. And so I'm pleased to announce I'll be sponsoring Corporal Jakeman. He'll attend St. Thomas's Hospital Medical School. I know he'll make a fine army surgeon."

The guests applauded and many raised their glasses. Jakes's mouth dropped open.

Elissa grabbed Jakes's arm. "Carlisle arranged everything. You'll be on furlough until your training is completed. He's going to pay your tuition and living expenses while you're in school. When you finish, you'll return to military duty, only as a surgeon."

Jakes's mouth curved in a huge, open smile. He laughed. Looked stunned, overwhelmed, thrilled. He shook Carlisle's hand.

Surprise and happiness for Jakes lifted Cam. No one was more deserving. No one would make a better or more compassionate surgeon. But underlying his happiness, knots of dissatisfaction cinched tight. Carlisle had accomplished the impossible—the unheard of—and seeing Elissa's shining face, Cam knew why. For her.

Carlisle had been shrewd enough to know she wasn't a woman to impress with jewels or other fine things well within his ability to give her. Instead, the duke had chosen to use his influence to help someone she cared about. That help would transform Jakes's future. His life. Carlisle, the benefactor, would reap the reward of Elissa's gratitude and admiration.

Cam wanted to be the man proving his value. His reliability. To make the impossible happen. He wanted to do something that made her eyes shine and her face glow.

Carlisle turned to the servant who stepped up beside him, holding a case. As soon as Cam saw it, he knew what it was. A surgeon's kit. He'd received his own the day he graduated, a gift from his father.

"One last thing." Carlisle opened the case, revealing scalpels, knives, forceps, hooks. A tourniquet. Saw. Bullet probe. A bottle of chloroform. Scissors. Needles and silk suture. The catgut suture wouldn't be useable by the time Jakes graduated, but that was of no consequence. It was a fine kit.

"I—I don't know what to say." Jakes couldn't seem to tear his gaze away from the array of instruments. His index finger traced the handle of a knife. "Thank you, sir."

"It'll be in your room," Carlisle said. Jakes closed the lid and the servant regained possession.

Dinner announced, Carlisle led the way with Elissa on his arm. Cam stood with Jakes, letting the other diners precede them. The guests smiled and offered their congratulations to Jakes as they passed.

Cam squeezed Jakes's shoulder. "I'm happy for ye, lad."

"I can't believe it. How can I ever thank His Grace, Miss Lockwood, and you enough?"

"Whoa, laddie. I dinnae have anything to do with it."

Sincere blue eyes raked Cam's face. "You don't know, do you? Carlisle may have given me the opportunity and the tools. But *you* gave me the desire. The example of what—who—a surgeon can be. What he can do. The difference he can make. If I can be even half the surgeon you were... I can't imagine anything would make me prouder."

"Laddie..." Cam's throat locked tight. He discarded any notion of speech and stared at the toes of his brogues. Jakes's words made pride fill Cam's chest, until he heard "were." Jakes no longer considered him a surgeon. It caused a wrenching pain where the pride had been, moments ago.

When he looked up, Jakes was grinning. "This means, someday I'm going to be able to ask Evie Riley to be my wife."

Good for Jakes.

CHAPTER THIRTY-TWO

A day later, Elissa entered the glass house and felt her tension ease. This was what she needed. Peace. Quiet. Time away from Carlisle and MacKay and servants and guests. She turned toward what Carlisle had termed the floral section. A number of plants were blooming, and the fragrant air seemed almost velvety when she took a deep breath. She strolled down the left aisle then sat on a bench positioned at the end.

Carlisle's guests were leaving this morning. Her own small group would leave on the afternoon train. It had been a successful weekend for Primrose Hill Hospital. Even more successful than the aristocrats weekend had been. It seemed industrialists with humble beginnings were especially generous.

She'd been anxious about spending two days near Cam, but now she was glad for it. Somehow, watching him and Carlisle had made her take a hard look at herself. Why was Carlisle so sure they could have a prosperous marriage, and she would make a successful duchess? He believed in her. Even knowing she didn't love him, Carlisle believed. Had faith. Trusted.

Yet she was convinced she and Cam would have an unhappy marriage. All because he wasn't a surgeon. What if he'd lost an arm? Would she feel the same way? She knew she wouldn't. Cam was special. Look at what he'd accomplished at Primrose Hill. Even without the surgery he loved, he'd found a way to help others and change their lives. *Why* was she so certain their marriage would be unhappy? What effect did his being a prosthetist have on their love? None. Didn't she admire him now as much as she had when he was a surgeon? Yes. He'd stopped drinking. He made innovative prosthetics. He encouraged the patients. Instilled them with confidence. And just one look from him turned her blood to fire.

He'd accused her of not trusting him. Could he be right? Didn't she believe their love would last? She couldn't imagine not loving him.

She knew she had trouble trusting. How could she trust in a future that could turn so fast and be so cruel? How could she protect her heart from a blow that would destroy her, if she let herself trust? Was she such a coward?

Sometimes life turned to the good. Carlisle had survived great pain, and used it as the cornerstone of Primrose Hill. So many wounded souls were being healed there. Cam had wrestled free of alcohol and the misplaced guilt of Logan's death. His eyes were clear now. He was writing a book that would help hundreds of surgeons and amputees.

Cam and Carlisle were brave. They'd faced their fears, fought through pain, and won. She needed to show Cam she was courageous, too. She took a deep breath. She'd been ridiculous. She needed to trust she could ride the crest of the future and fight her way out of the troughs.

Excitement bounced inside her, and suddenly she couldn't wait. She needed to see Cam.

A noise drew her gaze up to the glass overhead.

Through the glass she saw a man lying on his belly atop the structure. Had he climbed up there to clean the glass? Repair something? She stood, shifted, tried to get a better look. The sun glinted off something metal. A prosthetic hook. Archer. Holding a rifle pointed toward the mansion.

She pressed against the nearest pane, and looked where Archer aimed.

At Cam, striding up from the stables.

She grabbed the closest flowerpot and heaved it through the pane. The pot and its knot of green shoots crashed to the ground outside. Cam jerked his head toward the glass house, expression alarmed. She screamed, "Get down." But in the next heartbeat, she heard the shot, and saw Cam drop. "Noooooooooo."

She ignored the clatter of Archer above her. She couldn't think, couldn't breathe. Her heart and her head and her world had exploded.

Cam moved. *He moved.*

She ran for the vestibule. Just as she reached the outside door she looked up.

Archer stood above her, dropping the ramrod at his feet...bringing the rifle butt to his shoulder...taking aim through the glass roof...at her.

She pulled at the door, but it wouldn't open. *It wouldn't open.*

She threw herself behind a palm and settee, flattened, wedged herself in tight.

She jerked at the crack of a shot. Then came the rushing, crashing, whoosh of glass and man falling. Archer came down feet-first on the settee and fell to his side on the floor. Elissa scrambled to her knees, grabbed onto the back of the settee and pulled herself up.

He moaned and rolled to his side.

She moved her feet sideways, sliding out from behind the divan. Glass was everywhere. Cam kicked at the door, but it held. Archer coughed. Grimaced.

"Elissa, get back," Cam yelled. She saw him looking through the pane beside the door and relief overwhelmed her. He held a shovel, blade up.

She ducked behind the settee and Cam shattered the pane. She heard him striking again and again, breaking glass away from the edges of the pane. Shards hit the brick floor and tinkled like an ice storm hitting a window. As soon as the noise stopped she peeked and saw Cam coming through the window, other men behind him. She straightened and saw Archer leveling a pistol at Cam.

"No!" She pushed at the settee. Pushed it as hard as she could and shoved it into Archer, who cried out. Then Cam was on him. He kicked Archer's arm and the gun discharged, but not into Cam. The bullet went straight up and hit another overhead pane.

Something made her look up in time to see the pane break apart and plummet downward. She reacted instantly, without thought, and shoved Cam aside. Before a dagger of glass sliced into her.

#

Cam caught Elissa as her body crumpled. She made a funny, breathy little moaning sound as he lowered her and eased her down to her back. He muttered a curse or a prayer, he wasn't sure which, and she blinked at him.

There was blood—too much blood—flowing from around the wound. The shard, about four inches wide and as thick as the blade of a knife, had entered midway between her neck and her shoulder, just below her clavicle. A little higher, her clavicle bone might have displaced it. A little lower, and her corset would have provided some protection. Instead, it had buried into the vulnerable part of her chest, right where the top part of her lung would be. Right where the big vessels of the chest lay.

"Cam—" Her whisper shored him up, pumped strength into his arms, forced air into his lungs.

"Shhhhh, sweetheart. I've got ye." With great care he tore the fabric of her bodice away, exposing the glass shard and her wound. She was already pale, her breathing fast and shallow. A thin stream of blood ran from the lowest part of the wound into the fabric of her corset. "Don't move, 'Lissa. Not an inch. Don't even take a deep breath."

"Hurts. It hurts." Her heart beat so hard, so fast, her neck pulsed with it.

"A piece of glass impaled you, love. Try to rest while I work out what to do." One part of his brain—the part attuned to their safety— acknowledged the grooms tying Archer up, getting the door open, and hauling him out. The rest of his brain raced. Considered, discarded, reconsidered surgical strategies. There were few choices.

"MacKay? Should we carry her into the house?" Jakes. Here. Ready to help.

Some of the grooms and groundsmen stood watching. They parted as Carlisle pushed through. He jolted to a stop and cursed. "MacKay. Why aren't you doing something? Christ, man, *do* something."

Cam directed himself to Jakes. "We can't move her. The glass could shift, lacerate major vessels or her lung, if it hasn't already."

"Then pull it out," Carlisle ordered.

Cam shot an impatient glare at the duke. He didn't have time to explain every problem and decision. "The subclavian vessels could be lacerated, and the glass tamponading them. If I remove the glass I might not be able to control the bleeding." The vessels were large. Deep. He didn't know a surgeon who'd ever repaired a lacerated subclavian. The vessel was like a pipe. A pipe that could drain the body of blood in a few minutes. Finding the vessel when it was obscured by a pool of blood...

"I'll send for a surgeon," Carlisle said. He turned to one of the grooms. "Take Sultan. Tell Mr.—"

"Shut up." God give him strength. "There's nae time to bring another surgeon here."

"I thought you weren't able to perform surgery. That it made your hands shake."

Cam wasn't surprised Carlisle knew his history, although he had no idea how he'd found out. Neither Jakes nor Elissa would have told him. He thrust his hands out, fingers spread. "I'm not shaking." He wasn't. His hands were rock-steady. And the fear that they might shake was gone.

Very carefully he clasped Elissa's hand. Rubbed his thumb across the backs of her fingers, bumping the red stone of her ring. "Jakes. Get yer surgical kit. Towels. A sheet or tablecloth." What else? Elissa sometimes washed wounds with wine. "A basin. Wine or whiskey, a couple bottles. Go." Jakes tore off. Elissa's fingers curled around his. They were ice cold.

Cam glanced at Carlisle. "If ye want to help, ye can help with the chloroform. I'll need Jakes to hold retractors and clamps." Carlisle sank onto the settee and put his hand to his forehead. "And tell yer men to wait outside," Cam added.

Elissa's eyes opened. Looked right at him. "I trust you."

His heart stuttered. "What?"

"I trust you. And I'm not afraid to be happy."

Jesus. She was going to make him cry.

"Am I too late? Cam. Did I wait too long?"

"Nae, lass. My heart belongs to ye." He leaned down. Brushed her lips with his. "Rest now, 'Lissa. Save your strength. I'm going to give ye Jakes's chloroform. Stitch up this inconvenient hole."

The tiniest smile curved her lips. "Yes, I'd best rest. I'm getting a bit woozy."

He surged to his feet and went to the door. "Jakes," he bellowed. And there he was, racing toward him holding his kit, servants running after him with the other supplies.

The tablecloth was large enough to cover Elissa from the wound down, and a good portion of the floor. After spreading it out, Cam scrubbed his hands with whiskey. Dumped instruments in a basin and poured whiskey over them. Then knelt at her chest.

He spread towels around the wound, covering her chest. Then laid towels over her abdomen, atop the tablecloth, and placed the rinsed instruments there. Elissa would be asleep, and the instruments would be right at hand.

"Over here, Carlisle. Kneel at her head." Cam retrieved the chloroform and dropper while the duke got into position. Jakes had already rinsed his hands and kneeled on the other side of Elissa, opposite Cam.

"I'll administer the chloroform," Cam said. "Once she's asleep, ye'll keep her sleeping." For a moment Cam searched Carlisle's eyes, assessing the man's ability to hold up through the surgery. The duke had heard what 'Lissa had said to Cam. Had seen him kiss her. Carlisle knew he'd lost her, and Cam guessed the knowledge hit the man hard. Carlisle appeared pale but determined. His jaw looked like he could chew nails.

Satisfied, Cam turned back to the chloroform. He pulled his handkerchief from his pocket. Looked at the waiting instruments. Looked at Jakes, who gave him a nod. Cam was ready. For an instant, he recalled the day he met Elissa. She'd administered chloroform while Cam performed emergency surgery. She'd prayed with the patient, Riley, as he lost consciousness.

"'Lissa."

"Ummmph." Her eyelids twitched, but didn't open.

Urgency stabbed every organ. Every nerve. Cam breathed deep, pushing it back. "I'm ready. I'm going to give you the chloroform now." She didn't answer. Fear rose up faster, harder, darker than the urgency of moments before. He couldn't let himself think about the possibility of a horrific outcome. An outcome that was far more likely than its opposite satisfactory—and *happy*—conclusion.

The longer he waited, the greater the chance her body wouldn't rally. His brain screamed at him to *hurry*. But he made himself pause. Bow his head. He didn't often pray, but today, for her, he would. Pray for strength. And for God to guide his hands. When he raised his head, he thought it might have been the shortest and most fervent prayer ever sent to God's ears.

He tented his handkerchief over her nose and mouth and began dripping chloroform on the fabric. He wasn't sure she was still cognizant of the world, but he had the overwhelming need to comfort her. He could think of no better way than to offer her the same prayer she'd shared with patients in Koulali. So he spoke the Lord's Prayer as he employed the eyedropper and the powerful anesthetic ushered her to sleep.

She succumbed within a few minutes. Once she was deeply under, he passed the chloroform and dropper to Carlisle and gave him quick instructions.

Cam turned to his patient. *Elissa.* Remembered her voice saying, "*I trust you.*" Determination filled him.

He began. No hesitation. No indecision. He forced his mind to the challenge of the surgery before him.

Cam pressed a towel into Jakes's hand. "Once I move the glass shard, she may start to hemorrhage. She's already lost a lot of blood, and she's going to lose more. We can't let her lose too much. When I withdraw the glass, press down on the wound as hard as ye can." While Jakes held compression, bleeding would be stopped, or at least as minimal as possible. Jakes gave him a terse nod.

Cam took hold of the glass shard and, slow and steady, pulled it straight out of the wound. The thing was longer than he'd hoped, shorter than he'd feared. Jakes applied the towel and put muscle to it. "Now it gets ticklish," Cam muttered.

He picked up two skin hooks. He needed to open the wound wide in order to assess the damage. "All right, Jakes." Jakes lifted the towel. Cam hooked each edge of the wound and pulled it open. It filled with blood before he could get a look. "Ach." Jakes applied the towel.

With the glass removed, the bleeding was heavier. He shot a look at Carlisle. "Put down the chloroform. I'll tell you if she needs more. Right now I need another pair of hands. Rinse yours and be quick." For an instant Carlisle stared as if Cam had punched him. Then he launched into action.

"Take the hooks," Cam directed when the duke was ready. "Keep the wound spread apart." Carlisle took the skin hooks and Cam helped him apply the correct amount of tension to hold the laceration open.

Cam placed a clamp next to the wound, where he could grab it quick. Another clamp he held ready, just to the side of Jakes's towel. "Do yer best to sponge up the blood and keep the field clear, Jakes."

Cam nodded at Jakes and he lifted the towel. Cam clamped into the bottom of the wound. He couldn't see where the blood was coming from, but hoped the instrument would clamp the source of bleeding. With the bleeding stopped, he'd be able to get a good look and assess the injury.

Cam grasped the second clamp and Jakes pressed his towel against the wound. As soon as Jakes released pressure and lifted the towel, Cam applied the second clamp. Press, clamp. Press, clamp. After the fourth clamp, when Jakes lifted his towel the wound didn't fill.

Cam sat back on his heels and dragged in a deep breath. "That's better." He looked at Elissa. Breaths shallow. About as pale as a living person can look. He pressed his fingers to the pulse in her wrist. Fast. Weak. Skin cold. He could still feel her heart's pulsations at her wrist, though, and didn't have to use the large carotid artery in her neck. That made him feel a bit better.

"I'll attend to one point of bleeding at a time. Release one clamp, look for the site of bleeding, re-clamp. Once I find the bleeding vessel I'll tie it off." He had plenty of experience tying off vessels, during amputations. Elissa's deep chest wound just made it much more complicated. In an amputation he applied a tourniquet to the leg to stop circulation. It was then relatively easy to locate and ligate the stump vessels. Cam picked up the whiskey-rinsed needle and ligature and threaded the suture material through. "Thank God this kit had catgut." Without it, he'd have been forced to resort to cautery. Elissa's laceration was too large for cautery, but even if it weren't, tying off vessels was the modern, and far superior, technique.

Suture ready, he bent over Elissa. Released a clamp. As blood welled, Cam identified the lacerated vessel. He'd gotten lucky with this first one. While he tied off the vessel with the absorbable catgut, Jakes kept blotting the wound. After getting the vessel tied, Cam waited a few moments to make sure the bleeding had stopped and the suture would hold. Satisfied, he went on to the next clamp.

They weren't all as easy as the first. When Carlisle growled, "How much blood has she got?" Cam wanted to bash him, but ignored him instead.

The last clamp was deep. Cam positioned a retractor down in the laceration. Pulled on the instrument, widening the wound. Told

Jakes, "Hold that," and Jakes replaced Cam's hand on the retractor with his own. Blotted and compressed with the towel in his other hand. Between Jakes's compression and sponging and Cam's ligation of bleeding vessels, the bleeding had slowed to a trickle.

It allowed Cam a good look at the vessel he'd somehow managed to clamp. A look that confirmed what Cam had suspected and didn't want to contemplate. It was the subclavian.

He repositioned instruments so the injured part of the vessel lay between two clamps. Nicked, not sliced through. Fear and relief battered his brain, his chest, his belly with needle-sharp barbs. Relief because the vessel wasn't severed. Fear because the subclavian connected to the heart. He didn't think a person could survive without a working subclavian.

The catgut was too thick. The vessel too fragile. He swiped sweat from his forehead with the crook of his arm.

Like a building cyclone, anguish began a slow spin in his chest. He grabbed a clean towel. Ignored his inner turmoil and wiped blood from his hands. How did he stitch that delicate tissue, and leave the vessel functioning? Jakes's surgical case sat on the floor beside Cam. There were several needles, and one was small and curved. Cam picked it up and dropped it into the whiskey.

He'd never sutured anything as fragile as a blood vessel. He imagined taking tiny stitches with the little needle. He used cotton or silk thread for suturing skin, but those materials couldn't be used inside the body. He needed something with the delicacy of a very fine silk thread. Something as fine as—

He reached up to Elissa's hair, separated out a single strand, and plucked it.

"MacKay?" Jakes sounded hesitant and disbelieving and hopeful.

Cam retrieved the little needle and dipped Elissa's long strand of dark blonde hair in the whiskey. His glance must have communicated something good to Jakes, because the orderly's brows shot up. Cam still had her blood loss and the possibility of infection to worry about, but she was going to survive this surgery with a neatly sutured subclavian.

When he finished the last internal suture, Cam sat back and stretched his neck. His shoulders and arms moved like rusty springs, and they ached. Almost done.

He trimmed the catgut short, something he'd discovered resulted in fewer infections than the standard practice of leaving long catgut tails coming out of the wound. Last, he closed the wound with silk suture and washed away as much blood as he could. Once he got her to bed, he'd remove her corset and the rest of her clothing and put her in her nightgown.

He washed and dried his hands and pressed the flats of his fingertips all around the wound, up to her shoulder and down to her corset. No crepitation—the crackling-like sensation caused by air in the tissue. He'd have felt crepitation if the glass shard had lacerated her lung. He'd continue to check, but—thank God. He knew it had been a narrow miss.

Cam gathered her into his arms and prepared to stand.

"Let the footmen carry her," Carlisle said. "They can make a stretcher out of a blanket."

"I've got her," Cam said. He carried her inside the mansion, up the stairs to her room, and closed everyone out. Then he thought better of it and motioned a housemaid in. The two of them removed her bloody clothes, washed her, and got her into her nightgown.

Once he had her clean, comfortable, and covered, he opened the door. At Cam's request, Carlisle's footmen moved a large upholstered chair, placed it close beside the bed, and Cam collapsed into it.

Thank God he'd been here. And thank God he'd had those years as an army surgeon, getting the kind of experience he needed to perform that surgery. He had so much to be thankful for. That Carlisle had given Jakes a surgical kit. That the glass hadn't been an inch in any other direction. He swallowed. That she'd lived. He closed his eyes, folded his hands, and prayed.

CHAPTER THIRTY-THREE

Just ahead of the footmen, Jakes was first through the opened door. Without Cam telling him, he built up the fire. He ordered sandwiches and coffee for Cam, broth and tea for Elissa, and sent word to the cook to make custard.

A little bit later, after swallowing two long gulps of coffee, Cam took the pins from her hair. Jakes located her hairbrush and Cam brushed out the tangles, smoothing it over her uninjured shoulder in a long, shiny stream.

Jakes pulled up a ladder-back opposite Cam. "How long will she sleep?"

"Hard to say. She lost a large quantity of blood. She may sleep awhile, even after the chloroform wears off. As soon as she wakes, we need to start plying her with broth and sugared tea. As much as we can get down her."

Carlisle walked in, stood at the foot of the bed and gazed at Elissa. "How is she?"

"Still asleep. I'll know more when she wakes, but the wound isnae bleeding. I'll stay a few days, if I may? I think Primrose Hill can get along without me for that length of time." He'd post a letter to Fletcher tomorrow, telling him to find a temporary prosthetist. He intended to take care of Elissa.

Carlisle looked at Cam. "Certainly. Anything you need, please ask. I'll have one of the housemaids stay in the room and attend her. I don't employ a lady's maid, but Mary helps with the ladies when there's a need."

"Where's Archer?" Cam asked.

"Tied up in the cellar with two men watching him. The magistrate should be here soon."

Cam rubbed the back of his neck. "Elissa saved my life when she broke the window and yelled." He'd dived just as Archer fired. That close, sighting with a rifle from an elevated position, he doubted Archer would've missed.

"My valet recognized him," Carlisle said. "Says Archer's been calling himself Agnew and seeing one of my London housemaids. She'll have to be questioned, but I think we'll find he used her to get information. It was no secret you were to be my guests here."

"That's the connection. How he knew to come to Brighton," Jakes said.

Carlisle crossed his arms. "The man wanted you and Elissa dead. This was more than retaliation for tossing him out of Primrose Hill after he assaulted her."

"He hated Miss Lockwood in Turkey," Jakes said. "From the very beginning. Her position was superior to Archer's, and he couldn't bear a woman telling him what to do. He was jealous of how the doctors respected her."

"He detested me," Cam said. "I reprimanded him for his demeanor with patients and when he didn't improve, reported him. His biggest grievance was my recommending him for transfer to the battlefront. He confronted me in Turkey and again in the Crimea."

Carlisle rocked heel to toe. "Ergo, it was your fault he lost his arm."

Cam nodded. "He blames me, but the truth is, I saved his life. He needed surgery days before he had it. When I saw the condition he was in, I got the attention of a surgeon. He amputated a few hours later."

Jakes sighed. "Archer was always an uneasy bloke. Working at the front and losing his arm twisted his mind."

Carlisle faced Cam. His eyes narrowed. "He knew you cared for Elissa," he said in an I'm-Lord-Chief-Justice-and-you're-guilty voice.

Cam stood and faced Carlisle. Glared. Accusations of blame from Carlisle he dinnae need. The hell of it was, the man was right. "It's one of the reasons he gave her trouble at Primrose Hill, but she'd earned his ire at Koulali by demanding excellence. If I'd known how dangerous he was—" His own voice sounded savage, and he didn't give a damn.

Carlisle took a quick look at Elissa then returned his gaze to Cam. "But you didn't know."

He also didn't know if Carlisle meant it as a concession or indictment, but he wasnae making excuses to His Grace.

Carlisle's mouth tightened. "The magistrate isn't here yet. Do you want to question Archer? Or…maybe you'd like some time with him. Alone."

A powerful temptation. An offer he wanted to accept.

He gave Carlisle a one-sided smile. "Nae. But thank ye." He *couldn't* see Archer. Given the opportunity, he might kill the bastard.

Carlisle dropped his arms. He looked at Elissa, gave a slow nod, and turned to the door. "I'll stop by later. My servants are at your disposal."

Jakes watched Carlisle leave and groaned. "Pleeeeease don't fight with the duke. He's my patron now. My friend. I'm going to be a surgeon because of him. You know, if you fought him, I'd have to take your side, and that can't happen."

Cam gave an almost soundless, breathy laugh. "I'll do my best. It made him feel better, unloading some of his misery on me. He lost Elissa."

"He never had me." Elissa's voice flowed through Cam like the sweetest honey.

He leaned in and smoothed his hand over her forehead. "Ye're awake." He checked her pulse. A little slower and stronger than before. It would improve as her body produced blood. Which would take days. Weeks. "Can ye drink a little somethin'?"

"Mmmm."

He took that for a yes and spooned sugared tea into her mouth. Her eyes watched him—smiled at him—the entire time. The tightness in his belly eased. His chest filled with hope. He kept looking in her eyes, his tension draining away, gladness building. He scarcely noticed when Jakes slipped out the door. After a few minutes of her diligently swallowing the liquid, he let her rest.

"You cobbled me together."

"Aye. Ye'll feel weak and dizzy for a while. Ye lost a lot of blood."

She reached out, and he set down the teacup and took her hand. Interlocked their fingers.

"Do you remember me saying I trusted you?" Elissa asked.

"Aye." He'd never forget.

"I wasn't afraid. I trusted your skill and determination and ability to do the surgery. But it was more than that." The tip of her tongue moistened her lips. "I've never been so certain of anything. *I knew.* Knew I was safe. Knew you'd be strong for me. I felt your love, and I hung on to it."

"Love makes us strong." Loving her taught him that.

"My doubts are gone. My arrogant assumptions are gone. It's love that matters." Her fingers were cool, but strong enough to hold on to his. "I'm not afraid to love you. With my whole heart, whole body, whole mind."

Her eyes were clear. Steady. Sure. A pure, sweet shaft of joy pierced his heart.

"Ye'll marry me." It wasnae a question.

EPILOGUE

Elissa, watching from her front window, saw the hansom arrive. "They're here." Cam's arm slid around her and pulled her close to his side. He pressed a long kiss to her temple, and she felt his lips curve against her skin. She turned her head and smiled at her husband then smoothed her hands over her belly. The bump was still small. Hidden by her petticoats.

"Are ye goin' to tell them?" Cam asked.

Elissa nodded. "We're already celebrating two events. We might as well add a third."

They moved to the door and Cam swung it open as Evie and Jakes reached the front step. "Welcome, Assistant-Surgeon and Mrs. Jakeman," Cam said. "Come in."

Elissa hugged Evie and saw Cam and Jakes share a vigorous handshake.

"It's official," Jakes said with a flourish of his hand. "My tailor delivered the uniform today." He wore the dress of his new regiment—blue trousers, and a blue coat with standing red collar and red cuffs.

"Ye do the 4th Light Dragoons proud," Cam said.

"I can hardly believe it's true," Jakes said. "One of the Queen's Own. I'm fully qualified and a member of the Royal College of Surgeons."

"I'm so happy for you both," Elissa said. "Come into the parlor and sit. I want to hear everything. All about your qualification, your orders, and your wedding trip." They moved into the parlor, which had the window with a view of the street. Elissa patted the divan, and Cam sat. Like usual, he sat close enough to touch. Close enough, she could look into his green eyes and see the little bits of brown mixed in.

"Do ye have orders?" he asked.

Jakes grinned. "Garrison duty here at home. Being newly married, it's welcome."

"We loved Scotland," Evie said. "It was perfect. We want to go back."

"My father wrote he'd seen ye."

Elissa's resentment of Cam's father had lessened since their marriage. He'd come to their wedding, and a number of long conversations had eased the breach between father and son. His father admitted he'd always felt responsible for the death of Cam's mother. His guilt for not remarrying and giving his sons a mother added to his sense of failure and shame. When Logan died in Cam's hands, his father saw himself in Cam—failing, and plowing a trench through his center that could not be filled or bridged. The rage that erupted, and lasted eight years, had been fused with the anger he held for himself. The wrath he'd punished Cam with had been outrage he wanted to rain on his own head. Twice, Wallace joined Cam and their father, with Wallace realizing he'd let his father's influence warp his judgment.

"He and Wallace acted like the Queen and Prince Albert had come to visit, instead of Evie and me," Jakes said. "Your father's proud of you. He loved talking about how much attention your book has received, your work at Primrose Hill, your private surgical practice, and," Jakes dipped his head, "your marvelous wife."

Cam gave her a look that asked her permission. She nodded and felt heat rise in her face.

"He'll soon be braggin' about his grandchild," Cam said, his voice proud and amazed and grateful. Hearing his happiness made lightness fill Elissa like the purest blessing.

The Jakemans grinned and voiced happy congratulations. Jakes's face had matured a bit since Koulali, but his blue eyes still held the same earnestness and youthful appreciation for life Elissa had always enjoyed. She loved Grace, her good friend from home, and Evie, but she felt closer to Jakes than anyone, other than her husband.

"Congratulations," Jakes said. "It's wonderful, and what better proof you're truly well."

Someday soon she'd stop thinking about when she came close to dying. She'd come through weeks of fever and pain, and months of weakness. Yes, she'd forget all that, but she'd never forget Cam, loving her through it.

She took his hand. Strong and warm, his fingers wrapped around hers. He wasn't the man she fell in love with. He was more.

AUTHOR'S NOTE

One of the delightful things for me in writing this book was the way I happened upon a number of references that added significantly to the book's historical detail. Thanks to the published journal of a Koulali Hospital lady volunteer, and a history of the British Medical Service in the Crimean War, I was able to accurately describe much of the general area, the hospital and grounds, and the patient care delivered. Some details (such as the large number of rats cavorting about the nurses' quarters) I didn't include, thinking them a shade too gritty. For those wondering why I chose to gift a character with a name so similar to my own, it isn't fiction. In 1855, a man named Humphrey was Koulali Hospital's principal medical officer.

In a letter published in the *Journal of the American Medical Association* in 1910, a physician tells of using human hair to suture mucous membranes, conjunctiva, and facial lacerations in the late 1800s. Any woman's hair could be used, with the hair absorbing and wounds healing nicely. He references a letter published in *JAMA* at an earlier date from a physician who'd used human hair to suture blood vessels.

Some Victorian prosthetic hands were carefully shaped and painted, made to appear as lifelike as possible. Advanced prosthetics with joint movement were available for the wealthy, while the poor made do with peg legs.

The one significant exception to historical accuracy I made was the existence of Primrose Hill Hospital.

It wasn't until the end of the First World War that the first hospitals to incorporate rehabilitation (as we think of it today) were established. In 1917, a Joint Committee of the Ministry of Pensions on Institutional Treatment was formed and, with the help of the Red Cross, made provisions for the treatment of discharged men disabled while serving in the military.

What did exist in 1856 London were Specialist hospitals that focused on specific conditions. Devoted to a single disease such as tuberculosis, or disorders of single medical systems such as conditions of the heart, lungs, skin, eyes, throat, bones and joints, and others, these hospitals were frequently funded by wealthy patrons. It seemed reasonable to me that a Specialist hospital for amputee veterans *could* have existed, and so Primrose Hill Hospital was born.

Thank you for reading ***The Seduction of Cameron MacKay.*** I hope you enjoyed it.

~ Sheri Humphreys

ABOUT THE AUTHOR

Sheri Humphreys used to be an Emergency Room nurse, but today applies bandages, splints, and slings to the characters of her Victorian romance novels. She loves to ignore yard work and housework and reads—usually a book every one to three days. Having conjured stories in her mind her entire life, she wondered if she were normal. Then she began putting stories to paper and became a two-time Golden Heart® finalist. She lives with a Jack Russell-mix rescue, Lucy, in a small town on the central California coast. *A Hero to Hold* received a prized Kirkus Star and was named to Kirkus Reviews' Best Books of 2016.

Boroughs
Publishing Group

Did you enjoy this book? Drop us a line and say so. We love to hear from readers, and so do our authors. To connect, visit www.boroughspublishinggroup.com online, send comments directly to info@boroughspublishinggroup.com, or friend us on Facebook and Twitter. And be sure to check back regularly for contests and new releases in your favorite subgenres of romance.

Are you an aspiring writer? Check out www.boroughspublishinggroup.com/submit and see if we can help you make your dreams come true.

Made in the USA
Las Vegas, NV
16 December 2021

38242757R00157